Praise for Deb Kastner and her novels

"*Daddy's Home* by Deb Kastner sparkles with passion, emotion and stunning secrets."
—*RT Book Reviews* on *Daddy's Home*

"Kastner's latest will grab the reader with familiar characters and engaging dialogue."
—*RT Book Reviews* on *Yuletide Baby*

"[A] sweet second-chance story."
—*RT Book Reviews* on *The Doctor's Secret Son*

Praise for Pamela Tracy and her novels

"Tracy delivers a warm and loving story of mistakes, forgiveness, trusting God and doing the right thing, no matter the cost."
—*RT Book Reviews* on *Daddy for Keeps*

"A delightful romance about misapprehensions, jumping to conclusions, and love that, when not guided by God, can lead to sad consequences."
—*RT Book Reviews* on *Once Upon a Cowboy*

"A quaint setting and charming characters."
—*RT Book Reviews* on *Once Upon a Christmas*

Publishers Weekly bestselling and award-winning author **Deb Kastner** writes stories of faith, family and community in a small-town Western setting. She lives in Colorado with her husband and a pack of miscreant mutts, and is blessed with three daughters and two grandchildren. She enjoys spoiling her grandkids, movies, music (The Texas Tenors!), singing in the church choir and exploring Colorado on horseback.

Pamela Tracy is a *USA TODAY* bestselling author who lives with her husband (the inspiration for most of her heroes) and son (the interference for most of her writing time). Since 1999, she has published more than twenty-five books and sold more than a million copies. She's a RITA® Award finalist and a winner of the American Christian Fiction Writers' Book of the Year Award.

Daddy's Home

Deb Kastner

&

Daddy for Keeps

Pamela Tracy

HARLEQUIN® LOVE INSPIRED®

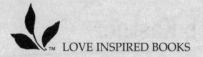 LOVE INSPIRED BOOKS

Recycling programs for this product may not exist in your area.

ISBN-13: 978-1-335-00664-6

Daddy's Home and Daddy for Keeps

Copyright © 2017 by Harlequin Books S.A.

The publisher acknowledges the copyright holders of the individual works as follows:

Daddy's Home
Copyright © 1999 by Debra Kastner

Daddy for Keeps
Copyright © 2009 by Pamela Tracy Osback

www.Harlequin.com

Printed in U.S.A.

CONTENTS

DADDY'S HOME

Deb Kastner

To my daddy, Jim Larkin,
for never letting me give anything but my best.
And for my girls' daddy, Joseph C. Kastner Jr.,
who never stopped believing.

He has showed you, O man, what is good.
And what does the Lord require of you?
To act justly and to love mercy
and to walk humbly with your God.
—*Micah* 6:8

Chapter One

"Christopher's back in town."

Jasmine Enderlin stiffened at the statement. Keeping a carefully neutral expression on her face, she met her grandmother's shrewd gaze. "And you're telling me this because...?"

"Don't be obtuse," Gram snapped, shaking a wrinkled finger under Jasmine's nose. "Don't you pretend I need to spell it out for you. I'm not buying. You know exactly what I'm saying, and you know why. Now, do you want to know the details, or don't you?"

"Yes," she whispered, not even sure Gram would hear her. She released an audible sigh and turned back to the thick olive-colored sweater she'd been folding moments before.

Jenny's sweater.

Brushing the soft material across her cheek, she caught a whiff of Jenny's light, breezy scent on it.

She wouldn't have thought something as simple as the smell of her sister's perfume would set her off, but for some reason, today it did. Her eyes pricked with tears, and she brushed them away with a hurried swipe of her fist, hoping Gram wouldn't notice the furtive action.

Why would Christopher come back to Westcliffe at all, and especially now of all times?

As if to answer Jasmine's unspoken question, Gram shrugged her age-bent shoulders. "He wants his son."

"What?" She sprang from the bed, tipping a pile of freshly folded blue jeans into a heap at her feet. "What do you mean he *wants* Sammy? He can't have him," she added vehemently, hugging her arms to her chest as if protecting an infant there. *Her* infant.

A moment more and she would have dashed from the room to snatch up the baby boy sleeping soundly in his bassinet in the next bedroom, but Gram held up a finger in protest. "You haven't heard the story."

I know the story, she thought, her heart clenching. *Love. Betrayal. Desertion.*

That chapter of her life was over, she reminded herself, fiercely determined to remain in control of her emotions. She shook her head to detour the advancing thought, but it came anyway.

Jenny's dead.

Ugliness folded over her like quicksand. God didn't help Jenny. He could have, but He didn't. Guilt stabbed at her conscience, and she briefly wondered if her thoughts constituted blasphemy.

Maybe they did.

But how could she change the way she felt, the way she viewed things? What else was she to think? Three months ago when *she* hadn't been able to save Jenny. Not with all her years of medical training, not with so much love that she would have willingly taken her sister's place.

And God had done nothing.

"It isn't your fault, my dear," Gram said as she hobbled over to a high-backed Victorian chair and seated herself with the sluggishness of age. "You shouldn't blame yourself."

Gram, she reflected with an inward wince, had the annoying ability to read her mind. Even as a child when Jasmine lost both parents to a tragic car accident, Gram had known what she was thinking and feeling. Gram had raised her, knew better than anyone what she suffered now.

"Because Christopher came back all of a sudden, after a year away?" she asked, knowing full well it was not the question Gram was answering.

Her keen silver eyes fixed upon Jasmine. If she was disturbed by her granddaughter's persistent avoidance of the obvious, it didn't show in her gaze.

"I had my hair set in the salon today," she said, relating the story as if it were of no consequence. As if Jasmine's world hadn't come crashing to a halt the moment she'd heard Christopher's name. "Lucille Walters came in for a perm. She told me everything she knew. Said since it's January and all, he's looking for a new beginning. Clean slate, you might say. Seems he's bunking with her boys at the Lazy H."

"He's rooming with ranch hands?" she asked, surprise sounding in her voice. His parents, like hers, were with the Lord. And as an only child, he had no family to return to. But ranch hands?

"Seems a bit peculiar to me." Gram raised a gray eyebrow and cocked her head to one side.

Her laughter was dry and bitter. "Yeah, for someone who's scared to death of horses, I'd say it is." How quickly the old anger returned to course through her. Righteous indignation swelled in her chest. She embraced it, welcoming the heat that surged through her bloodstream like electricity.

It was her way of dealing with what she couldn't stand to face. Anger filled the empty spaces, leaving no room for more painful, tender emotions to surface.

It was a welcome relief. "Did you talk to him?" she queried, her voice unusually low and scratchy.

"No." Gram leaned forward and cupped a hand to her mouth as if to whisper a secret. "But he told Lucille he wants his son."

"Sammy is *not* his son!"

Sammy! Would Christopher take him away from her? That sweet baby had given new meaning to her life, given her a reason to live when all she wanted to do after Jenny's death was crawl into the nearest hole and die.

And Christopher could take it all away. The thought pierced her heart like a stake. Sure, she had the papers that said she was Sammy's legal guardian, but Christopher was Sammy's father. She pumped her fists open and closed to release the tension swirling through her.

Oh Jenny. Why did God take you away from us?

"Sammy's *my* son," she said again, more to reassure herself than to answer Gram.

"Not sure the law will see it your way." Gram's age-roughened voice broke into her thoughts. Her eyes were full of compassion as she reached forward to squeeze her granddaughter's hand. "Seems to me Christopher had some part in making that baby."

Jasmine didn't want to think about that. "Jenny's will makes *me* his guardian. Besides, a romp in the sack doesn't make a man a father." She snorted her derision. "He doesn't deserve to be a father to baby Sammy, as I'm sure the courts will agree. He abandoned Jenny long before his *son* was born. What kind of a *father* does that make him?"

Gram held up her hands as if to ward off a blow. "I'm not disagreeing with you, honey. No-sirree! I'm just concerned that he's going to fight you every step of the way. Mark my words! You know as well as I do that Christopher Jordan is a strong, stubborn man. He won't stop until he gets what he wants."

She knew. Better even than Gram did. Once, she'd known his heart and soul. Or at least she thought she had. "He won't get Sammy," she vowed, her voice tight.

Gram raised an eyebrow. "Well, girl, I've gotta say you can be just as determined as any ol' man when you put your mind to it." She chuckled. "My money's on you."

"Thank you for your confidence," she replied with a wry smile. "I'll fight him if I have to." No one would take Sammy away from her. *No one.* He was her baby now. And he was all she had left of Jenny.

Sammy's cry pierced the gray haze of rage and frustration that flooded Jasmine's mind. She dashed into the other bedroom and tucked the crying baby to her chest, speaking to him in an incoherent, soothing whisper.

At three months old, Sammy was already well able to make his desires known, she reflected with a smile. Not all the anger in the world could dim the gentle glow of love that filled her heart every time she held this sweet, precious child.

With the palm of her hand, she smoothed the tuft

of light brown hair covering his head. He had a cowlick on the left side of his forehead. Just like his father.

Christopher.

She shook the thought away. "Gram, if I change
Sammy's diaper, will you take him for a while? I want
to go through the rest of Jenny's clothes before I quit
for the night."

Gram came around the corner, smiling and cooing
as she approached Sammy. "Let's get you changed,
little fellow, so I can take you. Your Mommy needs to
get some work done."

Mommy. Jasmine felt less awkward after three
months, but still the term hovered in the corner of
her consciousness, taunting her to prove herself. She
wrapped a fresh diaper around Sammy's waist and
pinned it securely, barely giving a thought to her actions.

Some things, at least, were beginning to come easier for her.

It was she who rose each night for the two o'clock
feeding, she who burped and cuddled and changed the
boy.

She hadn't planned to be anyone's mother. Not for
years yet, in any case. If only…

"Don't you think you've done enough for one day?"
Gram asked, reaching for the infant and bouncing him
against her shoulder, patting his back in an age-old,
soothing rhythmic gesture. "You have to go to work
early tomorrow. Besides, you've been called out three
evenings in a row. Can't the people around here stay
out of trouble for a single night?"

She chuckled. "I don't mind, Gram. Really. That's
why I went to medical school. I survived my residency

with far less sleep than I get here. This town rolls up the carpet at six o'clock in the evening! In Denver, our worst hours were late at night."

"Be that as it may," Gram argued, "things have changed. You've got a little one dependent on you. You need to keep yourself healthy. For Sammy's sake, Jasmine, if not your own."

She laughed. "Gram, I've never been sick a day in my life, and you know it. I rarely even catch a cold!"

"For Sammy's sake," the old woman repeated, kissing the infant's forehead.

Jasmine sighed. "For Sammy's sake. Everything I'm doing is for Sammy's sake. Not that I regret a minute of it." She stroked one finger down his feathery cheek, enjoying the loud giggle that erupted from him. Staring down at him now, her heart welled with love.

"Take care of my baby."

Her sister's voice echoed through her head as if it were yesterday, and not three months past. Would that fluttery, empty feeling in the center of her chest ever really go away, or would she eventually learn to live with it? It caught her unawares at the oddest moments.

She closed her eyes and took a deep breath to steady her quivering nerves. "I've got to get back to these sweaters, or I'll never get this done."

Gram settled herself on the rocking chair in the corner of the baby's room and adjusted Sammy on her lap. "We'll be fine, dear. Just don't be too long. I think he's hungry."

"I'm not surprised. That baby eats more than most kids twice his size," she commented as she moved into the opposite bedroom. "There's a bottle ready in the fridge if he gets too restless."

She eyed the open closet defensively. Jenny's clothes—blouses crammed haphazardly onto hangers, blue jeans rolled and stuffed on the shelf top above, the one dress she owned to wear for special occasions—beckoned to her.

She'd already put off this unpleasant task too long. The time had come for her to finish packing Jenny's things away and to sell the bungalow.

She reached up to the shelf above her head and tugged on a pile of jeans, which came fluttering down on top of her. Something solid hit her head, making a loud, clapping noise and stinging her skin where it slapped. She instinctively threw her arms over her to protect herself from being beaned with further projectiles, but none were forthcoming. It was just one book.

A book had been rolled up in a pair of jeans? That was something she didn't see every day. Curious, she reached to retrieve the errant missile.

A Bible. Jenny had a Bible, hidden away like a treasured possession. Somehow she'd assumed Jenny had left the faith, if her actions were anything to go by.

Curious, Jasmine thumbed the pages, recognizing the flowing loops and curves in the margins as Jenny's handwriting. Even though Jenny said she hadn't made peace with God until the end of her life, this Bible obviously had held some significance for her. Bits of paper were carefully folded into the book, as well as a single white rose, carefully pressed and dried, softly folded onto the page with the family tree.

Jasmine brushed her fingers over the crisp, dry calligraphy. "February twenty-fifth. Jennifer Lynn Enderlin married Christopher Scott Jordan."

Tears burned in her throat, and she bit her lip to keep them from flowing. Would the pain never lessen?

She ran a finger over the black ink, the carefully formed letters. Jenny's handwriting had always been so much neater than her own. It had been a source of endless amusement for Jenny to be able to harass her older sister about the chicken-scratching she passed off as handwriting. It was, she had often teased, God's sure sign to her that Jasmine was meant to be a doctor.

She curled up on the floor against the edge of the bed, staring at the Bible. It was a tangible piece of Jenny. She could run her fingers down the cracked leather binding, read the notes Jenny made in the margins about the Scriptures she read.

Slowly, almost reverently, she opened the Bible, silently flipping page after page, pausing to read a comment here and a highlighted Scripture there. Jenny had obviously spent a lot of time in the Word before her death. Jasmine's throat constricted around her breath.

The doorbell sounded. She snapped the book shut and stuffed it under Jenny's pillow. Her thoughts whirlwinded as she considered who might be at the door. Perhaps someone was here to look at the bungalow, even though it wasn't listed yet.

"I'll get it!" she whispered, peeking into the extra bedroom. Sammy was sound asleep in Gram's arms, and it appeared Gram, too, had taken the liberty of a small nap. Her chin nestled against the baby boy, and her mouth had dropped open with the light buzz of snoring.

Jasmine chuckled quietly and moved to the front door. It was only when her hand was already on the knob and she'd half opened the door that it occurred to her who might be waiting.

"Christopher!" Jasmine confirmed, staring up at the tall, ruggedly handsome man before her. "What are you doing here?"

Her heart skipped a beat, then thumped an erratic tempo in her throat, blocking her breath. Anger, shock and a dozen other emotions buzzed through her like a swarm of angry bees.

A smile tugged at the corner of his mouth, but it didn't reach his eyes, which gleamed like cold, gray stones. Despite herself, Jasmine remembered how those eyes used to twinkle, changing in shade from a deep gray to a cobalt blue whenever he was happy.

He clearly wasn't happy now. The quirk of a smile changed into a frown, matching the twin creases between his light brown eyebrows.

"That's a fine welcome for an old…friend," he commented slowly, his scowl darkening.

"What do you want?" she snapped, her voice cold. She felt a stab of guilt for her rudeness, but she brushed it away.

The man didn't deserve better. In her book, anyone who deserted his family didn't deserve much of anything. Except maybe a swift kick in the backside.

"Cut to the chase, Christopher." The determined gleam in his eyes left no doubt he wasn't here for a social call. And the sooner he was gone, the better.

Every muscle in her body had tensed to the point of physical pain, but that was nothing in comparison to the wrenching agony of her heart at seeing him again. She had no idea it would be this difficult to face the man she'd once loved with all her heart. She clenched her fists, her fingernails biting into her palms.

I'm not ready.

She knew she'd eventually have to confront him, but she'd hoped to be doing it on her terms, in her time, on her own turf. Three strikes and she was out before she even got a chance to bat.

He was taller than she remembered, with a lithe frame and broad shoulders. He curled a steel gray cowboy hat in his fists, leaving exposed the cowlick that made his light brown hair cock up just over his left eyebrow. She remembered once telling him it gave him a roguish appearance. He'd just laughed and shaken his head. Maybe if he'd known just how much she'd wanted to spend her life with him—to marry him and raise a family with him—things might have been different. If only…

"Medical school has done wonders for your manners," he commented gruffly. "What do they teach you there? How to offend your neighbors in one easy lesson?"

The barbs found their mark. "You're not my neighbor." She scratched out the words, since her throat had suddenly gone dry.

He raised one eyebrow. "No? Whatever happened to the Good Samaritan? Or didn't you learn that one in church?"

Jasmine cringed inwardly. It wasn't like him to throw Scripture at her that way. He possessed a strong, quiet faith, which he neither took lightly nor tossed in someone's face like pearls before swine.

She wondered where that faith had gone. The past few months were proof of his decline. Choosing to marry Jenny over her without even the courtesy of a phone call, then up and abandoning the poor girl once she was carrying his child—the change was too great to fathom. The icy-eyed man standing before her was a virtual stranger.

"Maybe you haven't heard," he continued. "I'm living at Lucille's place now." He rolled the brim of his hat once more, then jammed it on his head.

"With the ranch hands," she added dryly.

"Mmm. So you did know, then. I was wondering how long it would take for the news to get back to you. Small town and all." He peered over her shoulder into the room. "Aren't you going to invite me in?"

She heard Sammy cry out, and wondered if Christopher heard it, as well. With lightning swiftness, she stepped out onto the front porch and quietly but firmly closed the door behind her.

"No. I'd rather not." She wondered if he heard the quavering in her voice, and determined to control it with all the force of her will.

Christopher appeared unaffected by her intentional rudeness. He placed a hand on the doorframe above her right shoulder and leaned into her, his face only inches from her own.

Her head spinning, she tried to inhale, tried to steady herself mentally. Instead, she breathed a heady whiff of his western-scented cologne.

Her favorite. The brand he used to wear especially for her.

Panicking, she stepped backward until her shoulders hit the solid strength of the door. This furtive movement was no deterrent for Christopher, who simply crooked his elbow to narrow the distance between them.

The brim of his hat touched her forehead, and he tilted his head to move in closer. His breath mingled with hers, his steel gaze never leaving hers for a moment.

She felt the way a mouse must feel when hypnotized by a snake's haunting eyes—knowing she would be consumed, yet powerless to look away.

He was going to kiss her. The snake wasn't even going to ask. Just take. And she wouldn't be able to stop him, so mesmerized was she by his gleaming eyes that looked so serious beneath the brim of his hat.

She closed her eyes. Despite her head screaming to the contrary, her heart beckoned him closer. It wasn't rational; in fact, it was quite out of the question. But knowing that didn't stop her from wanting his lips on hers just one last time. Perhaps it was a move toward resolution. She leaned closer, anticipating the moment their lips would meet.

"Where is he?" His low voice resonated in her ears.

Her eyes snapped open to meet his amused gaze. The twinkle had returned, and the dimple in his left cheek was showing. He was completely relaxed, and he was smirking at her!

Hurt and anger warring within her, she pushed both hands into his chest and shoved as hard as she could.

Christopher stepped back, but only because he wanted to. He didn't want to admit that his feelings hadn't changed, not in all these years, and not with all that had happened between them.

But now was not the time to pursue his feelings, though surely that time would arrive. He would *make* that time come, one way or another.

There were bridges to be built to gap the distance

between them, and that would take some time. He'd known from the moment he decided to return to West-cliffe that it wouldn't be easy. Not for him, and most definitely not for Jasmine.

She could be one stubborn woman, he thought, pressing his lips together. But then again, he was a stubborn man. He clamped his teeth down hard and stared her down.

"Get out of here, you snake." Her voice was a low rasp.

Snake? He cringed inwardly at her animosity. He'd hoped her anger at the situation would have dulled enough with time for her to listen to reason, but it was obvious she was no closer to being ready to accept the truth than she'd been a year ago. He set his jaw and narrowed his eyes on her. "Not until I've seen my son."

"*Your* son? *Your* son is doing very well without you, thank you very much. When did you decide to be a daddy, Christopher? Yesterday? It's not like a hat that you can put on whenever you please. What right do you have to waltz in and demand to see him? He's a twenty-four-hour-a-day responsibility, which I have been facing alone, I might add. He's a flesh-and-blood human being, not some toy you can play with whenever the urge strikes you!"

"Yeah," he agreed, tipping his hat backward and raking his fingers through his hair. Some things hadn't changed.

Jasmine Enderlin was as pigheaded as she'd always been. If she hadn't jumped to conclusions a year ago, he wouldn't be standing here like a stranger on her front porch. God willing, they would've been married.

But God wasn't willing. And Jasmine wasn't budging.

"Give me a break, Jazz. I've been busting my tail to get back here."

"Is that so?" she snapped, bracing her arms on her hips. "And I'm supposed to feel sorry for you because you worked so hard to get back here?"

He leveled his gaze on her and stepped forward. "That's *so*," he said, his tone hard. "And at the moment, I don't give a wooden nickel how you feel about me. I want to see my son. Now."

Chapter Two

Jasmine's breath came in short, uneasy gasps. Her head swirled with emotion. To have to see Christopher again, to face not only what he'd done to her heart, but to her family, was enough to daunt the strongest of women. But to have him waltz into town and demand to see his child with all the arrogance of the perfect father was positively the last straw.

Anger welled in her chest.

"What right do you have to demand *anything?*" she growled through clenched teeth, willing her throbbing heart to slow before it beat a hole through her chest.

Christopher pulled the hat down low over his brows and leaned toward her, his posture firm and menacing. For a minute he just stared at her, the ice in his gaze freezing her insides. When he finally spoke, it was in a whisper. "I'm his father, Jazz."

His voice cracked on her name, and for the briefest moment, she saw a flicker of pain cross his gaze, so deep and intense she almost felt sorry for him.

Without even realizing what she was doing, she reached out a hand to stroke his strong jaw, then withdrew it just as quickly, curling her fingers into her chest as if she'd been burned.

She didn't feel *anything* for Christopher Jordan, she reminded herself harshly. Not anymore. He didn't deserve her pity, or her compassion. Scriptural verses flooded her mind, words about mercy and forgiveness, but she refused to concede. Not for him.

It didn't take a genius to read the change in her demeanor, and his eyes quickly shaded, resuming the tint of frosty steel.

"I have rights," he reminded her, his voice as cold as his gaze.

Jasmine steeled her heart, preparing to do mental battle with the man who'd once been the love of her life. She'd fight him tooth and nail for Sammy, and in the end, that was all that mattered. Not the past. The good or the bad. She wouldn't let her heart betray her a second time.

"You lost any rights you had the night you left Jenny alone and pregnant," she snarled.

His lips thinned. He opened his mouth to speak, then abruptly shut it again.

"You *aren't* Sammy's father," she added abruptly, sensing her advantage.

The barb met its mark, if his sharp intake of breath was any indication. She rushed on before she lost her nerve.

"You can threaten me with a lawsuit if you want, but I'm not backing down. Jenny made *me* Sammy's guardian. I've got papers to prove it—papers that will stand up in *any* court of law."

Jasmine wasn't as certain of her claim as she sounded, but she wasn't about to let on. She made a mental note to speak with the family attorney, feeling pleased that she'd struck Christopher dumb, at least for a moment.

He swept off his hat, his gaze genuinely hurt and confused. "Who said anything about a lawsuit?" he demanded, blowing out a breath. "Shoot, Jazz, don't you know me well enough by now to know I wouldn't do that to you? Or to Sammy," he added, under his breath.

Hat in hand, he reached out his arms to her, beseeching her with his gaze as well as his posture. "Just let me see him. I won't stay long. I just want to see that he's safe and—" His voice choked, cutting his sentence short. "Please, Jasmine. Just for a minute."

She felt herself relenting even as her answer left her lips. "Forget it. Not now, and not ever. Go back from whatever rock you crawled out from under, Christopher. There's nothing here for you now."

Her heart felt like it had been through a paper shredder, and she whirled away from him before she gave in to the earnest pleading in his tone. She had to get away from him until she could think things through, knowing she couldn't put two straight thoughts together when he looked at her that way.

How could she not remember the man Christopher once was, the strong, gentle man she loved? But that man was gone, her dreams shattered by the same disheartening reality that was responsible for creating the sweet little boy in the bedroom.

Which only served to prove that good really could come from something bad.

No matter what, she had to protect Sammy. She opened the screen door and slipped inside, glancing behind her shoulder in time to see Christopher punch his hat on his head and move to follow her.

Her heart pounded as she reached for the door and slammed it behind her, barely locking Christopher out before he began pounding.

"And good riddance," she whispered, leaning her forehead on the door.

Jasmine was terrified Sammy would wake up and start wailing. If that happened, and Christopher heard his baby, he'd never leave. She slid down against the wall, cupping her hands over her ears. Why wouldn't he just go away and leave them alone?

After ten minutes, when she'd finally concluded he'd never quit pounding, she heard him stomp back to his truck and slam the door. She felt both relieved and yet strangely desolate now that she was once again alone.

Her heart was still in her throat as she peeked from behind the front curtain and watched him drive away in his old Chevy truck, relaxing only when she knew for sure he was gone.

He would be back. Christopher Jordan was a stubborn, vigorous man who actively pursued what he wanted. He wouldn't let this episode stop him from seeing Sammy. But at least it would give her time to think, to sort out her feelings so she could face him again without the emotions that earlier clouded her judgment.

Running a palm over her hair to smooth it, she took a deep breath and forced a smile to her lips. She knew Gram would see right through it, but she had to try.

Head held high, she walked as quietly and serenely as possible into the bedroom. Gram sang softly to the baby, rocking slowly back and forth with Sammy tucked in the crook of her arm.

It was such a peaceful scene, and so much at variance with the frantic pace of Jasmine's heart, that she nearly turned tail and walked out again. But Gram caught her eye and smiled.

"He's sleeping soundly, dear," she said softly, continuing to rock. "I fed him the whole bottle. He's probably down for the count. Can you help me lay him in the bassinet?"

Jasmine nodded and moved forward, holding Sammy a moment longer than necessary, inhaling his sweet, baby scent and enjoying the feel of his soft skin against her cheek. It was only the threat of losing him that made her realize that she couldn't live without him.

It was more than just the schedule changes, the responsibility that came with having a newborn. More even than knowing there was someone completely dependent on her for his every need.

It was the space in her heart that grew larger every day, ebbing and flowing with love for this little one.

There was no way she was going to let Christopher take him away. She'd once thought the gaping hole he rent in her heart would never be mended. But loving Sammy forced her to open up her heart once again, to feel and live and hope.

She kissed the infant on his soft forehead and pushed the thatch of downy hair from his eyes. She wouldn't let the little guy down. No matter what.

"Is he gone?" Gram asked gently.

With an audible sigh, she took her grandmother's elbow and led her to the kitchen, where she seated the elderly woman on a foldout chair. Jenny's financial straits were obvious by the card table she used in place of a regular kitchen table.

Sammy had the best of everything, most of which had been bought by Jenny before her death. She had sacrificed everything for her unborn son, showing the kind of sweet, giving person she was all the way up to her last breath. She would have done anything for her Sammy.

Jasmine felt a tug of grief, and made a pretense of looking through the cupboard in order to have a moment to fold those feelings back into her memory. She already knew what was in the cupboards, which amounted to a box of peppermint tea and a box of saltine crackers.

"Do you want some tea?" she asked, hoping her voice didn't sound as high and squeaky to Gram as it did to her own ears. It annoyed her to betray her feelings in her voice, especially to Gram, who was already much too perceptive. With a determined effort, she steadied her voice and continued. "I think I'll have a cup, myself."

"Are you okay?"

She took her time pulling two mugs from a shelf and filling them with water, before turning to face her grandmother. "Yes, of course. Why wouldn't I be?"

"I can't imagine," Gram replied dryly.

She set the cups in the microwave and turned it on, then sat down across from her grandmother. "You're too wise for your own good."

Gram met Jasmine's gaze over the top of her spectacles and chuckled. "I haven't been alive for eighty years without learning something."

Jasmine reached for Gram's hand and squeezed it.

"You've been so much help to me these past months," she admitted, her voice quavering with emotion. "I couldn't have made it without you."

"What's family for?" Gram said, waving off her comment with a slight grunt of protest.

The microwave buzzed, and Jasmine jumped up. As she dipped the tea bags into the mugs, she took a deep breath and plunged ahead. "It *was* Christopher at the door."

"Who else would it be? Didn't sound like he was in a hurry to leave, either."

"That's the understatement of the year," she agreed quietly. "I should have realized he'd be back, that he'd want to see Sammy at some point. I just wasn't prepared for him to show up today."

"And you sent him packing." It was a statement rather than a question, punctuated with a dry chuckle.

Jasmine laughed, but it didn't reach her heart. "You could say that. I slammed the door in his face."

"He'll be back." Gram nodded her head as if confirming her own words.

The flatness Jasmine felt when Christopher left wound itself more tightly around her chest. "I know," she whispered.

"What are you going to do about him?"

Gram was nothing if not direct, she reflected. No games. No beating around the bush. She just said what she thought and was done with it. One of the perks that came with age, Gram always said just before blurting out something outrageous.

Jasmine shook her head. "I don't know yet. Seeing him again confused me. I thought it would be easier. I thought…"

"That you hated him?" Gram queried gently, finishing the sentence for her. "Love doesn't give up so easily, my dear."

She shook her head fiercely. "No. I'm not in love with Christopher anymore." If her heart believed that, she wouldn't be quaking in her shoes, she thought acerbically. But she'd never admit it, not even to herself. "I've been over him for a long time."

"Have you?" Gram's questioning gaze met hers, and she looked away, afraid her grandmother would read the truth she knew must shine through her tears.

She couldn't love Christopher! Not after all these years, and especially not after everything he'd done to her and her family.

Then why did her heart leap when she saw him again?

She'd loved him since they were both in high school, she rationalized. For years they'd been inseparable. He'd been the man to whom she pledged her life, with whom she was ready to tie the knot.

Was it any wonder she would have such a polar reaction at seeing him again?

How could she not? It was only natural, after all, for her to have lingering feelings for a man who was such a large part of her past. Some of her happiest memories were with Christopher Jordan, and that was something his recent actions couldn't take away.

"My feelings don't matter," she said at last, shaking her head. "This isn't about me." She paused and took a deep breath, giving the bassinet a pointed look. "He wants to see Sammy. For all I know, he wants to take him away. And somehow, I've got to figure out a way to stop him."

Gram slowly stood and stretched, then shuffled to Jasmine's side, placing a consoling arm around her shoulders.

That the arm around her didn't have the power of former years mattered not a bit. Strength flowed from the elder to the younger with an intensity that only came from inner peace.

"I know this is hard for you, dear," she said, patting Jasmine's shoulder as she would to comfort a child. "But don't ignore your feelings. They are God given. Pray about it. Search your heart. And, Jasmine?"

"Mmm?"

"Talk to Christopher."

"*Talk* to him?" she screeched, her anger returning in spades. "Gram, I never thought *you'd* be on his side, after what happened to Jenny! Why should I *talk* to him?"

Gram's eyebrows creased as she frowned. "Don't you speak to me that way, young lady," she said, her tone brooking no argument. "I may be eighty, but I can still take you over my knee!"

Jasmine stepped back, surprised, then broke into a tired laugh, serving as a valve for the release of her anger. Gram was right, of course.

She hugged her grandmother as hard as the older woman's frail bones would allow. "I'm sorry," she said, her heart contrite. "I'm just confused. I'm sure I'll be all right after I pray about it." The words slipped out of her mouth from years of training, and she just wanted to bite her tongue. Pray about it, indeed.

Gram nodded, not appearing to notice the grimace Jasmine made. "I'll pray, too. It's the best we can do. The first thing, and the best. It'll all work out. In God's way, and in God's timing. We just have to look to Him and trust that He knows what's best."

Well, on that point, anyway, Jasmine couldn't agree more. God, if there was one, must certainly have something spectacular planned, or else He had a very peculiar sense of humor. If only she knew what He had in mind—and what role she was to play.

Christopher pulled a hard right off the gravel mountain road and drove into the brush, not caring that the pine trees were probably scratching the truck's exterior. When he was in far enough that he couldn't see the road, he slammed the gear into Park and shut down the engine.

This wasn't the way he'd meant it to be. He thumped a closed fist against the steering wheel. He hadn't meant to alienate Jasmine with the first words out of his mouth. What a big lug he was. Talk first, stick his big, dirty boots in his mouth afterward. He could certainly add his first encounter with her in a year to his ever-growing list of failures.

This one, however, he had to take full credit for. Much of what happened to him wasn't in his control, a part of God's will he couldn't understand. But this was completely his own doing, and he'd blown it big time. Not exactly a surprise, with his track record.

He'd been so certain he was meant to come back to Westcliffe. What else could he do? He loved Jasmine. He always had. To think of living without her—and Sammy—was unbearable.

But if his first encounter with her was anything to go by, he had a long way to travel to get back in her good graces. Her closed attitude left him shaken and unsure of himself. She didn't even try to hide how much she loathed seeing him again.

He lifted his hat and raked his fingers through the short ends of his hair. Frustration seethed through every nerve ending until his whole body tingled.

All he wanted to do was see Sammy, not run off with the boy like some criminal, though that's how he'd been treated. And Sammy had been in that bungalow. He'd heard the baby's cry and the soothing sounds of Jasmine's grandmother coming from the other room. What kind of a fool did she think he was?

The point of it—and that's what hurt—was that Jazz didn't want him to see the baby.

He understood her hesitance. He'd done a lot of things that needed explaining. But in the meantime, he'd hoped their years together would count for something.

He wasn't foolish enough to expect that he would be able to knock on her door and resume their relationship, where it had broken off before she'd gone off to med school, but couldn't she at least listen to him?

"Ha!" he said aloud, the sound echoing in the small cab of his truck. She hadn't listened to him then, and she wouldn't listen now.

Especially now. She wouldn't trust him any more than any other of Westcliffe's residents did. Far less, even, for she had more reasons to doubt him than the small town that virtually shunned his existence now that he was back.

The neighbors he could live without. Jasmine, he couldn't.

He'd hurt the woman he loved most in the world, and the knowledge sat like lead in his stomach. It was a burden he'd been carrying since the day she'd turned away from him and walked right out of his life. The day the world discovered he would soon be a father.

Jasmine thought he'd betrayed her, and mincing words didn't change anything. Pain seared through his chest.

He wasn't denying his actions, no matter how questionable the whole thing was in his mind. What else could he have done, under the circumstances? He thought he was doing the right thing. He thought Jasmine would understand, that she'd want him to take the actions he'd decided on for Jenny's sake.

But she wouldn't even listen. What she'd learned, she hadn't learned from him, and he would regret that for the rest of his life. He should have made the trip to Denver as soon as he found out about Jenny. But there was so much to do, and not much time in which to do it.

He'd been so wrapped up in the tailspin his life had taken that he'd put it off, thinking he'd approach Jasmine when the ruckus had died down. After he'd taken care of the necessities, and before she'd heard the truth from someone else.

She still didn't know the truth. He'd hoped to tell her today.

He'd even hoped she'd forgive him. It was part of what drove him back to town—to ask her forgiveness for his part in the tragedy that had become their lives, and to ask for a second chance.

It was obviously not going to happen that way. He clamped his teeth together until he could feel his pulse pounding in his temples. What he wanted didn't matter. Not yet, and maybe not ever.

He had another responsibility—Sammy, the baby

he'd never seen. He wasn't going to let that boy down. And if that meant postponing the inevitable confrontation with Jasmine on personal issues, so be it.

His resolution did, however, present a unique set of circumstances, since he had to go through Jasmine to get to Sammy. Emotional issues aside, Jasmine was a formidable woman. If she decided to make things rough for him, there was no doubt in his mind she would succeed.

Which meant he had to convince her otherwise. Make her see reason. They needed to put the past aside, sit down together and discuss the issues like the adults they were.

This wasn't some high school spat they could just ignore and expect to go away. They were dealing with the welfare of a child. For all intents and purposes, *his* child.

His throat tightened. He had actually been relieved to hear Jasmine had been appointed Sammy's legal guardian, though he would never tell her so. He couldn't think of a better mother for the boy. He could depend on her to take care of Sammy as if he were her own.

And he could leave.

He recognized that the moment he'd seen the determination on Jasmine's face. He could turn around, walk right out of Westcliffe, and never look back, knowing Sammy was in capable hands. Loving hands.

And he would be doing no less than what everyone expected.

Maybe that would be best. How was he to know? He wasn't ready to be a father. What did he know about babies? He hadn't planned to be a father for a few years yet, after he and Jasmine had settled down. Blast it anyway, he didn't even know how to change a diaper.

What kind of hole had he dug for himself? And all because he was trying to do the right thing.

He blew out a breath and started the engine, gunning it into Reverse and making the wheels spin as he pulled back onto the dirt road. He shifted into gear and put the pedal to the metal.

Heading back toward town.

He couldn't leave. He couldn't go without Sammy, even knowing he was in Jasmine's capable hands. And though he knew he would cause a lot more pain before he could start mending hurts, it had to be done.

He had to go back. He needed Sammy in his life.

Sammy—and Jasmine.

Chapter Three

Three days later, Jasmine stared over the rim of her coffee cup at the soft-spoken cowboy across from her. The term *cowboy* used loosely, she thought wryly. Christopher had been born and raised in this mountain town, but he couldn't ride a horse to save his life. Ranching wasn't in his blood.

He looked the part, though, with his form-fitting western jeans, snap-down western shirt and a steel gray cowboy hat. Of course, he'd taken off the hat when he'd entered the café, exposing his thatch of windblown brown hair.

Another cowboy trait.

Her mind was being perversely obtuse this afternoon, she thought. How she could find anything humorous to laugh about in her present state of mind was beyond her comprehension. It was as if her subconscious were seeking to avoid the inevitable confrontation.

The determined gleam in Christopher's eyes and the hard set of his jaw gave him away. Why else would he have asked her to meet him in a small café in Wetmore, a half hour's drive from their hometown and well out of the public eye?

She'd been surprised when he'd called yesterday and asked to meet her, but now she was as prepared as she'd ever be for whatever he would throw at her, though she still couldn't come up with a single acceptable reason for a man to abandon his wife and unborn child. And then return to claim his son after Jenny was dead. If he didn't want the boy before...

The familiar swell of anger rushed through her, but she tamped it down. She would listen. She owed him that much, whatever sort of torn and twisted man he'd become. He claimed he wanted Sammy, and today he would attempt to explain why.

Not that his words would make any difference. She already knew what her answer would be, despite anything he told her.

He couldn't have the baby. Not in a billion, trillion years.

Sammy was her son now. The papers declaring it so were firmly in her possession and valid in a court of law.

She'd fight him tooth and nail in court if she had to, but she prayed it wouldn't come to that. That was her true objective—to reason with him, to try to touch the man she once knew, the man buried deep inside the monster sitting across from her.

To make him leave quietly. And alone.

"What'll ya'll have?" said a waitress, tapping her pencil against her pad of paper. Her cheek near her bottom gum was plump with tobacco. Jasmine had heard of gum-chewing waitresses, but the thought of a tobacco-chewing waitress was more than her stomach could handle.

"A cup of hot tea for me," she said weakly, shifting her attention from the woman to focus on her queasy insides. "Peppermint, if you've got it."

She wasn't sure she could swallow even tea, but it occurred to her the peppermint might settle her stomach a little. She'd used it on Sammy's colic to good effect, so she could only hope it would ease some of her own distress.

"Double cheeseburger with everything, onion rings and a chocolate shake," Christopher ordered, smiling up at the waitress as if his entire life weren't hanging in the balance of this conversation.

Maybe it wasn't. Maybe he didn't care. Jasmine didn't know whether to feel relieved or annoyed.

It was obvious *his* appetite, at least, wasn't affected by their meeting. And *he* wasn't keeping his hands clenched in his lap to keep them from quivering, either. She pried her fingers apart and put her hands on the table.

Christopher cleared his throat and ran the tip of his index finger around the rim of his mug. "Remember when we used to sneak up here on Friday nights?" he asked, chuckling lightly. His gaze met hers, the familiar twinkle in his light gray eyes making her heart skip a beat.

Jasmine felt her face warm under his scrutiny. She knew what he was thinking, the memories this café evoked. Two carefree youths, so much in love, their lives filled with laughter and happiness. And hope.

"We thought we were being so underhanded, slipping out of town." His light, tenor voice spread like silk over her. "Remember? We were so sure nobody noticed we were gone. We really thought we were pulling one over on everyone. And all the time, they were probably laughing and shaking their heads at us."

Jasmine laughed quietly despite herself. "I'm sure Gram knew all along. She had such—" She was going to say high hopes for the two of them, but the thought hit her like a slap in the face, so she left the end of her sentence dangling sharply in the air.

How ironic that he'd picked this location to meet today. She'd been so wrapped up in dealing with her crisis that she hadn't realized the poetic justice in his choosing this café. She swallowed hard, trying in vain to keep heat from suffusing her face.

It was the place where they'd first said *I love you.* The night they'd pledged themselves to each other forever. The night he'd asked her to be his wife. Before med school. And before Sammy.

She could see in his eyes that he was sharing her thoughts, reliving the memories right along with her. Her chest flooded with a tangle of emotions. Anger that he had brought her here. Hope because he remembered, too.

Had he brought her here on purpose, she wondered, as a way to have the upper hand? Or was this simply a convenient spot to meet, away from the prying eyes of the world? Did he mean to remind her of their joyful past, to taunt her with what could never be? She pinned him with her gaze, asking the question without speaking.

In answer, he swiped a hand down his face. "I'm sorry," he said, shaking his head regretfully. "It was thoughtless of me to bring us here. I should have realized—"

"It's okay," she interrupted, holding up a hand. "Better here than in Westcliffe, where we might be seen." She closed her eyes and eased the air from her lungs. At least he wasn't trying to rub her nose in the past, and for that, she was grateful.

He let out a breath that could have been a chuckle, but clearly wasn't, from the tortured look on his face. "I prayed about this meeting before I called you," he admitted in a low voice.

He clenched his napkin in his fist and looked out the window, allowing Jasmine to study his chiseled profile. There were small lines around his eyes, and dark furrows on his forehead. They weren't laugh lines, she noticed sadly. He looked ten years older than his twenty-eight years.

"Truth be told," he continued, still avoiding her eyes, "praying is about the only thing I've been doing for weeks."

His admission wasn't what she expected, and it took her aback. She remained silent for a moment, trying to digest what he was telling her.

She'd assumed from his actions that he'd played his faith false, that he'd given up on God and was taking his own way with things.

Abandoning his family was hardly the act of a man walking with his Maker. But now he was telling her, in so many words, that his faith was still intact. That he believed God was in control. That he believed prayer would help this wretched situation. That God was *here*.

She barely restrained the bitter laugh that desperately wanted to escape her lips. Irony seethed through her. How had he kept his faith in God when hers so easily disappeared?

He smiled, almost shyly, as if his revelation had taken great effort. It probably had, though there was a time when there had been nothing they couldn't share between them.

In so many ways, she wanted to close her eyes, embrace his belief, wipe the slate clean and start all over again. To return to the time in her life when she believed, and when her belief had given her hope.

But that was naiveté. She wasn't a child, to believe in miracles. To believe in a close, personal God who would help her through life's problems. Her faith was ebbing and flowing like waves on rocks.

She wasn't even sure she believed in God, at least in a personal God who watched over His flock like a shepherd watching over His sheep.

She couldn't—and didn't—pay Him more than lip service, and at this point she was hardly doing that. Although she hadn't denied her faith outright, she hadn't set foot in a church in months.

The subject humiliated and frustrated her. All those years she considered her faith strong, yet it wilted with the first attack of trial.

Some Christian she was. Or maybe she never had been. She was too confused to know.

How could she believe in a God who would allow Christopher to get away with what he'd done?

And Jenny—what about Jenny? If God was there, why hadn't He helped her? Why hadn't He healed her? He'd forced Jasmine to stand helpless and watch her sister die, her head crammed full of medical knowledge and unable to do a thing to save her.

"Would you pray with me?" he asked when she didn't answer.

Prayer. Gram suggested it before, and now Christopher was bringing up the issue. Her heart clenched. It wasn't as if she never tried.

She had. Last night on her knees beside her bed. But the words wouldn't come, and the space between her and the heavenly realm seemed unbridgeable. God wasn't listening. Or He had cut her off. As she had once cut off Christopher.

She shook her head. "We're in a public restaurant, Christopher. Let's just get down to business."

She cringed inside as she said the words. It wasn't *business*. It was a baby's life they were talking about.

He looked vaguely astonished, but he didn't argue. Instead, his gentle smile tipped the corner of his lips as he reached for her hand, which she quickly snatched from his grasp.

Shrugging, he plunged into the reason they were meeting. "You know what I want. I want to see Sammy. I want to—"

"Take him away from me?" she snapped, heedless of the fact that she hadn't given him a chance to finish his sentence. Suddenly she felt completely unsure of herself as Sammy's guardian, of her ability to provide what he needed. Without thinking, she took her insecurity out on the man sitting across from her. "I don't think so, Christopher."

He opened his mouth to protest, but she gestured for him to stop.

"You need to understand something," she continued, her voice crackling with intensity. "You weren't around when Sammy was born. You didn't walk him up and down the hall at all hours of the night because he had colic and didn't want to sleep. You haven't changed him, fed him or bathed him."

"I haven't even—"

She pinned him with a glare. "I have. *I* was the one there for Sammy. And *I* am going to be the one to raise him."

"But I want—" His voice closed around the words and he coughed. "I want to do all those things. I want to be there for the boy. My..." He hesitated. "My son."

He looked petulant, and his eyes pleaded for her mercy.

Why, oh why did his mere physical presence affect her so? He once used those very same big blue-gray eyes to get his own way with her when they argued over which movie to see or where to go for dinner.

This wasn't one of those times. Nor was it a debatable issue.

"Let me explain something to you," she said, her voice splintering with restrained anger. "I very frankly don't give a snip what your story is. I don't even want to hear it, though I'm sure you've spent many hours rehearsing for my benefit."

His scowl darkened and he grunted in protest.

"No, really. It doesn't matter. Nothing you say matters. What *matters* is that I've bonded with this baby, and nothing is going to convince me to give him away. Most especially to you."

With a sharp intake of breath, he sat back in his seat and pounded a fist on the tabletop, making the silverware rattle.

Water from her cup splashed onto the surface of the table, and she quickly wiped it with the edge of her napkin, her face flaming with anger and embarrassment.

She hazarded a glance at the neighboring booths, wondering if anyone had noticed his outburst.

"Even before you've heard what really happened?" he asked through clenched teeth, his chest rising and falling with the exertion of each angry breath.

She lifted one sardonic brow. "Astonish me. You were abducted by aliens. You've been in a coma. You had amnesia. What, Christopher? What's your story?" As much as she tried to keep her voice low, it lifted with each word to a higher crescendo until she'd reached well beyond shrill and piercing.

Now *she* was the one causing the scene, and it was *his* fault. She didn't care how irrational and childish the thought was. She clamped her jaw shut and glared defiantly at Christopher, and then at the patrons staring at her. Life had freeze-framed, with everyone's attention on her.

She blew out a frustrated breath, furious that he had provoked her to make a display of herself.

"Jazz," he began, reaching out with both hands in a conciliatory gesture.

She threw her napkin down on the table and stood. "I thought this meeting was a good idea when you first suggested it," she said slowly, articulating each syllable in a low, precise tone. "I was mistaken."

She looked blindly out the window, then back to Christopher. "I love Sammy, and he's staying with me. End of subject." She met his gaze briefly, willing her strength to hold out until she could flee from his presence. "Goodbye, Christopher."

She turned and walked away from him, holding her chin high and staying steadfastly determined not to look at the patrons she felt were staring at her.

Christopher could pick up the tab on the check. It served him right. Her blood boiling, she wished momentarily that she'd ordered a full-course steak dinner instead of just hot tea.

When she exited the café, she pulled in a deep breath of mountain air, closing her eyes as fresh, cool oxygen flooded her lungs. If only she could dissipate the heat in her brain as easily.

Walking away from Christopher was the hardest thing she'd ever done. He was suffering in his own way, she realized, and her presence affected him as much as his did her.

All the more reason for them to stay away from each other, she decided, fortifying her decision with every justification available to her.

Her heart said a father should be with his son. Her mind said Christopher forfeited that right when he walked away from Jenny and his unborn baby.

She had to cling to reason, no matter what her emotions were doing. Sammy's well-being depended on it. Probably her own happiness, too. She loved that baby. And for now, maybe for always, that love would have to be enough.

Christopher ate his food in silence, ignoring the curious stares and speculative talk around him. His mind was so preoccupied with his troubles that he barely tasted his food, and had to order a second milk shake to wash the hamburger down his dry throat.

He loved Jasmine more than ever. He thought the feelings had faded some with time, but sitting across from her today, he knew he was fooling himself. The ache in his chest only shaded his deeper feelings. He would do anything to wipe the pain from her eyes, and it was the ultimate irony to know he'd been the one to put it there in the first place. Sure, Jasmine was being harsh and stubborn, but who could blame her? He knew it was her fear of losing Sammy that was speaking for her. She'd always been an all-or-nothing kind of woman, a fact Christopher admired. Her obvious devotion and loyalty to her nephew only made him love her more.

Pain lanced his temple, and he reached a hand up to rub it firmly across his brow. Nothing was going as he had hoped.

He knew without a doubt that when she walked away today, she wouldn't meet with him again, at least not intentionally. She'd run the other direction whenever she saw him, screaming inwardly if not in reality.

Which meant his next move must be furtive. He'd have to follow her around until an opportunity presented itself to speak with her again—in a time and in a location where she had no place to go except into his arms.

God would give him that opportunity. Or maybe he'd have to make his own.

Jasmine didn't immediately return to Gram's apartment, where she was staying with Sammy. She knew Gram would take care of the baby as long as necessary. And right now, Jasmine needed to be alone, to have time to think.

Not entirely conscious of where she was going or why, she found herself parking in front of Jenny's cottage. There was still a lot of work to be done, she supposed. And it was quiet here, a far cry from the hustle and bustle of the medical clinic.

Once in the small cabin, she started to absently box up Jenny's things, beginning with the books in her room. She picked up an empty apple box from the pile and began stacking various romance novels spine up, mixed with some hardbacked classic literature.

Jasmine laughed to herself, trying to picture her flighty sister reading the classics. Fashion magazines were more her style.

Had been her style. Jasmine quickly sobered. How well had she really known Jenny? She suspected not as well as she should have, especially in the last few years.

They'd been close as children, though there was four years difference between them. But they had drifted apart when Jasmine reached high school and got interested in friends, makeup and boys.

In Christopher.

And when Jenny caught up, she'd taken a different road than Jasmine, who'd been class president and received straight As. Jenny hung out with the flashy crowd, the ones with too much money and too much time. Jasmine had always wondered what Jenny could have in common with her friends.

She didn't have money, and she wasn't college-bound. She just didn't seem the type. But she appeared to be happy, and Jasmine had left it alone. How she'd ended up with a simple cowboy like Christopher was beyond Jasmine.

And then she'd gone off to college herself, thanks to the grant from the city, increasing the emotional distance between the two sisters. As far as she knew, Jenny had grown into a beautiful, self-assured adult, a relative stranger she greeted with a kiss on the cheek when she came home from the holidays. Had Jenny been seeing Christopher even then?

There was always laughter in the house during vacations and holidays. Jasmine puckered her brow, straining to remember if her sister had been part of the joyous festivities. Or had she been off with friends? Jasmine couldn't remember. Probably, she'd been too busy with Christopher to notice, a thought which gave her a guilty start.

Shaking her head to clear her introspection, Jasmine carried the box of books into the living room, where the rest of Jenny's boxed goods were stored, and went to Jenny's room to begin stripping the bedclothes. Her sister's sweet, airy scent still lingered on the sheets, and she brought a pillow to her face, inhaling deeply.

"We never said goodbye," she whispered aloud, hugging the pillow to her chest. She wished she had one more minute, just one, to give Jenny a hug and tell her how much she was loved.

Jasmine shook herself from her melancholy with some effort. Funny how grief hit her at the oddest moments. She'd think her emotions were under control, and then in a second's time, grief would wash over her and overwhelm her, sometimes for no apparent reason.

Those were the toughest times, the moments before she found the strength to tuck her grief back away and go on living, because that's what she had to do. Because she was here and Jenny was not, and baby Sammy depended on her.

She reached for the other pillow, but when she yanked at the corner to pull off the pillowcase, Jenny's Bible fell to the floor.

Jasmine had forgotten all about it. She'd slipped it under the pillow when Christopher had shown up. She was relieved to find it now. It was a part of Jenny she wanted to keep.

Heart in her throat, she reached down and scooped it up, tenderly smoothing the bent pages before closing the cracked leather. Sitting on the stripped bed with one leg tucked under her, she ran a hand across the front of the Bible, considering whether it would be right to read more of the notes Jenny had written in the margins.

She was so confused, so hurt. And she missed her sister terribly. Would it be a breach of trust to read a little, to bring Jenny near through her words, her thoughts and dreams and faith? Who knew but that maybe, in some small way, it would help her know what to do about Christopher and Sammy.

She could only hope for such a miracle, even if she didn't believe in miracles anymore.

Chapter Four

The next morning, Christopher eyed the two-room log cabin, turning over the possibilities in his mind. After leaving the diner, he'd phoned an old high school football buddy, who'd lent him this place for the weekend. If God was willing and he planned right, it would be his and Jasmine's for at least one completely uninterrupted, if not happy, day.

Loose gravel and pine needles crunched under his feet as he approached the cabin, his friend's fishing hideaway. Nothing spectacular—it didn't even have electric heat. But for what Christopher had in mind, it was perfect.

He'd purposely picked a cabin tucked up just far enough into the Sangre de Cristo mountain range to keep the clinic from sending in emergency equipment right away, yet far enough from town to warrant Jasmine's personal attention.

Not to mention high enough in altitude to get a good snow, if the weather cooperated.

He eyed the sky critically, wondering when the snow would start. The weather forecast indicated a major storm heading their way. It could snow five feet in a day here, given the right conditions.

He only hoped these *were* the right conditions, external and internal. And that Jasmine would come when he called, even if she knew about the impending snowstorm. If they sent a couple of paramedics from Wetmore after him, he was in a world of hurt.

He laughed despite his sour mood.

She would come. Jasmine Enderlin was the singularly most compassionate woman he'd ever known. She wouldn't give a second's thought to risking her own life and health in order to help someone who needed her, a quality that made her a terrific doctor and an even better person.

His respect for her was only superseded by his love.

If he could just blurt out the truth of the past and wipe the slate clean, things would be much simpler. *If* she would listen. *If* she would believe him.

And *if* he had only himself to consider. He wouldn't waste a second before telling her everything. And he sure wouldn't be at 9500 feet constructing ridiculous undercover adventures better suited to spy novels than to an old-fashioned man who couldn't give up his dreams.

But right now he'd do just about anything—including spy novel antics, in order to see her again.

Again he glanced at the sky, wondering how long he had left to prepare. He had wood to chop, dinner to make and a leg to break.

He chuckled softly at his own joke, then quickly sobered, drawing in a breath, clenching his jaw and pressing his lips together as he determinedly went to find an ax.

I married Christopher tonight. Mrs. Christopher Jordan. Jenny Jordan. How awkward that sounds!

I still can't believe things worked out the way they did. Everything seemed so hopeless, and then there was Christopher and...

He gave me a rose at the altar. A single, beautiful white rose. I've pressed it into this Bible as a keepsake—the only one I really have of my wedding day.

It all happened so fast. No photographer. No wedding cake. No guests. Except for Gram, who stood up for me, and Christopher's brother from Texas, his only living relative, for him. Jasmine was there in the back, but she didn't say anything.

Jasmine cringed inwardly. She'd only gone because she thought it would be spineless not to. And she wanted to show them she was bigger than that.

Oh, she was bigger, all right. Pouting in the back and glaring at everyone. She'd never even wished the couple happiness.

She shook herself from her thoughts and continued reading, picking up where she'd left off.

But at least I can keep this rose. I know what he was trying to communicate with a white rose rather than a red one. He doesn't love me. He loves Jasmine, and he always has.

But he's committed himself to me, now. Me and my baby. And Christopher is an honorable man. He won't go back on his word.

I hope, in time, he'll learn to love me, though

I know it will never be the kind of love he has for Jasmine. But no matter how he feels about me, he'll love the baby. And he'll be a good daddy. If there was ever a man who was meant to be a father, it's Christopher.

Jasmine barely restrained herself from crumpling the piece of paper in her hands. She'd found it tucked into the page with the family tree, where Jenny had carefully written hers and Christopher's names on the appropriate lines. She'd drawn a heart where their baby's name would go.

She tucked the paper deep into the binding and closed the Bible with a pop. Her throat constricted until no air could pass through, but it didn't matter. She wasn't breathing anyway. Constrained air lodged squarely in her chest, throbbing mercilessly against her rib cage.

Christopher still loved her, even when he married Jenny? Oh, sure, but Jenny was carrying his child.

She was more confused now than ever. Nothing Jenny had written made sense! She stared at the Bible for a moment, then tossed it away with a frustrated groan.

Jasmine nearly launched herself off the bed at the sound of her pager. Placing a palm to her chest to slow her rapidly beating heart, she reached her other hand for her pager and turned it off.

The sweet strength of adrenaline pumped through her, clearing her head. While she wasn't like some of the residents she'd linked up with when she was in Denver, to whom the excitement of the moment was their reason to serve, she couldn't deny the pulse-pounding anticipation of being needed. It thrilled her to have something to give back to the little town that had given her so much.

She reached the phone and dialed the clinic number. Jill, the county nurse, gave Jasmine a quick rundown. A man had called from a mountain cabin just above Horn Lake. He'd been fishing, apparently, when he slipped off a wet log and fell.

"He's all alone, and he's afraid to drive. And Jasmine— he says he doesn't have insurance and can't afford a hospital. Or a doctor."

Jasmine made a noise from the back of her throat that signaled her compassionate understanding of his situation.

She pictured a gray-haired widower finding solace fishing in a mountain lake, afraid even to call the clinic because of the expense. An old man, all alone, with a broken leg and no one to help him.

The picture in her mind was too much for her heart to take. She'd work for free if she must, knowing that her actions would open a whole other can of worms should she be discovered dispensing her charity.

"What are the coordinates?" she asked, balancing a pad of paper on her hip so she could write them down.

Jill gave her the exact location of the cabin, someone renting the old Wallaby place. Then she paused expectantly.

"I'm going up there," Jasmine said, answering Jill's unspoken question. She reached into her jeans pocket for the keys to her four-by-four. "I have my bag with me. As long as it's not too major, I can handle a broken leg on my own. If it's too bad, I'll drive him back to the clinic myself. An ambulance crew wouldn't want to hike up into the lake area anyway."

"It's starting to snow, Jazz. The weather forecast says we might be in for a blizzard," Jill warned. "You never know how bad it's going to be. Maybe you ought to let Wetmore's EMT take care of it."

There was more than one EMT, and they were all men. Jill didn't have to say it for it to be true. And she was probably right.

But this was Jasmine's call, and an inner prompting was telling her to go.

"No, it's okay. I can get there faster. The poor old guy is probably in a lot of pain." And it would give her something to do to keep her mind off Christopher and her problems, she added silently. "I have my cell phone. If I have any problems, I'll give the guys in Wetmore a ring. I promise."

"Jazz, I didn't say—" Jill began, but Jasmine didn't let her finish as she put down the phone and raced to her car. Checking her sports utility vehicle for gas and equipment, she quickly got on the road. It took her half an hour to drive the dirt road as far as it ran toward Horn Lake.

When she reached the end of the line, she pulled her parka snug around her chin, gathered her gear onto her backpack, and began the hike up to the lake. A breeze had picked up, stinging her cheeks with bitter cold. Gritting her teeth, she ignored the icy pain and concentrated on putting one foot in front of another.

Just when she was getting to where she was no longer able to ignore the cold, she spied the cabin she was seeking. It was a run-down old place, more of a summer home than a winter hideaway. Jasmine wondered at the old man living in such conditions year-round.

Could a broken heart cause such misery? Her own heart clenched, answering the question on its own. Jasmine knew too well the feeling of abandonment, and she prayed she'd be able to help this neighbor, whoever he was, in more ways that one.

It occurred to her then that she hadn't asked for her patient's name, a major oversight not like her to make. Maybe those short nights *were* getting to her.

Her mind had been preoccupied, trying *not* to think about Christopher, she reminded herself, knocking firmly on the door. When no one answered, she tried again. And again.

Finally, she pounded on the door with her fist, wondering if her patient had been hurt worse than she'd first imagined. "Hello? Is anyone in there? Can you hear me?"

She'd break the door down if she had to, but it occurred to her to try the handle first. It turned easily in her palm and the catch switched, making the door swing inward. Jasmine shivered and swallowed hard. It was odd for the door to be unlocked.

She ignored the uncomfortable feeling of a stranger making herself welcome and stepped inside the cabin. "Hello? I knocked, but no one answered! Sir? Are you here?"

The scene inside the cabin was anything but frightening. In fact, if she didn't know better, she would think it was the setting of a lovers' secret rendezvous.

The only light came from a fire crackling in the old stone hearth. It basked the room in a soft, flickering glow similar to candlelight, but with the sharp, pungent scent of pine. The wooden floor had been recently swept, and firewood was stacked neatly in one corner.

A meal was set on a checkered cloth on an old, rickety table whose spindly legs looked like they might collapse at any moment. A tingle went up her spine as she realized the meal was set for *two*.

Clearly, she was not the one expected in this cabin. Her first thought was that she'd made a mistake, gotten the coordinates wrong and entered someone else's cabin.

But that couldn't be. This was the old Wallaby place, though others owned it now. It was too hard to keep track of all the summer residents who came and went. She struggled to remember who might have rented the cabin after Grace and Chuck Wallaby moved to Arizona.

Suddenly she noticed that the rocking chair facing the fire was slowly tipping back and forth without so much as a squeak to give it away.

Someone was in the cabin. But why didn't he answer when she called?

She tensed, then forced herself to relax. Fear and mortification warred within her for prominence. There was no reason for her to feel embarrassed, necessarily, but heat flamed her cheeks nonetheless.

She was a doctor responding to a call, she reminded herself sternly, taking a deep breath and squaring her shoulders. His broken leg might not be much, if he was rocking in a chair with that pain, but his hearing left a lot to be desired.

"Excuse me," she said loudly enough to cause an echo. She moved into the firelight, wanting to see and be seen. She didn't want the poor guy to think she was sneaking up on him. "I guess you didn't hear me knock. I'm Dr. Enderlin, and I've come to see about your—"

She paused, the breath cut off from her throat, as her eyes met a warm blue-gray gaze and her heart slammed into her rib cage.

"Christopher!"

"I see you made it," Christopher said, tipping his head toward her in greeting. "I was going to go looking for you if you didn't show up soon."

He neglected to mention that it had taken all the force of his will not to bolt into the winter chill to search for her when she didn't arrive as quickly as he'd expected. Only knowing he'd ruin any chance of convincing her to stay and listen if she discovered his scheme too soon kept him glued to his chair and praying for her safety.

Night came swiftly onto the mountains. Horn Peak quickly blocked out the feeble rays of the winter sun as it set for the night. It would be dark in a matter of minutes.

Her cheeks, already flushed a pleasant pink, rose in color, contrasting starkly with the silky weave of her sable hair. Her mouth opened briefly before she clamped it shut again and stood arms akimbo, a glare marring the sheer beauty of her face.

"You're angry," he said aloud, realizing as he spoke that he was stating the obvious.

She made a pointed glance down one of his legs, which were crossed loosely at the ankles, and up the other one before coming to rest back on his face. Her gaze made his skin tingle all over, and he shifted in his seat like a man with poison ivy.

Guilt tugged at his chest, and he shrugged at her

unspoken question. When she looked back at his wool sock–encased feet, he chuckled and wiggled his toes.

"Please tell me you didn't call me up here on a ruse," she said, her voice hoarse, whether from restrained emotion or from her walk in the chill night air, he couldn't say.

He cleared his throat, struggling between feeling mildly guilty and very self-satisfied. She was up here, wasn't she? Even if she *had* come under false pretenses, his intentions were good.

"Well…if you mean do I have a broken leg, then I guess the answer would have to be no," he drawled, tipping up the corner of his lip in a half smile he hoped would endear himself to her and not further raise her ire. He wasn't nearly as cocky as he used to be about the easy cowboy charm that had always worked with Jasmine.

"I see," she said, swinging her backpack off her back and holding it in front of her like a shield. Her fists clenched the material, her knuckles white. Christopher flinched inwardly, offering a silent prayer for the right words to say. Why did it have to be like this between them, when it used to be so good?

"I didn't call you up here on a ruse," he denied flatly.

"Really? Then what *do* you call it?"

"Embellishment. I stretched the truth a little because we need to talk."

"A little?" One eyebrow rose as she glared at both of his perfectly sturdy legs. "I drop everything to make a risky call in the middle of a major snowstorm, and you say you exaggerated a *little*?"

"If it makes you feel any better, I think I sprained my ankle chopping wood for the fire."

Her eyes were glowing, and he knew her well enough to know she was holding back a smile. But he could tell she was still harboring her irritation and resentment, and with good reason, he had to admit.

"I'd never do anything to hurt you, Jazz. Five more minutes and I would have come after you. I'd never put you in danger or let you get hurt, not when it's in my power to protect you."

"How comforting," she said dryly, turning away from him and surveying the room. "A knight in shining armor who tosses his damsel in distress to the dragon before attempting to save her." She turned back and smoothed a hand down her hair, which was attractively disheveled by the hood of her parka. "Does this place have a phone I can use?"

"Of course. On the far wall, next to the table."

Shedding her coat, she walked over to the antique phone and dialed a number, talking in hushed tones to the person on the other end of the line.

Christopher watched, a smile playing on his lips, as she picked at the cheese, crackers and fruit on the table as she talked. Things were working out far better than he'd anticipated. He half figured he'd have to hog-tie her to get her to stay with him, and here she was taking off her coat and eating the food he prepared for her all of her own volition.

Perhaps she knew how critical it was that the two of them worked things out. He was the first to admit it would take far more than a good talk to untangle this mess. But it was a start.

And afterward, he was prepared to follow up those words with action, to slay her dragons and bring her home to safety. Jasmine—and Sammy, too.

He wondered if she noticed the bouquet of red roses lying next to the bottle of sparkling cider. And if she did notice, would she realize the flowers were for her? Hope swelled in his chest and he swallowed hard.

He sat back in the rocking chair, giving her privacy to finish her conversation. She was probably calling Gram about Sammy, and he didn't want to pressure her.

She hung up the phone and went to stand by the fire, holding her hands palms out toward the flames. It was all Christopher could do not to join her at the hearth, wrap his arms around her tiny waist and bury his face in her long, soft hair.

It was something he would have done, in the past. They would have stared at the fire and talked in hushed tones about their future, reaffirming with every look and caress the strength of the love that passed between them.

It was like being run through with a bull's horn not to be able to hold her now. He stopped rocking, holding his breath through the endless moment of silence.

Finally, she turned and met his gaze, her dark eyes warm with emotion and the glow of the fire. "I want you to know that I'm just warming up here by the fire for a few minutes before I head back to my truck. I'm not staying, if that's what you're thinking."

"Jazz, you can't just turn around and walk out of here!" he began, but she cut him off when he tried to continue.

"I made it up here just fine, and the hike is downhill from here." She blew out a breath. "I can't stay, Christopher. Please. Don't try to make me."

The spur in his gut raked his insides like a cowboy's heels on a bucking bronc.

She wet her bottom lip with the tip of her tongue and continued. "Since it appears there's no medical emergency, I'm needed in town."

"I didn't call you up here to be a doctor, Jasmine, no matter what I said to the nurse on the phone."

She paused and breathed heavily, as if testing her words in her head before speaking them aloud. "I know," she said, her voice a low purr. "And I think I understand."

"Then stay."

She shook her head. "I appreciate what you're trying to do here, but—"

He would have interrupted her again, but her pager beat him to it.

Jasmine turned the blaring instrument off and glanced at the number. "I need to use your phone again," she said, her voice dull.

"Go ahead."

He rose and stood behind her as she made contact with the clinic in town. This conversation he wanted to hear, and he didn't think she'd mind his eavesdropping.

"Doctor Enderlin here," she began, then stiffened. "What?" Her voice went unnaturally shrill, sending a shudder of premonition through Christopher.

He reached out with a tentative hand and withdrew it again twice before finally laying a gentle palm on her shoulder. She tensed for a moment, then eased back into the stronghold of his arms. It only seemed natural to wrap his arm around the front of her shoulders in a move that was equally firm and gentle.

A silent offering to lend her strength. Her whole body quivered beneath his touch, and he knew it was the voice on the other end of the line that was making her shake.

And it wasn't good news.

"Forward her call to me," she said in a pinched voice. As she waited, she pulled a notepad and pen from her breast pocket, scribbling madly when the voice on the other end of the line resumed. She paused every so often to ask a question or clarify a response, but through it all, her trembling increased.

Moments later, she hung up and redialed the clinic. She put her notepad down and plastered her grip on his forearm, her gaze seeking his for reassurance. He gave her everything he had, tightening his hold just enough to let her know he read the terror in her eyes. And to let her know he was there for her, no matter what.

He watched in amazement as the doctor in Jasmine surfaced, masking the fear. Her features composed and relaxed and a determined gleam lit her eyes. So complete was the transformation that Christopher wondered if he hadn't imagined her alarm.

She squared her shoulders, which he took as a cue to drop his arm from around her and step back. "No, his leg wasn't broken. Minor *sprain,*" she said, tossing him a glance that made him cringe. "I've already taken care of it."

No you haven't, he disagreed mentally. *We haven't even started.*

But if someone needed her medical attention, she'd leave. And he'd let her go, of course. Shoot, he'd go with her.

"I'm only a ten-minute hike at most from that cabin. I can reach her."

A ten-minute hike. In this weather? Ten minutes

would seem like an hour. He picked up her parka. It was soaking wet. He moved it close to the fire, knowing it wouldn't have time to dry before she left. And a damp coat would make that hike every bit more excruciating.

"Who's injured?" he asked when she hung up the phone. She drew a breath and pinned him with her gaze.

"Not injured. Amanda Carmichael is stranded alone in her cabin, and she's having her baby. *Now.*"

He didn't miss the fear that briefly flashed in her eyes. Was she remembering Jenny's death?

He muttered a prayer for her comfort under his breath, and steeled himself to do what he could to answer that prayer on his own. If all he could do was stand by her and support her, then that's what he would do. And he might even surprise her.

His mind clicked into gear, reviewing the things he had learned. During the last year away from Westcliffe, God had given him the opportunity to prove himself as well as to help people in need.

The Carmichaels lived a short distance away, thank God. "We'll use the snowmobile," he said, thinking aloud.

"What?" she said, looking confused.

"I'm going with you."

Chapter Five

"There's no need," Jasmine said. The words were so firm and frosty they would have rivaled the air outside, but he wouldn't be moved from his purpose.

"I know there's no need. I *want* to help."

"You'll just be in the way."

"Maybe," he agreed, reaching for her parka and wrapping it around her, wincing at how cold and damp it still felt. "But I'm going anyway."

Jasmine met his gaze square on. Probing. Testing. He held perfectly still, barely breathing as he let her see inside his heart.

After a moment, she shrugged and turned away from him. "Whatever. But I'm leaving now."

Christopher snatched his own coat from a rack near the door and quickly zipped it up. "It'll only take me a minute to warm up my snowmobile." He planted his cowboy hat on his head by the crown and straightened the brim with his fingers.

"Good idea. We'll get there in half the time. I'll wait," she said, looking as if she weren't very happy about it but was determined to follow through.

Christopher warmed up the engine, then went back inside the cabin to get Jasmine, who was by this time pacing the floor. He hid a smile. She never had been the patient type. Probably why she was a doctor.

Ugh. He shook his head. His puns were getting worse by the moment. Could stress do that to a person? The thought nearly made him chuckle, if he wasn't so cold and the situation so serious. "Bundle up, darlin'. It's a raging blizzard out there, and we're heading right smack into it."

He wasn't kidding, Jasmine thought as she mounted the snowmobile behind Christopher. It was freezing and then some. The wind was blowing so fiercely the falling snow was almost horizontal to the ground.

"Hang on tight!" he yelled over the wind, and Jasmine tentatively wrapped her arms around his waist. It was funny how an action could be at once so awkward and yet so disturbingly familiar.

She clung tightly to him as the vehicle bounded over the snow toward the Carmichaels' cabin. In the brief conversation she'd had with Amanda, she was reassured that the labor was progressing along normally, if quickly.

Amanda was certain she would have the baby any moment. Unusual to have such a short labor with a first baby, but Jasmine had seen odder wonders in her time at the hospital in Denver. The best and the worst.

She swallowed hard and squeezed her eyes shut, trying not to think about Jenny. Trying not to think about death, when she should be concentrating on welcoming a new life into the world.

There was nothing to worry about, she reassured herself, praying all the while God would make it so.

She'd spent her requisite time on the maternity ward during her residency. She knew how to deliver a baby. She had all the necessary equipment, unless there was a problem, in which case she'd call for a back up.

She'd known coming back to Westcliffe that, while most expectant mothers made it to the hospital in Pueblo for their labor and delivery, she would be called on from time to time to deliver a baby.

And she'd had confidence in her baby-delivering skills until Jenny died. Watching her sister hemorrhage and knowing she was powerless to stop it was nearly the end of her medical career, never mind the permanent scars it left on her heart.

She knew how irrational it sounded. Jenny's death didn't have anything to do with delivering Sammy. But that didn't stop Jasmine from remembering, and the memory made her shaky.

It had taken all her effort to continue serving as the doctor to the town, and it was only her sense of obligation to its people that kept her there now.

What she really wanted to do was run away, hide her head in the sand like an ostrich. Now more than ever. How could she help Amanda and act as if nothing troubled her?

She could, and she would. She clenched her teeth together and concentrated on reining in the strong wash of emotion coursing through her.

She was a doctor. Doctors sometimes lost patients, and it wasn't their fault. If she internalized guilt every time something went wrong that was beyond her control, she would go crazy.

But Jenny wasn't just any patient, and Jasmine couldn't just lightly brush it away. The knowledge that she might not be able to help Amanda Carmichael shook her to the core. Women died in childbirth, even in the twentieth century. The shiver that coursed through her had nothing to do with the cold.

Christopher took one hand away from the handlebar and placed it over her clutched fingers. She leaned her cheek into the strength of his back and sighed. It felt good to be in his company again. Good, natural and right, as if she'd never left.

And despite the offhand manner in which she'd answered him back at the cabin, she needed him now. Desperately. She needed his strength and assurance, and most especially his faith.

He pulled the snowmobile up to the front of the house, a small A-frame log cabin similar to the one from which they'd come. Modest, but made for the weather, the building was a solid fixture against the raging of the storm.

Christopher removed the key and dismounted in record time. He held his gloved hand out to her, his lips pressed together grimly.

By the look on his face, Jasmine couldn't tell if he was angry or worried. Maybe a little of both. But she knew him well enough to know he'd put his own feelings aside long enough to help another human being out of a jam. Even if she was that person. And Amanda, of course. He would ignore the tension between them for Amanda's sake, as well as the baby's.

He saw her face and flashed her an encouraging smile. Reassured, she reached for his hand.

She expected him to release her fingers when she was free of the machine, but instead he tucked her hand under his arm and gave it a reassuring squeeze. "I'm here for you, Jasmine," he whispered gruffly, then gave the thick oak door a solid knock.

It wasn't likely Amanda would hear them knocking over the wind, so she wasn't surprised when no one answered. Christopher knocked again, then looked to her for guidance.

She stepped forward and tried the doorknob, which moved easily in her hand. "Amanda?" she called, stepping into the cabin out of the snow and wind, noting that Christopher followed her in. She heard a muffled cry from the back of the cabin and gestured for him to sit while she found Amanda, who was in the back bedroom, looking tired and peaked. Her pale green eyes gleamed with a mixture of anxiety and excitement. Her short, curly auburn hair was stuck to her forehead where streaks of sweat had dried, and the freckles that marked her face became more pronounced with her pallor. Her small frame looked thin and skeletal, except for the pronounced bulge of her abdomen.

She was a small woman, like Jenny. Small women sometimes had more trouble delivering. Jasmine cut off the thought before it could reach its completion.

"Dr. Enderlin!" she exclaimed, attempting weakly to sit up on the bed. "I'm so glad you're here! My water broke, and these contractions hit me real hard! I thought I was going to be popping this kid out all by my lonesome!"

"Well, that isn't going to happen," Jasmine replied, laying a comforting hand on her arm. "We're here now. Lie back on the bed and rest while you can. You're going to need all your energy for pushing."

Amanda nodded.

"Do you know Christopher Jordan?" she asked, her

voice clipped with the calm, emotionless demeanor she used with her patients.

"Sure."

"He's here to lend me a hand. Is that okay with you?"

"I don't care who helps," she said sharply, curling into herself as another contraction hit. "Just get this baby out of me!"

Jasmine ignored Amanda's terse words, knowing it was pain speaking and not the voice of her neighbor. "I'll be right back with Christopher, and we'll see what we can do about getting you out of pain and introducing you to your new little one."

As she went back to get Christopher, she took a moment to breathe deeply and regroup. She hadn't been prepared for the stab of panic that attacked her when she saw the writhing woman on the bed.

Contractions were a natural part of childbirth. Pain, too. But it still rattled Jasmine to see a woman in so much agony and not knowing the outcome her pain would produce.

A healthy baby, she reminded herself. A big, beautiful, healthy baby to lie in his mother's arms. She couldn't bear even to consider anything else.

"Can you give me a hand?" She gestured to Christopher, who was sitting in a wicker chair that appeared two sizes too small for his long legs.

"She's okay with my being here?" he asked, his voice and his face lined with compassion.

"Sure. And I can use all the help I can get. She's on the verge of having this baby. I've got to check both mom and baby out, then prepare her for delivery."

"You can count on me," he said, tossing his hat onto

the chair and moving quickly toward the bedroom. Jasmine followed on his heels, her medical mind clicking into gear, going over the procedures she'd need to accomplish in the next few minutes.

Christopher stepped into the room and combed his fingers through his hair. "You're in good hands, Mrs. Carmichael."

Amanda smiled weakly. But to Jasmine, his words had the same effect as turning on her hairdryer and dumping it in the tub while taking a bath. She darted him a surprised glance. He'd been told how Jenny died, and she'd bet her last dollar he knew she'd been there when it happened. He nodded solemnly, his gaze full of compassion.

She swallowed hard as he flashed her a reassuring grin. It will be okay, his eyes said. He knew, and he cared.

Amanda grasped her abdomen and groaned.

Jasmine and Christopher broke eye contact and rushed to her side, each taking one of her arms as she breathed through the contraction.

In-two-three-four, out-two-three-four. Jasmine counted the age-old rhythm in her head, verbally cheering Amanda on as the contraction peaked and receded.

"How often are they coming?" Christopher asked quietly, adjusting the pillows for Amanda's comfort.

Jasmine shot him another startled look. *She* was the doctor here. She should be the one asking the medical questions, and he was playacting someone out of a medical drama.

What did he know about a woman in labor? A tide of animosity washed over her, though she quickly stemmed the flow as she'd been trained to do in medical school.

She knew more than anyone that this was no television show where everything always worked out. The last thing she needed was some couch potato playing EMT.

Christopher's body didn't suggest he spent a lot of time watching television, but his attitude reeked of it. Maybe he just watched medical thrillers.

Amanda smiled weakly. "About every two minutes."

Jasmine settled her attention back on the woman. "Are you more comfortable on your side or on your back? Have you tried walking around?"

"On my side," she said, her voice dull. "I'm too tired to walk." Suddenly she doubled over as another contraction hit.

Christopher looked across the struggling woman and met Jasmine's gaze. "That wasn't two minutes."

"No," Jasmine agreed, "it wasn't. Amanda, I think this baby's ready to meet you face-to-face." Her heart leaped into her throat to do a little dance, then moved up to pound furiously in her skull. This was where the rubber met the road. And she hadn't even assessed Amanda's health yet, or the tiny infant whose life depended on her care.

Jasmine quickly searched through her case for her fetascope and a number of vacuum-packed sterile instruments. She didn't know how much time they had left before the baby would come, and there was a lot to do in the meantime.

"A stack of clean sheets?" Christopher asked, reading her mind.

"Yes, please. And some blankets to wrap the baby

in. Warm them in the dryer first. And kick up the thermostat. We need to keep the baby as warm as possible." She wondered again if his baby-birthing information came from the television, maybe an old western. She didn't have time to ponder.

Amanda curled in bed, screaming in exasperation, as another contraction racked her small frame. The hair on the back of Jasmine's neck stood on end. "I hope it's soon," Amanda mumbled through clenched teeth. "I can't stand this much longer."

"You're doing fine," Jasmine soothed, brushing Amanda's sweat-soaked hair away from her forehead. "I'm going to have a listen to this little guy's heartbeat when this contraction is over."

Despite the fact that she hadn't used a fetascope in a while, she found the baby's heartbeat with ease. It was strong and steady, without a hint of fetal distress. She let out a sigh of relief and offered a silent prayer of thanks.

Christopher returned, his arms laden with sheets and towels. Without a word to Jasmine, he unloaded his burden and began systematically laying out fresh, folded sheets on the bottom edge of the bed, gently moving Amanda's legs when necessary, offering quiet words of encouragement as he worked.

Jasmine took a quick breath and watched him with the woman, amazed by his careful thoughtfulness and the capable assurance of his movements.

He left the room momentarily and returned with several pillows. "I picked up every pillow I could find," he told Jasmine before focusing his attention on Amanda. "These will help support your back while you're delivering," he explained, laying the pillows next to her on the bed.

"Sit up?" Amanda queried with a weak smile. "I don't think I have the strength to move my little finger."

He chuckled. "You don't have to sit up until Jasmine says it's time," he reassured the groaning woman. "Hang in there, Amanda. Breathe through it. You're on the down side of this contraction. You're doing great, and you're going to be a terrific mother."

He looked to Jasmine, a question in his eyes. She answered with an infinitesimal shake of her head.

"Not quite yet," she said, speaking to both of them. "Probably within the hour. But Amanda, this is your first baby. We may be pushing for a long time."

Amanda winced. Christopher wet a washcloth and draped it across her forehead, his soothing tenor reassuring the tired woman.

If Jasmine was honest, it reassured her, as well. His *presence* reassured her. His instinctive knowledge of childbirth was a sight to behold, but that didn't shock her nearly as much as his bedside manner. Unlike the proverbial fainting man in the delivery room, Christopher was a pillar of strength, holding Amanda's hand in place of her husband.

"Where *is* Bill, anyway?" she asked aloud in a conversational tone, preparing the iodine solution she would use to disinfect everything and keep the area as sterile as possible. Keeping germs to a minimum was crucial. She couldn't have another woman die like Jenny had done, and infection was always an issue.

Please, God.

"He…" Amanda paused and gritted her teeth, breathing only when Christopher reminded her "…went out of town for a sales seminar," she finished, gasping as the contraction passed.

She realized too late the kind of question she had asked, how it might affect Christopher. She hadn't even considered the fact that he hadn't been present for the birth of his own son, and wondered how he felt about it now, watching another woman labor. Did he realize what Jenny had gone through to bring his son into the world?

She darted a glance at him. His jaw was clenched, and she could see the anger in his eyes. Anger at Bill for not being there for his wife, or at himself for the same offense?

Jasmine was definitely angry with Bill. What kind of a man would leave his wife in the middle of nowhere when she was due to deliver a baby?

Despite her misgivings, she picked up her thread of dialogue. Even if Amanda was angry at her husband, it would keep her mind off her pain. There was little or no break between contractions now.

Sweat was pouring from Amanda's brow. She appeared as frightened as she was tired. Jasmine knew, from her schooling though not firsthand, that the contractions at this stage were fierce and unyielding.

"His timing could have been better," she said lightly, glancing at Christopher.

At least he had the grace to look ashamed, she thought, noticing how the tendons in his neck tightened as if he were wincing. As well he should be. His own actions were reprehensible.

"It wasn't Bill's fault," Amanda exclaimed, panting for breath. "Not that I care *what* his excuse is at this point!" She stopped and panted. "His boss forced him to go. He'll be so disappointed that he isn't here for the birth."

Amanda cried out. "I've got to push, now, Doctor." Sweat broke out anew on her forehead.

Jasmine checked her again. "You're right, Amanda. You're fully dilated and effaced," she informed her patient, who looked as if she were beyond caring, now that the contraction was over. Amanda's eyelids drooped for the few moments between contractions, and her face was pale and haggard.

It was no wonder they called it labor. Jasmine wondered how a woman could fall asleep between contractions that were obviously wrenchingly painful. Some "experts" said it was a bad idea to let a patient fall asleep, but the poor woman looked so exhausted, Jasmine had to believe that any relief she found must help, be it ever so little.

"Your baby's coming!" Christopher said enthusiastically, gently wiping Amanda's face with a cool rag, and never letting go of her hand. "You'll get to see him any time now!"

Tired as she was, Amanda smiled.

"Christopher's going to prop you up with some pillows," Jasmine explained. "When your next contraction comes, take a deep breath and push for all you're worth."

Christopher gripped Amanda's hands and coached her through several contractions, each one tiring Amanda more. Jasmine wondered how much longer the laboring woman would be able to hold out.

"He's crowning!" she announced excitedly on the next contraction. "Amanda, I see your sweet baby's head!"

Amanda laughed weakly. "Can you…does he…?"

Jasmine smiled. "He's got a full head of thick, dark hair like his daddy," she confirmed.

"Oh!" This time it wasn't so much an expression of pain as it was of wonder.

Jasmine's heart jumped into her throat and lodged there. A baby was a miracle, and it was a joy to be a participant in the wonder of birth.

But they weren't out of the woods yet, and her mind wouldn't let her forget it, not even for a second. "Let's give another really good push, and I think his head will be out."

Christopher tucked the woman into the crook of his arm and wiped the sweat from her eyes. "This is it, Amanda. Give it your best."

Amanda nodded and gritted her teeth determinedly. "C'mon, kid, let's get this over with," she breathed. "I don't know about you, but I'm getting tired out here."

Jasmine and Christopher shared in her laughter, until another contraction hit and it was time for everyone to go to work. As Jasmine predicted, the head appeared, and she quickly turned the baby a quarter and suctioned the nose and mouth, clearing the air passageway.

"All right," Christopher said calmly, though excitement lined his voice. "The head was the hard part. The rest is easy. Just one more good push, Amanda, and you're finished."

How did he know that? Jasmine wondered again. Christopher continued to amaze her with his medical knowledge.

One more push was all it took. "It's a beautiful baby

girl!" Jasmine announced, accompanied by the happy sound of the baby's first wail.

"She's beautiful," Christopher agreed, his voice hoarse.

Their eyes met, and Jasmine was surprised to find he had tears on his face, running unashamedly down his cheeks. Excitement and wonder and joy skirmished for prominence in his gaze. But above all, there was love.

The other emotions confused her. Love made her swallow hard and turn away, focusing her attention on completing the afterbirth and getting Amanda resting comfortably in her bed beside her new daughter.

Again, Christopher was a great help, washing and caring for the baby as if he handled newborns every day. He talked and gurgled to the baby in the helium-high-pitched voice men automatically use with babies. Jasmine tried and failed not to let the scene affect her.

How could she help it? Seeing Christopher holding an infant brought up too many memories. Too many questions. And far too much pain. She gathered her equipment and tried not to think at all.

After spending several more hours monitoring Amanda and her daughter, Jasmine promised to visit her first thing in the morning. Jasmine gave Amanda instructions on what to do if she had any concerns as she prepared to leave.

Christopher interpreted her actions and pulled her aside. "I'm taking you back to the cabin," he said in a tone that brooked no argument.

As if she had enough strength left to argue. She didn't much care *where* he took her, as long as it was warm, and quiet, and she could find someplace to lie down and curl up under a blanket. It was after midnight, and she was physically and emotionally exhausted.

She wondered if Christopher could sense she was near her breaking point. He was solicitous on their way out, taking her bags for her and insisting he keep an arm around her to prevent her from falling on the ice.

She yawned and tucked her head into his shoulder. Tomorrow was soon enough to ask him the questions that had paraded through her mind in constant succession throughout the entire ordeal. For now, all she could think about was sleep.

Chapter Six

Christopher woke to the sound and scent of bacon being cooked in a skillet over an open fire. His neck crimped painfully and his shoulders were unbearably tight from sleeping in the old wooden rocking chair in front of the fire, leaving Jasmine to the privacy of the only bedroom.

He'd carried her to bed the night before. By the time they'd reached the cabin, she was barely holding on. He'd gripped her hands tightly around his waist for the last mile, hoping she wouldn't slide off the snowmobile. The cold had been her breaking point, and she hadn't made a whimper when he pulled her off the back of the snowmobile and into his arms.

Admiration rose in his chest. She was so strong for others, giving every bit of herself until she was completely drained. She was the type of person who naturally put others' needs before her own. He wished he could voice his respect for her, but she wouldn't believe him anyway.

What saint wanted praise from a sinner? And that's what he was, at least in Jasmine's eyes.

He figured she'd sleep, at least, but it appeared *he* was the slugabed this morning. He yawned and stretched, ruffling his hair with the tips of his fingers.

He couldn't help but enjoy the sight of Jasmine, dressed in the rumpled clothes she'd slept in and looking all the more attractive for it, humming quietly as she turned bacon.

His breath caught in his throat at the domestic scene, the warm, cozy atmosphere she'd unintentionally created. The world had ceased to exist except for the two of them in this cabin. Maybe today, finally, they could work out their problems and move on with their lives. He didn't dare to hope they could move on together. Yet.

"Smells wonderful," he said, moving to crouch beside her under the pretense of warming his hands at the fire. "Breakfast for two?"

He heard her breath catch as she swung her gaze up to meet his. The flash of startled surprise in her eyes stabbed him like a dagger to the chest. The guilty knowledge that he'd placed himself in this position was his penance, his punishment.

He'd have to live with the pain he'd caused her for the rest of his life.

"I was kidding, Jasmine. Relax. I'm not trying to put you under any pressure." He restrained himself from brushing back the lock of hair that had fallen in her eyes. Her beautiful, shimmering green eyes.

"I know," she said, her voice low. She gave him a wavering smile. "I'm not afraid of you, Christopher."

He swallowed hard, certain his heart had stopped beating altogether. "I'm glad to hear it," he said, his voice gruff.

"I couldn't find any muffins, but I mixed up a batch of pancakes. I thought we could fry some in the bacon grease, if you think your cholesterol can handle it," she teased, a sparkle in her eye.

It was good to see her smile. "You don't have to worry about me," he said, puffing out his chest and flexing his biceps. "I'm the very picture of health."

The smile dropped from her face as she hastily turned back to her cooking.

"What did I say?" he asked gently, laying his hand on her arm.

She shook her head. "Nothing. Can you get the pancake batter from the table?"

"Sure." The message was clear. She wanted him to back off. He was invading her space. He thrust his hands through the spiked tips of his hair and moved to do her bidding.

Grabbing the batter, he handed it to her, then stepped back, folding his arms with his open palms tucked close to his chest. If she wanted room, he had no choice but to give it to her. Even if what he really wanted to do was take her in his arms and erase the distance between them entirely.

"Why didn't you wait for me?"

Her question was spoken in such a soft tone, Christopher wondered if he'd imagined it. But when she turned to him, there was no denying the challenge in her gaze. Challenge, and pain.

He had no doubt of her meaning. She'd bridged the gap between them, said the torturous words that would open dialogue.

And now the ball was squarely in his court. They'd promised to marry as soon as Jasmine's internship was complete. He'd been so young, and so in love, the wait had seemed short. Now, it loomed before him.

"I couldn't wait," he said, surprised at how difficult the words were to say, though he'd rehearsed them a thousand times. His voice was rough and gravelly. "I had no choice."

Her shoulders tensed, and she turned back to her pan, breaking eggs one by one into the skillet. The hiss as each egg dropped into the pan reminded him of the torment of hell he was in.

"Oh, I see," she said finally, sarcasm lacing her voice. It was obvious she didn't see at all.

"Oh, Jasmine," he groaned, slumping back into the rocking chair and holding his head in his hand. The pulse at his temple threatened to burst through, and he pressed against it with the palm of his hand. "If you only knew what really happened!"

She picked up the skillet with a towel wrapped around the handle and slid the eggs onto a platter, then stood and wiped her fingers on her jeans. Christopher dropped his head, unwilling to see her perform such a normal, everyday task when real life was so off-kilter.

He didn't see her approach, but suddenly she was there in front of him, kneeling down before him and reaching for his hands. "I want to know, Christopher. Tell me."

He expected her to yell, to argue with him the way she had the other times they'd met. She had every right to be angry, and she was a spirited woman. But her gentleness, the glimmer of tears in her eyes, was his undoing.

He wrapped his arms around her and pulled her into

his chest, burying his face in the glorious silky soft-
ness of her thick, black hair.

He inwardly groaned, expressing the agony that was
his. For no matter how much he wanted to be with
Jasmine, she could never know the whole truth. How
could he confess it and risk losing Sammy? It would
hurt so many people if the truth came out, including
Jasmine. He couldn't be so cruel. He pulled her tighter,
closer to his heart.

Jasmine didn't think. She just wrapped her arms
around his neck and tangled her fingers in the short
ends of his hair. For just one moment, she would give
herself the pleasure of being in Christopher's arms
again, feeling the strength of his arms like steel bands
around her waist, taking joy in the sheer, masculine
power of his broad shoulders.

She'd missed him, more than she'd thought possible—
until this second.

She'd been only half-conscious when he'd brought
her inside his cabin the night before. There was a moment of panic when he tucked her into bed. They'd
never been intimate, saving that most precious of relationships for the time when they joined as man and
wife; but Christopher was a different man now, and
she wasn't sure what he was capable of.

In the end, he'd placed a gentle kiss on her forehead and she'd drifted off into peaceful dreams. If she
were honest, it was the best sleep she'd had in months.
Sammy was safe with Gram, and though the dear old
woman wouldn't get a good night's sleep, Jasmine realized it was probably in everyone's best interests for
her to have this night away from all her responsibilities.

She clung to Christopher a moment more, wondering how she could ever have left his side in the first place. If she hadn't gone away to medical school, they'd be happily married right now, probably with two-point-five kids and a dog and a cat.

But she had a dream to follow, responsibilities that went beyond her own limited vision and encompassed the world. At least she thought so at the time. She'd been so sure of herself when she'd expressed these thoughts to Christopher, urging him to go on with his life. It wasn't fair of her to ask him to wait for her.

He'd argued, but she'd been firm, certain she was doing the right thing. Sometimes now she wondered if that vision she'd so readily embraced was nothing more than a specter created by an overzealous teenage girl who desperately wanted to be part of something bigger than herself.

A husband, two-point-five kids and a dog and a cat would never be enough for her. She'd wanted to be a doctor for as long as she could remember, and had never veered from that objective. Again, she questioned her convictions, and came up with nothing but a blank.

Not that it mattered now. She shivered when Christopher moved his head down, his lips grazing the tender skin of her earlobe before planting tiny kisses against the nape of her neck.

With a surprised gasp, she pushed him away. "Christopher, no."

The tortured look on his face was almost enough to send her back into his arms. *Almost* enough. The memory of Jenny's casket being lowered into the ground stopped her cold.

Her stomach lurched, and she wondered if she was going to be ill. Jenny was dead, and she was consorting with the enemy! It was enough to make even the strongest constitution weak and queasy.

Christopher stood suddenly and walked away from her, raking his fingers through his hair. "I'm *sorry,* Jasmine," he growled before stomping to the side of the room and slamming his fist into the thick log wall. He winced with the impact. "What else can I say?"

She remained silent as he shook his grazed knuckles, pressing her lips together to keep herself from murmuring something sarcastic or unkind. She'd never seen him angry enough to punch something. Christopher wasn't prone to emotional outbursts, which made him all the more unpredictable now.

"You can tell me the truth."

He turned on her, his eyes dark as granite. "The truth?" He laughed cynically. "I don't know what the truth is anymore."

"No? Let's start at the beginning." She paced the room, ticking off a list on her fingers, beginning with her thumb. "I distinctly remember you saying you loved me, that you'd wait for me as long as it took."

He grunted in defense.

She shook her head. "I know. I was the one who insisted we break up while I went to medical school." Her throat closed around the words. "But I didn't exactly mean for you to take up with my sister!"

When he stayed stubbornly silent, she continued. "I guess any old Enderlin woman is good enough to date, doesn't matter which one," she jibed sarcastically.

"I never *dated* your sister!" he snapped back. "Not ever, Jasmine. I was faithful to *you.*"

"Except for when you tied the knot with Jenny, you mean," she corrected acerbically. The knowledge that he'd been intimate with her before their marriage slashed just as deeply as the wedding itself. Maybe more so. It gave a new dimension to her pain, making her feel unattractive and unwanted.

It was irrational, she knew. Christopher had never denied his physical attraction to her, and it was a mutual decision to honor God and wait for the wedding. And she had been the one to break off their relationship before med school. But she still felt he'd turned his back not only on her, but on *God,* when he welcomed Jenny into his arms.

Poor, sweet, innocent Jenny. At least he'd married her when she discovered she was pregnant with his child.

Married her and then abandoned her.

All the old anger came rushing back, and she turned on him, her face flushed with fury and her gaze condemning him before he opened his mouth.

"You said you would listen," he said quietly, shaking his head. "But you've already accused, tried and found me guilty."

"Aren't you?"

He swiped a hand down his face. "I don't know, Jasmine. And that's the honest truth."

"Please tell me you're kidding."

A dry laugh burst from his throat. "I wish I was. Everything was in such an uproar. But I didn't—" His words dropped abruptly and he turned away.

Christopher had been about to say *sleep with Jenny at all.* Not even after the marriage. He was there to give the unborn child a name and a roof over his head, and that was as far as it went. Jenny's health was declining rapidly, to his dismay. But if everyone knew the mar-

riage hadn't been consummated, others had leverage
to use against his claiming Sammy as his son.

"I did things in the wrong order," he said gruffly.
"I'll admit my responsibility to that."

Jasmine winced, then straightened her shoulders and
pierced him with a cold glare. "How gallant of you."

"I'll tell you what happened," he said, his voice low
and scratchy. "You can figure out the rest."

She nodded miserably and slumped into the rocking chair, wrapping her arms around herself protec-
tively. He wanted *his* arms wrapped around her. But
she needed to hear this story, and she needed to hear
it from him.

"Jenny called me up and asked me to come over and
spend the evening with her and Gram." This wouldn't
be news to Jasmine. She knew how close he was to
her grandmother. "But when I got there, Jenny was in
tears and Gram was nowhere to be found. Jenny told
me later she was out of town visiting relatives."

He was silent a moment, allowing Jasmine to sort
through the issues. It didn't take her long to reach her
own conclusions.

"Are you telling me she called you over on a ruse?"
she asked, disbelief gleaming from her jade green eyes.

He paced over to the rocking chair and squatted
to her eye level, wanting to be sure she could see the
truth in his eyes when he spoke. "That's exactly what
I'm telling you."

"Hogwash," she snapped. "Why would Jenny need
to trick you? She could have just called you."

"Yes. And I would have come. I'd do anything for
your family." He'd certainly proved that, even going

to the length of ruining his own life in the process. He *had* to win Jasmine back, or his life was *worth* nothing.

He took a deep breath, wondering how to tell her what happened next. "Jazz, your sister was…emotionally unstable. She was a basket case by the time I got to the house. That's the only reason I stayed."

"Jenny was sensitive. She cried easily. But she was *not* a basket case!"

Christopher held up his hands. "I'm sorry. I don't mean to upset you more. I know Jenny was a sweet girl. But she was really upset that night. Smashing glass vases against the wall, turning over furniture—"

He stopped when he heard her sharp intake of breath.

"What…" Jasmine swallowed hard. "What happened? What was wrong?"

"She didn't tell me. At least not then."

She pinned him with a glare.

"I'm serious. She wouldn't tell me. She kept mumbling something about a low-life scumbag, but I never got her to elaborate any further than that. She just burst into tears again."

Jasmine's jaw clenched. He stood and put his hands in his front pockets to keep from touching her. She needed someone to ease the lines of strain from her face, to knead the knots from her shoulders.

Someone. But not him.

"This had something to do with a man?" she asked, her voice choked.

"I believe so. I stayed with her. Cleaned up the mess. Cooked her dinner. She'd calmed down by that time, and… she begged me not to leave her alone."

Compassion and sympathy flashed across her face,

replacing the fierce lines of anger. Christopher swallowed hard. Jasmine had the gift of looking beyond the obvious to find the heart of the matter. Hope flared in his chest and his pulse raced.

"So you reached out to her, trying to comfort her, and…" She left the end of her sentence dangling.

"No!" Christopher closed his eyes and willed his emotions to the back of his mind. Her words weren't full of condemnation anymore, but reluctant understanding. "It wasn't like that! You don't understand!"

"I think I do."

"No. I didn't *comfort* her…that way. I went out and rented a couple of those old movies Jenny liked so much and popped some popcorn."

"And?"

He pulled in a breath. "And fell asleep on the couch, somewhere in the middle of the movie. That's all I can tell you."

"A woman doesn't get pregnant by a man sleeping on her couch, Christopher." Her sarcasm was back, a sure sign she was getting defensive again.

Anger tore at him as his face warmed with the necessity of talking about something so personal, so intimate, in such a clinical way. There was no love lost here.

He couldn't tell her why he left, or one of the two main reasons he returned would be null and void. He couldn't let that happen. "That's all I can tell you."

"That's all I want to hear." Jasmine stood suddenly and whisked around the room, gathering her personal items and her doctor's bag. "I'm going back to Amanda's to check on her and the baby."

"I'll take you."

"No," she countered far too quickly. "I want to walk."

"Walk?" he protested. "In case you didn't look out the window, there's over a foot of new snow on the ground!"

She tilted her chin up and glared at him. "So?"

"So…you can't just go *walking* to Amanda's."

"Watch me."

"Of all the stubborn, mule-headed women…"

She wrapped her parka around her and pulled up the hood. "I'm sure you've known plenty."

The barb met its mark. He clamped his jaw shut and scowled. Stubborn. Mule-headed. And he loved her with every beat of his heart.

"You don't believe me, do you?"

"What's to believe? That Jenny's baby was an immaculate conception? I don't think so, Christopher."

"I'm telling you the truth." He faced her off, his head only inches from her own. Her green eyes were flashing fire. Anger rose in his chest. All their history together, and she couldn't see the truth when it was staring her in the face. Maybe he couldn't say the words aloud, but she should *know*.

The injustice of it branded him through the heart. "You don't believe me?" he asked again. He willed every bit of his heart into his gaze. Surely she would be able to see that of all the people in the world, he could not lie to her. Not now. And not ever.

"As a matter of fact, no," she said, tipping her chin up to pierce him with another glare. "I don't believe a word you say."

"Then believe this." He took her firmly by the shoulders, tightening his grip when she tried to squirm away.

If she didn't know his intentions to begin with, he was aware of the very moment when she read it in his gaze.

He waited until that moment, until she knew what he meant when his lips descended on hers, tormenting him with their sweetness. In his kiss, nothing would be hidden. She would know the truth.

He shifted his weight so he could draw her closer and slid his hands up her shoulders so he could cup her face in his palms, sliding the smooth material of her parka hood away from her head. She was so soft, so sweet, and the unusual, tropical scent that was Jasmine enveloped him.

"And the truth shall set you free." The Scripture flooded his mind even as she melted into his embrace.

Would the truth set them free? In the eternal sense, he knew the answer to that question, but what about the rest of their lives?

She clutched at the front of his shirt like a drowning woman. Instead of pushing him away as he expected, she pulled him closer, hoarsely whispering his name between kisses.

Warmth rushed over him at the sound of his name on her lips. He loved this woman.

He'd always loved her, since the first time he'd looked up into a giant elm and seen her dangling from a branch when he was seven and she was six. Nothing had changed. And everything had changed, leaving him with nothing but the tattered cover of his life. And leaving him without Jasmine.

He broke the kiss off before his passion overrode his good sense, knowing she was too emotionally drained to be the strong one now. He tucked her into his chest and inhaled sharply, trying to slow the runaway rhythm of his heart and steady his ragged breathing. He wanted the moment to go on forever, but knew that his wish went beyond the bounds of reality.

After a moment more, as he expected, Jasmine stiffened and tried to pull away. He caught a glimpse of regret in her eyes and reached for her elbow, but she yanked herself out of his grasp. With a huff of breath, she pulled up her hood and marched determinedly for the front door.

She opened the door and a snowy gust blew in, chilling Christopher instantly. She appeared not to notice, stepping out onto the porch as if it were a bright summer day and not the aftermath of a Colorado blizzard.

At the last moment, she paused, then turned back to him. A single tear slid down her cheek.

His breath caught in his chest as his gaze met hers. He clenched his fists at his sides, hating that he'd hurt her, wondering if kissing her had been the wrong thing to do. He wanted so much for them to be together, but…

"I believe you," she said quietly. "I'm very confused right now. I don't know how to reconcile the facts. But I believe what you told me today is the truth."

"And the truth shall set you free."

Chapter Seven

"*O*ne more push, Jenny, and you're finished! Your baby is almost here!" Sweat poured from Jasmine's forehead, rivaling that of her laboring sister. Breathing heavily, she wiped the sting of salt from her eyes with the edge of her sleeve, careful not to contaminate her iodine-splashed hands with germs.

"I can't do this anymore," Jenny whispered, her voice cracking in agony. "I can't! I'm too tired to push." Panic in her voice rose to a fevered pitch, then dropped suddenly as her head sagged back onto the sweat-soaked pillow and her eyes drooped closed.

"You can do this," Jasmine said, giving Jenny's leg a reassuring pat. "With the next contraction. Then you can rest all you want." She noticed her voice quavered slightly. She couldn't quite maintain the clinical detachment necessary for a doctor. Not with her own little sister.

Well, not so little anymore, she reflected, automatically clearing the baby's airway as she worked. Jenny was having a baby!

Christopher Jordan's baby.

*Jasmine felt a slight rush of envy, but didn't allow
the feeling to persist. Christopher might be the biological father. But where was he now?*

Gone. And it was just as well.

*Jenny groaned. Another contraction was com-
ing. One more good push and Jasmine's first niece
or nephew would put in an appearance. Excitement
mounted.*

*Jenny rolled up and clenched her jaw as she pushed,
but it was not enough to keep her from screaming when
the baby slid out into Jasmine's waiting hands.*

*A perfectly formed little boy. Jasmine counted
quickly—ten fingers and ten toes, then cut the cord
as the child let out a lusty yell.*

Worse than a nightmare, the memory of Jenny's
death haunted her waking moments. Jasmine pulled
her four-by-four into the driveway of Jenny's house and
wiped a hand across her eyes to dispel her thoughts.
She sighed and gripped the steering wheel, steady-
ing her labored breath. In the semihypnotic state that
driving sometimes induced, she'd let her thoughts run
away with her.

Jenny's bungalow was becoming more and more of
a haven to Jasmine, and she was beginning to wonder
at the wisdom of selling the quaint old place. She unlocked the door and stepped inside, inhaling the light,
lingering scent of cinnamon potpourri—her sister's favorite aroma. Jenny was an almost physical presence
here, where her thoughts, hopes and dreams had once
meandered through the hallways.

Where Sammy had been born. And where Jenny
had died.

Jasmine didn't want to remember the sad things

anymore. She was tired of trying to think through the issues, wrestle with the nuances of truth she was learning. She couldn't stop the thoughts from coming, but she continued to shove them into the back of her mind.

That, and trying to forget what Christopher had said. How would she ever sort through the mess that had become her life? His revelation, and her response not only to the words but to the man, had her running from that cabin at top speed, afraid to look back lest her heart become more entangled than it already was.

After visiting Amanda and reassuring herself that the mother and baby were fine, she'd hiked back to her vehicle and made the treacherous trip back into town. She'd spent a couple of hours with Sammy, then she put him down for a nap and headed straight for Jenny's, determined to finish the bittersweet job of preparing the bungalow for sale and get it over with.

Grabbing a box, she opened the drawer to Jenny's nightstand. She'd left this job until last, because she suspected many of her sister's personal items would be in this drawer.

Low-life scumbag. That's what Christopher said Jenny had been mumbling that night. It almost sounded as if she were talking about a man, the sort of statement a woman used in regard to a relationship gone wrong.

But Jenny hadn't been involved in a relationship. Surely not? That she hadn't said a word about a special guy was proof positive that Christopher was lying— wasn't it? She'd certainly never brought a man home to meet the family that Jasmine knew of.

A beat with the echo of a canyon pounded in her temple. She and Jenny were too close for Jenny to keep secrets, especially about romance. Her sister had been the first person Jasmine shared her secrets with, and thought Jenny had done the same.

You kept your engagement to Christopher a secret, her mind taunted. If she'd just told Jenny the truth, maybe none of this would have happened. Jenny wouldn't have run to Christopher, and he wouldn't have—

She cut the thought off. Her whole thread of thought was assuming Christopher was telling the truth. She'd told him she believed him, and she did, though it was completely irrational to do so. Something in his look when he told her the story was so honest, so sincere, that she could do no less than give him the benefit of the doubt.

Of course, his explanation did nothing to the fact that he'd neglected to tell her of his upcoming wedding to Jenny, nor his subsequent abandonment of his wife and unborn son.

With a grunt of protest, she pulled on the drawer, wondering if it would reveal answers to her questions, or if it would merely reveal more secrets to unfold.

It was locked.

"Great," she said aloud, fuming inside. "Calm down and think this through rationally," she demanded of herself, willing her blood pressure to settle. "Where would Jenny put the key?"

She ran her mind over the possibilities. She'd already been through the dresser and the closet. She'd packed Jenny's kitchen items into boxes. She hadn't run across any keys, much less a small drawer key.

She sighed, frustration seething from her lungs. One obstacle after another, with no end in sight. Weariness spread through her bones, dragging her down with its weight. Maybe Gram was right, and she did need a break. But that would leave Westcliffe without a doctor.

Unless…

Jasmine made a dash for her purse and dumped the contents onto the bed. She snatched her date book from the hodgepodge of items and flipped through the pages, then reached for the telephone, which she'd not yet had disconnected.

"Marcus? It's Jasmine," she said without preamble when a man answered. She could tell from the deep sound of his booming bass voice that it was her dear friend from med school, so she didn't see a need to make small talk.

She'd met Marcus White at a campus Bible study during her first year as a resident. When her world had fallen apart, Marcus had been a rock, believing for her what she couldn't believe for herself.

He showed her in the best way, in word and deed, that everything she'd grown up believing wasn't in vain, and that God still worked in people's lives. She wasn't sure she believed it still, but not for his lack of trying.

He knew her present circumstances, at least about Christopher's dumping her for her sister. He didn't yet know about Jenny, never mind Sammy, but that could wait until later. She would explain the particulars when she saw him face-to-face.

She refused to give a thought as to what Christopher might think of Marcus's sudden arrival in her life. She knew he wouldn't be happy about it. Just one more obstacle he had to surmount. At least that's how he'd look at it.

Her eyes clouded as she remembered telling Christopher about Marcus. She and Christopher were secretly engaged at the time, and though he hadn't said anything, the left corner of his lip had turned down. He'd looked for all the world like a little boy who'd just been told to share his favorite toy. She'd kissed him and promised him the world that day, and he'd quickly lost his surly mood.

She shook her head and swallowed hard, dislodging yet another memory. They seemed to plague her today. It was none of Christopher's business who she brought to Westcliffe, she quickly reminded herself. *She* would be happy to see her old friend, and that's what really mattered, wasn't it?

As soon as they'd discussed how Marcus's own plans to return as a doctor to the inner-city neighborhood he'd grown up in had backfired, Jasmine enlisted his professional help.

"I'd be there even if you didn't need me as a doctor," he replied immediately. "I told you that you can always count on me. I'm here for you, girl. You just give me directions from the airport."

Jasmine breathed a sigh of relief. "I'm glad to hear that. I didn't dare to hope when I called you. And of course I prayed that your situation would work out in your home neighborhood."

"I appreciate your prayers," he said, sounding as if he were choking out the words. "Rest assured, God answered them."

Jasmine felt the familiar flare of animosity rise in her chest, the anger that jumped out when she was least prepared for it.

That he was holding back his emotions was blatantly obvious to her, yet his words were filled with strength and calm. For some unexplainable reason, that riled her.

"It was just a figure of speech, Marcus. How can you say God answered your prayers?" she demanded. "You aren't accepted as a doctor in your very own neighborhood. It was your dream."

"That was God's answer," Marcus explained patiently. "He wants me to serve elsewhere. When He's ready, He'll change my dreams."

His voice was firm. He really believed what he said, and that shook Jasmine to the core. She'd once believed herself to have the kind of faith that could move mountains. She made a grunt of disgust.

Deep down, she couldn't deny God existed. The beauty and artistry of His creation was enough to prove otherwise. But she'd come to believe He stood aloof, didn't dirty his hands with the affairs of men and women—at least not common, everyday country girls like she was. Where her life was concerned, she was on her own.

"I wish I had your faith," she said, her tone petulant.

"You don't need my faith," Marcus replied, laughter echoing from the deep recesses of his chest. "You have your own. It just hasn't resurfaced yet." He paused as if giving her time to consider his words.

When she didn't respond, he continued. "Now, getting down to business. What is it you need me to do for you? Tell you to take two aspirin and call me in the morning?"

Jasmine laughed weakly before filling him in. When she hung up, she returned to the locked drawer, deciding it wouldn't hurt to attempt to pick the lock. She tried a hairpin, a credit card slid into the top of the drawer, and the keys from her own chain, but nothing worked. She racked her brain for another idea.

Determined pounding on the front door interrupted her work, and she sighed in frustration. Yet another difficulty was just exactly what she didn't need right now. And she had no doubt it *was* a major trial on the other side of the door. A six-foot, broad-shouldered, sweet-talking problem.

No one but Christopher Jordan and Gram knew she was here. The rigorous beat on the door left no doubt which of the two wanted to see her. And it was not Gram.

"Pizza man," he coaxed from behind the door. "Open up, Jazz, I know you're in there."

"What do you want?" she demanded as she stomped to the door and swung it open. "I'm really not in the mood for company right now."

Christopher tipped his cowboy hat from his head and smiled as he tucked it under his arm, extending the pizza box he held in the other. "Why is it every time you answer the door you bite my head off? Something about knocking make you churlish? Maybe I should in-stall a doorbell to make things easier for you."

His tone was so light and flippant she had to chuckle, and the aroma of sizzling pepperoni was making her mouth water. "Oh, that would help," she quipped back. "Then you could interrupt me with a bell when I'm loaded under with a ton of boxes, instead of pounding my door off its hinges."

"Man with food doesn't work for you?" His smile was adorably contagious, and she found herself smil-ing too.

Just food would be best. The *man* in question was

already making her heart skip erratically, something she could do without.

"I knew you wouldn't be able to resist pizza," he said, stepping around her and into the bungalow. "I stopped by your place first and talked to Gram."

Sammy! Panic stabbed through her, but quickly ebbed. If he'd seen his son, he sure wouldn't be here now, offering her a pizza.

"She said you hadn't eaten—did you catch lunch in town?"

She sighed. "I haven't been to town. And no, I didn't have lunch. We had a big breakfast, remember?"

He shook his head. "You've got to eat regular meals, Jazz, or you're going to hurt yourself." Placing the pizza box on the table, he tossed his hat onto the counter and pulled out a slice of pizza, waving it invitingly beneath her nose.

"You sound just like Gram," she said, scowling.

Even as she wished everyone would stop trying to run her life, her fickle mouth was watering at the tantalizing aroma. She licked her lips.

"Hungry?" he asked, cocking a grin.

"Starved, actually." She didn't realize just how hungry she was until he'd arrived. She snatched the slice of pizza from him and bit into it, savoring the rich flavor of the mozzarella cheese and the tangy spice of the pepperoni. "Mmm. My favorite."

"I remember." His voice was husky.

She tried to catch a glimpse of his face, but he'd turned back to the table to get himself a slice. "You still haven't said why you're here," she reminded him, a little annoyed and a lot confused.

"Isn't it enough that I want to be with you?"

Her breath caught. "Under the circumstances, I'd have to say *no*."

The smile disappeared from his lips and his eyes turned a smoky gray. "Gram said you might need some help finishing up here."

"Gram talks too much."

"Now, is that any way to talk about your grandmother?" He squinted one eye at her, and she could see laughter lurking just below the surface.

"It is when she butts her nose into someone else's business. Especially mine."

"She's worried about you."

Reaching for a napkin, Jasmine wiped tomato sauce from the corner of her mouth. "I know she is."

Their eyes met and locked. Christopher's eyes were the smoky blue color that radiated love and passion and made her heartbeat triple. He was a vibrant, passionate man, applying everything he had to whatever he did, just as the Bible said. Whether it be in work, or play—or love. How often had he teasingly reminded her of that verse as his eyes turned smoky?

"In case you're curious, Gram wouldn't let me see my son," he said gruffly, answering the question she hadn't asked.

"I figured."

"I didn't ask." His voice sounded strained, almost tortured, when just a moment ago he'd been laughing.

Her eyes widened. She wouldn't blame him if he'd sweet-talked Gram into seeing Sammy.

When he'd first shown up on her doorstep, her only thought was protecting Sammy from his clutches. But now, despite the myriad of unanswered questions, she wondered at the wisdom of keeping Christopher from his son.

It was clear he cared about the boy, though he'd never seen him. Christopher was acting very much like the man she once knew and loved, the man who put others' needs ahead of his own, who always tried to do the right thing. Who would love and cherish his children.

"I'm not ready," she said aloud. "I know you want to see Sammy, but—"

"He's my son, Jazz."

"I know." *But you ran away.*

The barrier was still there between them, as potent and ominous as the Berlin Wall had once been. She blew out a breath. They'd been down this road before.

She needed more time to think, to sort things out, before she made any decisions. If she allowed herself to be led by her emotions, she wasn't the only one who stood to get hurt. "Did you come here to talk about Sammy?"

He wolfed down another large bite of pizza and shook his head. "No. I came to help. But—" he continued between bites, gesturing toward a pile of boxes "—it looks like you're finished."

"Almost finished," she corrected. "Everything except Jenny's nightstand. I'm going to give it to charity, but I wanted to clean it out first. The stupid drawer is locked, and I can't find the key."

"Have you tried to pick the lock?" he asked, wiping his hands on a napkin.

"Yes, but you're welcome to try again. It's not like I'm a master thief or anything."

"What did you use?"

"Hairpin, credit card, screwdriver. Any other ideas?"

"Do you have any idea where Jenny might have kept the key?"

"I don't have a clue. This is my last project. I've scrubbed this house from floorboards to ceiling, and haven't found a single key."

"Would she have put it somewhere special?"

It was as if a light bulb had flipped on in her mind, so quickly the answer came to her.

The Bible.

It had lots of pages marked with lumps made by various items—maybe the key was one of them. It was worth a try.

She rushed to the living room, where Jenny's Bible was sitting on top of a small stack of boxes of items Jasmine was keeping.

Jenny's favorite sweater. A photo album to give Sammy when he was older. And she was keeping the Bible, whether or not she ever read it.

She could throw it away, she supposed, but someday, maybe, she would give it to Sammy so he could know a little more about his mother, have something personal of hers, something to remember her by.

His *real* mother.

That he would only remember *her* as his mother both thrilled and terrified Jasmine. And now, if Christopher had his way, the boy would know his father, too. The situation suddenly didn't seem so awfully bad, for the boy, at least.

If Christopher wanted to play a part in Sammy's life, which appeared to be the case, Sammy would be able to benefit from a male role model. But it also meant she would be forced into close proximity with Christopher on a regular basis for the rest of her life.

Any hope she had of getting over him and moving on with her life, perhaps even finding someone else to love, died an instant death in her mind. There could be no other man. It was as if Christopher had been made for her, complementing her strengths and augmenting her weaknesses. She glanced to where he stood, his arms crossed over his broad chest, one shoulder leaning casually against the far wall.

She used to think that he *was* made for her, God's choice for her perfect mate. She squeezed her eyes shut against the tears that burned there, then opened the Bible and shuffled through the pages.

In the middle of it, tied with a small piece of golden embroidery thread, was the key. Jasmine pulled it out and snapped the book closed. "I've found it."

She felt rather than saw Christopher follow her into the bedroom. His gaze on her was almost tangible, and though he remained silent, she knew he felt her tension at the questions yet remaining. She sat on the edge of the bed, her spine stiffly straight, the key poised and waiting in her hand.

It slid easily into the lock, clicking softly as she turned it. "It fits," she said, knowing the verbal confirmation was unnecessary. He dropped his large hand on her shoulder, lightly rubbing the tension from the back of her neck.

The drawer wasn't nearly as full as she expected it to be. A box of tissues, a couple of paperbacks, a pair of reading glasses. And a picture, an old newspaper clipping that looked like it had been handled frequently.

Curious, Jasmine picked up the photograph. A

clean-cut young man dressed in tennis whites with a sweater draped over his shoulder stared dully at the camera, as if annoyed that he was once again being photographed. He was leaning against the railing of his yacht. A smiling bleach blonde had her arms around the man's neck. She, at least, didn't mind being photographed.

There was something disturbingly familiar about that woman, she realized with a start. She looked closer.

"That's *Jenny!*" she said aloud, astonished. Without thinking, she looked to Christopher for help. He merely clenched his jaw and looked away.

How could the woman in this picture be her sister? The Enderlins were a far cry from the country-club type, of which there were none in Westcliffe. A few in Pueblo, maybe, and definitely Denver. But not from around here.

What disturbed her most of all was the foreign look the woman who was her sister had on her face. There wasn't a trace of the sweet girl she'd grown up with. The woman in the picture looked comfortable on a yacht on Pueblo Reservoir where the rich hang out, and in the newspapers. Excited, but not giddy.

Jasmine swallowed hard. "How?" She choked out the word, then gasped for a breath.

"I didn't want to have to tell you." Christopher's voice was low and strangled. Turning toward her, he clenched and unclenched his fists. He opened his mouth to speak, then closed it again, scowling.

She waited, barely remembering to breathe. Her fingers were shaking where she held the worn photograph, the last picture taken of her sister. Nothing was as it seemed. Everything she believed in played her false.

Christopher. God. Now even Jenny. She wondered if she had the strength to hear what he had to say. Christopher reached for her, enfolding her in his arms without a word. Her quivering turned to trembling, and her trembling to quaking as the events of the past few months caught up with her.

She didn't cry. Her tears were spent. But the tension in her body welled up in her like lava in a volcano, finally exploding into tremor after tremor.

He buried his face in her hair and stroked her temple, murmuring until the shock had passed. When she no longer shook, he kissed her forehead and released her.

"Things changed around here after you left for med school," he said, carefully enunciating each word as if the syllables themselves caused him pain. "There are some things about Jenny you need to know."

Chapter Eight

Christopher didn't know how much to tell her. He wasn't sure he should be telling her anything at all. She'd been through so much already. But there was still so much she didn't know.

How could he make her understand how her leaving affected those closest to her? With both their parents dead, Jenny had been dependent on Jasmine, looking up to her as a role model, almost as a mother figure, though they were only four years apart.

All through junior high, Jenny had walked in Jasmine's shadow, doing the things she knew would please her sister rather than developing her own interests. But when Jasmine left for med school, Jenny changed.

Jasmine sat on the bed staring up at him, her wide, green angel eyes shimmering with emotion. Words he never planned to say hurdled over one another to leave his mouth. Without conscious thought, he related the story.

"After you left for med school, Jenny got into trouble. She made new friends—friends apart from the church and the community. She made a lot of trips to Pueblo, staying away for days at a time, even."

"I didn't even know she was hanging out with the jet-setters," she whispered.

"You had all you could do to keep up with your studies," he reminded her gently.

"But I could have *helped* her!"

"Maybe. Maybe not. Jenny had the strong will of an Enderlin, Jazz. She could be nearly as stubborn as you." He tipped up the corner of his lip, trying to smile, but feeling like he was grimacing instead. "I'm sure Gram thought it was just a stage, that she'd grow out of it."

"And she did, didn't she?"

"In a way. When she found out she…was carrying Sammy, she walked the straight and narrow."

What had her sister been seeking? The urge to pull her back into his arms was strong, but he resisted. Since he'd been back, he'd been reaching for her.

This time, he wanted her to reach for him first.

"She went back to church. Got straight with the Lord. Grew up in a hurry so she could raise a baby. She would have been a good mother to Sammy," he concluded softly.

"Do you know the man in the picture?" she queried, handing him the worn newspaper. Steeling himself for what he might see, he glanced at the picture. He had ample reason for his hesitance.

This was the man.

He handed the picture back to Jasmine with such alacrity her eyes widened in surprise.

He'd seen the young man in the photograph, though he couldn't place him right away. He knew it hadn't been with Jenny—he would remember that. The face was familiar, but beyond that he couldn't say.

Bart Pembarton. The biological father of Jenny's baby. That was the man pictured, Christopher realized a minute later.

"I don't think I know him," she said slowly, taking the picture back. She stared down at it another moment, as if trying to read something into the picture that wasn't there. "You know what's odd?"

"Hmm?" he murmured distractedly, his gaze tracing the line of her jaw to her full, wide mouth, which was even now curled down in a girlish frown.

"This doesn't look like Jenny at all, but even so… she looks happy."

"I don't see how."

"Maybe *happy* is the wrong word. Content? No, not that, either. I would have thought she'd be uncomfortable with rich people. But something in her eyes, I guess, makes me think…oh, I don't know. Like she really cared for the man in the picture. Maybe my overactive imagination is running away with me."

"If you want to believe she was happy, then believe it."

"But you don't."

He clenched his jaw. "I can't say. All I know is that she ran with a bad crowd. She made sure she was quite visible—almost as if she *wanted* you to hear about her behavior."

"I'm surprised I didn't."

"Like I said, Jazz, we all thought it was just a stage she was going through. If I would have guessed—"

"No, you're right," she interrupted. "You had no way of knowing."

Christopher picked up the nightstand and balanced it in his arms. If he stood still a moment longer, he would spontaneously combust. "Where do you want this thing?"

Jasmine pressed her fingers to her temples and squeezed her eyes shut as if staving off a headache. "Out in the living room with the rest of the boxes."

Just before he left the room, he saw her tuck the picture into the front pocket of the flannel shirt she had on over her T-shirt. Anger flooded through him.

He wished Bart were here now. He had two fists to introduce him to. He didn't even want to talk to the man, just show him in a way he could understand what happens when you mess with one of the Enderlin women.

But that was impossible. Bart was dead.

He wanted—no, needed—to help Jasmine. But all he succeeded in doing was to dig himself in deeper. He wasn't able to ease her pain. All he could do was stand by and watch, powerless, as the plot thickened.

More than anything, he hated this feeling of helplessness. He needed to do something, to take some positive action instead of just sitting here twiddling his thumbs.

There must be something he could do. But what?

He ground his teeth in frustration, barely resisting the urge to slam the nightstand to the floor and stomp it to pieces. It wouldn't do him any good to break Jenny's furniture.

Jasmine shuffled from the bedroom, refusing to meet his gaze as he stooped to settle the nightstand next to the boxes.

"Sammy..." she began, then hesitated, looking every direction except at him.

He dropped one knee to the floor, afraid his legs might buckle from the powerful, potent force of the single word. His breath jammed into his lungs and refused to be released.

She cleared her throat and tried again. "Sammy and I will...be walking in the park tomorrow afternoon."

She stopped again, and this time pinned him with a gaze so direct and open it knocked the stubborn breath from his chest in a whoosh of air. "At one o'clock."

Swallowing hard, he forced a trickle of oxygen back into his burning lungs.

Her meaning was unmistakable.

She would let him see the baby!

The memories haunted Jasmine even in her dreams.

Jenny was fading fast.

Instead of the regular joyful recovery of bringing new life into the world, Jenny was growing more peaked by the moment.

Jasmine felt for a pulse. It was weak and erratic. Something was terribly wrong.

"It hurts," Jenny rasped weakly, rolling her head from side to side on the sweat-soaked pillow.

It shouldn't hurt. The baby boy, wrapped in a blanket next to Jenny's side, was wiggling and gurgling contentedly. The afterbirth should have been easy.

Jasmine wiped her hands on a clean towel and stood slowly so as not to alarm Jenny. Her mind was screaming in panic, but her training as a doctor pulled her through. She would remain calm. If Jenny sensed her anxiety, it would only make things worse.

She needed to use the phone, she'd said.

To tell everyone the good news?

Sure. That was it. Her voice quavered with the lie. She'd only be a minute.

But the helicopter couldn't come soon enough. There wasn't anything anyone could do.

Not even a doctor. Jasmine knew it, and so did Jenny.

Her sister had looked up at her with the pained, wise gaze of someone who knew her time was near. She reached for Jasmine's hand, and it was all she could do to keep from shaking, from bursting into tears. From screaming to God for mercy.

"Grieve later," Jenny had said. "There are more important things to do right now." The hospital helicopter was on its way, and there wasn't much time. At least that's what Jenny said. The truth was much harder to hear.

Jasmine merely nodded, unable to speak. She wanted to run, to cry, to scream in rage. Instead, she took her sister's hands and waited.

"I've already made arrangements for my funeral," Jenny whispered, her voice hoarse.

Jasmine felt as if a thousand pins were pricking her body. This couldn't be happening.

Jenny nodded. "Yes. I knew I was dying. I've got cancer, Jasmine."

Jasmine gasped in pain and shock.

"I'm okay with it," Jenny was quick to assure her. "I've made my peace with God."

"How...when?"

"I found out about the cancer the same day I found out I was having Sammy. He's the sole reason I've

been hanging on. It's my time, Jasmine. I'm not going to fight it anymore."

"What about your baby?" What Jasmine really wanted to say was "What about me?" but she knew how self-centered that sounded.

How could she ever live without Jenny?

Jenny laughed weakly. "He's going to be fine. I know you'll make the best mother in the world. He's a lucky little boy."

"Me?" She swallowed around the lump in her throat.

"The papers are already drawn up. I want you to be Sammy's legal guardian." She reached weakly for Jasmine's hand. "Please."

"Of course," she assured, her voice scratchy. "Of course I will."

There was a moment of silence as Jenny's spirit seemed to fade away. Her breath became shallow and her eyelids drooped. Then, with what appeared to be a monumental effort, she opened her eyes and focused on Jasmine.

"Take care my baby." A single tear formed at the corner of Jenny's eye, then meandered slowly down her face.

Jasmine watched the progress of the salty drop of water as if in a trance. "You can care for him yourself when you get better."

"You and I both know that won't happen."

Jenny's fingers were cold as they squeezed her hand. "Promise me."

"I already did." The sting of tears met with Jasmine's stubborn opposition.

Jenny pulled the infant close to her chest, her tears

coming in earnest now. She stroked his cheek, his nose, his ear, then planted a gentle kiss on his forehead. With a sob, she handed him to Jasmine.

"I'm so sorry." Her words were growing slurred and faint. "Forgive me."

Jasmine wasn't sure if Jenny was speaking to her or not. Her eyes had closed, her face contorted in pain.

"And Jasmine, find... Christopher..."

Jasmine sat bolt upright in her bed, sweat pouring from her brow. Sammy's shrill infant cry had wakened her from the nightmare that was so much more than just a dream. Her breath came in deep, angry waves, her lungs burning with exertion. Jenny's final words echoed in her head, and she wrapped her arms around her legs, hugging her knees to her chest.

And tomorrow—or rather, today, she amended, glancing at the clock on the nightstand—she would introduce Sammy to his father.

She scooped the boy from his bassinet, murmuring gently and rocking him against her breast. She used her index finger to peep through the venetian blinds, which affirmed that the world still lay heavily under the shroud of darkness.

She yawned and rubbed her eyes. Sammy was pretty much sleeping through the night lately. She wondered what woke him, and hoped she hadn't inadvertently yelled in her sleep. She put a bottle of formula in the microwave and settled with Sammy on a rocker, humming softly.

She didn't even recognize the song she was singing, at first, but as the melody progressed, the lyrics soon followed.

"Great is Thy faithfulness…morning by morning new mercies I see."

There was no mercy for one such as she, though seeing the innocent, wide-eyed pleasure of the chubby baby boy in her arms made her wonder.

Where did God's plan end and hers begin? The road was narrow—had she missed it altogether?

She certainly felt she'd wandered off onto some mighty big highway, covered with cars and semis, without a shade of grace or mercy.

She closed her eyes, hesitantly pointing a prayer toward the ceiling, nudging gently to see if the wall between heaven and earth was as firm as she'd once felt it to be.

It budged. No, it did more than budge. The floodgates of heaven opened and God's grace shone upon her like the sun, lighting even the darkest recesses of her heart. The experience was at once so jarring and so gentle that she barely heard the beep of the microwave signaling the baby's bottle was ready.

Sammy heard it, though, and began doing baby jumping jacks in her arms, flailing his round little limbs wildly to get her attention. She opened her eyes and laughed, breathing in the peace that passes understanding. Not really knowing, but *knowing* anyway.

Nothing had changed, yet He had changed everything. She was still meeting Christopher to introduce him to Sammy. They still had a wide gap to bridge between them, and a million details to work out where Sammy was concerned.

What was different was *her*. She'd just made a tiny step toward the right road. A step toward discovering what God wanted her to do. She prayed for the strength and courage to do His will when she knew what it was.

She wasn't the wide-eyed innocent she'd been before she went off to school, she thought, appeasing the squalling baby with his bottle, then settling back down on the rocker.

She was a world-worn woman with a chip the size of Texas on her shoulder. She knew life wasn't full of easy answers. She no longer expected black to be black and white to be white. There were lots of other colors in between black and white.

But then, she reflected, tired but content as she rocked her baby boy, maybe that was why God made rainbows.

Chapter Nine

Christopher was as nervous as a teenager on prom night. After all this time, he was finally going to be able to see Sammy, maybe even hold him. Checking his image in a mirror, he smoothed back his hair with his palm and planted his hat on his head.

He didn't know why he was making such an all-fired effort to look good today. It just seemed right for him to present himself in the best light for his...*son*. The word stuck in his mind and refused to dislodge. He swallowed hard.

It wasn't every day a man met his son for the first time.

He was nervous about holding Sammy, even though his EMT training in Pueblo had taught him how to hold a newborn. He'd been fine with Amanda's baby, but his own son was another question entirely.

Thank goodness Jasmine would be there. She would show him how.

Funny how he fell into his easy dependency on Jasmine after all this time. She was his beacon in the night. Suddenly, he recognized the care he was giving his grooming was as much for her as it was for Sammy.

A family.

No. He wouldn't think about that now. He would meet the baby, and let Jasmine see his dedication to the child with her own eyes. Then she would understand he meant what he said.

The park was a mere five-minute drive from the ranch. He arrived early, thinking he'd find a seat on the bench next to the playground to wait. But when he got there, he changed his mind.

He didn't want to inadvertently put Jasmine on the defensive. Better to wait in his truck until he saw them, so he could approach from a distance, and make sure he didn't catch her off guard.

Not that she'd really be off guard. He knew the herculean effort it had taken her to comply with his wishes. She was offering her trust when no one else would give him the time of day. He wasn't only asking for *her* trust, either, but for her to risk what was dearest to her in the world—Sammy.

His breath caught in his throat when he saw her crossing the lawn toward him. She'd clearly seen his truck, waving in his direction when he looked up. He swallowed hard and waved back.

Her long black hair waved like silk in the breeze, gently caressing the smooth skin of her cheeks. She glanced down at the carriage and made a face, laughing at whatever response she created.

He bolted from the truck, then stopped short at the lilting sound of her croon. "That's a good boy, Sammy. That's my big boy."

He *was* her boy. The knowledge jolted through his

system. All of his senses snapped to life, appearing to magnify of their own accord. The scent of fresh-clipped grass assaulted his nostrils, an unusual aroma for the middle of winter in Westcliffe. The wind was crisp and sharp against the edge of his jaw. And Jasmine's sweet voice melted into him like liquid gold.

One thing was sure—she would never give up Sammy. To him or anyone. Without the boy, she would wilt up just as sure as any mother deprived of her infant. He'd already caused enough of a ruckus in the Enderlin family to last a lifetime and beyond.

But he couldn't just turn around and walk away. He wouldn't. He clamped his jaw against a bitter chill that swept through the air. For better or for worse, Sammy was his responsibility. And for better or for worse, Jasmine would have to get used to his presence in her—in *their* lives.

She startled visibly when he tentatively reached for the carriage, her movement as instinctive as a deer caught in headlights. She might be here, but there was obviously still a part of her that was afraid he would grab the baby and make a run for it. That knowledge didn't hurt him as much as the uncertainty in her eyes.

Would he ever be able to prove himself? He resisted the impulse to turn and stalk off the way he came. Frustration and anger seethed through him, vying for prominence, but he held it in check and tipped his hat off his head.

"How is the little nipper?" he asked, awkwardly opening the conversation.

"Good."

Terrific. She wasn't going to help him any. He met

her gaze and stepped forward slowly, his movements painfully obvious.

Releasing her breath, she nodded toward the carriage. "I suppose you want to see him."

A low rumble of laughter left his chest as she stated the obvious.

She laughed with him. "That was dumb. Sorry. I'm as jumpy as a rabbit today."

"Me, too," he agreed. Somehow it was easier knowing she experienced some of the same awkwardness he was feeling. Even if it was awkwardness *he* had created.

"You can pick him up."

"I…" He hesitated, unsure of himself. What happened to showing Jasmine what a perfect father he was? He was afraid to pick up the baby.

He scooped Sammy up and cradled his head, making soothing noises. He tried to remember everything he'd learned. Support the neck. Tuck him in your arms.

Suddenly Sammy pumped his arms and legs wildly, nearly rolling off Christopher's arm. He made an exclamation and grabbed for the boy, who let out a delighted squeal which sounded very much like, "That was fun, let's do it again."

Christopher and Jasmine both laughed with him.

"You don't have to support his neck," Jasmine said. "He's old enough to do that on his own."

"He's a sturdy little guy," he commented, reaching tentatively to touch the baby's hand. His throat tightened as Sammy wrapped his little fist around his index finger and brought it to his mouth, smacking noisily.

"Sure he is. Sammy's my happy baby, aren't you, big boy?" she asked in a sweet croon. "Mommy's big boy."

Mommy.

She called herself Sammy's mother. He supposed he shouldn't be surprised. It was best for Sammy and a natural thing for Jasmine to do, but for some reason it made his throat constrict until he couldn't draw a breath.

"How old is he?" he asked gruffly.

The question made Jasmine scowl. "Three months."

Had it been that long? He would have been back sooner, had he not been in the middle of his EMT training in Pueblo. It had been his way of dealing with Jenny's death, losing himself in his studies, following God's call. But it kept him from Sammy. And Jasmine. Guilt stabbed at his chest.

"Can you show me how to hold him?"

"You said yourself he's sturdy," she replied, the lines creasing her eyebrows together easing as she stroked the boy's downy hair. "Just grab him under his shoulders."

He released the breath he'd been holding and adjusted Sammy, holding him under his arms. Christopher was surprised to discover how heavy the boy was already, and how slippery, when Sammy began wailing and squirming.

He tightened his grip on the boy, still holding him at arm's length. This baby-holding business sure was awkward. "Easy, little fellow," he coaxed.

Jasmine laughed. "He likes to be cuddled close to your body, Christopher. Give your son some loves."

He flashed her a surprised look, but was quickly diverted by his wiggling son. He pulled the boy up to his chest until the baby's soft cheek rested against his rough chin. He gave the boy a hesitant kiss on the top of his head.

To everyone's surprise, Christopher's most of all, Sammy immediately settled down. The baby lounged back into the crook of Christopher's arms and gurgled contentedly, one fist planted firmly in his mouth.

"He likes me," said Christopher, astonished.

"Well, of course he does. Babies know these things, you know. I'm sure he can sense you're his father."

That was stretching it, Christopher knew. He would hate to find out what would happen if Sammy had been exposed to his *real* biological father. Not that Bart wanted anything to do with him.

If only he could tell Jasmine. But everyone was better off if he kept his mouth shut. Sammy was safe, and Jenny's name wouldn't be dragged through the mud.

In all the ways that counted, he was Sammy's father. The baby sensed his sincerity, if not his genetic connection. It would be much harder to convince Jasmine, but he'd manage. He was Sammy's dad, and he'd prove it.

"Does he like to swing?" he asked, gesturing to a swing set.

"He loves to swing," she answered, nodding for him to lead the way.

The three of them spent over an hour playing in the park. He carefully pushed Sammy in the baby swing, laughing out loud when he squealed. Jasmine held the baby on one end of the teeter-totter while he worked the other end. She even convinced him to climb up the ladder and squeeze through a narrow opening to take Sammy down a slide.

He couldn't remember being happier. He was with

his son and the woman they both loved. And they were happy.

He hadn't laughed so much in years, and it was nice to see Jasmine with a grin on her face and a rosy glow on her cheeks. She'd been so unhappy lately.

Somehow the time they shared was unexpectedly intimate, something special only a family unit could experience. He wondered if Jasmine sensed it as well. It was almost as if it were floating in the air, permanently binding them together with every moment they spent together. They were a family.

A *family*. That was the answer.

"I've got to get Sammy back to the apartment. His little hands are like ice cubes."

Jasmine's statement dashed his thoughts and brought him abruptly back to the present. "I wouldn't want him to catch a cold," he said, concern lacing his voice.

She chuckled and adjusted the baby's hood over his head. "He'll be fine, Christopher. I just think we need to be heading home."

"I—" He floundered, having so much to say and not knowing how to begin. "You can't go yet."

She lifted an eyebrow. "Oh? And why is that?" He could still hear laughter in her voice, and he crooked a smile in return.

"I have a question to ask you."

"Ask away, then. I've got to put Sammy back into his stroller anyway."

"Okay." He took a deep breath of the fresh mountain air and hoped desperately the words forming in the back of his throat came out in English and not in some alien language.

Stalling, he crouched down to stroller level and

kissed Sammy on the cheek. He was feather soft and smelled so sweet and clean. Christopher had a feeling it was going to be difficult to walk away from the little nipper, even for a day.

"We're off," she said brightly, turning the stroller around.

"Wait!" His heart hammered double time.

She turned toward him, looking mildly annoyed.

"Marry me."

Jasmine's jaw dropped, and she struggled for a good minute to wipe the stunned look from her face. "Excuse me?"

"That didn't come out right," he said, color rising on his face. "I'm sorry, Jasmine. You deserve a marriage proposal with all the trimmings, but under the circumstances, I thought it best to bring up the subject now. Best for Sammy, I mean. And...er...us."

She sat down on the cold grass, not trusting her weak knees to hold her weight. Her insides felt like gelatin. Marry Christopher?

She pulled her knees up to her chest and wrapped her arms tightly around them, as if she might fall apart were she to loosen. She wanted to marry him—it was what she'd always wanted. That was what made the moment so difficult. What she wanted didn't matter.

"Give me one good reason I should marry you," she snapped, deciding to take the offensive.

He crouched down to her level, hat in hand. "I can give you two," he said, his voice low and strong. "Number one, Sammy."

"Sammy?" she repeated dumbly. She didn't know what she expected Christopher to say, but it certainly wasn't to start off discussing his—*their* son.

She shook herself mentally. What else would he be talking about? Surely not love. "What about Sammy?" she asked suspiciously.

"He needs a family."

"He *has* a family. *Me.*"

"I won't dispute that, Jasmine. I've seen today what a good mother you are to Sammy. Great, actually. But doesn't Sammy deserve a home with both a mother and a father present?"

She remained silent, feeling his argument weighing her down like a cement block on her feet. She wanted to bolt from the scene and from Christopher's logic, but instead simply set her jaw and tightened the hold on her legs.

"Don't you see?" he continued, softly pleading. "I can give Sammy a name. I can give him security. I can be a good male role model for him. And most of all, I can point him to his Heavenly Father by being a good father on Earth."

Jasmine shut her eyes, unable and unwilling to meet his persuasive stare.

"I'll do right by him. By both of you. And Jasmine—"

She opened her eyes then, to find Christopher's face only inches from her own. He was looking at her with such love and passion that she couldn't mistake his meaning.

He crooked his adorable grin and Jasmine felt her heart do a loop the loop. Why couldn't she resist him? She should, but when he was this close to her, all she could think about was holding him near to her and never letting him go again.

"The second reason our marriage is a good idea is because I love you. I always have, and if you search your heart, I think you'll discover that truth for your-self."

He was speaking the words she wanted to hear. But he was also presumptuously speaking of their marriage as if it were a fact. She embraced the anger that welled in her chest, finding it much easier to deal with that emotion than the frightened tremor of a cornered animal.

There were too many questions, facts Christopher was elusive on or flatly refused to discuss. It was time to throw the ball back at him in spades. "Okay."

"Okay?" He tipped off balance and landed hard on one knee on the frozen ground. "Yee-haw!"

Jasmine cleared her throat. "But before you throw your hat in the air and start celebrating, you might want to hear the conditions to this agreement."

He smacked a big kiss on her lips and stood, anxiously shifting from foot to foot. She stood as well, dusting off her backside and cringing at the feel of ice on her jeans. She'd been so steamed up she hadn't realized until this moment how cold the ground was.

She glanced at Sammy, afraid it was getting too cold for the baby, but he was sleeping soundly, his head tilted awkwardly to one side, his breath coming in little white puffs. It calmed her heart just to look at him.

"Honey, I'll do anything for you and Sammy. Just ask."

"Then tell me the truth. I know why you married Jenny, but why did you abandon her? How do I know you won't do the same thing to me?"

His scowl darkened. He looked like a man frozen in ice.

She nodded. "I thought not," she drawled acerbically. "What else could I have expected?"

"You could admit your love for me," he countered. "You could follow your heart for a change, instead of rationalizing everything."

"Oh, like how a man runs out on his wife? That's a tough one to rationalize, Christopher." Inside, her heart was breaking, but she was cool and crisp on the outside.

It was happening again, the betrayal, the utter abandonment she felt when she'd first learned about Christopher and Jenny. The pain felt every bit as fresh and new as it had way back then. Only now she stood to lose Christopher a second time, and with him, Sammy.

Christopher was Sammy's father. She wasn't sure, but was afraid the courts would find in his favor. It was a blessing, really, that he hadn't already filed a law suit. Instead, he'd come up with the ridiculous notion that marrying her would solve everyone's problems.

Well, it would only add to hers. "Then I guess the answer is no," she said, surprised at how even and stable her voice sounded.

Christopher clenched his fists, fighting desperately to control the anger and hurt warring inside him. He couldn't tell her why he left. "Why can't you just love me enough to trust me regardless of the way things look?"

He saw her wince, and reached out to hold her, only to withdraw again when she pierced him with a glare.

"How dare you lay this on my shoulders?" she snarled through gritted teeth.

Because I love you, and I think you love me. He was about to answer when he was interrupted by a man's low bass calling Jasmine by name.

Jasmine whirled around, relief evident in her expression. Christopher broke his gaze away from her, seeking the man that could bring such happiness to her features. He felt his insides crunch as she launched herself into the big African-American man's arms.

"Marcus!" she shouted merrily. "I'm so glad you've come."

Christopher didn't see why she had to be quite so jubilant, unless she was just putting on a show for his benefit. He'd startled her with his sudden proposal, and he knew it. But she didn't have to hang on the man just to make a point.

Marcus kissed her firmly on the mouth, and she joined in his low laughter. He swung her around as if she weighed nothing, then gently placed her back on her feet.

Christopher scowled. Marcus. He'd heard this name before. He searched the recesses of his mind for the occasion.

Of course. Marcus White. Her friend from college. But what was he doing here?

And what was he doing kissing Jasmine?

Chapter Ten

"You arrived just in the nick of time, you knight in shining armor, you," she teased, giving Marcus one more affectionate squeeze before releasing him.

He chuckled, a sound that echoed from the depths of his barrel chest. "You need saving, fair damsel?"

"Call me distressed," she promptly replied.

"And I suppose the man with the stroller glaring daggers at me would be your Christopher?"

"He's not—" she began, but Marcus cut her off with a look.

"Save it for someone who'll believe you."

Jasmine made a face. "I forget how well you know me."

He wrapped an arm around her waist. "Are you going to introduce me, or do I wait until he knocks my block off first?"

They walked arm in arm to where Christopher was standing, scowling at Marcus and rocking Sammy in his arms.

"Marcus, I'd like you to meet Christopher Jordan," Jasmine said shakily.

"And who's this little fellow?" Marcus reached for Sammy as if he held babies every day, causing Christopher's scowl to darken even more.

Jasmine knew there was going to be an eruption the size of Mount Saint Helens if she didn't avert a disaster here and now. She laid a hand on Christopher's arm and said, "That's our baby, Sammy."

Marcus started so abruptly he almost dropped the baby. "But that's impossible," he muttered under his breath.

Christopher relaxed his posture and reached for the baby. "Nope. This is my son. Say hello to the man, Sammy," he said in a high, tight voice. He waved the baby's pudgy little arm at Marcus.

Jasmine laughed at the astonished look Marcus flashed her. *I'll explain later,* she said with her gaze. He nodded imperceptibly.

"Christopher, I really do need to get Sammy indoors."

He eyed Marcus again, then held the baby to his chest. "I can take him for a couple of hours if you want to—" he stopped and ran his tongue slowly over his bottom lip, eyeing Marcus with distaste "—renew old friendships," he concluded, his voice low and coarse. "I'll drop him at Gram's apartment in a couple of hours."

Jasmine didn't know what to feel, never mind what to say. Christopher obviously loved Sammy, but could he be trusted to care for the boy? What if he ran off and she never found him again? She couldn't bear the thought of losing both of them.

But she couldn't very well confine him, big ox that he was. And even if she could, freedom was a rare commodity. She felt God nudging her to trust Him, and to trust Christopher.

"The stroller converts to a car seat," she said, standing on tiptoe to give Sammy a kiss. When she moved away, Christopher took her elbow and drew her back, brushing a gentle kiss across her lips.

His eyes met hers, and they were gleaming with joy and relief. "Thank you," he whispered for her ears only. "I won't let you—or Sammy—down."

She believed him. Despite his past and the web of mystery still entangling them, she believed him, and her heart was at peace.

"Be sure and buckle him in real tight. Oh—and there's a diaper bag stuffed underneath the seat of the stroller. You should have everything you need—formula, bottles, diapers. You do know how to change a diaper, don't you?" she asked half in teasing and half in distress.

He smiled down at her, his eyes twinkling affectionately. "Think I can handle it."

His mouth straightened to a firm, thin line as he nodded grimly at the other man. "Marcus." He turned away and put Sammy in the stroller, then straightened. "Take good care of my lady."

Jasmine's heart nearly bolted right out of her chest. *His* lady? It gave her shivers just to think about it, but she didn't let herself smile. Instead, she attempted to look every bit as grim as Christopher. "I can take care of myself."

Marcus burst into low laughter. "You got that right, girl."

Christopher just shrugged, indicating his frustration, and stalked off in the other direction, pushing the stroller ahead of him.

Jasmine turned to Marcus. "You, dear friend, are a lifesaver."

"Sweet as candy, you mean?"

She chuckled. "Oh, you!"

"Well, whatever else I am, color me confused. I haven't the slightest idea what just happened over here, but I can tell you one thing—one and one aren't adding up to three, if you know what I mean."

"I told you it's a long story. Things have gotten rather confusing."

After filling him in on the past three months, Jasmine sighed. "I've missed you, Marcus."

He settled an arm on her shoulder. "Missed you, too, girl. I have this peaceful feeling inside me like this is really where God wants me to be."

"I hope so. I need you."

"I'm here in the flesh, girl. Now you just tell ol' Marcus what he can do for you."

"Well…" she begin, then hesitated. "You can't wave a magic wand and wipe the past away, nor can you wipe *my* slate clean, so let's try helping me keep the town clinic running. It's turned out to be more than I can handle with a baby."

"I'm not surprised."

"Yes, well, Gram helps out as much as she can, of course, but she has her own physical limitations to worry about."

"You're living with your Gram?"

"Yes. She was gracious enough to take me in. Nags me incessantly about taking care of myself. She'll be glad to hear you're here to lend me a hand."

"Hand, foot, eyeball. Whatever you need."

"Gross!"

"Sorry. Male humor."

She rolled her eyes. "That's something I don't think I'll ever get used to. Christopher always comes up with the most outrageous—" She cut her words off abruptly, mortified by what she'd said.

Marcus hadn't missed her hesitance, for he squeezed her shoulder lightly. "What are you going to do about him?"

For some reason, Jasmine wanted to break out into bitter laughter. She remained silent as her emotions warred within her, guilt, bitterness, anxiety, anger, pain, grief. She closed her eyes and felt herself weave against Marcus.

He tightened his hold on her. "Question of the day?" he asked seriously.

"I guess." She took a deep breath of the crisp mountain air and let it cleanse her insides. "Christopher—asked me to marry him just before you got here today."

"Really?" Marcus ran his free hand across his jaw. "No wonder he was glaring at me, poor man. What did I do, interrupt the romantic moment?"

"Oh, no, quite the opposite, in fact."

He cocked an eyebrow.

"I was trying to figure out how to gracefully disappear off the planet after I declined his offer."

Marcus dropped his arm from her shoulder and whirled her around to face him. "Girl, you continue to astound me! The guy you moped around med school for asks you to be his wife, and what do you do? Say no."

"It's a little more complicated than that."

"Don't you let a little jealousy get in your way. If Christopher was a big enough deal to mourn about for a year, he's a big enough deal to marry."

"I'm *not* jealous," she denied, even as butterflies of envy fluttered through her stomach.

"Seems like a perfect solution to me. Christopher is Sammy's biological father, and you are his adoptive mother. Christopher loves you, you love him and everyone loves the little tyke. Talk about your fairytale endings."

"Don't I wish." Jasmine paused, trying to figure out how to phrase her next statement. "Christopher abandoned Jenny, Marcus. Before the baby was born."

"*Abandoned* her?" He brought up a fist and shook it as if threatening an intruder. "Why, I'd like to—"

"We all did. And he was such a good Christian, too."

"Good Christians don't knock a girl up and then abandon her."

"This one did."

"Then why did he come back?"

Jasmine sighed. "I've been asking myself that for days now. Naturally I'd assumed he'd walked away from his faith, but he hasn't, Marcus. I can feel it in my heart."

"Then what?" His voice, a deep bass to begin with, dropped another octave, and he scrubbed a hand across the short, tight curls of his hair.

"I don't know. And every time I ask, he clams up like a soldier at Buckingham Palace. All he says is that I need to trust him. Oooh!" she exclaimed, releasing her pent-up frustration. "I think I'm getting a headache."

"That's what you get for trying to think," he teased, attempting to lighten the mood.

"How would you know?" she rejoined, glad to back off from the subject of her life. She'd rather not think about it at all, much less talk about it.

"Do you trust him?" Marcus asked, breaking into her thoughts.

She met his gaze. "I don't know. Right now, my heart is saying one thing and my head is saying another."

"Then wait," he said, grinning to show a full, straight line of shiny white teeth that were enhanced by the dark features of his face. "You'll know when the time is right to act. God will put your heart and your mind in one accord, probably in some incredibly amazing way. All you have to do is wait."

Chapter Eleven

"What now, Lord?" Christopher whispered, tucking Sammy's head under his chin. "Where do I go from here?"

He'd spent his two hours with Sammy just rocking him in his arms. His little cabin on the Walters's ranch wasn't exactly secluded, what with all the other ranch hands living in similar quarters all around him. But cozy was just right for the afternoon with his son. He fed him a bottle and even changed a diaper. He'd done well for his first try at diaper duty, even if he did say so himself.

Sure, he put it on backwards the first time, but he quickly realized his mistake and had everything in the right place in no time flat. And no one could accuse him of making the same mistake twice.

He wished Jasmine could have been there to see. Then, perhaps, she would see what a great father he wanted to be. He'd be a great husband, too, but that would be harder to prove. Especially since she'd turned him down flat.

How could he walk away? This baby was as much a

part of him as if he *were* the biological father. Sammy was his responsibility. But he was also his son.

Marrying Jasmine had seemed the obvious answer to everything. They could be together, and he could be with Sammy. And it *was* best for Sammy.

Darn the stubborn, mule-headed female race, one woman in particular. Why couldn't she trust him, look past his actions and into his heart?

And to think that this whole blinking mess got started because he was trying to help her sister, thinking that's what Jasmine would want him to do. Remind him never to attempt to read a woman's mind.

So, what was the next step? Somehow, he had to make Jasmine see reason. He had to make her see what a good husband and father he'd be.

Or else he needed to show Jasmine what her life would be like if he and Sammy weren't in it.

He stroked his chin and pondered the thought. It could work. Jolt her so she spoke with her heart and not her head. Whether she was ready to admit it or not, she was meant for him. He, Jasmine and Sammy were meant to be a family. He felt it in the very core of his being.

He tried to focus and pray, but he was too jittery, unable to sit still. He laid Sammy in the middle of his king-size waterbed, placing pillows on either side of him to keep him from rolling off.

"Sleep well, son," he whispered, kissing Sammy's forehead. "Daddy's home."

He paced the halls for another hour, trying out one scheme in his head and replacing it with the next. By the time the clock struck five, he had a mental waste-paper basket full of shredded ideas.

Glancing at the clock, he felt his shoulders tighten. Jasmine would be expecting him to return Sammy any time now. Well, she'd just have to wait. The boy was sleeping, and Christopher wasn't about to wake him up. He'd wait until the boy woke on his own.

Or at least that was the excuse he gave mentally. Deep down, he was glad he'd be a few minutes late. Maybe missing Sammy would give her time to think. Think about what life without him and the baby would be like. Maybe she'd meet him at the door with open arms and welcome him into her heart and home. And maybe his tennis shoes would sprout wings and fly.

She'd no doubt think he'd up and run off with the kid. His jaw tensed. He'd actually considered it. For at least a millisecond. How could he not, with the possibility of being torn from his son forever lingering on the horizon?

But he wasn't a fool. Running away would be the absolute worst thing he could do. Jasmine already didn't trust him because of the last time he'd left Westcliffe. And the fact that then, as it would be if he left now, there had not been a single moment where his soul didn't long for Westcliffe and to return to Jasmine's side, wouldn't hold much weight with her.

If he ran, it would be with the thought of eventually reconciling with Jasmine. But if he ran, reconciliation could never happen. So he had to find another way.

There *was* another way. It came to him clearly and quietly, a way to startle Jasmine into searching her heart for the truth. She'd mentioned it herself the first night he was back.

It was difficult to consider the option, but what other

choice did he have? He had to do something to shock her. And this was going to make Jasmine fighting mad.

"Where is he?" Jasmine demanded for the tenth time in as many minutes. She peered through the front window shade, watching the parking lot below for lights or movement.

Marcus was stretched out on Gram's sofa, snoring quietly. Gram was sitting in a rocking chair, sipping at a cup of hot tea.

"You're sure you knew what you were doing when you let him take Sammy?" Gram asked, her voice scratchy. She often coughed at night.

"Of course I knew what I was doing!" she snapped, then grimaced. "Or at least I thought I did. What's taking him so long? Do you suppose they got in an accident?"

"He's probably just enjoying time with his son, Jasmine," Gram said gently. "It's their first time alone with each other. Don't rush them. Besides, you should be enjoying this time off baby duty. It's going to be nice to have another parent around."

"He sure swung you over to his side in a hurry," she commented acerbically.

"I wasn't aware there were sides," Gram snapped back, every bit as brittle.

Jasmine sighed. Even she had to admit the sides were getting a little gray around the edges.

"Why don't you grab a cup of tea and sit down? We haven't had a good chat in ages."

Jasmine did as she said, feeling more relaxed just holding her steaming cup of tea.

"That Marcus fellow is certainly nice," Gram said in a transparent attempt to change the subject.

"Yes. He's a good friend. It was really great of him to agree to help me out at the clinic. I hope you don't mind his crashing here overnight until he can find a place to live."

"I'm always open to entertaining strangers," Gram agreed quickly. "You never know when you're going to offer your hospitality to an angel."

Jasmine laughed. "Marcus is a real sweetheart, but he's hardly an angel. He'd be the first one to tell you that. But I'll concede he's prayed me out of more than one pinch. His faith in God is strong."

"Is that the only reason you invited him?"

Jasmine stiffened. "If you mean do I have feelings for Marcus, no. At least, not in that way. We are dear friends, and that's all we will ever be. He knows how I feel about—" She wasn't about to finish *that* loaded statement.

"Christopher," Gram concluded for her.

She winced, folding her hands in her lap to keep them from shaking. Gram would notice her anxiety in a moment if she wasn't careful to hide it from her.

"But that wasn't what I was asking. It appears to me you might use Marcus to hide behind so you don't have to deal with said *problem*."

Jasmine didn't fail to notice how Gram avoided speaking Christopher's name a second time. "I'd never do that to Marcus!"

"Maybe not intentionally, honey, but it would be easy to do without even meaning to."

"I don't think so."

"Think about it. You and Marcus are close. It would

be easy to give Christopher the opinion you were more than friends, without ever letting on to Marcus what you were doing."

"What are you getting at, Gram? Are you trying to plot me a way to get rid of Christopher for good?"

"No, of course not. I'm just trying to point out what might happen. You're bound to get hurt. You could lose Christopher *and* Marcus."

"I don't *have* Christopher," she denied, her mind freezing on the first part of Gram's statement.

Gram cocked a silver eyebrow. "No? I've got news for you, sweetheart. That man loves you within an inch of his life."

"I don't see what difference that makes." Gram of all people knew how impossible the situation was.

"It's your call, Jasmine. I just want you to remember the Lord's admonition to forgive. Christopher has done a lot of bad things. But he's back now, and it looks to me like he's trying to atone for his sins."

"I don't know what that means to me."

"Give yourself time. God will help you work it out."

She had God to help her work it out. That was a comfort, anyway. She'd been praying and reading the Scriptures every day since she'd made a commitment to walk in His steps. He'd been opening her heart to considering new paths.

It was part of the reason her feelings about Christopher were so contrary. And another of the many reasons she could not even consider marrying Christopher at this point.

"I've been feeling restless lately," she admitted quietly.

Gram nodded.

"I always thought the only thing I wanted in the world was to become a doctor and move back to Westcliffe. I wanted to be a country doctor, taking care of the people I've known all their lives. I wanted to bring all my high school friends' babies into the world. I've never even considered any other path. But lately…"

"You've discovered there's more to life than just your career."

"Yes, for starters. I'm sure you remember how much a newborn baby changes your world. I view everything as a mother now, not just a woman. Family means more to me than I expected."

"Enough to give up your career?"

"No. I don't think I could ever give up being a doctor, at least in some capacity."

"Dr. Mom," Gram teased.

"I don't think that's quite enough," she said, laughing. Tears followed close behind the laughter, for no reason she could fathom. "I'm a small-town girl who is strongly tied to her roots. I love the Wet Mountain Valley, the beautiful mountain range. History runs through the town like Main Street itself. Two years ago, I was pining for home, thinking that once I was back I would never want to leave Westcliffe again."

"Come here, love," Gram whispered, opening her arms.

Feeling like a young, frightened girl again, Jasmine knelt before her grandmother and laid her head against the old woman's breast. She closed her eyes, inhaling the powdery scent that was distinctly Gram, and losing herself in the gentle caress of Gram's hand on her hair.

"I think God's calling me somewhere else," she admitted, reaching for a tissue.

"Any place in particular?"

She wiped her tears away, her mind wandering to the missionary information packets she'd been studying in every bit of her spare time. "I think I'm going to take Sammy and go to Ecuador."

She expected Gram to be surprised, but she just nodded like a sage old owl.

"Why do I get the feeling you already knew this?"

"I didn't know where. I just knew. Why Ecuador? Are you going down as a doctor?"

"There's a hospital in Quito. And I already know Spanish. I learned it in college and used it a lot in Denver at the hospital."

"I'm glad you're seeking God again, Jasmine."

She smiled through her tears. "Me, too. But I'm scared to death to be stepping out in faith."

"He's ahead of you, on the left and right of you, and behind you as well. He's your fortress, and a twenty-four-hour-a-day watch guard. Rest in Him."

"I will, Gram." She blew out a breath. "Whew. It sure is nice to have that off my chest. I do worry about you being here all alone."

"I'm not alone. God is here. And I have lots of friends in this town. I was born here, you know."

And I'll die here. The words were left unsaid, but hovered in the air anyway, putting a damper on Jasmine's rising mood. She made a mental note to explain Gram's situation to Marcus when she talked to him, so he would look in on her regularly.

That is, when she had that big, long, unavoidable heart-to-heart talk with Marcus. The mere thought of it made her stomach cramp. What would he say when he learned she was prepping him to replace her rather than just help her out?

Her thoughts were interrupted by the doorbell. She jumped to her feet and lit to the door like someone had set her tail on fire. Behind her, she was aware that Gram had stopped rocking, and that Marcus was wearily rousing himself on the couch.

No one said a word, but she knew they'd all thought the same thing. Deep down under layers of reassurance was the lingering doubt that Christopher might have been planning to steal Sammy away all along, and she had conveniently handed the baby right into his hands.

"Christopher," she announced loudly as she swung open the door, her hands shaking with relief. Her heart wanted to burst with happiness when she saw him and the baby, but instead, she scowled. "You're late."

"Sorry, Mom," he replied, tipping his hat back and giving her that toe-curling grin of his. Her heart was hopeless to resist his physical presence, but her mind was pressing for answers.

"This is where you come into the house, remove Sammy from his seat and give me a really good excuse why you thought it was okay to worry me half to death."

"I had you worried?"

"A figure of speech, I assure you."

Gram burst into laughter, but when they both turned to her, she was looking away out the window and humming softly to herself.

"The little nipper was sleeping," he offered, unbuckling the straps on the baby carrier and lifting Sammy out of the seat. He kissed the baby's cheek and handed him to Jasmine.

Her heart immediately settled now that Sammy was back in her arms. He was a perfect fit. His sweet, baby scent was pleasant to her nose, and his happy squeal music to her ears. She really was becoming a mother.

She didn't feel quite whole without him any more. And maybe just a little of it had to do with Christopher being here with her as well.

"Were you giving your daddy a hard time?" she asked Sammy, who bounced and kicked in her arms.

"Da!" he said, then, pleased with himself, said it again. "Da!"

Christopher whooped in delight. "Did you hear that? My baby boy just called me Dad!" He thrust his chest out like a rooster and strutted around the room. "How 'bout that? Sammy's first word is *Daddy*."

He couldn't have been grinning any wider, Jasmine thought, somehow irritated, feeling as if she'd been betrayed. Of course the baby didn't know what he was saying, and she'd be hearing *Mommy, Mommy* soon enough. Still...

He pulled his hat off his head and rolled the brim in his fists. "Will you walk me out to the porch?" He glanced covertly at Gram and Marcus.

She stared at him wide-eyed for a moment, then nodded slowly. "As long as you promise this won't be a repeat of this afternoon. I can't handle that yet."

"Oh, it's definitely not a repeat of this afternoon," he muttered under his breath.

"In that case, let me give Sammy to Gram and I'll be right there."

He nodded and planted his hat on his head, sauntering out to the porch. He took deep breaths to try to slow his heartbeat. It was downright cold once the sun went down. He could see his own breath coming in white puffs of mist, and the breeze nipped the skin on his face despite his five o'clock shadow.

She appeared suddenly, and immediately wrapped her arms around herself against the cold. Christopher wished he'd thought to remind her to bring a coat out with her.

"I won't be long," he promised.

"Um, okay," she said, looking perplexed. Her bottom jaw was starting to shiver. She looked small, defenseless and entirely adorable.

He put his hands on her shoulders and rubbed down her arms to help restore the circulation. Then he lightly swept his fingers back up her shoulders and cupped her face in his hands. He brushed a light kiss on her forehead, her nose, her lips, her jaw.

Then he took a deep breath and plunged ahead. "I can't live without my son, Jazz," he began.

"I don't expect you to."

"But you won't marry me."

She stiffened in his embrace. "You promised you wouldn't ask me that. I can't think about it right now."

"I wasn't asking, just stating facts. I know you feel it's more than you can handle right now, but it really is the best thing for everyone concerned."

"I asked you not to talk about it anymore," she snapped, turning away and staring off toward the shadowy, jagged outline of the Sangres.

He moved up behind her, putting an arm around the front of her shoulders and drawing her firmly against his chest.

She stiffened in his arms, but didn't try to move away.

"Can you really not trust me?" he asked, his voice husky. "Isn't it enough that I've returned?"

"No. And no. You've given me no reason to trust you, and how am I supposed to know whether or not you are staying for good?"

He *wouldn't* be staying in Westcliffe for good. It was part of what held him up from returning for Jasmine and Sammy. But now wasn't the time.

"What if I told you leaving was something I had to do, that it wasn't meant to hurt anyone? And that the reasons are, at this point, beyond explanation?"

"In other words, you plain just don't want to tell me. You don't trust me, but you want me to trust you. To be your wife." She turned in his arms until they were face-to-face. She looked up at him, confusion rampant in her deep green eyes.

He wanted to forget his intentions and kiss Jasmine like he did in the old days, when they dated in high school.

But he was a man now, and the kiss he would give her would be a man's kiss. It was far too dangerous to risk. His self-control was thread thin as it was. And he had an agenda tonight.

Cupping her hips, he pushed her back a step. She stroked a hand down his face and sighed. "Don't you see, Christopher? I can't marry you with secrets between us. A husband and wife are one. They should share their lives in every way, and that includes trusting the other enough to tell the truth."

Her voice cracked and she stopped, nibbling on her full bottom lip as she considered what to say next. "If you believe I love you, then you've got to know that whatever dark things are in your past, I can hear them. I can forgive you. And I'll go on loving you."

It was incredibly tempting just to blurt out the truth and have it done with. He more than anyone was sick to death of keeping secrets. If it would be like Jasmine said, he'd willingly divulge the whole agonizing truth.

If she loved him and forgiveness was real, she'd understand why he'd kept silent, and would join in his silence to keep Jenny's memory untarnished and Sammy's reputation pure. There would be no more bitterness between them. They'd marry and raise a big family, with Sammy as their eldest son.

But it wouldn't happen that way. Anger would overwhelm the lesser sentiments, and then Jasmine wouldn't allow him to see Sammy at all. If he told the whole truth, she'd have ample authority for making it so Christopher never saw Sammy again.

And that, he could not risk. It wouldn't be right. He owed it to Sammy to keep the truth to himself. More important, he loved the boy.

"I can't tell you, Jazz. I'm sorry, but I can't."

"Then it appears this conversation is over. I'm freezing out here, anyway. Good night, Christopher." She ducked under his arm and started toward the door.

"Wait!" he called, reaching for her elbow to stop her. "If you won't accept my marriage proposal, what are we going to do about Sammy?"

"Sammy?" she asked, looking perplexed. "Oh, I see. You mean can you see him again?"

Christopher nodded.

"You've proven yourself, as far as I'm concerned. We'll make plans for you to see him on a regular basis. Every other weekend or something."

His jaw dropped, then he clamped it shut. He was good enough to see Sammy every other weekend? What was this, some kind of contest or something, and Sammy was the door prize?

"Why don't you go out and buy yourself some baby furniture? You can use my car seat stroller, but you'll need a crib, some baby blankets, diapers and a few toys."

She sounded so detached, too clinical. He yanked his hat off and slapped it angrily against his thigh. "I'm afraid every other weekend isn't good enough for me."

"What's that supposed to mean?" she snapped, sounding alarmed.

"It means if you won't marry me, I'm taking you to court for full custody of Sammy."

Chapter Twelve

The cabin was cold and empty when Christopher returned. He poked at the ashes inside the wood stove in the corner and got some kindling ignited, then slumped into his large easy chair and spent ten minutes staring blankly at the television and channel surfing with no real heart.

He was bluffing, and he was more afraid than he'd ever been in his life.

The whole thing was nothing but a ruse to catch Jasmine off guard. It had as much chance of failure as success—the act of a desperate man.

He looked around at the cabin and snorted in disgust. This place wasn't fit for anyone, much less a tiny baby. Besides, it wasn't his. He couldn't even imagine what the Walters would have to say about it if he brought a baby on their land.

He supposed he could look for something else, except he really wasn't looking for something more permanent. Because he wasn't going to be staying in Westcliffe.

Now, however, it looked as if he *would* be staying,

at least until he could prove to Jasmine his heart hadn't changed, that he wasn't the scoundrel of a man who walked out on her sister. He was still the man she had once loved and to whom she'd pledged herself.

He wasn't leaving without Jasmine. And if that meant another six months or another six years, then so be it. God's timing was better than his, he knew, but he was impatient.

He'd played his ace. Now all he could do was sit back and see if he won the hand. This was Dead Man's Draw, winner take all.

The irony of it was the secret he was carrying was the reason he *couldn't* take Jasmine to court for custody of Sammy. There, under oath, he would have to tell the world that he was not Sammy's father. And even if he lied, which he wouldn't do under oath, the paternity test they'd no doubt make him take would be just as revealing, probably more so.

And in Westcliffe, real news was scarce. They were sure to make the front page of the newspaper, maybe even as far as Pueblo. And Sammy would become a public entity.

He couldn't let that happen. He *wouldn't* let that happen. Bart Pembarton hadn't been man enough to own up to what he'd done, to do the right thing, marry Jenny and claim his son—not when Mommy and Daddy might object. And object they did, when Christopher confronted them with the facts after Bart's death. Bart's parents had warned Christopher not to let Sammy become a public entity. He sensed their threats were real. No matter what, Christopher had to protect Sammy.

Without realizing where his thoughts were heading, the night of Bart's death replayed in his mind, as clearly as if it had happened yesterday. It was a hot, damp night in Pueblo, and he'd been working on duty as part of his EMT training.

They'd been called to the scene of a fatal traffic accident. The wreckage was a once shiny BMW lodged between a light pole and a building, as if the driver had been attempting to drive on the sidewalk.

There were no drugs or alcohol involved, and the fatal accident remained shrouded in mystery. But the driver had been the man in Jenny's photo. Why had Bart crashed his car?

Christopher's stomach knotted. He'd made a decision to forgive the man for getting Jenny pregnant. It was a conscious struggle to make that decision truth. He still got angry just thinking about it. But forgiveness, he reminded himself, was an act of the will. His feelings would eventually fade, and God would help him through.

Responsibility definitely hadn't been Bart's middle name. Of course he hadn't wanted a child to slow down his jet-set lifestyle, especially with his parents holding the purse strings.

The Pembartons might have money, but money wasn't what a child needed most in life. Only he and Jasmine could give Sammy the home he deserved. He knew he couldn't do it alone. The picture wasn't complete until Jasmine was in it, binding their hearts together as one.

Which is why he'd taken so great a risk in announcing he was taking her to court. The last thing he wanted to do was hurt her, and he knew his words had hurt her.

But it couldn't be helped. He'd tried affection, now he hoped intimidation would work.

If it didn't, he was in a world of trouble. He clenched and unclenched his fists, wanting to punch something just because it was there.

He was a man of action, and he'd just relegated himself to sitting back and waiting for Jasmine to come to him. All he could do was pray she'd want to talk about a compromise, which would give him another chance to convince her marrying him was the best solution.

If only he didn't hate waiting so much.

"Oooh! That lousy, no-good, rotten—" Jasmine vented, stomping across the floor and back again. "If he thinks he can intimidate me, he has another think coming."

Marcus grinned up at her from the kitchen table, where he was eating a big bowl of oatmeal. "You were so quiet last night, I knew there was something wrong."

"I didn't want Gram to worry. But Marcus, what he did to me last night was like a slap in the face."

He chuckled, a low, deep sound from his chest. "You haven't exactly let the cat out of the bag yet, girl. What exactly did he do?"

"He said he's suing for full custody of Sammy."

"He wants *full* custody? He wants to take Sammy away from you?" he said quietly, in wonder. Then he took her firmly by the shoulders and reassured her with the strength of his gaze. "You've got rights, Jasmine. And friends who will fight tooth and nail to keep Sammy with you. Myself being first and foremost, of course."

"I know." She sighed wearily. It had been a long,

sleepless night, fighting emotions that ranged from passionate, self-righteous ire to fear and apprehension such as she'd seldom known before.

She'd spent at least an hour raging in her own fury before it occurred to her the best thing to do was to seek a Higher Authority in the matter.

She'd sought God on her knees, begging for His interference in her cause. She knew that God, more than anyone on this earth, understood what it meant to be separated from His Son.

She'd pondered through the middle of the night on the incredible mercy and love of a God who would give His own Son to die in her place. What sacrifice Jesus made for her, to come down from heaven and be made a Man. And His Father willed Him to go.

She knew she was not that strong. She couldn't give Sammy up, not even to Christopher, who she knew would love and care for the baby.

She prayed for peace, and she prayed for answers. But by morning she'd still not been able to come up with any long-term solutions to the problem, short of running away and changing her name as she'd seen ladies on television crime shows do.

Would she be a hunted woman? Would Christopher put the FBI on her case? Her mind had raced with the possibilities, and the questions answered themselves.

She couldn't force Sammy to live that way, living hand to mouth and always looking behind her for shadows. It wouldn't be fair to him. She had to find another way to fight Christopher and keep Sammy.

"Are you taking me to the clinic today?" Marcus asked, cutting off her thoughts.

"Actually, today would be perfect. I'll show you

around and get you settled. This afternoon I've really got to try to hook up with one of those charity organizations in Pueblo so they can come by Jenny's bungalow and pick up all her things."

Marcus nodded, but didn't comment.

"I hate to be leaving you on your own on your first day, but the county nurse will be there, and being such a small town, the receptionist is very knowledgeable."

"No problem. Relax."

"Of course, I'll be wearing my pager, and I always have my cell phone with me, if you have a problem."

He barreled out a deep, hearty laugh. "Will you *relax?* I've been alone in a clinic before. I think I can handle it. Besides, I'm getting kinda fond of this country living."

"You've only been here a day."

"Fondness grows quickly. I feel like I'm home here in Westcliffe, with its horses and hayfields. Funny for a man born and raised in the ghetto, I guess. But I can't help it. This place just feels right to me. Like I could put down roots here. It'd be a great place to raise children," he concluded, with a pointed look at Jasmine and a sly grin.

She was relieved to hear it, more than he could possibly know. That Marcus might want to stay on as the doctor for this town was looking like more and more of a possibility.

And if that happened, she'd have the freedom she desired to pursue the new dreams God had given her. If she could work things out with Christopher and Sammy. At the moment she was bound hand and foot.

She had three choices. She could run, but she'd already ruled that one out. She could go to court, but with Christopher's paternity proven, she had the sinking feeling he'd get Sammy in a heartbeat, no matter what she said on the witness stand.

The other option, and the one that galled her to the core of her being, was that she could go back to Christopher and beg. Beg for time with Sammy, even if it were just every other weekend, as she had suggested Christopher do.

For a moment, she found herself in his shoes, only able to see their son once every two weeks, and then for only a couple of days at a time. It was no wonder he'd said it wasn't good enough. If he felt even half the agony that she did at the thought, his heart was being ripped out of his chest in little pieces.

It startled her to have put herself so much in Christopher's position, and she immediately shut down her thoughts and emotions on the subject. Her only desire and responsibility was to see she kept Sammy, whatever the cost.

"You look like that famous thinker statue guy. The de-e-e-ep thinker," he said in an exaggerated tone. "Keep that up and you're going to make your headache worse."

"Are you ready to go down to the clinic?" she asked, her voice sounding annoyed despite her best efforts.

"Not thinking about Christopher won't make him go away," Marcus said gently. "Eventually you are going to have to face him again and try to work this out."

"That may be," she snapped, seething in frustration. "But I don't have to think about him, talk about him or most especially talk *to* him, today. I would appreciate it if you didn't bring his name up again."

"Hey, girl, whatever you say," he replied easily, ignoring her tone. "I think we ought to get to the clinic right away. Do you think I might be able to search out a place to live after work?"

"Well, sure. The clinic closes at three today."

"I'm looking to buy, Jasmine. I hope that doesn't alarm you."

"On the contrary, I'm very pleased."

He opened the front door and gestured her through. "After you, Dr. Enderlin." She'd been called a doctor since the beginning of her internship, but suddenly the title felt too tight, as if it were strangling her.

Funny how something she had worked so hard for and been so single-minded about could feel so awkward and uncomfortable to her now.

Well, no matter. She loved being a doctor. At least *that* hadn't changed. She'd just discovered there was a big, scary world out there and shades of gray all over the place.

"Jasmine? Are you coming?" Marcus asked in his soft, low voice.

Jasmine. At this point it was all she could do just to be Jasmine, never mind mother, doctor, friend. And now Christopher was asking her to be his wife. She wanted to scream in frustration.

That is, if he still wanted her as his wife. Taking her to court was a pretty drastic move in the opposite direction. But she wouldn't think about that now, she reminded herself again.

Today, she would just be Jasmine. Okay, and Dr. Enderlin, at least for the afternoon.

As it turned out, Jasmine wasn't able to contact a charity group in Pueblo as she'd planned. An avalanche at the nearby ski resort kept Marcus and her busy well into the night, tending to major wounds, X-raying broken appendages and arranging for helicopter flights and ambulances for those who needed to be hospitalized.

Days flew by as Jasmine made rounds, introducing Marcus and caring for the less serious injuries. It seemed to Jasmine that at least a third of the town had been skiing that day, though she was certain she was overestimating.

Her real surprise was in Marcus. She already knew he was a fine doctor with a heart for the people, but she was truly amazed at how well everyone had taken to him. She'd heard compliment after compliment from those healed by his medical expertise.

He was so patient with the children, kind to the elderly and straightforward when a patient needed to hear something about their recovery. More than once she'd just hovered in the background and watched him work his magic on others.

Marcus found a house, and because it was vacant, the closing went quickly. At the end of the first week, he'd moved into his new home.

By the end of the second week, Jasmine was physically and mentally exhausted. The only good thing was that she hadn't had time to think about Christopher. She checked on baby Sammy during her lunch hour and tried to spend time with him in the evening, but more often than not she fell asleep on the rocking chair with a wiggling, bouncing Sammy in her arms.

Marcus insisted that she take a week off. The clinic had slowed down to a dull roar, and she needed time to recuperate so she could be at her best for Sammy.

She didn't even argue, which was very unlike her. Instead, she went to bed and slept for two days, rising only to eat and care for Sammy. Gram assured her everything was under control and that Jasmine should rest before she became ill.

It wasn't until after her extended session of sleep that she felt ready to face the world again, and the first order of business was finding a charity to take care of Jenny's things. After arranging for one to come that afternoon, she put a sandwich together and took off for Jenny's bungalow.

As always, the smell was the first thing that caught her when she entered the house. Jenny's smell. She wondered why a house would have the owner's smell about it once the owner was gone. She didn't notice any smell in her own house. She wondered if others did, and if so, what kind of smell hers was.

Jenny's was light and breezy, just as Jasmine remembered her personality as being. But then she remembered the newspaper photograph.

The newspaper photograph! What had she done with it? Her hand flew instinctively to her left breast pocket, where she vaguely remembered placing it. But of course it wasn't there now, since she wasn't wearing the same clothes.

What *had* she been wearing? She strained to remember. She'd worn her grubbies that day, which meant...

The jeans with the holes in the knees. A black T-shirt. And...

Her red plaid flannel shirt. That was it. The photograph was in the pocket of her red plaid flannel shirt. Except, where *was* her flannel shirt?

She leaned against a wall and slid slowly to the floor, cupping her face in her hands. How could she have been so stupid as to lose the picture?

She was overreacting, she knew. It was just a lousy newspaper photograph, and not even one that showed Jenny in her best light. But for some reason, it was important to Jasmine, a part of Jenny that she wanted to keep.

Odd as it seemed, she felt it must have meant something special to her sister, being locked up in her nightstand as it was. She could just picture Jenny carefully unlocking the drawer and pulling out the picture, staring at it with the glassy-eyed look of someone in love, and then hugging it close to her heart with a sigh.

She threw her head back until it was touching the wall, and it was there that she spotted her red plaid flannel shirt. Jasmine broke into strained laughter. Here she was getting all stressed about a shirt that had been right in front of her nose all along. Now that she'd noticed it, she remembered getting warm—more by Christopher's gaze than the heat in the house—and shedding her flannel to work in her T-shirt.

The doorbell rang, and Jasmine jumped, putting a hand to her chest to still her racing heart. Why was it every time the doorbell rang in this place she jumped out of her skin? She'd be glad when this was over and she could sell the bungalow. The strain of Jenny's death was getting to her again.

She welcomed the charity people in, gesturing at the boxes to be taken. When one of the men picked up the apple box with her personal items in it, Jasmine reacted immediately.

"Wait," she exclaimed. "I'm sorry. That one's mine.

I apologize. I meant to get it out to my car before you gentlemen got here."

The trucker, a boy in his late teens, grinned and handed the box to her. "Sure thing, ma'am. No problem."

She took the box and turned away from him before she scowled. She hated when people called her *ma'am*. It made her feel like her grandmother. And this young man was no exception.

Where did that come from, she wondered as she packed the box in the back of her four-by-four. She shook her head. It wasn't as if she were an old maid or anything. Lots of people established themselves in their careers before they married and settled down, didn't they?

Besides, she'd already had two bona fide offers of marriage, right? Okay, so both were from Christopher. But still… She tipped her chin in the air and marched back into the house, determined not to let it bother her.

"This is yours, miss?" the other trucker, a middle-aged man with jocular features asked, waving her flannel shirt. *Miss.* Now that was *much* better. She smiled widely. "Oh yes, that's mine."

She heard the crumple of newspaper as she took the shirt. The men would be there for a while loading the truck, she decided, and it would be best to stay out of their way.

She found an out-of-the-way corner where she could watch them without fearing they would trip over her, and sat down cross-legged on the floor. Gingerly, she felt for the pocket and pulled the newspaper clipping from it.

It was crumpled. She laid it against her thigh and

smoothed out the wrinkles with the palm of her hand. The same proud man stared at her, and there was Jenny with her arms thrown around him and a silly grin lighting her face.

But there was love in her eyes as she looked at that man. Jasmine had no doubt of it now. Jenny had found true love, the way she had with Christopher.

Probably no one but a sister would notice. And it did make her wonder about Jenny's relationships before Christopher. The man in the picture obviously had money. It was odd that Jenny would settle for a penniless, small-town cowboy, even a guy as wonderful as Christopher.

Her skin tingled at the thought, and she shook her head. Back to the man in the picture. He was blond, buff, and, if the look on his face was anything to go on, conceited as all get-out.

She read the caption, searching for his name. "Barton Pembarton III," she read aloud, as snooty and regal as a butler announcing a guest.

She glanced back at the picture. "Barton Pembarton III enjoying a Valentine's Day cruise with his yacht *Celebration* on the Pueblo reservoir."

Of course, no mention of Jenny. She wasn't media material, even in a skimpy bathing suit. Jasmine wondered how Jenny had taken that slight, or if she'd even noticed. Perhaps she was used to playing second fiddle to the rich playboys she hung out with.

Jasmine, that's not fair! she chastised herself. She didn't know for a fact Jenny led that sort of lifestyle. She was the last one who should be judging another on circumstantial evidence, especially her sister.

She tucked her thoughts away with difficulty and

returned her attention to the truckers. The men were finished with the boxes and bid her farewell on their way out.

There was a strange mixture of sadness and relief swirling through her chest at finally putting an end to all that was Jenny. It was almost as if she were being forced to say goodbye once again. She clutched the newspaper clipping to her heart.

The house was so empty and barren, devoid of life. Even the boxes had given it some sense of humanity. But now there was nothing. Nothing except herself and the photograph she held in her hand.

Chapter Thirteen

Jasmine glanced at it one last time, intending to tuck it into her wallet when she was through. She stared at Jenny for a long time, then ran her fingers over the caption.

Suddenly she noticed the date in the upper right corner of the clipping. *It was dated last year!*

Last year. Last Valentine's Day. But how could that be? She was with Christopher by then, carrying his child. Jasmine was a doctor—the math involved in pregnancy came naturally to her.

Sammy was born in early October, and he was two weeks overdue. That put his conception somewhere square in the middle of January. Which meant what?

She stared at the newspaper clipping in disbelief. Had Jenny been two-timing Christopher with this Barton What's-his-name? Christopher appeared to stiffen a little when he'd seen the photograph, but not nearly enough for her to believe he'd just discovered he'd been cuckolded.

He was a proud man. Whatever else he would do, he wouldn't accept his future wife out *playing* with another man. Besides, why would any woman want to cheat on Christopher? He was the most gallant, loving man a woman could want.

She swallowed hard, trying not to think of Jenny in Christopher's arms. She'd conquered her anger, but the stab of pain that accompanied any thought of those two together would never go away. Some wounds even time couldn't heal.

Jasmine turned her mind back to the puzzle at hand. Okay, so Jenny was pregnant with Christopher's baby and was hanging around with Bart. Where was Christopher?

She struggled to recall exactly when she'd learned about Christopher and Jenny's impending nuptials. She closed her eyes, trying to remember what she'd been doing when she heard the news.

Maternity. She'd been serving on the ward, learning firsthand how to bring new life into the world. And dreaming every time the miracle of birth happened of her own children, the ones she would have with Christopher.

Okay, technically, they weren't speaking to one another. And she was dating Richard, a radiology intern. But deep in her soul, there was only Christopher, and she knew she was kidding herself to believe otherwise. Richard was a nice, sweet guy, and that was it. It was only pique and pride that kept her from apologizing to Christopher and making things right.

She'd just finished a twelve-hour shift and was getting ready to drop into bed when her phone rang. Groggily, she answered, only to find Mrs. Rulitter jabbering something about Christopher getting married and was

Jasmine going to be able to make it back to town for the wedding day, short notice as it was, and all?

A dazed Jasmine had pulled the handset away from her ear and stared at it, bemused. Of course Christopher was getting married. To her. But it wouldn't be until after she was finished with her internship here in Denver. And anyway, it was highly unlikely she'd miss her own wedding.

Mrs. Rulitter was spouting nonsense. She was on the verge of telling the meddlesome gossip so when she heard something else on the line. The constant chatter hadn't ceased. Apparently Mrs. Rulitter wasn't even aware she didn't have an audience.

Somewhere in the prattle, she'd heard her sister's name. Jasmine pulled the phone back to her ear and cleared her throat loudly. When Mrs. Rulitter didn't take the hint, she resorted to rudeness.

"I don't mean to interrupt you, Mrs. R., but I'm afraid I missed what you said about Jenny. Is she in some kind of trouble?"

She couldn't imagine what her sweet sister could have done to have become the object of town gossip. Whatever it was, though, it was good and juicy enough to warrant Mrs. Rulitter's long-distance call.

"Has she asked you to be her maid of honor?" Mrs. Rulitter answered a question with a question.

"Maid of honor!" she exclaimed. "Jenny is getting married?"

"Of course. That's what I've been telling you. Jenny and Christopher are going to tie the knot in a month's time. Shotgun wedding, if the gossip—er, news—I've gotten has the least inkling of truth. Can't say I blame

the girl. It's tough when you've got a good-looking cowboy like Christopher."

Jasmine's head was spinning, and she sat down hard on the bed.

"Shotgun wedding," Jasmine repeated dully, her extremities going numb. Now she was not so much afraid of passing out as simply turning into sludge and melting into the sheets.

That meant a baby. Jenny was having a baby?

Christopher's *baby*.

She tried to breathe, but couldn't. "Are you sure about this?" she squeaked through a dry throat when she could speak again.

"Sure as shootin'," Mrs. Rulitter promptly replied. "Jenny probably hasn't asked you to be maid of honor yet because of—well, you know, your past with Christopher. Bless me, I thought you and he were gonna tie the knot. You sure were little lovers in high school. Oh well, I'm sure you both grew up and grew out of each other. Happens all the time."

Grow away from Christopher? Her every thought, at least in her free time and often at work, was about Christopher. But of course, that was how it must look to an outsider.

It was almost laughable, if her stomach didn't hurt so much. Jenny was bubbly and flighty. She'd drive calm, cool Christopher mad in a day. And as far as Jenny was concerned, surely she considered Christopher as more of an older brother than a love interest.

Lines were crossed somewhere. That was all there was to it. She'd make a simple phone call to Gram's apartment, and it would all be straightened out in a heartbeat.

Or else she'd pinch herself and wake up. This was more like a nightmare than reality. Christopher and Jenny. What a laugh!

Or was it? Her mind flashed back to the night before. She'd just come in from a date with Richard when the phone rang. A glance at the call display screen on her telephone warned her the call was from Christopher.

Annoyed, she'd handed the phone to Richard and requested he answer, knowing that would bother Christopher more than any futile argument. Looking back, she recognized how juvenile it was, and felt a moment of regret.

It appeared his call had been much more serious than she could have imagined. Had he called her to tell her he was getting married?

With shaky fingers, she punched the numbers on the keypad. She hoped Gram would answer. At least she would be straightforward. Gram always told the truth, no matter if it hurt.

The phone rang, then rang again. Finally, a light, tenor voice answered on the other end of the line. She might have thought she had the wrong number, but she recognized that voice instantly, and intimately.

Christopher.

She cleared her throat, suddenly flustered. Why was Christopher at Gram's house? Talking to him was even worse than trying to sort it out with Jenny.

She blew out a breath, hoping he couldn't hear how shaky it sounded. "Hi, Christopher. It's me."

"Jasmine!"

Under usual circumstances, she would have thought

he was excited to hear from her. But what she heard in his voice was shock and alarm.

So it was true. Suddenly Jasmine knew, without his having to say the words. Their souls had been connected for so long she could even tell long distance what he was feeling.

"I understand I'm to wish you happiness," she said, trying but not succeeding in masking the bitterness lacing her tone.

She heard his deep intake of breath. "Jazz, I—"

She cut him off. "Save your breath, pal. Let me talk to Jenny."

"I tried to call you. I was going to drive up but—"

"Frankly, I don't really want to hear. Will you get Jenny for me, please?" she asked, annoyed that she couldn't keep her voice from shaking.

She'd heard Christopher curse as he put the phone down. He never cursed, and Jasmine felt a perverse pleasure in driving him to it. It was the least he deserved.

Jenny picked up the receiver, exuberant. "Oh, Jasmine, I'm going to have a baby!"

Nothing about Christopher, only the baby.

"So I heard," she said dryly. "When?"

"Well, Chris just took me to the doctor in Pueblo this morning. He says the baby is doing great, and I should expect her in early October. They did an ultrasound, and I got to see her little heart beating."

Jasmine had cringed at the use of Christopher's name. In elementary school, he'd given anyone who called him Chris a black eye. She'd always thought of him as her Christopher. But Jenny had broken all the rules.

"You know it's a girl already?"

"Well, no. Not really. I'm only ten weeks along. The ultrasound technician said she wouldn't be able to tell me the sex of the baby for sure until she was much bigger. And if it is a girl, they might not be able to tell me at all. Little boys are easier to spot," she concluded, giggling.

After that came the quick calculation. How long had they been seeing each other behind her back? It was Saint Patrick's Day, so Jenny had been seeing him for at least two months, probably much longer, since they were intimate.

Christopher simply wouldn't pressure a woman on the first date. He'd never pressured her at all. Maybe Jenny had pressured him. But in any case, they'd been seeing each other awhile.

Yet he'd been with her, Jasmine, during the Christmas holiday, which meant he'd been lying to her. The time they'd spent together was a hoax. He'd probably been with Jenny all along, right behind her back.

She'd felt as if gravity had tripled, pulling her whole body down into the earth.

Jenny had filled the silence with her babbling. "Can't you just see Chris bouncing all those curls and pearls on his knee? Or teaching his little girl to dance? He's going to be the greatest daddy in the world."

She'd paused and waited for Jasmine to answer her questions. As if Jasmine hadn't pictured Christopher as a father a million times.

"This is okay with you, isn't it? I mean about Chris and me?"

Jasmine gasped for air, but her throat was closed.

"He said it would be. That you'd understand. I re-

ally hope you'll wish me happiness, Jasmine. It means
a lot to me. And of course I want you to be my maid of
honor at the wedding."

A maid of honor. When she should have been the
bride! she felt her head spin, and nausea was coming
in waves. "Yes, of course. Congratulations. Unfortu-
nately, I'm calling long distance, so I won't be able to
stay on the line. And I have a class in just a few min-
utes, anyway. Goodbye, Jenny."

Jasmine had clanked down the phone in the re-
ceiver, grimacing at her lie. She had no class to go
to. She was done for the day. She just couldn't stand
to listen to the sound of Jenny's happy voice while she
was in such agony. She lifted a prayer to God, asking
Him to forgive her. She hadn't known what else to say.

She sank down beside the bed, seeking heavenly
comfort. Only God could help her now. She'd been so
exhausted when she first came into her room, but now
she wasn't sure she'd ever sleep again.

After what had seemed like hours of praying and
crying out to God, she'd dozed off, still on her knees.

Jasmine awoke with a start. The little bungalow was
shrouded in darkness. Feeling displaced, she wrapped
her arms around herself and took deep breaths.

She rolled to her knees, exclaiming as the cramped
muscles in her neck, arms and thighs made themselves
known in spiked bursts of pain.

Her voice echoed in the small room, making her
feel even more alone. Something crunched under her
left knee. Her newspaper clipping! She carefully set
the clipping aside, then continued her slow, laborious
crawl to the other side of the room. She reached the

door and barely missed smacking her head against the solid oak before she reached the light panel. She flicked the switch, flooding the room with bright, cheery light.

Jasmine breathed a sigh of relief. She wasn't afraid of the dark, or of being alone, but the light was certainly welcoming to frighten away her dark thoughts. The day her own dreams died. A day she'd never forget.

March 17! Of course. That's what she'd been trying to remember. She dashed back across the room and snatched up the newspaper clipping.

She pieced it together in her mind, bit by bit, trying to create a timeline that made sense.

Sometime in early January, Jenny gets pregnant.

February 14, Jenny is seen on Barton the Snob's boat. At least he looked like a snob. She's clearly in love with him, or at least is making cow eyes at him.

March 17, she's engaged to Christopher.

She hadn't learned about the engagement all that long after it happened. Jenny had assured her they'd only made the decision to marry the night before. She went over the facts again. There was something she was missing. Jenny had cancer. Did she know of her illness at that point? Was she trying to live it up as much as possible before her death, even if she made Christopher suffer?

And Christopher—did he know about Jenny's illness? Is that why he allowed her to play around with another man? He wasn't the type of man to sit around blindly ignoring the obvious while he was being cuckolded.

Or…

Jasmine's thought was so astounding she felt as if

her entire body had been pricked with thousands of pins and needles. Her blood pressure skyrocketed.

Or Sammy was not Christopher's son at all.

It made sense. Jenny and Bart. The thought was enough to make her cringe. Could Sammy's biological father be Barton Pembarton III?

She cringed, and her stomach swirled. That possibility was far worse than Christopher sleeping with Jenny, though that, too, must have been, or else why would he have married her?

The questions collided in her head like bumper cars. None of it made any sense, and yet it did. Too much so. And if Bart *was* Sammy's biological father, that created the possibility, however slight, of *his* claiming the boy, a thought that chilled Jasmine right to the core.

She shook her head, astonished. Things weren't anything like they appeared, and for every answer she concocted there arose five or six new questions. Like why wasn't Bart in the picture now, if Sammy was his son?

Bart's son. That meant Christopher *couldn't* pursue custody of Sammy in court. He had no right if he couldn't prove his paternity. That he was married to Jenny would mean nothing, especially in light of his past behavior in running out on his wife and unborn baby. They'd surely ask him for a cheek swab to check his DNA. And if the court didn't order it, she would, knowing what she now knew.

And if she could disprove Christopher, she would be free and clear to claim Sammy as her own. She'd work off the assumption that Bart didn't want anything to do with his son, or that he didn't know about him in the first place. She wasn't sure what was ethical in this situation, but she'd work that out later.

For now, she needed to find out the truth. And the one person who could tell her what really happened was Christopher. It was time to pay the man a visit and lay it all on the line.

The more she thought about it, the more she believed she was right, despite the nagging doubt that Christopher wouldn't take her to court in a custody battle if he wasn't absolutely certain he was the father of the child.

Well, there was only one way to find out. Confronting him would only save her the time and effort of having to go to court to make Sammy her son, if her hunch was correct. Sammy's adoption could proceed as scheduled, and her life could go on as well.

She refused to consider that life wouldn't truly go on without Christopher. She loved him, and she always would. It was more than likely she'd never marry. How could she, with Christopher always on her mind?

But she didn't have to be married to have a full life, did she? She had Sammy, and she had an exciting missionary vision she believed God had placed in her heart. Surely she could be happy with that. The question was, what to do now? She had to take *some* kind of action.

There was no way Christopher would continue this mad ploy to take her to court for custody if he discovered she knew the truth about him. About Sammy. No wonder he was so closemouthed about the whole thing.

She wondered again why he would take her to court when he wasn't the biological father. He had to know they'd demand a paternity test, and he'd be disproved in front of everyone.

Which meant, if everything she suspected was true,

all his huffing and puffing about taking her to court was nothing more than a worthless threat.

The realization hit her like a bullet in the chest. Why that foul, no-good beast of a man! He wasn't really trying to take her to court to take Sammy away from her. That had *never* been his intention. He was bullying her into accepting his marriage proposal! It made perfect sense and explained nearly all his actions over the past month, save why he left Jenny after marrying her. *That* he still needed to explain.

And if he thought his little ploy to get her to tie the knot was going to work, he had another think coming. He was probably sitting around right this minute waiting for her to come begging for mercy.

Oh, she'd fulfill his wishes all right. She wasn't even going to wait until morning to pay that man a visit. But boy would he be surprised when she showed up at his door and cut the line to his threat like a snip with a pair of scissors.

She was out the door, her car key in her hand, when a thought occurred to her, one that put the brakes on her anger and sent her head spinning again.

If Christopher wasn't Sammy's father, why did he call him his son? And why did he want the baby boy as his own?

Chapter Fourteen

Christopher was tired of waiting.

He clamped his freshly shaved jaw closed as he pulled his left boot on, then his right. It was time for action. He'd considered and discarded a number of scenarios before settling on one. The right one. And the toughest.

He was going to tell Jasmine the truth. He stared at himself in the mirror, scowling at the man he'd become. A man of secrets. And what were secrets but lies left unspoken?

He should have told her the truth in its entirety the moment he'd crossed the town line into Westcliffe. No, that wasn't right. He should have driven up to Denver the second he and Jenny made their plans.

He *should* have talked to Jasmine before he made any plans at all.

He swiped a hand down his face and turned away from the mirror. A million *should-haves* wouldn't mend his broken world. He had to deal with the way things were now. And right now he had an irate, stubborn, wonderful woman on his hands that he couldn't decide whether to shake silly for being so headstrong or kiss thoroughly just for being herself.

He hoped for the opportunity to kiss her again. Over and over for the rest of their lives. But come what may, he couldn't keep up this ridiculous ruse and sit around waiting for her to come meekly and mildly offering to compromise.

He knew it wasn't Jasmine's style. He should have known it wasn't *his*. He'd spent the better part of the afternoon praying, asking forgiveness for his deception and for strength to reveal the truth to Jasmine when the time came.

He stuffed his cowboy hat on his head by the crown and adjusted the brim with his fingers. Now was that time. And it wasn't getting any easier by putting it off.

His mouth set in a grim, determined line, he opened his front door, then stepped back with a muffled exclamation of surprise.

"Jasmine!"

"Christopher." She was dressed in black jeans and a fringed western shirt. A small gold cross, set with a tiny diamond in the center, was the only jewelry she wore. Her long, shiny black hair was pulled back from her face with a clip, exposing her firm jaw and determined eyes.

If he didn't know better, he'd think he was looking at his reflection in a mirror. Jaw set, eyes sparking with stubborn pride and resolve, shoulders squared with purpose.

"Going somewhere?" she asked, gesturing to his hat.

"Er, yes. I mean, no. Actually, I was going to see you."

"You were?"

She looked every bit as flustered as he felt.

"Would you like to come in? The place isn't much to look at, but it's a roof over my head and walls to keep out the cold," he rambled, suddenly overaware of his humble surroundings.

"Not a problem," she said, shedding her coat and draping it across his armchair. She seated herself on the floor near the woodstove.

"Okay," he said, recovering slowly. He shut the door and tipped his hat off his head, returning it to the rack behind the door where he usually hung it.

He wondered where he should sit. If he sat in his armchair, he'd be sitting above her. Same with his desk chair. It might give him a slight mental advantage, but he wasn't sure that kind of advantage was what he wanted tonight. Then again, he was a gawky jumble of long arms and legs sitting on the floor.

But at least then he'd be face-to-face with Jasmine. He sat on the floor.

Actually, he stretched out right in front of her and propped his head on his hand, like he would have in the old days. With only a single lamp for lighting, it was dark, comfortable. Intimate.

"So…" Jasmine began, then stopped.

"So…" he repeated, feeling suddenly nervous.

"Did you want to go first?"

He swallowed hard. Did he? He probably should. She might have come to ask for compromise, which would be unnecessary once he'd spoken. But how did a man start such a conversation?

It was going to be a long night. Maybe he should offer her some coffee or something.

He took a deep breath and opened his mouth to

do just that when she jumped in and beat him to the punch line.

"I could use some coffee." She gestured to a worn aluminum coffee percolator sitting cockeyed on the woodstove. "Is this the pot you use for coffee? You don't happen to have a microwave, do you? I don't much have experience with cooking on a woodstove. I'm a modern woman, if you know what I mean."

She was babbling, a sure sign that she was nervous. Christopher grinned inwardly and reached for the pot. "Now, don't you go fussin' over this here coffee," he said in his best imitation of John Wayne. "Why, this is the way the old cowboys used to make it. Threw the grounds right in to brew, they did."

She made a face, indicating she didn't believe him for one moment. She still knew him that well, at least.

"It'll put hair on your chest," he drawled, laughing when her mouth dropped open.

"Oh. Now *there's* something I need," she said, laughing. "A furry chest."

Christopher felt himself blush to the roots of his chest hair. He coughed and made a beeline for the door, unable even to come up with another line of conversation that would put the old one to rest.

Excusing himself, Christopher stepped outside to the pump and filled the pot with fresh spring water, then filled the aluminum cup with coffee from the barrel on the porch. Settling the lid on top, he took a deep breath.

Thankfully, she didn't follow him out, and he had a few moments to collect his thoughts and clear his head. He was going to be the first to reveal what was in his heart. It was imperative he be thinking about what to

say, but Jasmine's presence made it excessively difficult for him to think of anything besides how much he
loved her, how he wanted to take her into his arms and
never let her go again.

It had startled him immensely when she'd shown up
at his door at the very moment he was leaving to see
her. But he had to admit in some ways it made what he
had to do easier, in the privacy of his little cabin where
they wouldn't be disturbed.

And she couldn't kick him out if she got mad at
him, he thought dryly. He chuckled, creating a puff of
mist in the night air.

When he could stall no longer, he picked up the pot
and returned to the cabin. She was seated where he'd
left her, her arms wrapped around her knees as she
stared vacantly at the warm glow of the woodstove.

Seeing her there, her gorgeous black hair gleaming
like silk in the dim light, he once again wondered how
things could have gotten so far out of control.

He loved this woman with every beat of his heart.
And he sensed that her feelings for him hadn't died, no
matter how well she attempted to mask them with other
emotions. He'd always been able to read her gaze, and
he'd caught glimmers of what used to be in her eyes,
especially recently.

But her eyes were shaded as they turned to look at
him. Shaded, and angry. He wondered how her mood
could have switched in the time he'd been outside, but
he was afraid to ask.

Instead, he put the coffeepot to boil on the stove
and seated himself on his desk chair. "Are you sure
you wouldn't be more comfortable sitting on the armchair?" he inquired gently.

"No, thank you."

They sounded like strangers. It was enough to make Christopher want to pound something, but instead he leaned forward with his elbows braced on his knees, clenching his fists behind his forearms so Jasmine couldn't see.

She wanted him to go first, and go first he would. "I needed to see you today, Jasmine, because—"

"Wait!" She stood abruptly and began to pace the small room. "I don't want to hear it. All you've ever told me about what happened between you and Jenny are lies."

He shook his head in vehement denial, but she held up her hands in protest when he tried to speak.

"Half-truths then. You're hiding something, Christopher Jordan, and I've come here tonight to find out what."

"Jasmine, if you'd let me explain," he interrupted, biting off his frustration before he lost his temper. What was with her tonight, anyway? She wanted answers to her questions, answers he was finally ready to give, but she wouldn't let him get a word in edgewise.

It was almost as if she were subconsciously trying to avoid hearing what he had to say.

"Are you going to tell me the truth, or aren't you?" she demanded, looking down at him with her arms braced on her hips.

"I'm *trying* to tell you," he snapped back, standing to tower over her. "*If* you'd let me speak."

Her sparking green eyes widened slightly, then narrowed upon him. She was not the least bit intimidated by his greater height.

"Good," she said firmly, reaching up and caressing his jaw with the palm of her hand, gently bringing his head down until his face was mere inches from hers. He closed his eyes, savoring the feel of her gentle fingers.

"Since you're in the mood to talk," she whispered, still stroking the line of his jaw, "Why don't you start with the fact that you're not Sammy's biological father."

Jasmine wouldn't have gotten such a strong reaction if she'd slapped him hard in the face. And in that moment, she knew that her theory was, indeed, fact. Christopher *wasn't* Sammy's biological father.

She'd come here with the intention of confronting him and being done with it. But she certainly hadn't meant for things to happen as they did. He'd stepped out to get water for the coffee, and she'd sat inside and stewed. It was a nervous reaction to coming face-to-face with him when he'd returned. He was standing over her, near enough to touch, his broad shoulders like a shelter. It had taken all her strength not to step into the haven of his arms. As it was, she couldn't help herself from touching his face, running her fingers across his clean-shaven jaw.

His cologne, a western scent, was strong, wreaking havoc on her senses. She'd almost succumbed to the love she still felt beating strong in her heart.

And then she remembered the impassable wall between them, the wall created by Jenny. And Sammy.

She'd just blurted out what she knew with no warning, no warming up to the subject.

Christopher had exhaled as if someone had sucker punched him and whirled away from her, raking his hands through the tips of his short brown hair. He stood facing away from her, and she could see his hands trembling.

"I see you're not denying that you really aren't Sammy's biological father."

"How long have you known?" he asked, his strained voice a good octave lower than his usual smooth tenor.

"I only began suspecting it this afternoon. I didn't know for sure until this moment." In an instinctive move borne of love, she stepped forward and reached out for him, stopping just short of touching him.

"I guess you're really laughing now, aren't you? I played my trump card and lost everything."

He sounded so genuinely miserable that Jasmine flinched. What he said was true, but she knew she had put some of that agony in his voice. Oh, *why* hadn't she gone home and spent the night praying before blustering up here like a misguided whirlwind?

She muttered a quiet prayer for God's help to untangle the entire mess once and for all. Then she reached up and gently placed her hands on his shoulders. "I'm sorry, Christopher," she whispered, her voice cracking. "I shouldn't have blurted it out that way. I've hurt you."

He stepped away from her touch and turned to face her. Instead of the tortured expression she expected to see on his face, she found him scowling so darkly she took an instinctive step backward.

"Don't apologize, Jazz. I've had it coming for a long time. I'm not surprised that you loathe me."

"I don't—" she began, but he cut her off.

"It's time for you to hear the whole story. It isn't pretty. But it's time you knew the truth."

Jasmine sighed. "Well, at least we agree on one thing."

He led her to the easy chair and bade her sit. Reluctantly, she did, and he knelt before her. It felt too much like a knight paying homage to his queen for Jasmine's tastes. She would have preferred to be on an equal level. She tried to move onto the floor, but he wouldn't let her.

He took her hand and turned it over, palm up, staring at it so fiercely it was almost as if he were trying to find the answer to their dilemma in the lines of her palm.

"I'm asking for forgiveness, Jasmine, though I don't expect you'll be able to give it right away. I want you to—" his voice cracked and he paused, swallowing hard "—to be able to put this episode behind you. To go on with your life and…find happiness."

This sounded like a eulogy. Jasmine's heart sank. She'd been so angry. She still was. But even so, she wasn't sure she was ready to say goodbye to Christopher forever.

God was calling her to missionary work in Ecuador. She'd have to say goodbye to Christopher one way or another. But it just didn't feel right.

"Go on," she said at last, when he didn't continue.

"I also want you to know I never meant to hurt you."

She lifted an eyebrow. That was pushing things a little bit. He had, after all, dumped her for her sister and then—but no, Sammy wasn't his baby.

"It might not seem that way now."

She nodded, barely restraining a bitter laugh. Lately she'd discovered nothing was as it appeared.

"I told you how Jenny called me one night, asking me to come to dinner with her and Gram. Gram wasn't there, and Jenny was a wreck."

Jasmine pictured the scene in her mind. "I remember. You said she was throwing things."

"Yes. She was hysterical. Completely beside herself. But Jasmine," he said, his voice low and earnest, "that night—it was the night I tried to call you and that guy answered."

"What?" she shrieked, then clapped a hand over her mouth. "I thought—"

"That the night in question had been much earlier. Otherwise, how could I have been Sammy's father?"

"But you're not…"

"Exactly. Anyway, to continue the story, I calmed her down and we watched a movie. After the movie, Jenny was herself again. She told me the real reason she invited me over. She needed help. She—" Again he cut off his sentence.

"She was pregnant with Barton Pembarton the Third's baby," Jasmine concluded, the scene coming clear in her mind. "She'd tried to call me, but I wasn't home. I remember the message on my machine, now. It said to call her right away, but I was pulling an all-nighter."

She had closed her eyes as she pieced the facts together, but snapped them open when Christopher's hands closed firmly on her arms.

"How did you know?" he asked in amazement.

"How did I know what?" She was having trouble following him, steeped as she was in chronologizing the facts.

"Know Pembarton's name?"

"The newspaper clipping we found in the drawer. Remember?"

"Yeah. That's the first time I'd ever seen what he

looked like." He clenched his hands. "Man I'd have loved to give him a piece of my mind."

Jasmine chuckled. "You'll have to stand in line. I expect there's a number of people in that category."

"When Jenny told him about the baby he refused to acknowledge it."

"What?" Jasmine stood. "Why, that—"

"That's not the worst of it." Still on his knees, Christopher reached for her hands and drew her down beside him on the floor. "He told her he was engaged to marry a Denver socialite. His parents' choice for his bride."

"Poor Jenny," Jasmine whispered.

"Well, you can understand why she was so upset." He looked away. "And she'd learned she had cancer and didn't have long to live. I didn't even know what to say."

"I can imagine."

"I was her sister's boyfriend. I felt so awkward even discussing such private issues. But she was hurt, and needed to talk."

"Is that what she wanted you to do?"

"Yes. She already loved her baby, and despite everything, loved the baby's father. It was her family she was worried about—the stigma of her having a child out of wedlock."

"She should have known we'd all stand by her and support her."

"Yes, but Westcliffe is a small town. Things like illegitimate children are remembered forever. It isn't like Denver where single moms are the norm and a person can just fade into the background."

"That still doesn't explain how you and she ended up together," she reminded him, bracing herself for the answer she'd been waiting so long to hear but in truth was afraid to know. "Or why."

"I thought it was the right thing to do, that God had placed me where He did for that reason," he said with a bitter laugh. "I thought it's what *you* would have wanted me to do."

"Marry my sister and not tell me about it?" she snapped, the old hurt rising to the surface. He'd known about Jenny's cancer. "Where did you get a cockeyed idea like that one?"

He blew out a breath and looked away. "I meant to tell you everything." Suddenly he stood and pulled on his jeans to straighten them. "Coffee's ready. You still want some?"

"I guess." She looked away from him. Coffee didn't even sound good anymore.

He returned with two steaming mugs and handed her one before sitting back down. He propped one arm on the seat of the easy chair and sighed. "Jenny was more concerned for you and Gram than she was about her own reputation. And of course, she worried about the baby."

Jasmine drew in a loud breath. Of course Jenny would think of Sammy first. Hadn't she been that way the whole time she was pregnant?

Christopher continued. "She didn't know what to do. She was just talking it all out, really, trying to come up with a feasible solution that wouldn't hurt anyone."

Her breath froze in her chest. Did they really think their actions wouldn't hurt anyone? Did they not consider the ache ripping through her heart when they planned all this?

But of course, Jenny had sacrificed so much more.

She'd given her life for her baby. Who knew but that chemotherapy would have prolonged her life, perhaps even saved it?

Jenny hadn't so much as mentioned her cancer to Jasmine. Did she fear Jasmine might try to change her mind? But how, *how* could she have believed it would be okay to marry Christopher?

"I was the one who convinced her," he said, answering her unspoken question. "She wanted nothing to do with it, not knowing what you'd say, how you'd feel. But I knew you'd understand, so I talked her into it."

"You knew I'd understand," she repeated dumbly, wondering why everyone else in the world presumed to know what she would think and feel when she couldn't even figure that out herself.

"She was young, alone and scared. And pregnant. If we announced our engagement, everyone would just assume the baby was mine. He'd have a name, and he'd have my protection."

He paused and made a fist. "Bart Pembarton was a weak, irresponsible boy, still tied to his mother's apron strings. I wouldn't let him near someone I care for, much less a baby. Jenny knew it as well."

"Then why was she with him?" Jasmine blurted angrily. "Where was her head, Christopher, for her to go and get pregnant by someone like Bart?"

He pinned her with a glare. "That's exactly what the town would have said. Don't you see that?" She was shocked into silence.

"He's dead now, so the point is moot."

He didn't say how Bart had died, and Jasmine didn't think to ask. The news only added to the depth of her wounds. Poor Jenny. She'd been so fortunate that a man like Christopher would come into her life when he did, would offer her the solace of his name and take on the burden of her illegitimate child.

"That explains who, what, where and why," she said, ticking the list off on her fingers. "But there's one thing you haven't answered."

He lifted an eyebrow.

"How were you planning to handle *me? Oh, Jasmine, by the way, I decided to marry your sister instead of you?* Only you never got a chance, did you? Because dear old Mrs. Rulitter thought she should be the one to break the news to me."

"Oh, come on, Jazz," he snapped, his face flushing. "Give me a break, here. I'm sorry you had to hear it that way. But that's not how I meant it to be. You know I tried to reach you."

Jasmine stood and crossed her arms to stave off the chill settling in her heart. She was trying to understand, she really was. But the sense of betrayal that she'd been struggling to tamp down just wouldn't stay put. It bubbled up in jealous swirls all around her insides.

"Tell me then, Christopher, how it was supposed to be."

"Yeah, well, think about this, Jasmine. What if you had been there that night? What if you had picked up the phone and heard Jenny wailing on the other end? What if she had told *you* her story. What would you have suggested she do?"

The air seemed to get thicker in the room. Her mind raced for a pithy answer, or even a serious one, but nothing came.

"Yeah, that's what I thought," he drawled. "It was

the only thing I could think of. And it would have worked. If things hadn't gotten out of hand so fast."

"Meaning if I hadn't found out the way I did."

"Well, yeah, sure, that's what I mean. I tried to tell you. But obviously, I didn't succeed," he finished miserably.

"Just for curiosity's sake, what were you planning to say? Were you just going to break things off with me and leave me dangling?"

"Of course not!" he nearly shouted, then looked away. "I was going to explain everything. You were supposed to see how heroic I was being, and how perfectly everything would turn out. I mean—" he cleared his throat "—as perfect as things could be, under the circumstances."

"In spite of the fact Jenny was dying."

"You're still not seeing the whole picture, are you?" he demanded, thrusting his fingers through his hair.

"Evidently not," she said wryly. "I haven't quite figured out how I was supposed to play into all this. Or whether I was just supposed to fade out of the picture completely," she added on a pique.

"You were supposed to marry me, you mule-headed woman!" he stormed. He stalked across the room and leaned one arm against the wall.

She laughed out loud, but it was a dry, bitter sound. "Oh, I see. You were going to be a bigamist. That surprises me. Somehow I always pictured you as a one-woman kind of guy."

"I am," he declared, the passion of his statement making his neck redden. He was by her side so quickly she didn't even see him move before he swept her into his arms and kissed her firmly and thoroughly.

She was breathless by the time he raised his head. His eyes were glowing with conquest. Her heartbeat roared in her ears, and she thought if he let her go, she might well fall to the floor.

Never in all their years together had Christopher kissed her with such strength and passion. To her surprise, she wanted more. If he leaned down and kissed her again, she wouldn't so much as mew a protest.

But he didn't kiss her. He gently pushed her away and into the easy chair, where he knelt before her.

"I'm a one-woman man," he said, his voice husky. "And I always have been. Jasmine, that woman is, was and always will be you."

"But you married Jenny, anyway." She could have slapped herself once the words were out of her mouth, but she couldn't help it. Her wounds were recently reopened and raw to the touch.

He tipped her chin so their eyes met. "Yes. I did. And I'd do it again. Jenny was dying. She wanted you to raise the baby. She knew I was going to marry you, so it was the perfect solution. I would marry Jenny and proclaim myself the legal father of the baby. When she died, you, Sammy and I would be the family Jenny wanted us to be. She really loved you, you know. You were supposed to be in on the plan."

Tears rolled down her cheeks at the thought of her sister sacrificing everything for her baby. And all Jasmine had been able to think about was the way she'd been jilted. Her sister hadn't told her about the cancer, and now, perhaps, she knew why. Jasmine had backed away from her relationship with Jenny, letting her sense of betrayal get the best of her when she should have been trying to forgive.

She should at least have been trying to find out the truth. She hadn't even done that. How many actions had she based on misconceptions? How much hurt could she have spared everyone? She knew Jenny suffered from the breach in their relationship at least as much as she had.

Maybe more.

And how much more she would have made of the short time with her sister. If only she had known.

"You okay, Jazz?" Christopher asked uncertainly, reaching for her hand.

She snatched it back and cradled it against her. She was so ashamed of her words and actions, she could barely think. "Why didn't you just tell me the truth?"

He groaned. "If you remember, we weren't exactly on speaking terms when we first saw each other again. I lived in constant fear of flying projectiles."

She couldn't even find it in her heart to chuckle. Her sorrow was nearly overwhelming, and she knew if she didn't escape Christopher's cabin soon, she'd break down completely and wouldn't be able to go anywhere.

"And then it became too difficult. Insult piled on insult until no one could break their way through." He paused and wet his lips with his tongue.

"I'm as much at fault as you."

"I was going to tell you everything the day I came back to Westcliffe. But then when some of the facts came together, I stood to lose Sammy. I knew you'd be a great mother for him, but I just couldn't rest until I was part of the picture. I wanted Sammy to have my name. And my protection, what little I could offer."

"But he's not your son. You could have just walked

away." *Like you did before.* But she didn't need to say the words.

"That boy is my son, Jasmine, in every way that matters. I love him, and I want to take care of him. I didn't want him—or you and Gram—to face any more scandal than you'd already dealt with. And I guess I didn't really want to be the one to have to tell you about Jenny. Or that Bart's parents rejected Sammy as their grandchild. It seemed easier to remain quiet."

Revealing Jenny's shame would only add another scandal to the family record. Dear Christopher had done all he could to shield the Enderlins from harm. It just appeared that they—*she*—got into trouble faster than he could play the rescuer.

"I've got to go," she said suddenly, snatching up her coat and dashing out the door without looking behind her.

Christopher called to her, but she refused to listen, to stop her headlong flight into the darkness of the night. It was where she belonged, in the dark.

She knew the way back to her four-by-four, and her feet put themselves one in front of the other without conscious thought.

He'd given everything, and she'd done nothing. She hadn't proved her love with faith and trust. Instead she'd made every one of his gallant actions twice as hard for him to make.

He must hate her. And if he didn't, it was only because he was the best, kindest, most honorable man in the whole wide world.

And she didn't deserve him.

There was a new wound in her heart, one that made the others small by comparison. She wanted to cry but her eyes were dry, for what use was crying when the wound in question was self-inflicted?

She was every kind of fool. And she'd discovered the truth too late.

Chapter Fifteen

So much for confessing the truth, Christopher thought, lifting himself gingerly from his easy chair. It was very early in the morning, judging from the thin stream of light beaming through the window. He'd spent the night half-sleeping, half-praying on the chair, and every muscle in his body was screaming for release.

And he was no closer to resolution than he'd been when Jasmine had left the night before. He didn't know what he expected God to do.

He knew better than that. God wasn't going to solve his problems for him, or undo the mess he'd made. A man had to live with the consequences of his actions, even when it meant watching the woman he loved walk out on him.

He deserved it, of course, but that didn't make it any easier to swallow. To have fought so long and hard for their happy ending, and then to have it dashed from his hand by his own foolishness was its own penalty.

She wasn't coming back. He'd seen the disillusionment and disappointment in her eyes, heard the anger sounding from her voice. She no longer trusted him.

And not all the words in the world could unscramble the disaster that his life had become.

Heading out the door the night before, his heart had been light. He'd found hope that she might hear what he had to say and forgive him. That they might have that happily-ever-after ending they used to dream about. Sammy would only add to their bright future.

His chest clenched, thinking about Jasmine and the baby. Despite the circumstances, God had given him such a love for baby Sammy he could barely contain it. It was like a fountain overflowing. And now he'd lost Sammy, too.

He found himself at the stable, where he looked around uncertainly. It occurred to him that here was a good getaway, to ride off into the Sangres until he figured out what to do next.

He had plans, at least. He'd felt God's call into ministry. He finally knew what he wanted to do with his life. But he'd hoped with all his heart his future would also include Jasmine and Sammy.

A dark bay nudged Christopher with his muzzle and he jumped back, laughing shakily. "Guess you just want some hay, now, don't you, fellow?" he asked, not knowing if he spoke aloud to reassure the beast or himself.

"Hey, Chris. Whatcha doin' in the barn?" Old Ben, one of the ranch hands sidled up to him and slapped him on the back. "Goin' riding?"

"Thinking about it," he admitted, sliding a glance toward Ben.

"Kinda green with horses, ain't ya?"

He chuckled. "You could say that. I've been on a horse all of twice in my life."

"I still don't see how you could have been raised on a ranch in Westcliffe and don't know how to ride."

He sighed quietly. This wasn't his week. He was going to have to divulge another secret just to get a horse. "Twice being when I fell off backward," he clarified. "I was six."

"Shoot, boy, you should've climbed back on. Who was teaching you? They should've known that."

"Unfortunately," he commented dryly, "I was teaching myself. And as far as I was concerned, taking one topple was enough to prove I wasn't cut out for the rodeo."

"But you want to ride now." It was a statement, made with an undertone of humor.

"I expect so. If you'll help me saddle a horse, that is."

"Well, I'd hate to keep a cowboy from his cows, if ya know what I mean. But I gotta tell you, I don't have a broken nag in the bunch."

"You don't have a single horse I can handle?" Maybe this was a bad idea and he should take his truck up to Horn Lake or something. At least his truck wouldn't throw him off. But for some reason, maybe it was guilt, he wanted to ride a horse.

"Commander might be a safe bet," he said, stroking the white stubble on his jaw. "Recently gelded. Ought to be a safe ride."

"Which one's Commander?"

"This dapple gray over here." He reached into his pocket and produced a carrot, which he fed to the nickering gelding.

Christopher tugged his hat lower over his brow and set his jaw. Commander. Sounded intimidating to a man who didn't like horses. He reached out a hand to stroke the horse's muzzle, but quickly withdrew it when he bucked his head and whinnied.

Old Ben laughed. Christopher scowled.

"Are you *sure* you don't have another one for me to ride?" he asked, ready to give the plan up completely. "I only want to go up by Horn Lake for a while."

Old Ben scratched his head, then his eyes lit up. "As a matter of fact, I think I *do* have something you can handle."

"What's his name?"

"He's a she. And her name's Fury."

Fury. And he'd thought Commander was bad.

A good night's sleep could make a world of difference to a woman, Jasmine reflected as she rose and glanced at the clock. Nine o'clock. She never expected to sleep as well as she did. It was amazing how clean a freshly scrubbed soul could feel. She'd come straight home from Christopher's cabin and slipped into the apartment so as not to wake Gram or Sammy.

She'd dropped into bed, exhausted from thinking and sobbing. So depleted, in fact, that she wasn't sure she had enough left in her to pray. Which is why it surprised her at how easy confession came from a quiet mind.

She didn't have to speak aloud and list every sin, or kneel in the proper posture of prayer and make her pleas to heaven from there. She merely had to lie still and *be*. God did the rest, sweeping in and taking the burden away from her, replacing it with the peace that passes understanding.

Be still and know that I am God.

The Scripture had soothed her wracked nerves, unhinged the stress from her shoulders. She'd made a thousand mistakes, but God was greater. Thank God, He was greater.

This morning, all that was left was to go back to Christopher, this time for good. She'd unjustly condemned herself, she realized now. Yes, she'd made more than her share of mistakes, but then again, so had Christopher. Surely they could forgive each other and finally be at peace.

She laughed out loud. He was every bit as stubborn as she was, the big lug. They'd butt heads more than once during their marriage, but she couldn't think of a rosier future or a brighter dream. She'd have the two men she always wanted, Christopher and Sammy, to love and spoil for the rest of her life.

"Where are you going looking so chipper, young lady?" Gram asked suspiciously as Jasmine entered the living room where Gram was rocking Sammy, who sucked noisily from his bottle.

"Hey there, little guy," she said, kissing Sammy on the forehead and Gram on her weathered cheek. "And hello to you, too, lovely Gram."

"Now I know something's up," she complained good-naturedly.

"I'm going to see your daddy! Yes I am!" she said in baby talk, as Sammy wrapped a pudgy hand around her finger. "Daddy's going to take good care of his little boy."

"Now, this *does* sound interesting," Gram said with a crackly laugh. "Do tell."

Jasmine couldn't help but smile. "I love him, Gram."

"Oh, now *there's* news."

"And I think he loves me, too," she concluded with a sigh.

Gram rolled her eyes. "And it took you *how* long to figure that out?"

"He's not the bad guy in all this."

"I never said he was," Gram reminded her.

"No, I guess you didn't. But you never offered me an easy way out."

"The easy way out isn't always the best way out. The road is narrow, and that sort of thing. Besides, I didn't know anything for certain. I just suspected that young man of yours wasn't the type to change his character so radically. He's always been a good fellow, that one."

"Oh, he's that," Jasmine agreed with a laugh. "That, and *so* much more."

"You've ironed out all the issues?" she asked gently. "Come clean with each other?"

"Well, pretty much. I guess." She experienced a sudden flash of apprehension running through her, but it abated as quickly as it came.

"Good. Then you can tell me why he left Jenny before Sammy was born, especially since you knew she was dying. That's the one thing I've never been able to figure out."

She blanched. "I…er…that's one of the things we haven't discussed yet."

"Jasmine," Gram exclaimed in exasperation. "Don't you think that's one of the biggies you want to have cleared up before you make any long-term plans with the man?"

"Well, yes, sure," she agreed, stammering slightly. "But Gram, the point is, I trust him. I don't know why he did what he did, but I trust that he had a good, honorable reason for doing it."

Gram raised a bushy white eyebrow, and Jasmine held up her hands in her own defense.

"Even—maybe especially—about his leaving Jemy."

"I cannot even fathom."

"Well, neither can I. But I'm not going to speculate, either."

"There you go, girl," Gram said, her voice filled with encouragement. "You're off to see him, then?"

"Yes, after I check on Marcus at the clinic. I need to have a long chat with him, anyway."

"Just don't get distracted," Gram teased.

"Oh, Gram! You know I won't. There's nothing to keep me away from Christopher now."

She made a beeline for her four-by-four, hoping to corner Marcus as fast as possible and be off to see Christopher. She still hadn't mentioned to Marcus that she wanted him to be her permanent replacement, but then it occurred to her that she hadn't yet mentioned Ecuador to Christopher, either.

Well, of course she hadn't. They weren't exactly on speaking terms. She couldn't just blurt out that God was sending her to a foreign country to work as a missionary. And it could be that Ecuador would have to wait.

She felt it so strongly, so certainly in her heart, this need to serve as a doctor in that little hospital in Quito. But if God allowed her to be with Christopher, she would choose that first. If God really meant her for Ecuador, the rest would fall into place in His time.

For once she would trust God and see what happened. It could only be good. She was certain of that.

She was more nervous about speaking to Marcus than she was to go see Christopher. Somehow she felt she'd deceived Marcus, and perhaps she had at that.

She found him in a back office, cheerfully working on a pile of paperwork higher than his head. He was singing a hymn under his breath and tapping his pencil in time to the beat.

"You can take the man out of the music, but never the music out of the man," she said with a laugh.

He looked up quickly, a startled look quickly replaced with a welcoming grin. "You said it, girl. Don't be thinking you'll be takin' the music out of *this* man any time soon."

"It's good to see you so happy," she said gently, her heart welling up with joy.

"I've never been so content, Jasmine," he agreed, placing a hand on her shoulder. "I'm glad you brought me out here. New York wasn't the place for me. I just didn't know it."

She smiled up at him and gave him an impromptu hug, which he returned.

"I told you God changes your dreams. Now all I want is a small country clinic like this one and a roof over my head. Beautiful mountains on one side and a gorgeous valley on the other."

"I've been meaning to talk to you about that dream," she inserted, taking the opening.

"Oh, so the time has come already. You feel rested enough to get back to work?"

"No, no," she exclaimed, shaking her head fervently.

"I didn't mean that at all. I was wondering if you'd like to stay on here as *this* clinic's doctor!"

His face brightened immediately, but then his brows fell in confusion. "You know I'd take this job in an instant," he said, his voice low even for him. "But if *I'm* the doctor, where does that leave you?"

"Happily unhindered and pursuing the Lord's work," she replied promptly.

"Huh?" he asked, justifiably confused. "But I thought *this* was the Lord's work for you."

"Maybe it was. But not anymore." Her excitement bubbled over, and she smiled widely. "I'm getting married, Marcus!"

"To Christopher, I assume," he commented, sounding mildly cynical.

"Well, he hasn't asked yet—again—but I'm hoping he will today. And I plan to accept. There's more," she said, and she proceeded to fill him in on her plans to go to Ecuador to be a missionary.

Marcus laughed aloud. "Girl, you better be goin' to tell your honey that information right away. That isn't the kind of news you surprise him with on your wedding night."

"I know. I'm on my way to see him now. I wanted to see you first."

"Tell him I wish you both the best."

"I will, Marcus. Thanks." She blew him a kiss and dashed out of the clinic, eager to find Christopher and throw herself into his arms.

Nerves finally hit her as she walked up to Christopher's cabin. She hadn't actually planned what she'd say when she got here, and now she could think of a million reasons why she shouldn't be there at all.

She knocked on the door and waited, tapping her toes in time with the hymn running through her head. The same hymn Marcus had been singing, she realized with a smile.

When he didn't answer, she searched his empty cabin, then headed to the mess hall. Frustrated and feeling her anxiety rising, she decided to find a moment's peace and shade inside the stable. She inhaled deeply despite the crisp air. She loved the smell of horses.

Quite a contrast, really. Next to the hustle and bustle of a hospital emergency room, there was nothing she liked quite so much as the respite of a stable, with its pungent combination of fresh hay and fresh manure, and the horses stamping and whickering lightly in the background.

She walked up to a friendly gray and rubbed her hand along his neck, making soft, horsey sounds with her tongue. She'd been riding since she was three. Though they didn't own any horses now, she occasionally borrowed a mount from here at the Walters to take a picnic into the mountains.

"That's Commander," said a voice from behind her.

She jumped and put a hand to her pounding heart. "You startled me, Ben," she said, turning back to the horse. "Well, there, Commander, aren't you a pretty boy?"

"That he is," Old Ben said fondly. "The poor fellow was recently gelded, so he's still got some stallion to wean out of him. But he'll be an excellent mount after a month or two."

"Yes," she said, speaking to the horse. "I'll bet you'll

be a beauty, won't you, my boy? I'll have to take you on a ride sometime so you can show off what you can do, won't I, big boy?"

Old Ben laughed behind her shoulder.

"What's so funny? I've been riding since I was three," she said, offended.

"It's not that, Jasmine. I know you can handle this mount. But this morning—" He snickered and wiped the corner of his eye with the sleeve of his flannel shirt. "This morning, Christopher Jordan wanted to ride Commander." He promptly burst into another round of laughter.

Jasmine knew it was polite to laugh along, but she couldn't. She didn't know what jolted her more—the fact that Old Ben had seen Christopher this morning, or that the crazy love of her life wanted to ride a horse!

"You didn't let him, of course," she prompted.

He chuckled again. "Not on your life. The guy was heading into the hills. Said he wanted to go up by Horn Lake. On a *horse.* Oh, man."

Jasmine smiled along with him as her mind processed the information. Christopher was clearly trying to find somewhere quiet to think things through. Up to that point, he was being rational. But why on earth did he want to ride a horse, when he could just as well have driven himself up to Horn Lake?

"Thanks for not giving him a mount," she said, smiling at Old Ben.

His pale blue eyes widened and he scratched his day's growth of beard. "Oh, I gave him a mount."

"What?" Jasmine screeched, clasping her hands together.

"Sure." He smiled. "I put him on Fury."

"I don't believe this." She turned and stomped out of the barn, heading straight to the mess hall. Christopher was somewhere in the Sangre de Cristo mountain range on a horse called Fury. And he was alone.

Ben might think it a joke, but to Jasmine, Christopher on a horse was deadly serious. He knew nothing about trail riding, and there were a million hazards to best even a good rider.

After getting Cookie to pack a lunch for two, Jasmine rushed out the door and made her way steadfastly back to the stable. Ben stood where she'd left him, looking bemused.

"Don't just stand there," she barked. "Help me saddle up Commander."

He raised his eyebrows at the order, but did as she requested. Jasmine ran back to her car for a few emergency items she always kept with her and stuffed them in the saddlebag. Ben had already tied her lunch to the other side.

"You going to be warm enough?" he asked, concern in his eyes.

Jasmine picked up the reins and led Commander to the front gate. The horse had a nice, easy pace, and Jasmine didn't anticipate any trouble. "I expect so, Ben. Don't worry about me."

"Okay, I won't," he responded, walking out beside the horse. "But, Jasmine—"

She cut him off with a "Hee-yah." She set off at a canter, leaving the stable, and Old Ben, in the dust.

The last thing she heard as she turned around the corner of the drive, was Old Ben muttering, "—about Fury…"

Chapter Sixteen

Christopher lay flat on his back with his hands clasped behind his head, staring at the clear blue Colorado sky. A cushion of snow and pine needles made his bed a comfortable one, and it wasn't too terribly cold with the sunshine streaking through the trees.

God's country. He didn't get up here enough to ponder God's creation and wonder at His magnificence. It sort of put things in perspective for him.

His life was in God's hands, and he wouldn't have it any other way. He'd apologized to Jasmine, and tried to set things right. That was all he was able to do. He regretted the fact that he'd let his temper get the best of him, but he supposed he'd apologize for that too, when the time came.

He was trying to imagine a life without Jasmine and Sammy, but it just wasn't fathomable. They *were* his life. But he'd done everything he could to make them a family, and everything he'd done had failed. He could only hope for a miracle, now.

In the meantime, he supposed he should go on pursuing the call God had given him for the ministry. He'd put his application in to the local seminary, right here in the Sangres, only about a mile from where he currently lay. The president of the seminary had already assured him of a spot in the next class, which would start at the beginning of summer.

At least he would remain close to Jasmine and Sammy this way. He couldn't even consider not being able to see his son, and his dear, sweet Jasmine on a regular basis. He thanked God again for the blessing of Sammy, who would bind him to Jasmine forever, in a way, even if it wasn't the way he would have chosen.

He heard the sound of hoofbeats approaching only seconds before Jasmine launched herself from the saddle and landed in an ungraceful heap of arms and legs right on his chest, knocking the breath from his lungs.

If the shock of her landing didn't stun him, the fact that she was feathering kisses across his face and neck certainly did. And there were streams of tears rolling down her cheeks. He stared up at her stupidly, unable to move.

"Oh, my darling Christopher. Oh, my dear, crazy love. I came as soon as I heard. I brought supplies in the saddlebag. Oh, just tell me where you're hurt, my love, and I'll make it better." She was half laughing and half sobbing as she continued to rain kisses down upon him.

It occurred to him that he didn't really *want* to move, or to be taken from the heaven in which he'd suddenly found himself. He had no idea what Jasmine was about, but as her silky hair fell down around him, he thought he might have found the most pleasant way to smother to death that the world had ever known.

She stood up as quickly as she'd descended on him.

For a moment she just glared down at him, then turned and stomped to her horse, yanking a paper grocery sack off one of the saddle strings.

She stomped back and threw it at him, again pelting him in the chest. He grinned despite his best efforts, and swung to his feet, casually leaning his back against a convenient pine tree.

"I thought you were injured," she said, enunciating each word unnecessarily, "because Old Ben told me he let you ride out on Fury. And—"

He tried to interrupt her, but she held up her hands and continued on.

"*And* there you were, lying on the ground like some corpse or something and I thought... Oh! Who cares what I thought? The point is, you're fine."

"You sound as if you'd rather I wasn't," he remarked dryly.

"At this point, don't push it," she said, and then broke into laughter.

He laughed with her, relieved. Apparently she was here with some purpose other than to cause him bodily harm. They met each other's gaze and laughed even harder. He reached out and hugged her to him, wanting her back in his arms. She didn't resist.

"Uh, Jazz?" he asked when they'd both somewhat recovered. "About Fury..."

"You must be a better rider than I thought. Or else a quick learner."

He shook his head and tried not to grin. "Not exactly."

She lifted an eyebrow, and he shrugged and pointed to the glen, where Fury was tethered.

Jasmine had been honestly terrified when she

tracked him up here, but she turned her gaze to where he pointed and felt her mouth drop open in surprise. "That's *Fury?*"

An ancient gray donkey with one droopy ear looked back at her, his expression one of mild annoyance. He had a clump of grass in his jaw and was chewing slowly. He couldn't move beyond turtle speed, she was certain of that just by looking at him.

At least now she knew why Old Ben had been laughing. "He's a little short for a man with your long legs, don't you think?"

Christopher turned a deep shade of red, and reached to retrieve his cowboy hat from the ground. "Fury is a she, thank you very much, and it just so happens that we got along fine."

"In other words, no one saw you trying to ride the beast," she teased.

He tugged on his cowboy hat and grinned from underneath it. "That, too. But really, she's perfect for me. One speed, slow. And since my legs can almost touch the ground when I ride her, I don't have that *liable to take a digger* sensation I get from riding a horse."

"Oh, Christopher." Before she could consider her actions, she slid forward, framed his face in her hands, and kissed him soundly on the lips. She loved him, every crazy inch of him, and she wanted him to know that.

"I didn't think you'd be back," he admitted, settling her into his arms. "I was trying to figure out what to do next."

"And what did you decide?" she murmured, locking her arms around his waist and snuggling under his chin. "There's food in that bag, by the way."

"Then we should eat. I missed breakfast this morning."

"Yes, I know." Kneeling, she ripped the sack open to bare the contents—fried chicken, cheese, biscuits and a couple of apples.

Christopher shined up an apple on his flannel shirt and took a big bite. "You make it your business to know whether or not I eat breakfast?"

"I make it my business to know a lot of things," she teased. "Like how you planned to get along without me."

"I couldn't do that, and you know it. You and Sammy are all the world to me. But—" he paused and stared down at his apple.

Jasmine felt her chest tighten, as if she were once again going to lose control. But control wasn't hers to begin with, she reminded herself. It belonged to God.

"What I was thinking about up here," he said, crouching down to face her, "is that I'd like to go to seminary. In fact, I've applied to the one here in Westcliffe. I believe God is calling me to the ministry."

She took in a deep breath, then laid a hand on his arm. "Oh, Christopher, that's wonderful." She stroked his forearm up, then down again, loving the texture of flannel under her fingertips. "Are you going to pastor a church?"

"I'll do whatever I have to in order to stay near you and Sammy, but—" He removed his hat and swept a hand through his hair before planting the hat firmly back in place, brim low over his eyes. "But recently I've had other ideas with what I might do for the Lord."

"Such as?" She sensed his hesitance, and wondered if she ought to tell him she'd follow him to the ends of the earth if necessary. That was, after all, what true love was about.

Still, though Christopher was being affectionate enough, he'd spoken of being *near* her and Sammy instead of *with* them. She kept her thoughts to herself and her mouth firmly closed.

"I want to go to Ecuador, Jazz. There's a hospital there where you could do some work if you wanted. After I left Jenny, I got an EMT certificate in Pueblo."

"So *that's* where you learned to deliver a baby," she said, the light bulb in her head going off.

She was still reeling about his wanting to go to Ecuador. It cleared up any lingering doubts she had about whether or not the two of them should be together, but she wasn't quite prepared to express her thoughts in words. For now, she simply wanted to experience the sheer joy of a match made in heaven.

After a moment, she sighed aloud. "Will you be angry if I ask you a question?"

He sat down beside her and laced their fingers together, squeezing gently. "I love you, Jazz. I want to marry you. If there's anything else we need to clear up between us, let's get it over with now. Let's start fresh from today, okay?"

"Okay." Her heart thumped loudly in her chest as she wondered how to phrase the delicate question. "I want you to know up front that it doesn't matter what you say. I love you and I'll marry you, and the answer to this question isn't going to make a bit of difference."

His Adam's apple bobbed as he swallowed. "It means a lot to me that you trust me."

"I do. But there's no sense in leaving a nagging question behind. Why did you leave Jenny, Christopher? Everything else makes sense, seen from your viewpoint. You acted in a gallant and honorable manner. But then how could you leave?"

She held her breath, wondering if she'd been too harsh.

He smiled gently, and sadness lurked in his eyes. "Another thing I didn't want you to know about Jenny." He blew out a breath. "She knew when I married her that my heart did and always would belong to you. She knew I planned to tell you, though the thought humiliated her. But you had to know, for the baby would one day be your own."

"Yes, but you didn't tell me."

"No, I didn't," he replied gravely. "And because I didn't, Jenny got it into her head that I might come to love her, and that the three of us might be a real family."

"I can see how that would happen." It hurt to think about it, but Christopher was a magnetically attractive man. What woman could sleep with him and not fall prey to his natural charm and stunning good looks?

"She was young," Christopher explained. "And idealistic. I tried to ignore the tension building between us, but she wouldn't let us be. One day she demanded that I—well, uh…"

Understanding dawned on her, and she swiped a hand down her face as if clearing the cobwebs. "What are you trying to say, Christopher? That you didn't consummate the marriage?"

"That's exactly what I'm trying to say. Jasmine, you didn't think that I'd—"

"I'd think that if you gave me no reason to believe otherwise."

"I love you, and I've always loved you. We made a

pledge long ago to save ourselves for each other, and I've never broken that promise. Not even when I made my pledge to Jenny."

Tears pricked at the corners of her eyes. After all this time, all she'd been through, they would still have the joy of a previously unexplored wedding night together.

"The long and short of it is, Jenny threw me out. She was in love with me and couldn't bear the thought that I was in love with you."

"But why did you leave? Everyone blamed you." *She* had blamed him, when all the time he'd been suffering for her.

"One takes the bow, one takes the blame, Jasmine. That's just the way things are. Jenny threatened to expose herself if I didn't leave town. She told me not to contact her at all, and not to ever try to see the baby."

"Do you think that was jealousy talking?"

"Oh, I'm sure it was. And immaturity. I'm not holding a grudge."

"Another man would," she said, feeling as if she were missing some fact, something important that was lurking just outside her reach.

"I'm not another man."

"That's the understatement of the year." She hugged him close and closed her eyes. Jenny's face sprang to mind, just after she'd had Sammy. Her last words— she was trying to say something about Christopher.

"I love you, Jazz kitten."

"I love you, Christopher cat," she replied, using the pet names they called each other in high school. "And honey?"

"Mmm?" he asked, his face buried in her hair.

"I think Jenny wanted us to get back together. At the end…she kept saying your name."

"There you go, then. Happily ever after."

She smiled, knowing he couldn't see. It was time to share some of the joy in her heart with him. "Not completely, my dear."

"No?" He leaned down on one elbow and looked up at her, his normally gray eyes a smoky blue, shining with love for her. "What have we missed?"

"Oh, something about Ecuador."

He smiled up at her. "God will work it out in His own time, if it's meant to be," he said, reaching a finger up to stroke the line of her jaw.

She leaned into his caress. "He already has. I've had my application to Quito in for months now. I'll just tell them to put me on hold for a couple years so you can finish seminary and I'll continue to work part-time at the clinic with Marcus."

"Yeah?" She put a hand to his chest and could feel his heartbeat pumping wildly. "Well, praise God!"

"Yes, let's," she said, smiling.

"Marcus is going to stay and work at the clinic?" he asked belatedly.

"Marcus found he has a liking for country living. We've already made arrangements for him to stay on here."

"*Now* can we have our happily ever after?" he whined like a petulant little boy.

"*Now,* my love. And let's not rush it. We have the rest of our lives together."

Epilogue

Considering the fact that the Enderlins were still in questionable social status, nearly everyone in town showed up for Jasmine's wedding three weeks later— the soonest Christopher and Jasmine had been able to convince Gram she could arrange a proper wedding.

The church was so full they were bringing folding chairs in, and it occurred to Jasmine, as she stood in the back of the room to watch the proceedings, that perhaps they should have used the grange hall.

But of course she wanted a church wedding, with her pastor decked out in his finest vestments up in front, and she gliding up the aisle in her white gown like a fairy-tale princess.

She felt like a princess, on this happiest of days. The only sadness to mar the event was that her parents and sister were not here to see her wed to Christopher. She wondered if they could see their loved ones from heaven, if they knew that today was her wedding day.

People quieted as the organist began the wedding march. She had no bridesmaids, as a sign of respect to her sister. She tightened her grip on Marcus's arm and bowed her head, saying a little prayer of remembrance.

"Hey, girl, you aren't nervous, are you?" he whispered, sounding surprised. "This here's your big finale."

"No it's not," she whispered back, scowling. "It's only my grand entrance."

"Touché," he said, and bowed. He was handsome in a white tux with tails, especially when he smiled in that big, toothy way of his. "We're on."

Jasmine gathered her dress and her thoughts, but in the end, all she could think about was putting one foot in front of the other. She didn't even look up until she reached the front row, and then she was so stunned she couldn't think at all.

Christopher stood waiting, his eyes alight with love. In his arms, in a matching silver tux with ruffles and gray cowboy hat, was his son. He'd insisted Sammy be part of the ceremony, and Jasmine was glad he was. Now she was walking up the aisle to her two handsome men, and her future couldn't look any brighter than this moment.

Marcus patted her hand as they reached the front, and the minister held his hands up for silence. He intoned the requisite opening and asked who would be giving the bride away.

"I am," Marcus boomed in his resonant bass. "In place of her mother and father, and in memory of her sister."

He placed Jasmine's hand in Christopher's, and she

was relieved to feel his own hand shaking beneath hers. Or maybe it was her hand shaking them both.

"Thanks, buddy," Christopher whispered as Marcus moved away.

He turned back and winked at them both. "You take care of my girl, mister."

Usually Christopher would have bristled, but today he merely grinned. "You can count on it."

The minister directed them to face one another and hold hands in order to exchange vows and rings. Jasmine had seen a dozen real weddings and who knew how many more on television, but she had no idea how completely her life would flash down to this one moment. She was certain she wouldn't be able to say a word.

"Are you ready?" Christopher whispered, squeezing her hands.

"I've been ready for years," she whispered back.

It seemed only moments later that the ceremony was complete and they were turning around to be introduced for the first time as Mr. and Mrs. Christopher Jordan. And their son Samuel. The many times she'd dreamed it as a teenager didn't hold a candle to the real thing.

Tears ran unbidden down her cheeks, but she didn't even bother to wipe them off. They were here, the three of them, a family at last.

"Happy, my love?" he whispered in her ear.

"Oh, yes."

"Then promise me you'll never look behind, but only to what's ahead." He gestured down the aisle and out the door, to where a limousine waited to take them to the airport.

It was an easy promise to make. And one she intended to keep.

* * * * *

DADDY FOR KEEPS

Pamela Tracy

To every mother who gave her heart
at first sight, first touch, first cry.

Plus, special thanks to Mark Henley,
who shared bull riding expertise.
The ride in the last chapter is really his.
And to Wendy Lemme, who read the book
in its final stage and helped with fine-tuning.

Every good and perfect gift is from above, coming down from the Father of the heavenly lights, who does not change like shifting shadows.
—*James* 1:17

Chapter One

The billboard on top of the grocery store featured a picture they'd taken straight from his mother's photo album. Lucky Welch, headliner of this year's Selena Rodeo, shook his head and hoped no one recognized the bull in the background. It had belonged to his grandfather and was a family pet named Whimper.

Pulling out his cell, Lucky punched in his mother's number. She didn't even bother with "hello." Instead, in a no-nonsense voice, she said, "Lucky, I'm right here with Bernice. She says it's silly to pay good money to stay at a campground when you're surrounded by family."

Surrounded by family was a bit of a stretch, but Lucky knew better than to mention that detail. "Mom—" He paused, knowing that no matter what he said, he'd be staying at Bernice's. That Bernice Baker was his mother's best friend from childhood and not really family had never been an argument that worked. Nope, his mother always had one better, like…

"Bernice has already changed the sheets in Mary's room."

The changing of the sheets for company, at least in his family and most West Texas families, for that matter, was a time-honored tradition and not one to mess with. Plus, Lucky had met bulls easier to win over than his mother. Well, okay, one bull, to be exact: Whimper.

An hour later he pulled his truck into Bernice's yard and waited for the fireworks. They came in the shape of his mother and her best friend, who exploded out the front door and down to meet him.

Since his brother's death six months ago, his mother had taken excitable to a new level. After assuring her he was doing just fine—well, fine for a bull rider who'd put 52,000 miles on his truck this year—he unpacked in Bernice's oldest daughter's bedroom. He stuffed his rigging bag into a closet already full of old clothes, old shoes and old suitcases. He piled his Blackwood spurs and hand-tooled leather chaps on top of a hope chest that Mary had often referred to as hope*less.* Slightly older and full of jokes and mischief, Mary had taught him that girls could be tough but that sometimes the toughness was an act.

His mother and Bernice waited for him on the porch, enjoying the sunset. Polar opposites, they'd been friends since their first day of high school. Lucky's mother, Betsy Welch, had ridden the bus an hour each way from a neighboring town. She stood almost six feet tall and still favored the big hair of her generation. Bernice had always called Selena, Texas, home. She edged just over the five-foot mark and was nearly as round as she was tall. She still wore her hair tied back in a simple ponytail. She'd been the tomboy; Lucky's mother had been the princess and Selena's rodeo queen when she was just eighteen.

"We're going to have fried chicken later on," Bernice said.

"Sounds good, but I want to check out the town."

"You mean the competition," his mother guessed.

"Yup."

Lucky headed for his truck. Bernice's young son, Howard Junior, called Howie by everyone, followed Lucky down the path. "I'm gonna be a bull rider when I grow up," he bragged.

Ten-year-old Howie looked like he should still be pushing cars on the ground, watching cartoons or carrying a snake and chasing girls—not planning to hop on the backs of bulls. "You practice every day?" Lucky asked.

"Nope."

"Then you're not gonna be a bull rider."

"Yes, I am," Howie insisted stubbornly.

"You gonna practice every day?"

"Don't haf to."

Lucky grinned and ruffled Howie's hair. "Okay, if you say so." Howie scowled in return, as Lucky put the truck in gear and headed to a town temporarily doubled in size because of the rodeo *he* headlined. The town was one long street of businesses flanked by modest homes. Tonight, the bowling alley had a full parking lot, the restaurants had long lines and music blared from a bar on the corner of Fifth Avenue and Main.

Man, he wanted to take the highway to the Lubbock rodeo. His buddies were all there, and the purse was way bigger. When they heard he was doing Selena, they'd either laughed or offered condolences. He couldn't decide which was more fitting. Most claimed his absence from the Lubbock rodeo was the answer to their prayers.

They had less competition, and he had a very happy mother.

Her roots were in the Selena area and although now she was a big-city girl, he knew deep in her heart she'd rather be here. If this rodeo made her happy, fine, he'd do it.

He found a parking spot at the end of the street, walked to a hamburger joint and stood in a ridiculously long line. He watched teenagers talking on their cell phones instead of to each other. Husbands his age divided their time between watching their children climb on the indoor jungle gym and talking with their wives.

Life.

That's what he was witnessing. Ordinary, daily life. People who were doing the most routine activities: talking, eating, playing, sharing. Not at all like his own solitary life. Lucky shook his head to clear his thoughts. Man, he needed to shake this melancholy mood. Since Marcus's death, dark moods and the desire to be alone kept popping up at the most inopportune times. His gloom had already cost him too much money and too much time. Tonight, the need to get away and brood had cost him homemade fried chicken.

He finally snagged a meal and headed for a seat. Bowing his head, Lucky spoke to his Heavenly Father, asking for forgiveness, healing and help.

When he lifted his head, not only were the fries cold but also his appetite. Maybe it took a bit more than six months and a thousand prayers to get over the loss of a brother, a brother who'd loved Bernice's fried chicken, a brother who had also loved the rodeo life.

Yup, this part of Texas brought back all kinds of emotions. When Marcus and Lucky were young, they'd left the overcrowded streets of Austin and spent memorable summers with their grandparents in a town even smaller than this one, just forty-five miles west of here. They'd even come here for the Selena Rodeo, not only because his mother loved her memory of being a rodeo queen but also because during his younger days Grandpa had been a bull rider. He'd ridden in the first Selena Rodeo. He'd started the passion. And he'd emphasized the danger.

Lucky paid attention; Marcus didn't.

Now Lucky had spent the last six months trying to forgive his only brother for dying.

Dying before he found his way back home.

Six months ago and on his fifth ride of the day, Marcus made his eight seconds, jumped from the bull and was knocked unconscious by a quick turn of the bull's head. Then, before the clowns could intervene, Marcus was stepped on, butted, trampled and broken in front of hundreds. And Lucky had seen it all, hopeless to stop the tragedy.

A friend had kept Lucky from climbing the fence and running to his brother while the bull still raged.

Marcus died.

In a matter of seconds.

He died.

Lucky unwrapped the hamburger he didn't really want and took a bite that had no flavor. A toddler stumbled by with a French fry clutched in one hand and a tennis shoe in the other. He hit the ground, bounced back up, grabbed the French fry from the floor, shoved it in his mouth and moved on. One of the women laughed, and suddenly, Lucky noticed just how beautiful she really was. How alive. Even as she cleaned the face of a high-chair-bound baby, she touched her husband's hand.

"...But the woman is the glory of man." Lucky unwittingly recalled the familiar Bible verse. Lucky had not experienced the glory of a wife to call his own, but Marcus had married once.

It lasted five months, probably because Marcus was seldom around. After that, his brother had spent the next three years in and out of relationships. Most had lasted weeks, one quite a bit longer, but never with women who could be considered the "forever" type.

Lucky shook his head. His thoughts didn't bode well for tomorrow's rodeo. Thinking about his brother hadn't made the last six months easier, hadn't helped his standings on the circuit, hadn't put money in his pocket. Good thing the previous three years had. He had almost quit after Marcus died. Truthfully, Lucky stayed in only because of the memories. That and the Sunday morning worship that gave Lucky hope that maybe he'd help some other Marcus find his way home.

Lucky threw the remains of his meal in the trash can and headed outside. The dark Texas sky greeted him. He didn't want to go back to Bernice's or head for the bar to see who he knew, *who he could drive home.* He leaned against the restaurant wall and looked down Main Street. There were at least four bars, two restaurants, a bank and a church.

Lucky wished there were four churches, two restaurants, a bank and an empty bar with a For Sale sign in its window. Some of the circuit riders called Lucky a preacher because he carried a Bible, could quote scriptures without hesitation, and, yes, frequented the bars when the rodeo came to town.

Not to drink. Nope, he'd put down the bottle the first time a drunk Marcus was hauled to jail after wrapping his truck around a tree. Lucky had come to despise the bottle after watching Marcus pour his money, talent and friends down the drain while under its influence. Now Lucky frequented bars in order to drive his friends to their motels, their trailers and, yes, even to the homes of the girls who followed the rodeo, "buckle bunnies," who were so lost Lucky didn't know what scripture to begin with. Lucky crossed the parking lot, climbed into his truck and pointed it down the familiar street.

Tears—hot, instant and completely unwelcome— blurred yet another oversize image of Lucky Welch. Natalie Crosby almost turned on the windshield wipers, but windshield wipers only worked when it was raining outside the vehicle, not when the wetness came from her own eyes.

Gripping the steering wheel of her aged Chevrolet, she managed to avoid running into the rodeo fans clustered at the gate. The poster beckoned rodeo fans to come to the fairgrounds, have fun and cheer on their favorite riders. What Natalie needed—wanted—was a giant dart and an even bigger target. Since that wasn't an option, it looked like a little emotional overload would have to do. Sensibly, she pulled into a parking spot a little farther from the entrance than she liked. It was either that or plow into a horse trailer.

"Mommy?" Robby wiggled in the backseat. He could see the activity outside and didn't want to be confined. Add to that Natalie's strange behavior, and no wonder she had a fidgety, confused little boy.

"I'm okay, Robby. Sit back." Natalie wiped at the tears and succeeded only in spreading the evidence of her despair instead of removing it.

After taking several deep breaths, she looked at the poster again and reminded herself there was no need for virtual darts. The man wasn't Marcus. Couldn't be. No way would Marcus be headlining Selena's premiere event of the year. He'd drawn the death bull six months ago, and his rodeo career ended with a ride in a hearse instead of a ride in a parade.

This rodeo rider was Marcus's little brother, Lucky. Some called him the Preacher. She'd never met him, but if she'd heard correctly, he was the antithesis of Marcus. He preached instead of partied and carried a Bible instead of a little black book.

Her cousin Tisha, who shared Natalie's last name, had little to say about Lucky, except that he didn't seem to like her much.

Right now, the image of Lucky faced the crowd with an oversize, mirthful grin and impossible dark brown eyes that demanded notice.

Natalie checked the tiny rearview mirror she'd attached to her windshield. It allowed her to check on Robby while driving. She intended to make sure he had everything he needed, especially a good and stable home. Robby was responsible for her attendance today—Robby and this overgrown bull rider. Natalie hadn't graced the Selena rodeo in a decade and definitely didn't want to be here today.

"Mommy, why we sit still?" Robby battled with the buckle on his car seat. He was growing up way too fast, wanting to do things for himself. Still, she'd rather he battle the seat belt than notice the battle taking place in front of him.

Natalie gritted her teeth. No way could she explain her fears, her conflicts, to a three-year-old.

Someone thumped on the back fender of her car. Walter Hughes, her dad's best friend, waved as he hurried by. "We need to talk later," he mouthed. She was grateful he didn't stop. Questions would only make her rethink what she had to do, and Walter had known her since she was born. No way would he accept that she had stopped by the rodeo "just for the view."

For the last two weeks, since her father's death, Walter had called every evening to ask if she was all right.

Am I all right? Are we all right?

He probably knew that although she kept saying yes, the true answer was no. There was a huge hole in her world, one that tapped her on the shoulder every few minutes and whispered, *Wrong, everything feels wrong, something's missing.* She'd buried her father— made the phone calls, called in the obituary, filled out the forms, arranged the funeral, said all the right things—and today, she still felt wrong.

Walter was just as sad as she was. He'd gone to school with her father, been the best man at his wedding and, since retirement, they met almost every morning for breakfast at the café in town.

The hole that Natalie felt was no stranger to Walt. Plus, Walt felt a sense of responsibility for her. His family owned Selena's only bank. Although Walt no longer put in an eight-hour day, really not even an eight-minute day, he knew her situation—about the low checking account balance, about the surprise loan her dad had taken out just five months ago, using his business as collateral. Today, the business belonged to her dad's partner, who was as mystified by the sudden turn of events as she was. Natalie was left with nothing. It was Walt, one hundred percent, who did not believe her dad had left her in financial trouble.

Natalie wondered at the conviction of the banker. Surely as a banker, he knew that most Americans were one paycheck away from being homeless. Walt simply said that Leonard Crosby was not "most" Americans. He'd take care of his own. Walt wanted to look at the will, wanted to help, wanted to believe in something that just wasn't there.

Natalie could only think about what was there. She had a son and a home to take care of. Her part-time job as a Web designer allowed her to support herself and be a stay-at-home mom while her father was alive. But it wasn't a career that could support the large home that had been in her family for more than a hundred years. It was not a career that could pay for a college education for Robby. At least not on the hours she worked. She could do—would do—more. But to keep her family home she needed money now.

Worry, combined with overwhelming loss, was keeping her awake at night, staring out windows and trying to figure out a way to make a go of her—their—life.

And the billboard and posters all over town announcing the headliner of the Selena rodeo offered a dangerous solution that just contributed to her sorrow and angst.

It made her reconsider options she shouldn't be thinking about. It got her out of bed this morning as the clock radio glowed a bright orange six o'clock. It had her standing in front of her closet remembering what it felt like to dress as a participant. She'd almost cried at the combination of longing and fear that enveloped her.

Natalie pushed open the car door and stuck one leg out.

And froze.

Why'd they have to put the poster at the only entrance?

Lucky was well-known for his participation in Cowboy Church, right? Surely that should count for something—some sort of commitment to responsibility. Natalie hadn't been to church since childhood, but she remembered some of the lessons. Jesus told His flock to take care of the widows and orphans, right?

Natalie wiped the last tears from her cheeks as Robby's "Mom! Mom! Mom!" caught her attention. She finally stepped out of the car carefully and went around to get her rodeo-clad son. Yup, Pop Pop, Robby's grandfather, had spent plenty of money creating a miniature cowboy, and this morning Natalie allowed Robby to dress the part. He wore a belt with his name, tiny boots, and even a pair of chaps. The only request that went unfulfilled from her son's Christmas wish list was a horse.

Pop Pop was willing; Natalie was not.

"Can I ride on a horse today?" Robby skidded down Natalie's leg and hit the ground. Natalie bit back both a yelp of pain and a too-abrupt comment. Robby wasn't old enough to understand her limp or her fears, and she didn't want to transfer her negative feelings about horses to him. Truth was, going to the rodeo had her in a sweat, and she didn't know what to blame for her troubles more: the rodeo or the rodeo cowboy.

"You can't ride a horse today, but there will be plenty of other things to do."

He glared at her, an accusing look on his face. Fun, she was denying him fun. Well, today wasn't about fun. It was about survival because today was the day she intended to confront Lucky Welch.

Salvation or ruination.

And what should she tell Robby? One thing for sure, she couldn't just lie down and die, or give up. She took Robby by the hand and led him to the poster. It was past time to take action, and Robby was three and could understand more than she gave him credit for. "This man…"

His face brightened, and he tried to help. "A cowboy?"

For a brief moment, Natalie considered pointing out the thick brown hair, dark brown eyes and strong chin so unlike her own blond, blue-eyed, elfin look.

And so like Robby's own thick dark hair, brown eyes and still-forming strong chin.

"Yes. I think I might know him."

"Really?" For the first time in days, Robby's eyes brightened. "A cowboy! You know a real cowboy? Can I meet him, Mommy?"

She opened her mouth to answer, but the words didn't come. She couldn't do this. Not right now. Not when her father had just died. Not when she was in danger of losing her home. But the loss of her father, the danger of losing her home, were exactly why she was standing here today, contemplating making the worst mistake of her life.

Because it might not be a mistake, it might be salvation.

The high school band warmed up in the distance. Two children eating cotton candy walked by. Natalie took a breath and managed a smile as nostalgia took her back to the days when the rodeo was a good place to be. *She and her dad, on rodeo day. Cotton candy sticking to her fingers.* And the rodeo still smelled the same, a mixture of popcorn, sweat—both human and animal—and excitement. Yes, excitement had a scent. Natalie first noted the aroma at the age of eight. She'd been leading her pony, Patches, in the children's parade. To think she'd worried the rodeo might have changed.

Well, everything else had.

Excitement attached itself to this rodeo, always had, and it buzzed with an energy that even Robby picked up on. If she hadn't put her hand on his shoulder, he'd have been all the way to the ticket gate before she got her bearings. "There's no rush. The day is just beginning."

He bobbed his head, clearly wishing he had free rein. *No way, not here, not today.*

She turned, taking a step toward the entrance.

"Natalie, it's been forever since I've seen you at one of our rodeos. You need any help?"

"No, thanks, I'm fine." Natalie nodded and forced herself not to rub her thigh. "Good to see you, Allison." They'd been fast friends during school, practiced together and competed against each other in local barrel races events. Allison Needham, like Natalie's cousin Tisha, had gone on to be a rodeo queen; Natalie reigned as a couch potato. Allison came back from the road about three years ago, a quieter girl with a baby on the way, and she didn't talk much about the past. She didn't talk much to Natalie, either.

Natalie figured she had her cousin Tisha to thank for that.

"Good to see you, too. Travis is competing for the first time. He'll be tickled to know you got to see it."

She and Allison had pushed her baby brother, Travis, in his stroller, and now he was all grown up.

"I'll watch," Natalie promised.

Robby waited at the ticket booth. Natalie plunked down her money and pushed through the gate. T-shirts were to her right, Native American art to her left. Robby headed straight to the food and smiled. "Hot dog?"

"We just ate breakfast."

"But I still hungry, Mommy."

"Nothing tastes better than a rodeo hot dog, Natalie." The comment came from one of her dad's friends, manning the concession booth. "My treat."

Natalie swallowed. This was harder than she'd thought possible. Why had she imagined that she could attend this rodeo and just melt into the crowd? She'd lived in Selena all her life, and she knew this was a time-honored event. Everyone would be here—from her old kindergarten teacher to the bank teller who handled the Crosby transactions.

"I appreciate the offer, but I'll pay." She added a soda for herself and held Robby's hand as they followed the crowd. He stopped to gape at the cowboys sitting on the fence.

Lucky Welch wasn't one of them.

The bleachers were already pretty full, and Robby frowned at the people who'd beaten him to the most coveted seats. "Mommy, we sit there." He pointed to a spot near the top. People were pressed together, and the walkway was crowded with spectators.

"Over here!" Patty Dunbar, her best friend, waved from the crowded bottom row. Robby headed right over and plopped down in Patty's lap.

"Oomph, I think you've gained a ton since the last time I saw you." Patty settled Robby next to her own son, Daniel, and scooted to make room for Natalie. "I cannot believe you're here."

"Me, neither. Where's the baby?"

"With my mother, and don't change the subject. Why are you here?" Patty whispered the question so only Natalie could hear. Ten years ago, Natalie broke her hip at this very rodeo. That had been enough reason to keep Natalie away. But, of course, that wasn't why Patty was asking.

Natalie knew exactly what Patty was really asking because Patty was the only one in Selena, besides Natalie, who knew who Robby's father was.

Before Natalie could respond, the "Star-Spangled Banner" boomed from the sound system and the grand entry began. Everyone stood, and the cowboys took off their hats. Natalie saw him then, in the arena, standing amidst a straight line of competitors with his hand over his heart. He was more compact than she'd imagined and looked more serious than some of his peers. He actually looked like he believed in, enjoyed, the national anthem.

Natalie spent the next few hours watching the steer wrestling and the team roping. She took Robby to the bathroom twice and then for a walk during the barrel racing, denying it was planned timing, not that Patty believed her, and the whole while Natalie pretended not to look for Lucky. Bareback bronc and saddle bronc riding were next; Robby was mesmerized. After that, she watched her son attempt to catch a greased pig and pretended not to look for Lucky again. This, of course, was followed by another trip to the bathroom.

Finally, it was time for the evening's final event— bull riding.

The term "crowd favorite" took on new meaning when Lucky Welch's turn came. He rode often, and he rode hard, scoring in the eighties on a bull named Corkscrew. To Natalie's eye, Lucky looked like a rag doll with one hand tied to a moving locomotive. She felt faint. What if he was killed? It only took one fall, one wrong move! She knew that from experience. So did Lucky. Just down the bleacher, a woman yelled, "You can do it, son!"

Leaning forward, all Natalie could see was big hair. Lucky's mother had been introduced to the crowd a few hours ago. Standing alongside Allison and other past queens, those who'd bothered to show up, Betsy Welch smiled, but the smile didn't quite reach her eyes.

Yes, the Welches would still be grieving Marcus the way Natalie and Robby were grieving her dad. Difference was, as Walt kept pointing out, Pop Pop took care of his own. Or at least tried to.

Marcus had only taken care of Marcus.

Next to Lucky's mother sat Bernice Baker. For the last year, really since Robby stopped looking like a baby and started looking like a Welch, every time Natalie saw the woman, she headed the opposite way.

Bernice Baker was probably the only person in town who might notice how much Robby looked like a Welch.

Long shot, but a shot nevertheless.

Natalie almost chuckled. Since Robby was a baby, she'd been worrying about Bernice, about Marcus showing up. Now she was willingly looking for Lucky Welch and thinking about confronting him. She was even worrying about the match between him and the bull.

The woman yelling "son" was only a basketball toss away, and Robby had no idea she was his paternal grandmother. Oh, no, no. This was not something Natalie could do after all. She changed her mind, started to stand, but she chose the wrong moment. She was stuck. She couldn't pull Robby left or right. Not while the crowd was this worked up, not at the climax of the rodeo. She stretched her leg, trying to ease the stiffness, and watched as Lucky Welch made the eight seconds and jumped from the bull to land on both feet. The bull made a move, Lucky ducked behind a clown, and it was over. The crowd roared. The scores to be announced, but finally the day's events ended. A human surge began exiting the rodeo. Robby, who'd never been to a rodeo, finally felt overwhelmed by the crowd and clutched at Natalie's hand. Daniel, a rodeo veteran at just five, headed for the edge of the arena. Patty was right behind.

Natalie panicked. If she saw Lucky, and he was alone, she'd approach him, she really would, but if she—

Suddenly, Lucky was heading straight for her with a swagger that screamed pure cowboy. His belt buckle was even bigger than his confident strides. He wiped dust from his hat, smiled, and Natalie thought maybe he had the whitest teeth she'd ever seen. Another bull rider walked beside him.

Natalie stopped in her tracks. Lucky stopped, too, and caught her eye. "Do you want an autograph?"

Oh, no! He thought she was a buckle bunny.

In a way, his assumption knocked down the defenses she'd so carefully erected while she was watching him. Unfortunately, she forgot to consider that the other side might not have a safety net. "No," she blurted, "I don't want an autograph. I want help with Marcus's son."

Chapter Two

Lucky had spent a lifetime learning how to harness control, and he wouldn't lose it now. Even if a buckle bunny was trying to tarnish his brother's memory.

The cowboy next to him looked at Lucky with a relieved expression, said, "I think this one's for you," and took off for the cowboy ready room.

The threat of paternity suits was a real issue to the boys on the circuit. Most played hard and all too often got mixed up with women who wanted bragging rights and/or a piece of the purse. Well, this gal had really missed the boat. What kind of woman showed up six months after a bull rider's death and...?

Lucky backed up. The noise of the crowd had boomed only a moment before, but now he didn't hear a thing. He could only look at the woman and the little boy by her side. She looked right back at him, young, curvy, blond, her eyes wide with fear. To his dismay, something registered, a glimpse of a memory.

No, it couldn't be.

"Tisha?" It had been over three years since he'd last

seen her. She looked different, but then hard living had a way of changing people.

It had certainly changed Marcus.

The woman's eyes narrowed. Tears disappeared, replaced by anger.

Marcus had dated Tisha Crosby for just over a year. She'd wiped out his bank account and his heart. Marcus hadn't been the same afterward. Maybe this was why. Lucky didn't know that much about kids, but the boy could be the right age. Plus, he had the look—the Welch look. Thick, dark brown hair, piercing brown eyes and the square chin that made shaving a time-consuming venture. Something akin to fear settled in Lucky's stomach.

Looked like the family roller coaster was about to switch into high gear again—thanks to Marcus.

The woman—it must be Tisha—clutched at the boy and pulled him close. Regret washed over her face, replacing the anger. Well, at least she cared for the boy. From what Lucky remembered, she'd been a cold, calculating woman. Not everyone saw past the beautiful facade she presented. Marcus hadn't.

"Never mind," she whispered. "We were wrong, so wrong, to come here. Come on, Robby, let's get out of here." She stumbled between two people. Robby—eyes wide—tried to hurry and keep up with her.

"Wait!" Lucky was at her side in two seconds.

"Leave us alone. It was my mistake." She held up a hand, stopping him, and somewhat regaining her composure. "We want nothing to do with you."

He started to follow her, and he would have, if he hadn't seen the tears streaming from the boy's eyes.

Lucky didn't want the boy—his nephew maybe?—to be afraid of him.

"Everything all right?" Three men, strong farmer types, materialized in front of him, blocking him. Their words were directed at the woman; their granite gazes were aimed at him. Lucky stopped. As for Tisha, she wasn't taking the time to answer. Just like that, he lost track of Marcus's son. The woman had him by the hand and was hurrying him through the crowd.

"I just need to talk to her," Lucky said. He took one step then halted as the men angled for a block. They looked meaner than the bull he'd just ridden.

"It looks like she doesn't want to talk to you," the biggest one said.

"Tisha!" he hollered. He took a step and then noted that, if anything, the three men had moved closer. He considered his options. Three against one was more than he bargained for, especially when some blond-haired woman, her purse all primed to bash him upside the head, joined the fray.

"Tisha," the blonde spat. "You think she's Tisha?"

"Isn't she?" Lucky croaked.

"No, that's Natalie. She happens to be Tisha's cousin, but that's all the resemblance there is."

He saw the woman then, leaving the front gate, with the little boy. He could see now that her uneven gait wasn't fatigue, the earlier stumble was not clumsiness. She stopped by a small car parked in a handicapped spot. Yup, the limp was real.

He'd have to rethink this encounter, which might have been his all-time low.

The next time he said a prayer, he'd have so much to say it might take him a year to get to "Amen." Especially since he had no intention of sharing this information with his family until he was sure. It wasn't the first time Marcus had been accused of fatherhood. But this time, the child looked like a Welch, and somehow Tisha was involved.

He nodded at the three men before they could move any closer, skipped the ready room and, still in his gear, headed for his truck. Intuition told him Robby was indeed Marcus's son. More than intuition told him his mother would never understand Lucky not sharing the discovery with her immediately. In essence, he was robbing her of precious days of grandmotherhood.

But gut feelings were not always reliable. Otherwise, Lucky would hold a few more titles and have a lot more money and a whole lot fewer broken bones. He'd look into this Natalie woman and wait before telling his mother, even though keeping the secret might be a crime he'd pay for later.

Once Lucky had opened the truck's door and climbed behind the wheel, he dialed his lawyer—not that he expected the man could be reached on a Saturday night. After letting the phone ring until it went to voice mail, Lucky left a quick message for him to call, hung up and stared out the truck's windows. Without exception, the festive mood of the rodeo carried over to the dirt parking lot. Exhausted-looking children clutched treats, toys and their parents' hands. Adults laughed, took sips of soda and reached for the ones they loved.

Normal, so normal.

Once again, Lucky's emotional roller coaster crested a steep incline.

"Every good and perfect gift is from above, com-

ing down from the Father of the heavenly lights, who does not change like shifting shadows."

The Bible verse came suddenly and comforted his spirit. He pocketed his phone, shed his gear and headed into town. There was a dance, there were bars, there were plenty of places to go to find out what he most wanted to know. Based on how quickly the farmer types had circled, Lucky figured Natalie was well-known and well-liked in Selena. Before he met up with her again, he wanted a little history, some semblance of equal footing.

On her *and her cousin Tisha.*

He drove down the middle of town, intent on stopping somewhere but seeing no place where he'd feel comfortable. The tent on the fairgrounds holding tonight's dance was too crowded and upbeat, the bars in town too crowded and dark. He turned around and cruised again. Finally, he settled on a 1950s-style diner on the edge of town with plenty of horse trailers in the parking lot. Surely he'd run into not only peers but also locals inside. As long as the three farmer types were content to stab chicken-fried steaks instead of him, he'd be good.

He didn't even make it inside the door.

"Lucky Welch. Wow, I enjoyed watching you! Where you going next?"

The man was a young local and today had been his first competition. Travis Needham, Lucky remembered. He had spunk but was as clumsy as a puppy. He hadn't known how to handle his draw, scored dead last and had enjoyed every minute of the rodeo. Lucky envied him. The first few years he and Marcus rodeoed had been magic.

"Not sure," Lucky said as he looked around. There were plenty of familiar faces, but most were seated at tables with no empty spaces.

"Join us," Travis invited. *Us* looked to be a young woman and older man, both looking a lot like Travis.

Never look a gift horse in the mouth. His grandfather had actually been talking about horses when he shared the proverb, but today Lucky knew it had more than one meaning. "Thanks." He sat next to Travis and directly across from the older man. Putting out his hand, he said, "I'm Luc—"

"I know who you are, son." The man put down his fork and returned the handshake. "Travis has been talking about you for months, ever since you accepted the invitation to headline the rodeo. I'm Fred Needham. Guess you can tell by looking, these two belong to me. Sure enjoyed seeing a pro today."

"Selena holds a nice rodeo."

"I've seen you compete quite a few times." Travis's sister didn't hold out her hand although she'd set her fork aside the moment he sat down. If anything, she looked a bit reticent.

"Allison, don't bring it up," Travis urged.

"Bring what up?" Lucky asked.

"I was at the rodeo, the Denton rodeo," she whispered. "I'm sorry, so sorry."

Denton…six months ago, where everything went wrong.

"Yeah, I'm sorry, too." He looked at Allison. She looked right back at him, and he got the feeling that if it had been up to her, he would not have been invited to join them. He didn't know why. He'd never seen her before. "Did you know Marcus?"

"I knew him because of Tisha."

Fred frowned. Lucky waited a moment, trying to figure out if the frown came because of Marcus or Tisha. If he were a father, he'd keep his daughters away from men like Marcus and his sons away from women like Tisha.

Finally, Travis filled in the silence. "Allison and Tisha were roommates for a while. Allison used to rodeo. She was in Denton cheering on a friend."

Allison nodded. "I used to rodeo. When I practice, I can do the cloverleaf in eighteen seconds without touching a single barrel. When it's the real thing, the barrels move in front of me."

Travis nodded. "I've seen them sprout legs. Ain't pretty. Now, the way you ride that bull is magic, Lucky. I didn't realize your mama had been a one-time rodeo queen here in Selena."

"I told him," Fred said. "He just didn't listen."

A harried waitress found their table, refilled the Needhams' ice teas, cleared plates and took Lucky's order.

Travis took a long drink and then said, "Man, it was a treat to have you competing. This turned out to be the biggest rodeo Selena ever hosted. We had cowboys show up today who always bypass us in favor of Lubbock."

Lucky smiled. "I had fun."

"Where'd you learn to sit the bull? My dad's always helped me, plus all the guys around here do bull outs on Saturday night."

"You know where Delaney is?"

Fred nodded. "It's about forty-five miles west of here. Not much there."

"My grandparents lived there. Grandpa actually competed against the legend Jim Shoulders. I don't think Grandpa ever won a thing, but man, he loved the bulls. He taught my brother and me what equipment to buy, which hand to favor, how to get off and how to get away."

"How old were you?" Allison asked.

"He started us when we were ten, but it was mostly play. Then, when we hit thirteen, he took us as far as we'd let him."

"Only forty-five miles from here." Travis shook his head. "I had no idea you were so close."

"It's a small world," Lucky agreed. "My mom even went to high school here in Selena."

There wouldn't be a better opportunity, so he looked at Allison and said, "So, you traveled with Tisha. Did you know my brother?"

Allison paled. "Tisha was just beginning to date him when I was bunking with her. Pretty soon I didn't bunk with her anymore. I went on my own—"

"Came back home," Fred interrupted.

"—soon after they started getting serious."

"I tried to warn you about that girl," Fred said.

Allison's lips pressed together in a look of agitation Lucky knew all too well. "Dad," she said. "Leave it be."

"Is that how Marcus met Natalie Crosby, through Tisha?"

"Natalie knew Marcus?" Allison looked surprised. "Really? I didn't know."

This was not the response Lucky was hoping for. He'd been thinking he'd hit pay dirt. Really, who would know better than an ex-roommate of Tisha's?

"Yeah, I think Natalie knew Marcus. We, the family, are still trying to put together the last few months of his life. He wasn't at home. We're not sure where he was staying. Guess it wasn't here."

"No," Travis said. "I'd have known if he was here."

Lucky's food arrived. He really wasn't hungry, but Texas hospitality would keep the Needhams with him as long as he was eating, and he had a lot more questions. He took a bite and said, "They look alike, Tisha and Natalie."

"That's 'bout all," Travis said. "Natalie's lived here all her life. Tisha just came for summers. All the guys liked Tisha."

"They like Natalie, too?"

"It was a different kind of like," Allison said, looking at Lucky with suspicion. It was definitely time to change the subject.

"What happened to Natalie's leg?" Lucky asked.

Fred answered this one. "The rodeo. All the girls, Allison, Natalie, even Tisha, were into barrel racing."

"Natalie was great," Allison said. "When we were fifteen, she could do the clover in twenty seconds. No one else could. Sure made Tisha mad."

"She fell during the rodeo you just competed in," Fred said. "Her horse went right and she went left. She landed on one of the barrels. We didn't know how bad it was until later."

"She finished the school semester in a wheelchair," Allison added.

"A few months later," Fred continued, "her dad sold all the horses. Natalie hasn't ridden since."

Lucky pushed his plate away. All that was left was a few crumbs. "She have a boyfriend?"

"Why, you interested?" Allison asked.

The table grew silent, and Lucky shook his head. "Just curious."

Fred pulled out his wallet and placed some money on the table. "Right now, Natalie doesn't need any more complications. Not with her dad so recently deceased." He looked at Lucky. "You do what? Way more than a hundred rodeos a year? Do you even remember the name of the last girl you paid attention to?"

This conversation had definitely taken a turn Lucky wasn't prepared for. He opened his mouth, but no words came out. Fred took that as an answer. Then, he stood and looked at Allison. "It's about time to set the baby-sitter free. What say we head home?"

Allison stood, looking relieved, shot Lucky a look he couldn't read and followed her dad out the door.

"I take it Natalie's a touchy subject?"

Travis just shook his head. "Not usually, but her father died just a few weeks ago, and some are saying he was having money troubles. Dad thinks she's in danger of losing her home."

"What about Robby's father? Is he helping?"

"No one knows who Robby's father is."

Later, Lucky stared out the window of Mary's room at a full moon. He didn't get along well with his father, never had, but Lucky couldn't imagine his dad suddenly being *gone*. Lucky should have asked more questions about Natalie's family. He weighed his options. Child support, money for Marcus's son was no problem, but it would certainly come with strings. His parents, especially his mother, would want to be involved in the child's life. There were also aunts, uncles, cousins, friends…

Lucky's last thought, before drifting off to sleep, was just how Marcus had kept this a secret and why?

Natalie stretched. All morning she'd battled fatigue and stress, and wouldn't you know it, she'd done some of her best work. Glancing at the printout, she then looked at the screen, checked all the spelling and once again made sure the video trailer she'd created took only seconds to load.

She usually didn't get to work this late in the morning. Usually, by now, she was watching *The Wiggles* with Robby. She'd been lucky seven years ago, when she'd created a Web site in a high school computer class. The teacher liked her design and introduced her to his wife, who'd started designing Web pages as a stay-at-home job. Natalie and she became business partners. When Natalie got older and her partner had two more children, Natalie took over the business and it grew.

It had paid for college so that her father didn't have to. It had helped support her and Robby. But it hadn't covered everything. Natalie needed to gain more clients now.

"Mommy, milk."

"Sure, Robby. When did you wake up?"

"When my eyes opened."

She pushed the laptop toward the middle of the table and stood. Julia Child had nothing to worry about. Natalie's idea of a good breakfast was a pancake she could pop in the microwave and a cold glass of milk.

Robby, a boy of few words in the morning, got himself a plate and paper towel, and then climbed up on Pop Pop's chair and waited.

A minute later, the newspaper hit the front door and the pancakes were ready.

Robby got the paper; Natalie set the food out.

The front page of the *Selena Gazette* featured the rodeo, make that the rodeo star.

A bit of pancake lodged in Natalie's throat. She tried to swallow, but coughed. Half of her glass of milk soaked the front of her shirt; the other half splashed onto the floor. She quickly grabbed a rag. Usually, it was Robby's spilled milk. Unlike her, he didn't cry over the mess. But then, she really wasn't crying about the milk.

After a moment, she sat back at the table and stared at Monday's newspaper. There he was. A winner. The picture had been taken yesterday, as Lucky conducted something called Cowboy Church. Standing next to him, with admiration written on her face, was a local girl, a Realtor's daughter.

She'd expected Lucky to show up yesterday. It had taken every ounce of courage not to turn off the lights, shut the curtains and move heavy furniture in front of the door. But instead of showing up at her door, the Big Bad Wolf had been at church.

She glanced at the newspaper article. Cowboy Church? Okay, maybe Big Bad Wolf was an unfair moniker. And, in truth, she'd started this fiasco—she and her big mouth.

Lucky had looked shocked by her announcement—and her demand.

Even from the grainy black-and-white picture, Natalie could see what made him more than a typical cowboy. He had a magnetism that upset her stomach. She wanted to blame the pancake, but in all honesty, it was Lucky who sent the butterflies fluttering in her stomach.

Natalie had wondered all along if Marcus hadn't told his family. That would explain why they'd left her alone. Until her dad's death, she hadn't cared, really, hadn't needed help or money.

She should have waited, thought this through, not acted on impulse. Of course, impulse was what brought Robby into her life.

Robby slurped the last of his milk. "I'm finished," he announced, pushing away the plate. In a moment, he was out of the chair, into the living room and back in the kitchen wearing Pop Pop's cowboy hat. Too big, it had the habit of falling in Robby's eyes, and he whipped it off and let out a whoop. Since yesterday, he'd continually ridden a broom around the house. Even worse, he'd gotten really good at pretending to fall off.

He hit the ground, pure rodeo landing, and she flinched.

Pop Pop would have had the video camera out.

What had Natalie been thinking?

She hadn't!

The loss of her father and the muddle of his finances must have rendered her temporarily insane. It was the only explanation for her behavior.

Robby galloped back into the room. "Mommy, go park?"

Natalie nodded. "We'll go to the bank, and then to the park."

That was good enough for Robby. He dismounted, carefully guided his broom horse to lean against the oven and ran to get his favorite train. After she'd cleared up the dishes and zipped Robby into his jacket, they were out the door and heading toward town.

Selena had one bank. Its claim to fame wasn't beauty. It was as rectangular as a cracker box and too small for the town. But change came slowly to Selena and not even the town's most forward-thinking seemed inclined to fix what wasn't really broken.

Mondays were busy, which explained why Natalie managed to get past the tellers without chitchat.

Unfortunately, Robby wasn't about to miss an opportunity.

"Hi, Allie," Robby chirped.

Allison Needham grinned at him, still counting money without missing a beat.

"Morning, Allison," Natalie said. On top of everything else, Natalie always worried that maybe Allison knew a bit too much. After all, she'd been Tisha's friend back when Tisha came to Selena to spend summers. Then, later, when Allison decided to give rodeoing a shot, she'd followed after Tisha, who was giving rodeoing a different kind of shot.

Just as Natalie walked toward the bank president's office, Walter Hughes came out of it. Seven years ago, it had been his office. Now, it was his son's. He stopped when he saw Natalie, handed Robby a peppermint from his pocket and said, "You need anything, little girl?"

"I'm hoping your son has a few minutes to give me."

Timothy Hughes, who'd sat across from Natalie in almost every class in grade school, and who'd been her first high school crush, came to the door. "Natalie? Come on in."

Walter looked at his son and Timothy nodded. "You mind if I sit in?" Walter asked.

Her eyes started pooling. Walt had thinning gray hair, like Dad. He wore the same kind of casual clothes. He still opened doors for women, and he made her miss her father all over again.

"No, not a bit."

"Let me pull Allison away from the front," Timothy said. "She can watch Robby for a few minutes."

Robby willingly took Allison's hand, and Allison headed out the front door and down the sidewalk. Robby loved to walk. He could walk up and down the street for hours, seeing the same sights, saying "hi" to the same people, and never get bored.

It took a few minutes for Timothy to gather the files and punch up her information on the computer. Walter chewed his bottom lip and perused a copy of her father's will. Yesterday, while Robby napped, she'd spent two hours itemizing what she had, what she didn't have and what she was unsure about. She'd gone over the will in detail and listed her tangible property. Now, she had very specific questions. Timothy couldn't answer her concern about the life insurance, but he could show how a good deal of money had gone into a new roof, new air-conditioning and taxes. After playing with the numbers, what she had and what she could earn, he agreed with her assessment. She could make it about three months.

Walter was the one with questions. "I think I know all of your dad's tangible personal property, and I'm as surprised as you are that he used the business as collateral for a loan, but, Natalie, were there deeds to any other properties?"

"None, and I would have known."

"And insurance?"

"The only one I found paid for his funeral."

Timothy's face finally changed expression. "Are you sure there's not something in your dad's safe-deposit box? Could you have missed seeing the policy?"

Natalie gripped the arms of the chair. She'd been so careful with the paperwork, with what was in the house. "I didn't even know he had a safe-deposit box. I certainly don't have the key."

Hope, Natalie started feeling a dim hope. It made her sit taller, but only for a moment, because the feeling of hope was just as quickly followed by fear. Why hadn't she known about the box? What if it was empty? Or what if it just held some of her mother's jewelry—worth a little but not a lot.

Still, hope flared a bit. What if the missing funds were somehow accounted for inside the safe-deposit box?

Then she'd have involved the Welch family for nothing.

"Think you can find the key?" Timothy interrupted her scrambled thoughts.

"I—"

"We're not messing with that," Walter said. "I'll make a call. We'll drill it open in no time."

"Dad, that costs almost a hundred—"

"Exactly what we should pay for not notifying Natalie about the safe-deposit box sooner."

An hour later, Natalie knew that approaching Lucky Welch for money was, indeed, the last thing she should have done. Her dad had kept his promise in the form of bank bonds, *lots* of bank bonds. Barring a catastrophe, they had enough to stay afloat for two to three years, not even counting Natalie's income.

It did raise a few questions while still leaving others unanswered. Natalie still didn't know why her father had cleaned out the checking account or borrowed against his half of the business.

"Mommy, we go park now?" Robby was at the office door, Allison behind him.

"It's like having Jasmin come visit me at work," Allison said. Her daughter was only a little older than Robby. "She loves to walk, too."

"Thanks, Allison," Walter said. "Natalie, I'm thinking you need some cash now. Would you like to turn in a few bonds and then maybe meet with your dad's financial advisor about what to do with the rest?"

Natalie could only nod.

Her money troubles were over *for now,* but she had new troubles and they were by no means over and *may never be.*

"Mommy, we go now?"

Natalie was more than ready to *go now.* And the park was the best destination. Home was too empty.

Twenty minutes later, feelings raw, she watched Robby at play. He had changed her whole life.

Amazingly so.

And all because she'd been home alone on a Friday night, studying for a math test.

She hadn't even known Tisha was pregnant, let alone that she'd given birth. That Friday night, after her initial shock, she'd thought she was saying yes to helping out, watching a tiny, two-week-old Robby for a night. Truthfully, she'd loved sitting in her little apartment a mile away from New Mexico State University and watching the little guy sleep. She'd unfortunately figured out by the next evening that the phone number Tisha left was wrong, that formula and diapers were expensive and that nobody—including Tisha's parents—knew where Tisha was.

She skipped the next two days of school and her dad had driven to Las Cruces. He'd stayed a week. With his help, she'd found a sitter for the remaining month of school, and by the time the semester ended, she'd realized what it felt like to be separated from Robby, like she could still feel the warmth of his little body in the crook of her left arm. It had taken her from the hallways of higher academia and back home to walking the hallways with a little personality who liked to touch her cheek and who smiled—yes, smiled—at the whole world.

Soon, her dad felt the same way, and they'd stopped looking for Tisha.

When the whole town assumed Natalie was Robby's mama, Natalie and her dad had gone along. At the time, it was easier than explaining, and Natalie didn't want Robby to ever see the kind of look that passed between judgmental adults whenever Tisha's name was mentioned.

Natalie had been an only child and had always wanted brothers and sisters. Her cousin Tisha had been the closest thing to a sibling, and Natalie loved her—flaws and all—even if she didn't always like Tisha or the choices she made.

Tisha at first claimed she didn't know who Robby's father was. A year later, when Tisha borrowed some money from Natalie, she'd mentioned Marcus.

She'd also mentioned Marcus's dad and how strict he was, how he always got what he wanted.

Natalie swallowed. Here she sat on her nice, safe bench while Robby played. Maybe the park was the only safe place. At home, there was the newspaper article featuring Lucky. She'd have to deal with her mistake. Figure out the right thing to do. What was right for Robby.

Maybe Lucky would saddle up and ride away. Yeah, right. Truth was, if what Natalie knew about Lucky was true, soon he'd probably be out on the playground, climbing the jungle gym, and teaching Robby how to do something dangerous like jump.

That's what her dad would have had done. It's what he'd done for Natalie. After her mother died, he'd swallowed his sorrow and stepped right into the role of both parents. He cooked dinner, went on field trips and even sat through ballet lessons. Of course, she only took the lessons after he convinced her that the grace of a ballet dancer would benefit a barrel racer.

Her dad had always taken care of her.

He'd taught her to jump, and he'd made sure she always had a soft place to fall.

Natalie swallowed. Robby, brown hair tussled by the wind and an unguarded grin on his face—was jumping just fine. He climbed the slide, slid down, got to the bottom, stood up and jumped. Then, he tried to climb up the slide instead of the steps. He fell, skidded and hit the ground. Natalie started to get up, wanting to cushion his fall, but Robby didn't need help. He managed on his own. Standing, climbing, falling and laughing the whole time. He was all boy.

Thanks to her father, she could take care of herself and Robby.

It was her own fault she had to deal with the Welches.

Chapter Three

Sunday had been pretty much a blur for Lucky. Otherwise, he'd never have allowed a photographer to take pictures after the morning service. What he did on the circuit could be sensationalized. What he did on Sunday morning in front of believers should not.

The girl in the photo was wearing next to nothing. And the adoring look she aimed his way was rehearsed. Luckily, the reporter knew how to gather facts: Lucky's rodeo win, his mother's rodeo-queen status, his brother's rodeo belts and recent death, and even Lucky's penchant for sermonizing, all made it into the story. Too bad God was at the bottom of the pyramid. The reporter definitely put the facts in the wrong order of importance.

God should have been first.

Lucky got out his Bible and turned to James. *"Every good and perfect gift is from above, coming down from the Father of the heavenly lights, who does not change like shifting shadows."*

He put his hand flat on the page. Sometimes, in the quiet of the early morning and in the twilight of the night, when Lucky was alone, the touch of the Bible felt like a pathway straight to God.

He reread the passage. To Lucky's way of thinking, no matter what Marcus had done or been, Robby Crosby was a good and perfect gift. One Lucky's mother would welcome and his father would shun.

Lucky closed the Bible, held it in his hands and stared out his window. It was just after five. Howard, Bernice's husband, was already taking care of the animals. Howie Junior should be with him. Those summers when Lucky and Marcus visited Grandpa and Grandma Moody, they'd been up at five.

Finally setting his Bible aside, Lucky started dialing the numbers in his cell phone. He'd devoted yesterday to God, prayer and meditation. Today he was devoting to Robby Crosby, who maybe needed to be known as Robby Welch. Surely, out of all the friends he and Marcus shared, somebody would know something. Two hours later, he lost the charge on his cell phone, switched to the landline in Mary's room, and he discovered what he'd suspected all along. Natalie obviously kept a low profile. No one seemed to know her or remember Marcus talking about her. Everyone remembered Tisha. And, like Lucky, most agreed that she had stopped following the rodeo after she stopped seeing Marcus.

No one had seen her in the last few years.

No one cared.

During the time she'd spent with Marcus, Lucky had felt displaced and his youthful prayers about her all had to do with her disappearing. He'd hated when Tisha accompanied them from one show to another. She'd been a wedge between him and his brother. He was older now, and maybe his prayers should take a different slant.

Marcus had probably been a father, and it looked like he had a son to be proud of. A tiny seed of suspicion settled in Lucky's gut. Could Marcus have cheated on Tisha with this Natalie woman? Or could Natalie have been a rebound because she looked so much like Tisha?

Either scenario might give some insight as to why Marcus had kept his son a secret.

Lucky headed for the kitchen and the beckoning aroma of pancakes. "Bernice!"

"I'm right here. You don't need to yell. What?" Bernice wore an apron over her jeans as she expertly flipped the pancakes while holding a gallon of milk in her other hand. "Don't tell me you're not staying for breakfast."

"I'm staying and I'm starved. Do you know Natalie Crosby?"

"Sure I know Natalie, ever since she was a little girl." Bernice looked at Lucky's mother. "You'd know Natalie's mama. Tina Burke. She was a freshman when we were seniors."

Betsy Welch shook her head. "I don't remember."

Bernice shook her head. "About the time your daddy died and the boys stopped coming here for the summer, that would be about the time Natalie started performing in the rodeo. About a summer or two later, Tisha started coming for the summers and got involved. It's a wonder that Tisha and Marcus met elsewhere—both of them have roots here." She patted Betsy on the shoulder before turning to Lucky. "I heard you burning up the phone line asking questions about that girl. I could have saved Marcus a passel of trouble if he'd listened when I told him she was nothing but trouble."

Lucky looked at his mother. She'd poured herself a cup of coffee and was taking a seat at the table. She didn't even glance at the plate of pancakes in front of her. The look on her face clearly indicated she knew something bad was about to happen. The name Tisha always had that effect on his mother.

"Did Marcus know Natalie?" Lucky asked.

"Not that I know of." Bernice set the milk on the counter. "You want to tell me why you're asking?"

"I met Natalie yesterday at the rodeo and, for a moment, I thought she was Tisha. Some of her friends quickly set me straight."

"Natalie was at the rodeo?" Bernice sounded surprised.

"Yes."

"Well, that's interesting. After her leg got mangled so bad, Natalie stopped going anywhere near horses. Her father sold off his entire stock. About broke his heart. When Robby started wearing a cowboy hat, you could just see Leo wishing he had a horse to put that boy on."

"You're not looking for Tisha, are you?" his mother asked slowly.

"It really shocked me, Mom, how much this Natalie looked like Tisha." Lucky sat down at the table and tried not to notice his mother's trembling hands. Tisha brought up bad memories. Marcus's drinking had gotten out of control during the Tisha era. His mom blamed Tisha, slightly unfair, but not completely unwarranted.

Bernice piled pancakes on a plate and set them in

front of him. His mother stared at the syrup bottle in front of her but didn't move. Finally, Bernice reached over and pushed it toward Lucky. "Don't worry, Betsy. Natalie's nothing like Tisha."

Betsy wiped away a tear, and Bernice started talking, even as she dug into her own plate of pancakes. "Everyone loves Natalie. She's a hometown girl. Family's been here since the area was first settled."

Bernice looked at Lucky. "At one time, that girl loved the rodeo as much as you do. Of course, Tisha did, too. My, my, those two girls could ride, but Natalie was a natural. She and little Allison Needham used to practice every weekend. I heard you asking questions about her, too, didn't I? My Mary said she wouldn't be surprised if Natalie made a name for herself. She wasn't too sure about Allison. I think Tisha only rode because she couldn't bear Natalie getting the attention. When Natalie was still a teenager, she got tossed during the rodeo. She was still using a cane when she graduated high school. If you look real close, you'll see she still has a limp to this day."

"I think I saw her," Betsy said thoughtfully, looking at Lucky and finally relaxing. "She came over to talk to you after the rodeo."

"Yeah, she did."

"I only saw her from the back. I didn't notice she looked like Tisha."

"Her boy must have convinced her to bring him. Can't think of anything else that would get her there. She's a good mother. Too bad there's not a dad in the picture. She went off to college and came back two years later with a little baby. Leo didn't even blink, and no one dared say a word or ask questions about

Natalie's situation. She and her dad dote, make that he doted, on Robby." Bernice looked over at Betsy. "Natalie's father died just two weeks ago. Heart attack. Real surprise to everyone."

Bernice turned to Lucky. "Natalie's dad owned part of the stockyard Howard works at. We all expected to hear that Natalie would take over the reins, but it seems just a few months ago, Leo took out a loan. He used the stockyard as collateral. It's gone now, Natalie's livelihood. Word is, she's hurting for money and might lose her home."

Lucky nodded. So desperation drove her to him. That she'd risk talking to him, asking him for child support, for help, meant she was pretty much at wit's end financially. No doubt she wanted money with no strings. He finished his plate and wasn't surprised when Bernice piled more on.

With each bite, he thought of his brother. Marcus had been a pro at keeping secrets from his family. He'd spent time in jail without placing his one phone call to them. He'd nursed an alcohol addiction that not even Alcoholics Anonymous had been able to counter. But of all his secrets, this one took the prize.

Then, a more subtle thought surfaced, adding one more turn on this roller-coaster ride out of control. Maybe Marcus hadn't known he was a father?

Suddenly Lucky's appetite was gone. "Where does Natalie live?"

"Three blocks past the church, turn right and go down Judge Taylor Road all the way to the end."

He stood. "I need to get going."

They didn't ask; he didn't tell.

He rehearsed his speech on the drive over, in between praying. There were two possible scenarios. One, Natalie was a decent woman who truly needed help. Lucky had watched decent women fall victim to Marcus. Two, Natalie was the same as Tisha. Then, possibly, Marcus had been the victim.

No matter which one she was, approaching her looked to be the hardest thing Lucky had ever done. The words he practiced seemed weak, hollow, accusing. As he pulled in front of the house, he was no closer to knowing what to say to the mother of Marcus's child.

Sitting in his truck in the driveway, Lucky bowed his head and one last time petitioned his Father. Never had he dealt with such a situation. He couldn't even come up with a Bible reference.

Natalie came to the door, stared at Lucky, disappeared inside for a moment, then stepped onto the porch. He admired that. She wasn't going to hide. She'd meet him head-on. He also had to admire the way she looked. White jeans, red button-down shirt. Perky and mad. On her, the combination looked good.

The boy wriggled up next to her. Grinning like it was Christmas and obviously hoping for escape. The tears Lucky evoked yesterday obviously forgotten.

Thank you, God.

Lucky stepped out of his truck. "Ma'am, can we talk?"

"Robby, go up to your room." She slipped her hands into the back pockets of her jeans and frowned.

"Why, Mommy?"

"Just for a little while. I'll talk to you later."

The boy peeked out. "Are you the cowboy?"

"I'm a bull rider," Lucky corrected, throwing an

apologetic look to Natalie. "A cowboy *and a bull rider,* much better."

"Better?" The boy looked interested.

"Robby." The one word did it. Robby bobbed his head, grinned and ducked behind her.

"I wanted to talk to you—" Lucky began.

"I owe you an apology," Natalie said. "I'm not sure what came over me yesterday. It was a mistake to come see you. We don't need money. Really."

Lucky shook his head. "Ma'am, we can worry about money later. Right now, I just want to know how it can be that my brother had a son the family doesn't know about."

She stumbled, then stopped to lean against one of the porch's white pillars. Suddenly, he wanted to go to her. Hold her up. Tell her he didn't mean to hurt her. Where were these feelings coming from? This morning, with the sun hitting the blond, almost white, highlights in her hair, she looked nothing like Tisha.

"So, you didn't know," she whispered before regaining her footing.

She drew herself up, standing proud, yet still whispering. "I always wondered."

"Ma'am, we had no idea. When I tell my mother about Robby, she's going to be so happy. I cannot even tell you how much that little boy will heal our family. I know we can work something—"

"No!" She took two slow steps down the front steps. The limp was more pronounced, as if the emotional pain robbed her physically as well as mentally. Still, she managed to keep steady. "I was so wrong to approach you. Robby and I are doing just fine."

"I believe you, ma'am. I can see how fine you're

doing. Little Robby looks happy and healthy, and this is a great spread you got here, but *I'm* not doing fine. For six months, I've done nothing but miss my brother, wish I could bring him back, and now I find out he has a son—a son who knows nothing about his father or his father's family? Tell me, ma'am, did Marcus know about Robby? Did you tell him?"

"Tell him? Why would *I* tell him?" The look in her eyes said it all. Marcus was pond scum. "We, my father and I, wanted nothing to do with Marcus, ever. We were glad he never came around. Robby's ours. We kept him, we love him, and he's ours. And keep your voice down. He doesn't know he's related to you."

"That's going to change. Robby has family, on both sides, who want to get to know him and love him."

Natalie's eyes narrowed.

"By not telling my brother about Robby, you deprived him of any opportunity to know his son." Lucky felt the words pool in his throat. Maybe knowing he had a son would have calmed Marcus down, grounded him, made him rethink what he did with his time and his money. "I know my brother. He would have taken care of Robby."

"No," Natalie said.

"Look, how and when did you meet him? What made you decide to raise his child alone? Why…"

She covered her ears. The pain on her face so evident that Lucky stopped.

"I can't deal with this right now," she said.

He started to argue, but tears pooled in her eyes and threatened to overflow.

"It's too much. I've dealt with losing my dad, losing my home, and now you're making me deal with losing Robby."

"No, not losing Robby, but introducing—"

She held up her hand. "No, not today, I cannot deal with this today." She took one step in his direction, and he backed up. He recognized anguish. He'd felt it every day since his brother died. Their eyes locked, hers blue and beautiful, then she pivoted and hurried quickly back to her front door.

A moment later, sitting in his truck in the driveway again, Lucky bowed his head once more and petitioned his Father, even as his heart pounded and his own anguish threatened to take over. He'd finally thought of a Bible reference. The story of King Solomon offering to cut a child in half when two women were arguing over who was the infant's rightful family.

When he looked up from his prayer, his eyes went right back to Natalie Crosby.

She stood at the front door, looking at him like he was either the Grim Reaper or an IRS agent.

Finally, he rolled down the window and leaned out. The smell of West Texas sage grass reminded him of being at his grandparents' house. Lord, he could use Grandpa's advice now. "Look, Natalie, you know you're going to wind up talking to me. I've got plenty of questions and seems you're the only one who can answer them." He shook his head. "Saturday you told me that I'm an uncle. Surely after that bombshell, you know I'm not going away."

Her expression didn't change. He'd dealt with friendlier bulls.

"Okay," he finally said. "The next time we talk, it probably won't be you and me. It will be you and me and my lawyer." The next words out of his mouth shamed him, but she'd left him no choice. "And I don't think you can afford that."

He fired the engine and backed out. Just when he hit the street, he paused, stuck his head out the window again, because he couldn't stand feeling this low, and shouted, "I'm staying at Bernice Baker's place. You can call me anytime. I know you can find her number."

With that, he pointed his truck toward Bernice's, but his white knuckles and clenched teeth convinced him that no way, no how, could he sit in Bernice's living room and not look like something was wrong. Holing up in Mary's bedroom wouldn't work, either. He was driving away from one headache and heading toward another. He needed to tell his family, and soon. Because if they found out about Robby from someone else, he'd never hear the end of it.

Selena in November was a riot of colors. The trees were shades of orange, red and yellow. The grass was turning brown but still had hints of green. None of the scenery matched Lucky's mood. He needed some black or at least a lot more brown. He drove out of town and headed toward Delaney. Maybe there he could recover some feeling of peace.

Delaney was even smaller than Selena and just as colorful. A small sign announced the town and its population. An even smaller sign pointed to a café and general store. Both were new. School was in session. The building, the same size as the combined café and general store, had four trucks and one Ford Taurus parked in front. Lucky turned at the corner and saw a playground much improved since the days he had climbed the metal slide or fallen onto dirt and grass from the monkey bars. He still wasn't seeing the colors that fit his mood. While the playground of old had been brown, green and silver, the playground of new was sunny yellow and fire-engine red.

Down from the school was the church his grandparents attended. It still looked good; getting declared a historical marker had that effect on property. Lucky pulled into the parking lot and almost couldn't get out of the truck. The church looked good but lonely. The minister who'd been there during his grandparents' time had passed away five years ago.

The sight of his childhood church looking pristine but unused did not help Lucky's mood.

He left Delaney's few businesses and traveled five miles of dirt roads, finally reaching his grandfather's house. He stopped just in front and let his foot hover over the gas as he reflected back on the best memories of his life. A discarded bike, a tiny pretend lawn mower and a wagon gave evidence that life indeed went on. Lucky didn't know the family who'd purchased Grandpa's land, but he liked them already. The place looked pretty much as it always had, even the horses running in the distance. The only thing missing was the carpet-covered barrels over by the barn and Grandma standing on the porch yelling at Grandpa to turn down the music so she could think.

Believe it or not, Grandpa said there was nothing like Jimi Hendrix to get the adrenaline pumping. He said it was necessary for bull riding.

Lucky relaxed enough so his knuckles returned to their normal color.

The cemetery was a good twenty miles away and one of the oldest and biggest in the area. He'd been to Grandpa's grave often, every time the rodeo brought him near, but today the pull was more than paying respect. It was a place to reflect.

He certainly could have handled his encounter with Natalie better this morning.

And it looked like he'd need to work hard to handle his mother now. In the distance he could see her standing in front of her parents' graves. On a patch of land that usually inspired the wearing of black, his mother wore a pink button-down dress and white high heels. Yup, she was an avid member of the June Cleaver fan club. At least that's what his friends all claimed. No one ever surprised Betsy Welch in an awkward moment. She always looked like she'd just left the hairdresser.

He parked alongside a Virgin Mary statue. The cemetery didn't have a fence surrounding it. To the best of Lucky's knowledge, the need to escape Delaney ended at the grave. It took him only a minute to join his mother in front of her parents' graves. The headstones were weathered yet dignified. A Bible verse was engraved under his grandfather's name:

Thomas William Hitch
1917–1999
He followed the Lord.

"We should have buried Marcus here." Her voice broke. "I don't know what your father was thinking. My family's here. The cemetery back in Houston is full of strangers."

"Mom, it's okay. Marcus really doesn't care where he's buried."

"But I care! And I should have brought flowers today."

There was a grave, fairly new, just one row up. The wealth of flowers stacked there caught the sunshine. Another wasted life? Or did the grave, like Lucky's grandfather's, denote he followed the Lord?

Lucky took his mother by the elbow and started leading her away. "We can come out again."

"I checked out that grave over there," his mother said.

"The one with the flowers?"

"Yes."

"Did you know that person?"

"No, but Bernice mentioned him this morning. Leo Crosby."

Lucky slowed his pace. "Natalie's father? Wonder why he's buried here instead of in Selena?"

"I checked around. There are lots of Crosby graves, some from as early as 1862."

"Hold on, Mom. I want to go take a look."

A moment later, staring down at Leonard Crosby's headstone, Lucky reassessed his day. He'd thought he'd come here for conversation with God and Grandpa. Instead, he got his mother and now Leo Crosby, who was lying under a covering of not only flowers, but also a brown teddy bear with a toy train nestled between its legs.

Maybe his mother was right. Maybe if Marcus were buried here, he'd have flowers on his grave and maybe even a little toy train.

He knew what his mother wanted—someone to listen, someone to understand and someone to grieve with her, someone to fill a void. Since his brother's death, it was the only thing she wanted.

A grandchild would surely comfort her grieving heart.

Chapter Four

Loss of sleep became a way of life over the next few days. Natalie didn't go to town, afraid of confrontation, and she didn't tell Robby the truth, afraid of his desire to know a real cowboy and just how much said cowboy *and his family* could change their lives.

On Friday morning, she took Robby for a walk around the property. It might be mid-November, but he only needed a sweater. West Texas weather was a bit like Robby, sunny one minute, tears the next, and oh, when he was mad, he certainly knew how to freeze a body out. Today, the ranch smelled like sage and felt like Indian summer.

After an hour, they headed back for a snack and some downtime. Okay, Robby wanted the snack; she wanted the downtime. He stomped into the living room and plopped onto the floor. Natalie made sure he was busy with his trains and then walked around the house, turning on lights and trying to ignore the feeling of loss that followed her. Even with Robby's noise, her father's absence was tangible.

His accounting books were still open on the kitchen

table. She no longer had so many questions; she had a few answers. Still, she needed to know what had happened to Dad's share in the business. Why was his checking account wiped out?

Slowly, she took a seat at the kitchen table and flipped open Daddy's checkbook. She should have taken an interest long ago. He'd always told her that he'd make sure she—they—didn't need to worry.

Hey, Dad, I'm worrying here.

She rubbed her finger over the black ink. He had tiny handwriting, always print, and it slanted ridiculously to the right. He'd chase down a penny if his balance didn't add up. Sighing, she pushed away the evidence she couldn't change, at least not at the moment and not in her current frame of mind.

Heading for the living room, she joined Robby on the floor. He'd managed to crawl under the coffee table and was running a little green train across a terrain of brown carpet. She started to get up, but he said, "Stay, Mommy, stay." He could play for hours and loved having her sit right beside him. He didn't want her to play, just to be by his side. Apparently, she hadn't inherited the I-know-how-to-push-trains-across-the-carpet gene. If she reached for one, he would say, "Noooo."

It was okay if Pop Pop reached for one, though, and choo-chooed around the room. And if one of Natalie's or Pop Pop's friends stopped by, they were welcome to play. Just not Natalie. There were other things for her to do, like hold her hand at the ready so Robby didn't bump his head when he finally wriggled out from under the coffee table. Her hand often made the difference between smiles and tears.

There'd been too many tears her hands couldn't prevent lately.

She leaned against the couch and closed her eyes. When she opened them again, Robby remained happily entertained, sprawled under the coffee table. Natalie stared at the photographs hanging on the living room wall. The earliest showed the ranch as it looked in 1910, with lots of brush and dirt, four cowboys, two dogs and six horses. Natalie didn't know if the building in the background was the beginnings of the ranch or an outhouse.

The newest photo, one taken by her father, showed a ranch with trees and lots of green grass, no cowboys, no dogs and, since her accident, no horses. The house—white, sprawling and two-storied—had two chairs on the porch and Robby's tricycle on the path.

The phone rang loud, unwelcome and jarring. She'd left it off the hook too often lately. Condolences from those who had loved her father seemed to deepen her sorrow, not relieve it. Then, there was Lucky Welch, the bull rider who was staying with the Bakers, who knew where she lived and who could definitely find her phone number.

She let it ring. Maybe he'd go away. Maybe hiding out was working. But she couldn't hide for long. The postman knew where she lived. Robby heard the sound of the mail truck. He loved the postman, who often had peppermints in his pockets.

"Mama!" Robby was at the door and twisting the knob before she made it off the floor. She needn't have hurried. The postman was out of his truck and coming up the walk.

"You got something official," he said. "Probably about your daddy."

Natalie took the envelope, the official-looking envelope, and stared at the return address.

She couldn't breathe.

She couldn't swallow, either.

Opening the screen door, she wandered onto the front porch and collapsed in a wooden rocker. The smooth wood creaked under her weight, or maybe it creaked because she held the weight of the world upon her shoulders.

How had it all gone so wrong?

And though it was the last thing she wanted to do, she went inside and opened the envelope. Inside was a single sheet on fancy letterhead. She'd been right to berate herself for a foolhardy action, right to worry about a custody battle, right to wonder what kind of man Lucky Welch was.

He wasn't his brother, that was for sure. No, instead, Lucky got things done.

Attending the rodeo and approaching Lucky had been stupid. She'd done this on her own. With no help from anyone else, she'd made her life a soap opera. Suddenly, losing her home didn't seem such a disaster, not when she compared it to losing Robby.

The lawyer's letter was straightforward. Lucas William Welch requested a meeting. The letter suggested it be in Selena. Lucky's lawyer would travel here, and it specified a date and a time next week. If the date and time were not convenient, she was instructed to call.

With trembling hands, she laid the letter on the kitchen table and looked into the living room where

Robby busied himself by pounding on the coffee table with a toy train.

"Robby, stop!"

He looked at her, looked at the train, and then gently tapped it on the coffee table.

For the past three days, she'd been faced with a curious child and no words to explain what had happened. Robby had so many questions. Who was the cowboy and why did he come to the house? Why was Mommy crying all the time? Why couldn't he go to a friend's house? She'd settled for telling Robby that she didn't feel well, and that the rodeo brought back old memories and so did Lucky. It wasn't a complete truth, but it certainly wasn't a lie, either.

Oh, what had she done?

For the last three days, instead of holing up, she should have been busy finding herself a lawyer because no way could she bear to lose Robby, especially so soon after her father's death, or any other time, for that matter.

Selena had two lawyers. One had been her father's. He was old-fashioned and spent more time patting Natalie on the hand when she asked questions about her dad's money than he had investigating where the money had gone. Sunni Foreman was brand-new to the community and trying to make a dent in what had always been, at least in Selena, a man's world. A quick phone call got Natalie an afternoon appointment. A second phone call arranged for Patty to watch Robby. Robby was more than ready for an afternoon of play with other kids, and he didn't even cry when she left him.

Sunni Foreman shared office space with an accoun-

tant and a wedding planner. They didn't share a secretary. Natalie noticed that the waiting room was clean
and had current magazines. The chairs looked new and,
before she could knock, Ms. Foreman, as the plaque
on the door read, stuck her head out of her office and
said, "Come on in."

The good news was that everything happened so fast
that before Natalie could get nervous, she was sitting
in a comfortable maroon chair in an office with a picture of George Washington on the wall and the scent
of cinnamon apples all around. Ms. Foreman started
to sit down, then left the room for a moment. "Call me
Sunni," the lawyer said when she returned, bringing
Natalie a glass of water.

Sunni stood over six feet tall, had frizzy blond hair
that certainly deserved the woman's moniker, and wore
a white top with a blue jacket over a pair of well-worn
blue jeans. Natalie had seen her around town at the grocery store, the library and such. She wasn't the type of
woman likely to be missed.

Opening her purse, Natalie handed Sunni the letter.

Sunni sat at her desk, reached for glasses and held
them instead of putting them on. "Before I read this,
why don't you, in your own words, tell me what's going
on."

Natalie took a drink of the cold water. Setting the
glass down carefully, Natalie took a breath, and the
words poured out of her so fast they tumbled right
over each other. She started with her father's death,
the money situation and the mistake at the rodeo, then
went on to finding out she did have money, and finally arrived at Lucky's visit to the ranch and the letter Sunni was holding.

When she finished, she almost felt better, but not quite. Her father's death wasn't the beginning, and with her lawyer, she needed to start at the beginning.

Tisha showing up at Natalie's place in New Mexico, a tiny baby in her arms, was the real beginning.

Sunni opened the letter from Lucky's lawyer and read. After a moment she said, "Seems pretty straightforward. By your own admission, Marcus Welch is the father. His family does deserve visitation, and you are the one who initiated contact. Tell me what you want out of this upcoming meeting."

"I—I want it so that nothing changes."

"That's a pretty broad request and judging by this letter, it's not an option."

Reaching down, Natalie put her hand in her purse and curled her fingers around a stiff manila envelope. She didn't bring it out, couldn't yet, because she didn't want to cry, didn't want to acknowledge the fear threatening to spill over.

The tick, tick, tick of the office's plain brown clock seemed to get louder before Sunni, who looked at Natalie like she could see right into her soul, gently continued. "Is there any reason to deny them a chance to get to know Robby? Fathers, and their families, have rights. Unless you're worried they might abduct Robby, I don't see why you need me. My best advice is to call this Lucas Welch, apologize for how you ended his last contact and ask if you can meet without lawyers."

Natalie swallowed. Nowhere in the television shows about lawyers, the books she'd read about lawyers and in the dealings she'd witnessed with her dad's lawyer had she heard the words...*without lawyers*. Well, she'd wanted an honest lawyer; looked like she'd found one.

Natalie's fingers still curled around the envelope. Now, she tightened her grip and slowly brought the envelope to the desk. "There's a reason why I need a lawyer and a reason why I don't want this meeting with the Welches." Leaning forward, Natalie asked the question that she most dreaded hearing the answer to. "Anything we discuss in here is private, privileged, right?"

"Yes." The lawyer waited silently, as if knowing Natalie needed time to regroup. Silence was a type of pressure.

"Well, um, the letter instructed me to bring one thing. Robby's birth certificate."

"Do you have it?"

"I do."

Before Natalie could change her mind, Sunni Foreman's hand reached across the desk and Natalie relinquished the packet.

Inside was a copy of Robby's birth certificate. Sunni pulled that out first, glanced at it, glanced at Natalie, and then pulled out the rest of the papers. After a moment, she looked at Natalie again. "Okay, I see your dilemma. What is it you hope I can do for you?"

"I can't negotiate any rights for Robby," Natalie said. "I can't sign any paperwork. But I want, I deserve, to be the one who calls the shots. That little boy is mine, and I want what's best for him."

"And you're what's best for Robby?" Sunni asked.

"I am."

Sunni nodded, leaned forward and said, "You've got no ammunition here, nothing to help your case, not even guardianship papers. Marcus's family will have the law on their side. You knew Marcus was the father but never informed him, so basically, you've been raising his son without his knowledge or permission."

"But Tisha—"

"Abandoned her son."

"I took him when no one wanted him."

"Don't even begin to go with that argument." Sunni tapped the letter from Lucky's lawyer. "This is just the first step in a long walk that leads to how many people want Robby."

"I…" Natalie stopped talking. Tears dripped down her nose. She'd spent more time crying this last month than she had her whole life, including when her dad sold off all the horses.

Sunni waited, her face a neutral mask of professionalism. It was just what Natalie needed. Tears didn't win wars; lawyers did.

"What do we do first?" Natalie finally said, bracing herself. She had no clue what advice the lawyer would give. She just hoped there would be advice.

"We get your cousin Tisha to sign over guardianship." Sunni picked up her pen. "What's Tisha's number?"

"I—" Natalie managed a weak smile "—have no idea."

Lucky was back at Bernice's after spending the weekend on the road. He'd gone to Vinita, Oklahoma. He'd already paid the entry fee, and he needed the purse. Plus, he was going stir-crazy hanging around Bernice's place, waiting to hear from the lawyer and forcing himself not to drive to Natalie's place. Then, too, he was feeling guilty about keeping a secret from his mother. She was still in Selena, at the end of what she called a two-week vacation. She'd be heading back to Austin next weekend. He needed to tell her soon. He needed to call his father, too, but not until he was sure.

He could only call the last few days educational. He'd learned that when on the bull, he indeed *forgot* everything else, so great was his concentration. Off the bull, he *couldn't forget* Natalie and Robby Crosby. He remembered the way her hand automatically went to Robby's shoulders, a protective move. He remembered how her blue eyes snapped, looking right at him.

And he remembered Robby, who he could clearly see now looked so much like Marcus.

His body had been at the rodeo; his thoughts were in Selena, but Selena wasn't a paycheck. While Bernice served up breakfast, Lucky took out his calendar and started checking dates. At Vinita, he'd walked— okay, limped—away in third place. Respectable, yes. Advisable, no. He'd met up with Travis Needham there, and he and the rookie decided to travel together some. Made sense since Lucky's new jumping off place was Selena. Still, the commitment also reminded Lucky of his last partner, his brother.

Where was Lucky due next weekend? Could he afford to miss a rodeo or two and deal with Natalie and Robby, or did he need the standings? Before he had time to make a decision, his cell phone rang.

"Wish you wouldn't bring that to the table," his mother scolded, glowering at the phone.

He checked the number. Finally, his lawyer. He excused himself. Ten minutes later, he returned to the kitchen, having reached an agreement with his lawyer and had a disagreement with his father. Bernice busied herself by pouring more orange juice. Howie Junior stomped off to get ready for school.

"You know what I wish?" Lucky said.

"That you'd done better than third?" Bernice guessed.

He had to grin. Trust Bernice to cut to the chase. Too bad she had the wrong topic.

"That Bernice was making fried chicken again tonight." This guess came from his mother. They'd played the game before. Lots of times. Usually with Marcus. Never with their father. He'd found it a waste of time. "If you want to say something, say it," he'd demand. If they didn't manage to say the words in a certain amount of time, Henry Welch would put on his hat and be out the door.

Marcus tired of the game after a while, but Lucky never had.

"I wish things never changed."

His mother nodded, and Lucky knew she was thinking about Marcus, maybe even thinking of when her two boys had been young and dependent on her.

"Things have to change." Bernice handed Howie his lunch and ushered him to the porch just as the school bus pulled up out front.

Lucky looked out the window, at Howie running to the school bus. He and Marcus had walked to school or their mother had driven them. Big cities had the luxury of schools every few miles. Not so here in Selena. As a matter of fact, his mother had been bused to Selena from Delaney. She'd spent two hours a day on the bus.

"I never did homework," she'd joked. "I always did buswork."

When Bernice came back in the kitchen, Lucky

pushed aside his breakfast and asked, "Bern, do you
have any pictures of us, me and Marcus, when we were
little? Say about four or five."

"Ten, twelve or a hundred, probably."

"Can I see one when Marcus was, oh, about three
or four?"

"Can you? Yes. May you? I don't know. Why?" She
gave him a strange look and went to get a picture.

A moment later, Lucky studied the photo. She'd chosen one taken at his grandfather's place. He and Marcus stood in front of a carpet-covered barrel. Marcus
wasn't looking at the camera. He concentrated on the
practice barrel, and Lucky, who knew his older brother
well, figured Marcus resented the time posing for the
camera took away from the pretend bull. Lucky, ever
the good son, looked right at the camera and grinned.
Even at four, he was a poser.

"Mom, Bern, do you remember when we were this
little?"

Bernice looked at Lucky's mom and took the picture. "Of course we remember when you were little.
This was taken when you were about four. I think Marcus was five. Am I right, Betsy?"

Lucky's mom took the picture. A slow smile crossed
her face. "Yes, I took the picture because every time
my mother tried to get Marcus to stand still, he ran
over and got on that barrel." Betsy chuckled. "Your
grandmother got so mad she stomped into the house
and said she didn't care if she ever got a picture of the
two of you together or not. Somewhere, we have five
or six pictures of Marcus standing on that barrel and
you looking up at him."

Yes, Lucky looked up to his brother, even during Marcus's dark days.

Whoever loves his brother lives in the light, and there is nothing in time to make him stumble.

The Bible verse echoed in his heart as loneliness slammed into Lucky's gut with a force that almost uprooted him.

He missed Marcus. Oh, how he missed his brother.

"Mom, tomorrow I'm meeting with my lawyer."

His mother laid the picture on the table. "Why? Are you thinking that rodeo doctor could have done something more, that maybe Marcus needn't have died?"

"No," he said slowly, surprised that his mother jumped to such a conclusion so quickly. He almost lost his nerve.

"Lucas." Bernice used his given name. Not a good sign. "Why did you want me to fetch that picture? You want to tell us what's going on?"

"No, I don't want to tell you." He was still speaking too slowly, but he couldn't seem to help it. "But I probably need to."

And he needed for his father to be here, but per the three-minute phone call, Lucky knew that wouldn't be happening *yet*. Henry Stanton Welch's absence proved some things, some people, never changed. A few minutes ago, after he'd hung up from the lawyer, Lucky had called his father. He didn't mention Robby. Lucky only mentioned a family meeting, an *important* family meeting, and when could he come?

His father's first response was that the important family meeting should take place in Austin, and by his tone, Lucky knew that the word *important* didn't impress one bit. Next, Dad got out his calendar and couldn't decide. Finally, Lucky did what he usually did when trying to get through to his father. He gave up. Yet, in the long run, Lucky's father would be mad at missing this meeting. No, come to think of it, his father would be more than mad that he wasn't put in charge of the *problem*.

But Robby was not a problem; he was a gift. *Every good and perfect gift is from above, coming down from the Father of the heavenly lights, who does not change like shifting shadows.*

With that verse resonating in his mind, Lucky looked at the two women who'd stayed silent while he fought his memories. "I'm meeting with my lawyer tomorrow with and concerning Natalie Crosby."

He got out of his chair and came to kneel on the floor beside his mother. "Mom, by any chance did you see the little boy Natalie had with her at the rodeo?"

"No."

"Little Robby," Bernice supplied. "He's full of spit and vinegar. When he was a baby, his grandpa Leo would take him everywhere. Carried that baby seat like it was just another arm. I think he got three marriage proposals based on the way he loved that boy."

"That boy," Lucky said slowly, "is the spitting image of Marcus."

His mother's mouth opened, but no words came out.

Bernice's eyebrows drew together, then her lips pursed for just a moment before she said, "Oh. Oh. Oh…."

She might have "oh'd" forever except Lucky took the picture from his mother and walked it over to Bernice. "Tell me I'm wrong. You've seen Robby since he was little. Tell me I'm wrong."

"Oh, my." She looked up from the photo. "I can't quite grasp this. You think Robby is Marcus's son? No, little Natalie and Marcus? I just can't see..." Her words faded, but her facial expression didn't. She did see.

"Yes, little Natalie and Marcus," Lucky said. "Marcus has a son."

A chair screeched across the kitchen floor and Betsy, a wild look in her eyes, grabbed the photo from Bernice's hand. "Marcus? Marcus has a son? No way. We'd know."

Bernice's mouth was still open in a perfect O. It looked like she wanted to say something. Silence didn't sit well with Betsy. Lucky's mom grabbed Bernice by the arm. "Why do you look so spooked? This cannot be true."

"Oh, it just might be. What was I thinking? I remember seeing Natalie at the grocery store with Robby and thinking he was a good-looking kid. Why didn't I realize where he got his good looks from? Oh, my. What are you going to do, Lucky?"

Maybe change my stupid nickname, Lucky thought. He sure didn't feel lucky. He felt kicked in the stomach. All this time, his brother's son had been living in the same town as his mother's best friend, really only a stone's throw from where his mother grew up.

"And little Natalie Crosby's his mother," Aunt Bernice repeated. "She's a town favorite, you know."

He knew.

Not exactly a hanging offense.

Just an annoying roadblock.

"How old is he?" Mom asked.

"Three, he's three," Bernice said. "I remember when Natalie showed up with him. She went away to college and came home a mommy. Remember? I told you. And I couldn't imagine what kind of man wouldn't step up to the plate." She covered her mouth with her hand. The unspoken name "Marcus" lingering in the air.

"Robby. I have a grandson named Robby." Betsy sat back down, as pale as Lucky'd ever seen her.

"And I'm going to find out our rights tomorrow, when we meet with the lawyer."

Lucky's mother slumped forward, her eyes closed. Dark circles huddled under her eyes. "Three years, and nobody told us. We need to call your father and—"

"Mom, we're not sure about anything, the whys, the whats, the hows. That's why we're meeting tomorrow with lawyers. Let's tell Dad after we have proof, something tangible."

"Betsy, I'm still going to say that Natalie's a good girl. I'm—I'm flabbergasted at this information. I cannot picture her with Marcus…"

"Marcus never had trouble getting females," Betsy mumbled. "They started calling him when he was in second grade. His father and I, we tried to teach him right from wrong."

It was like Lucky wasn't there. Or worse, he was a teenager again. The irritable teenager who stood in his parents' living room while everyone discussed his future. Which college he would go to; what he would major in; whether he should live in the dorm the first few years or would an apartment be better?

Marcus had endured the same and had packed up in the middle of the night, left, and didn't call for two months.

Lucky'd disappointed them, too, but he'd been a man about it. He'd told his parents his plans.

Dad said not to let the door hit him on the way out.

This morning, Lucky's mother had the same look on her face as she'd had that night Lucky had walked out. Disappointment in life, disappointment in her children.

Why couldn't Lucky have found Robby in Timbuktu? Away from family, away from a family history that was so hurtful, where he'd have time to set things to right?

Probably because Timbuktu didn't have a rodeo.

Chapter Five

Finding Tisha had become Natalie's number one—no, number two—duty. Robby came first. While Sunni searched the Internet for information on Tisha, Natalie used her dialing finger.

Neither venture garnered much progress. Sunni found three Tisha Crosbys, none the Tisha they were looking for. Natalie found the few postcards Tisha had sent. Since dropping off Robby, Tisha changed boy-friends and addresses about every six months, but judg-ing by the postal marks, it had been over a year since she'd last made contact. Natalie really didn't have a single phone number. Using the return addresses and the Internet, in a week's time, Natalie found and spoke to a movie-star boyfriend, a dentist boyfriend and, of all things, an animal trainer. He'd sounded nice.

The most recent postcard proved to be the most dif-ficult to track. According to Tisha's brief note, she was happy; he was wealthy. Natalie had an address and no name. At least on the earlier postcards there'd been names. It took Natalie three days to find a number. Judging by the clipped tones, Natalie figured Tisha hadn't made any friends in this household. According to the "Livingston Residence" Tisha'd been gone for two months, no forwarding address, and please don't call again.

At that point, Sunni made her next suggestion: hire a private detective to find Tisha.

Unfortunately, they'd only arrived at the decision yesterday. Today, Natalie and her lawyer had to meet with Lucky and his lawyer and hopefully delay any action.

Selena's courthouse was the oldest building in town. It was a redbrick monstrosity, a facade that misrepresented the town's size and importance. Natalie stepped from her car and pulled her coat tighter around her. Texas weather, ever fickle, had changed from warm to cold in the blink of an eye.

The chill seemed foreboding. The sting of the weather matched the biting fear that gripped her heart.

She saw her lawyer's car, but, unfortunately, she didn't see Sunni.

Robby was over at Patty's, enjoying a day on the farm and getting dirty. Patty would feed him candy and let him follow her own kids around. He'd eat dirt and have a wonderful time.

"Are you all right?"

Natalie blinked. She'd been standing beside her car, not moving. And, wouldn't you know it, Lucky Welch was now standing next to her.

"No, I'm not."

"I'm not, either," he said gently.

He didn't look like a bull rider today. He looked like an urban professional. He wore light brown slacks and a white dress shirt. Over it, he had a too-small brown jacket. One that emphasized the broadness of his shoulders, the strength in his arms. He still wore boots, well-worn and also brown.

"Can we just stop this?" Natalie asked hopefully. "Turn around and pretend I never approached you?"

"No," he said. "My mother's waiting at Bernice's. It was all I could do to keep her from attending. We need to come to some solutions today that work for both of us because I have to let my father know all that's going on, and the more we decide together, you and I, the easier it will be."

"This day is not going to be easy," Natalie predicted.

"It's going to be a lot easier than if my father was involved. If he were involved, you'd need a more expensive lawyer, and I wouldn't be using a man I love and trust who specializes in sports law."

Sports law? Lucky Welch was using a man he loved and trusted and not a cutthroat? Natalie studied Lucky's face. He looked sad, lonely, and maybe even wistful.

She wished she looked the same. She looked, felt, terrified, lonely and threatened. Not the combination she really wanted. But one she deserved. A moment's desperation, a rash act, had culminated in this.

She turned and walked away. Lucky Welch, the preacher, may have been sincere when he asked, *"Are you all right?"* But he was also sincere when he said, *"You're going to need a more expensive lawyer."*

He was not on her side.

They met in a conference room. It was as brown as Lucky's outfit and smelled like Lysol. Lucky's lawyer, Paul Wilfong, didn't act expensive. Lucky was dressed better than Mr. Wilfong. The lawyer wore jeans, a flannel shirt and boots that looked like they needed to be replaced.

Sunni nodded for Natalie to take a seat on one side of the table. She put a slim folder on the surface and sat beside Natalie. Before she could protest, Paul Wilfong was helping adjust her chair.

Sunni's lips pressed together.

Wilfong just grinned.

If this were any other place or time, Natalie might enjoy the show, but if this Wilfong fellow was putting on a show, it had better not be to disarm them.

"Let's begin," Sunni said after both Lucky and Wilfong sat down.

Wilfong looked at Natalie and remarked, "You sure do resemble Tisha."

Natalie felt Sunni's hand gently pat her knee. Good thing, because Natalie didn't have the breath to respond. Sunni said, "We're here to talk about the custody of Robert Crosby."

"No middle name?" Lucky said, seemingly to nobody.

"No."

Wilfong, apparently, didn't have a folder to place on the table. He also didn't carry a briefcase. He folded his hands in front of him. "Let's pray first."

Without argument, Sunni and Lucky both bowed their heads. Natalie sat stunned. Bowing her head seemed almost to imply an agreement, and she didn't want to agree to anything. And since when did a meeting requiring legal assistance start with a prayer?

Her father's lawyer never prayed.

After his "amen," Mr. Wilfong looked at both women. Then he said in a voice that sent a chill down

Natalie's spine, "I'm not a children's advocate. I've never handled a custody case. I do, however, know the right lawyer to steer Lucky to, and I also know, having children myself, that if you two can come to an agreement outside the courtroom, it's best for everyone. Madam, do you have something to say?"

Natalie glanced at Sunni. Sunni had been hoping to speak first. The prayer certainly one-upped that idea. Sunni had wanted to set the stage, the tone, and have the upper hand because, truthfully, the team of Natalie and Sunni had only one weapon to support their claim to Robby: the guardianship papers Tisha had yet to sign.

Sunni was looking at Lucky. Her hand was atop the folder. Inside that folder lay the birth certificate, a paper that would end the negotiations right now and Lucky wouldn't need a high-dollar lawyer.

"I say," Sunni said easily, "we leave the room and let these two see what they can come up with without us."

"I'd like that," Lucky said. If trustworthy was searching for a national spokesperson, then judging by the look on Lucky's face, the self-assured way he held himself, he'd be the man for the job.

"Natalie, say the words. Tell me to go or to stay. You're in charge," Sunni prodded.

Great, just great. If Natalie said no, she'd be the one dragging her feet, the one not willing to be a team player. If she said yes, she alone would be negotiating Robby's future. She swallowed and said, "I'll stay. You go."

Wilfong opened the door for Sunni. On the way out, her lawyer's eyes fell on the folder still lying on the table. Then, her eyes raised to meet Natalie's. One tiny nod encouraged Natalie that she could do it.

When the door closed, Natalie noticed that she and Lucky sat in a room without a window. She pressed her lips together. Trapped. In a hole she'd dug herself.

"You want to take a walk?" Lucky suggested. "We don't have to stay here." Suddenly, he appeared chagrined. "I mean, it doesn't hurt you to walk, does it?"

"What? I can walk." For a moment, Natalie was confused. "Oh, someone told you about the accident. My leg only hurts, really, when the weather is about to change or I'm really stressed."

Lucky grinned. "I'll take the fact that it doesn't hurt as a good sign. You're not stressed."

"Yet," Natalie said. "Or maybe I've been so stressed lately that my body no longer recognizes stress."

"I'm going to stand by my original thought, that you're not stressed." Lucky stood and came around the table. "Let's walk. I know it's cold, but there's a diner just down the street. I'd love some coffee, and we'll be in—" he looked around "—a little less sterile environment."

"Okay." Natalie stood and took the folder. It lay accusingly on the table, a constant reminder of how impossible it was to discern right from wrong *emotionally.* Folding it, she put it in her purse and prayed she wouldn't need to open it.

Lucky walked slow enough. While Natalie waved at people she knew, people who would be sure to call later and ask about the young man she was with, he rambled about the weather, about his mother, about Delaney and about his love for small towns.

Right. Sure.

Like some rodeo Romeo would be willing to settle for one choice at the movie theater, no McDonald's and streets that rolled up at nine unless you were a drinker.

Okay, his grandparents were from practically next door in Delaney, and it wasn't fair for her to compare Lucky to Marcus.

Right before the waitress seated them in a back booth, Lucky mentioned seeing her father's grave.

"When did you see it?" she asked.

"Last week. I headed for Delaney. I wanted to drive by my grandparents' place. Then I stopped at the cemetery."

"Makes sense. I probably should have realized. How many years has your family been in the area?" She was surprised to discover she really wanted to know. Lucky, either by the gift of gab or by a burning desire to make her like him, had managed to find topics that felt safe.

"My grandpa moved to Delaney in 1942, following his parents. They were in Abilene first. I think we've had family in West Texas for at least a hundred years."

"You'd love my living room," Natalie said. "Dad put up pictures from when the ranch was just starting. We have pictures of the Selena and Delaney area dating back more than a hundred years. My favorite old tintype shows what looks to me like an outhouse but I think is actually the original house."

"I'd love to see it," Lucky said.

Suddenly, the menu looked like a good defense. Natalie picked hers up and held it so it covered her face. What had she just done? Invited him over? No, no, no. Maybe the gift of gab was beneficial only to the speaker. She'd just walked into a trap.

When she put the menu down, not even noticing a single item she hungered for, Lucky was studying her.

"Natalie, I can't even imagine how uncomfortable you are, how threatened you feel, but, believe me, I, my family, we don't want to be the enemy. We want to help. We want to get to know Marcus's little boy, and if we can make this a win-win situation, everybody, especially Robby, benefits. Please meet me halfway."

The waitress came at that moment. Lucky ordered coffee and a cinnamon roll. Natalie decided on ice tea. When it arrived, she took a long drink and then said, "What do you want?"

He took a folded piece of paper from his pocket and stared at it. "Paul has a typed, more legalized version of this, but my notes are the same." Looking at her, he said, "My mother and I put this together yesterday." He slid the paper across the table. "Here."

He wrote in all capital letters. They were straight, and he seemed to like leaving extra spaces between each word. The top half of the paper was labeled "short-term." The bottom half was labeled "long-term." Each half had only three items.

Six altogether.

Six too many.

Short-term, he wanted Robby to be introduced to the Welches, first as friends, then as family. He wanted that to happen sometime next week. As if he knew right where she was reading, he said, "You can tell him on your own, or we could maybe have a cookout at Bernice's. Neutral territory. She loves you and says she can't imagine a better single parent. But you don't need to be a single parent. We'll help. Bernice said you dropped out of college to raise Robby. If you want to go back, we'll help with money."

"What?" She glanced at the paper, and then back up at him. Going back to school, for her, was listed under long-term, along with money negotiations and holidays.

"We'll help with money.…"

"Are you for real?"

He pinched himself, exaggerating, and with a grin on his face. It looked silly, but it did take an edge off the fear that was starting to pool in her stomach again.

"I'm for real."

"This is happening so fast. I mean, I've hired Sunni Foreman just to try to make sense of what legal rights—" she almost said *I have.* Instead, she said "—you have. She seems to think quite a bit. My dad says—said—not to completely trust lawyers. I'm pretty sure he'd also be inclined not to trust you."

"Your dad must have been quite a man. I hear he looked after Robby as his own. I'm only sorry that I can't shake his hand, thank him, on behalf of our family."

He reached across the table and put his hand over hers. She almost tugged it away, almost made a face, but again, he looked so sincere.

"I'm gone most weekends to rodeos, and people are counting on me. But I'm going to take to flying a bit more now and also make Selena my home base."

Well, that would take care of the next two items on the short-term list. After the initial meeting, Lucky wanted to take Robby to church on Wednesday evenings, and then he wanted the family to have permission to visit at least one Saturday a month.

Lucky continued, "I'm making Robby my business,

at least until we're all comfortable with where we fit in as a family. Please agree to the potluck at Bernice's. I promise, we'll take everything slow. First, this Saturday, and then we'll wait a few weeks before we either do church or a family outing. If it seems too fast for Robby, we can wait a little while before we tell him. But he needs to know us. We want to know him. We're going to make sure my brother Marcus's son has everything he needs. And, as Robby's mother, we'd like the same for you."

Natalie swallowed. The words sounded so innocent. And they were true. She'd dropped out of school to take care of Robby. Robby, who *was* Marcus's son, *not* Natalie's.

The son Marcus apparently hadn't known about.

"If I say yes to this meeting, to letting your family get to know Robby, all you want to do is help, be involved, not take?" Her voice broke. Just three weeks ago, she'd lost her father. He'd been taken from her. Today, sitting across from her, was the man who could easily take Robby away.

"All you want to do is help, get to know Robby," she repeated slowly.

"Yes."

The folder remained in her purse. She didn't need it. For a moment, she was safe. The list went with it. Lucky wanted to get to know Robby, take the boy to church, help financially and, so far, *without legal strings*. If she agreed, then the birth certificate remained hidden, at least for now.

"Okay," Natalie said. "We'll come to the potluck. Depending on how that day goes, I'll tell him you're related to his father."

She half expected him to whoop; instead, he bent his head. His lips moved, and she could hear his muffled words of thanks.

Lucky was thanking God for answering his prayer. Only Natalie knew that Lucky's prayer was misdirected and that he deserved a lot more than he was receiving.

The phone call came early morning Wednesday while Natalie uploaded, cropped and then enhanced jewelry photos for one of her clients. The finishing touches, and the ones that kept her clients with her, were the details. For this client, she added what she called diamond dazzle. When a prospective buyer went to the Web site, not only would the display be attractive, but the jewelry the client most wanted sold would sparkle, literally.

Playing with dazzle wasn't enough to keep Natalie from worrying.

All Tuesday afternoon and evening, she'd been expecting the ax to fall, expecting to find that the list that looked so simple was not. So hearing Betsy Welch's voice on the other end of the phone was no surprise.

After all, Natalie and Lucky had met just yesterday, sent their lawyers home and agreed on the short-term. But there were twenty-four hours between yesterday and today. Hours that were probably a long time to a grandmother who wanted to meet her only grandson.

Betsy Welch managed to turn Natalie's name into Nat-tal-lee. Natalie's own grandmother had done the same, and Mrs. Welch wept more than she spoke. Maybe the tears were more responsible for the name mangling than the Texas drawl.

Natalie left the computer. Mood always affected her

overall performance. Her client wouldn't want to see a digital smorgasbord of black, brooding diamonds when it came to his display. Instead of pounding on the computer keys, Natalie paced in front of the couch as Lucky's mother talked about wanting to get to know Robby, and about her son Marcus—she assumed, of course, Natalie really knew him—and about staying in Selena longer. Natalie winced at that pronouncement and kicked a toy train out of the way before bending down to pick up a pillow. One thing for sure, if this woman was wrangling for an invitation to the house, she wasn't getting one. Right now Natalie's living room did not look like something from the pages of *Better Homes and Gardens*. It looked like *Return of the Three-Year-Old Tornado*.

But Mrs. Welch didn't ask if she could stop by the house, pretend to be selling household goods or a church lady. Betsy wanted something else, something a little more convenient, something straight from the list, except that it was an item Lucky and Natalie had agreed to put on hold. "Let's meet at church tonight. Real innocent. Just let me see him. I need to see him. I—"

When Betsy finally took a breath, Natalie jumped in. "I'll think about it." A no-frills answer, and one that shut Mrs. Welch up, until Robby ran into the room, that is.

"Momma, who's on the phone? Why I no get to answer?"

"You were asleep, honey."

He nodded, an exaggerated response and reached for the phone. Until Pop Pop's death, they'd been letting

Robby pick up the beloved instrument and say "Hi" before taking the phone and giving a real salutation.

To Robby, getting to answer or at least talk on the phone was as good as Christmas.

"It's a lady I know. She's inviting us to church tonight."

"Church?"

"Yes, you know, where Patty and Daniel go every Wednesday and Sunday?"

"Oh, yeah. We go?"

"We're not sure." Natalie looked at the phone. Betsy Welch was still talking. Natalie could hear her asking, "Is that Robby?"

Maybe Natalie should call Sunni Foreman. Lucky had walked her to Sunni's office after she'd agreed to a Saturday outing at Bernice's and after they'd finished eating. It had been a long walk, all of fifteen minutes, and all Natalie could think of was that Lucky Welch was making this his home base just to be near his nephew.

Right. How long would it last?

He was rodeo from his hat to his heart, and he was in his prime.

It wouldn't last.

But Lucky wasn't Marcus.

And what really bothered Natalie was that after she repeated, "We'll think about it," and hung up, her first impulse was to call Lucky.

After all, it was his list she'd agreed to; it was his list she'd stared at last night when sleep refused to visit. Yes, church attendance was on it. But they'd agreed to start slowly, with Saturday.

One day after their initial meeting was definitely not

slowly. One day after their initial meeting, and things were already changing, meant Natalie had to tell Robby a few things about family, and pray that her family— namely Tisha—stayed away until Natalie could sort out what to do, what to say, *how long she could hide,* and the guardianship issue.

Mrs. Welch suggested an innocent meeting tonight. An "Oh, by the way, Robby, these are some people you need to know" kind of thing. And Natalie, already skittish, felt threatened.

By church as much as by Betsy Welch.

Natalie had gone to church with Patty when they were kids. Vacation Bible School was fun, lots of Kool-Aid and animal crackers, but other than that, it was a lot of sitting still and being quiet. It would drive Robby nuts. He wasn't a sit-still kind of child. What if he misbehaved? What if Betsy Welch determined Natalie wasn't a good mother?

Natalie hadn't agreed to attend, but she hadn't disagreed, either. It wasn't easy to say no to a crying grandmother. Her father would say she was prolonging the inevitable. Well, so be it. Then again, her lawyer would say she was tempting fate.

Her lawyer attended the Main Street Church. Yesterday afternoon, with Lucky's visitation wishes spread on the lawyer's desk, Sunni asked, "If the roles were reversed, and Robby was your kin and being raised by someone else, is this list more than, just right or less than what you would hope for?"

The list was less than she'd have asked for. Anyone who knew Robby, the kind of kid he was, the joy he brought, would know that no list of sporadic meetings here and there would be enough.

"It's a reasonable request," Natalie had agreed.

Just her luck to find a lawyer who reasoned and who valued right over money.

There'd be no Monday-night movie made about Sunni. What you saw was what you got.

Almost too perfect.

And right there in the office, Natalie had seen a picture of Sunni Foreman standing with a group of kids all wearing Main Street Church Bible Bowl Champions 2008 shirts.

"I wanna go to church. Let's go." Robby was up for anything and truly believed that the next place was better than the place he was. It was a characteristic he'd inherited from Tisha.

That comparison was so truly right-on, Natalie sank onto the couch and whispered, "Oh, no."

"What wrong, Mommy?"

"Nothing. Just something Mommy needs to do. Go get your trains while I make a few phone calls. When I'm done, I'll build a track with you."

Robby's eyes lit up. His favorite thing! Next to talking on the phone and going somewhere and Christmas. They were going to put train tracks together. Life just didn't get any better.

Oh, to be three again.

"We play train!" he jabbered excitedly.

"In just a minute." That's all it took. A moment later, Robby dug out his blue track and was sorting his trains by which had working batteries and which needed new ones.

Most of the trains needed batteries. Batteries had been Pop Pop's job. Natalie knew where they were, how to put them in, but she cried every time.

Batteries were Pop Pop's job.

Bandages were Natalie's job, but they didn't make one big enough to fix all that was wrong in their lives at the moment.

Chapter Six

The Main Street Church put every other building in
Selena to shame. It received a fresh coat of white paint
every year, and if Natalie didn't know better, she'd
suspect the minister, Tate Brown, even spray-painted
the lawn green.

Natalie, following the Selena church crowd's example, pulled into the parking lot at the exact moment
church began. Just two spots down, Patty was unload-
ing her kids.

"Girl!" she called. "I can't keep up with you. You
about knocked me down when you called. First the
rodeo, now church. Are you sure you know what you're
doing?"

"No, I'm not sure." And she wasn't, but Sunni
thought church more a neutral ground than Bernice's
house. Grandma Welch would have to curb her enthu-
siasm in front of a crowd of virtual strangers. Natalie
would be the only stranger, really, at Bernice's house
on Saturday.

After getting the go-ahead from Sunni, Natalie
phoned Patty to make sure she would be at church

that evening. No way did Natalie want to go without a friend by her side during the evening service.

Since her father's death, she'd felt so alone. Surprisingly, just being in the church parking lot diminished some of those feelings. The place felt alive as friends shouted back and forth, parents hurried bundled children toward the doors and her best friend from childhood opened her arms for a hug.

Robby hit the ground and headed toward Patty. He knew a good hug when he saw one. He hopped the whole way. "We go church!" he announced, not only to Patty but also to the couple parking their car next to hers, and to the elderly man who wisely stopped walking to let the three-year-old careen by.

Natalie shook her head. "How about I pack Robby up tomorrow and we come out to the farm for a whole day?"

"Perfect," Patty said, bending down and lifting Robby up. "We'll come up with a battle plan just in case you need warriors, I mean, friends."

Daniel let go of Patty's husband's hand and ran around to take Robby's. Without so much as a by-your-leave, they disappeared up the steps and into the church. Patty rescued her nine-month-old from the car seat before turning to Natalie.

"And, as concerned as I am about what's going on between you and the Welches, it's still good to see you here at church."

Natalie looked at the white clapboard building and suddenly realized it hadn't been all that long since she'd passed through the front door.

Her father's funeral.

Before her feet could slow or her mouth protest, the

minister opened the door and stepped out. The sound of singing spilled out of the auditorium. Still, as if he didn't care that he wasn't where he was supposed to be, his greeting was as enthusiastic as Patty's.

"Natalie Crosby! An answer to my prayers…well, one of them at least. Good to have you here. Patty, are you responsible for her attendance today?"

"Only if you count my prayers as responsible."

"Nat-tal-lee." The third greeting came from Betsy Welch. She'd followed the minister and now stood at the top of the steps looking down. Her hair was the same color as Robby's. And tall…this woman and her hair were tall. Nevertheless, Betsy had on cowboy boots with a more-than-decent heel. On a good day, Natalie might have headed up the steps and tried for an even match. On a good day, she'd reach Betsy Welch's shoulder.

But it wasn't a good day.

"Where's Robby?" Betsy asked.

"He already went inside with my son," Patty said. She gave Natalie a side look and went up the stairs. "I'm Patty Dunbar. You must be Mrs. Welch?"

Betsy nodded.

"We all love Natalie," Patty said, emphasizing every word. "She's a great mother."

"That she is." Lucky stepped up beside his mother. "Robby looks happy and healthy and—"

"I understand he looks like a Welch." Betsy murmured the words, but to Natalie, they might as well have shouted.

If Natalie read the minister's facial expression correctly, then the minister was quickly realizing that the group on the steps were not strangers, and that his job as a preacher just might be needed.

"Ma'am." He turned to Betsy, no doubt figuring she was the catalyst, along with Natalie. "Is there—"

"Mommy—" Robby appeared in the doorway "— you coming?"

"Oh, my." Betsy's hands fluttered to her chest.

Robby suddenly realized he was the center of attention and grinned. He took two steps toward Natalie and halted. Looking back up, he studied Betsy Welch. Then, before Natalie could move or say a thing, he bounded back up the stairs and held out his arms.

Betsy Welch was more than willing to bend down, pick him up and hold him *like she'd never let go.*

Lucky felt sorry for the preacher. The man didn't know who to go to first. Lucky took one step, heading down the stairs, thinking Natalie might need someone to lean on.

Looks were deceiving. Natalie, with only the barest trace of a limp, advanced up the stairs.

"Mom," Lucky said, standing still, somewhat of a block between Natalie and his mother. "This is Robby Crosby, the boy I was telling you about. He came to the rodeo Saturday. He's quite the little cowboy."

"Yes, I can see he is." Betsy stroked Robby's hair and jiggled him up and down, causing giggles and making the little boy hold her even tighter.

"I not little," Robby protested. "I big."

"I can see that, too," Betsy cooed.

The door to the church opened again, and the preacher's wife poked her head out. "Tate, we've gone through three songs, and the congregation is wondering where you are."

Tate obediently looked at his watch, then looked at the group on the steps and said, "We'd better go in."

Natalie had already reached the top of the stairs. Lucky's mother didn't even notice. Natalie held out her arms, and Robby obediently turned toward her but didn't acknowledge her arms. He shook his head. "No."

This time Lucky managed to be in the right place. He put one hand on Natalie's back and the other nudged his mother forward.

"Mom," he said gently. "It's time to go in."

His mother blinked, noticed Natalie and held on to Robby.

"Mommy." Robby was blissfully unaware of the tension. "There's choo-choo in the classroom. Can I have a gink?"

"Of course you can have a drink," Natalie said. "And remember, when we go in the doors you need to talk in your quiet, inside voice."

Lucky held open the door, glad the preacher was in a hurry and glad that his mother had been in the preacher's way so that she had to enter before everyone else.

"Sorry," he whispered in Natalie's ear. "She called you while I was outside showing Howie Junior what to do with his free hand when he's riding. I about fell over when she told me what she'd done."

"I about fell over when she called," Natalie admitted.

"I really appreciate your coming tonight. It's the first time since Marcus's death that she's been this happy. She practically danced as we were heading to the car for church."

Natalie didn't respond. She clutched her purse and hurried after his mother. It was almost comical. His mother practically floated, she was so happy. What Natalie, a good foot shorter, was doing could only be described as a march, a very determined march.

Gumption, she had gumption. If she were Marcus's rebound from Tisha, then Marcus was blind. This woman shouldn't be anybody's rebound.

That thought led to another. Maybe it hadn't been rebound. Maybe there'd actually been a courtship. The people in town knew nothing about it, but Natalie had spent two years in college, away from the prying eyes of the community.

Had she loved Marcus?

Oh, he hoped so. His brother deserved at least that. Of course, if she loved Marcus, *why didn't she contact the family after Marcus died?* Let them know then that Robby existed and needed family.

Did she need comfort? Of course she did. Especially now. She'd just lost her own father and so soon after Marcus's death. No wonder she was tense.

Since Marcus's death, Lucky had more than once sermonized how the Father's comfort had been his only comfort.

He had always wondered how the nonchurched had the strength to put one step in front of the other when sorrow struck. God was Lucky's strength.

"Praise be the God and Father of our Lord Jesus Christ, the Father of compassion and the God of all comfort, who comforts us in all our troubles, so that we can comfort those in any trouble with the comfort we ourselves have received from God."

"What?" Natalie turned to face him. She'd caught up

to his mother, and now Robby was more than ready to return to Natalie. Her hand was solidly against Robby's back, and the boy had placed his cheek right next to Natalie's and was grinning ear to ear.

"I didn't mean to say the verse out loud," Lucky said. Still, he admitted to himself, it was probably good that he had.

According to Bernice, Natalie didn't attend church and neither had her father. Robby was not being raised to know God. Lucky'd mentioned church as a long-term goal, and Natalie hadn't objected, but now he could see Natalie needed a church home, too.

"That was a verse from the Bible?" She sounded incredulous.

"Yes."

Her words softened, and he was gladdened by the look in her eyes.

"That's right," she said. "You're a preacher, too. No wonder you're glad Robby's here."

He could have corrected her, but he didn't.

He wasn't glad Robby was there. He was glad Robby *and Natalie* were there.

Wednesday-night services were a whole lot different from the Sunday mornings Natalie dimly remembered. Instead of going to an exciting Bible class and then sitting in the auditorium for a whole hour, they sat in the auditorium—Robby nestled between Natalie and Mrs. Welch—while songs were led, announcements read and a prayer offered. Five minutes in, Robby wriggled from his seat, got permission from Natalie and went to sit by Daniel.

Natalie forced herself to relax. Robby was mesmerized by a new place full of potential playmates and, in his opinion, full of noise. If all these people could sing at the top of their lungs, why couldn't he shout? He said "MOM" in a loud voice during lulls at least four times—each time with a bit more volume. She and Mrs. Welch both leaned forward and said "Shh!" When the congregation looked, most nudged each other and Natalie could just imagine their whispers. *"Is that the Crosby girl? Who's she with?"*

About the time she was ready to head for the foyer, Robby's hand firmly tucked in hers and the "inside voice" lecture at the ready, a voice from the podium boomed, "You are dismissed," and almost everyone stood. Robby, no dummy, used the opportunity to edge away.

Fifteen minutes had passed in a blink. "What are we doing?" Natalie whispered to Patty as they followed the masses into the foyer and down the hall, keeping the kids in sight.

"It's time for class. Robby's already found his."

Ah, yes, the choo-choo classroom.

Patty stayed by Natalie's side as they headed down a hallway and followed Robby into a room decorated with a pint-size table, a puppet box and lots of toy boxes. Five small children were already there. Two sat at a table putting together puzzles. One ran around the room, holding a paper plate and chanting, *"The wheels on da bus. The wheels on da bus."* Robby and another child had their heads buried in one of the toy chests. Five little trains were soon scattered across the floor.

"Good, we have a visitor tonight." The teacher— surprise, surprise—a man, boomed as he entered the room. Immediately, all save Robby headed for him, bashed right into his knees, and they all tumbled to the ground in laughter.

Robby put down a train, and after just a moment's contemplation, joined right in.

Nope, this was not the church service Natalie remembered.

Patty tugged at Natalie's arm, dragging her from the classroom and out into the hall again. "He'll be fine. Mr. Chris is an excellent teacher. I almost wish Daniel was still in his class."

"Where are we going?" Natalie asked as they moved down the hall again.

"Right now there are three adult classes offered. One is called 'Discipleship.' Um, probably not for you, *yet*. One is for young parents. I'm going to that one. The last is about Paul."

"Paul who?"

"Wow," Patty said. "I don't think I've ever been asked that question. Let's go to the young parents' class. I'll tell you later about Paul, but I'm going to need a lot more time."

"And what she can't tell you, I can," Lucky Welch whispered in her ear.

Only he wasn't whispering in her ear, he was simply standing behind her. For some reason, he felt so close, she could feel the words against her cheek like a caress; each word was warm, heated and deep, like the man who spoke them. One look over her shoulder and Natalie knew Lucky had no idea of his effect on her.

Better to keep it that way.

Against her will, she shivered as they entered a classroom already filled with about thirty people who were all chattering comfortably. They weren't all young, either. Natalie recognized the Pruitts, who were now raising grandchildren. Allison sat in the back of the room, a notebook in hand, looking exhausted. Natalie probably should join her and complete the single-mother corner. For the first time in a long time, she considered Allison her friend. If things had been different, if Tisha hadn't been in the picture, then Allison and Natalie would still be the best of friends, sharing Mommy stories, and swapping babysitting. But Natalie was too afraid of what Allison knew.

The rest of the classroom was occupied by young couples, mothers *and fathers*.

"My mother went to the class on Discipleship," Lucky whispered as they all sat down.

"Good," Natalie whispered back.

Patty's husband welcomed everyone and then started a video. Natalie relaxed. She wouldn't need to talk, share or even act interested. She was a master at zoning out when the television was on. Two full years of cartoons had perfected the art.

The segment on raising children, this night, focused on birth order. Natalie didn't close her eyes all the way. Maybe this would be interesting. She'd been an only child. The doctors didn't know why her parents couldn't have more, but she hadn't heard them complain.

During her adolescence, she'd complained, loud and clear. Onlys, especially those who lived a distance from town, didn't often have playmates. Onlys never won an argument because the only people around to argue with were parents. According to the program, onlys needed to be exposed to other children, playgroups and such. Natalie agreed. A few years ago, her dad finally admitted that keeping her from being a lonely "only" was why they'd had her cousin Tisha out so often.

Natalie figured Tisha's parents were partly responsible, too. With eight children to feed, having one out of the way might be a relief. Dad's younger brother was dirt-poor and when money came their way, it left just as quickly. The words *gambling problem* were bantered around. What Natalie remembered most about Tisha's visits was how Tisha thought Natalie's closet was her closet, and how Tisha seemed to know just where and what Natalie was doing and managed to get there first.

If this birth-order film was to be believed, Tisha did indeed have "oldest child syndrome." She believed she was superior and knew everything.

"I'm the baby," Lucky whispered.

Instead of responding, Natalie closed her eyes and tried to clear her head. Lately, Tisha'd been on her mind way too much, thanks to Natalie's own misstep inviting the Welches into their lives.

Lucky was supposed to give her money and then disappear, like Marcus had done with Tisha, not stick around and offer support, support and more support.

"Are you really a baby?" she finally whispered back.

"I think if I believe this guy, I'm more of a middle. I'm certainly not a prankster, but I am a salesman and an entrepreneur."

"Salesman?" Natalie questioned.

"I think all preachers are salesmen with a winning product."

"That's a funny way to think of it," Patty said doubtfully.

Someone coughed about then, and Natalie became

uncomfortably aware that quite a few people were watching them instead of the television scene.

So, birth order wasn't a given. Now in Dad's family, he had been the oldest and fit the stereotype. He'd been responsible and a leader. His much-younger brother, Allen, Tisha's dad, had been a prankster. He'd been kicked out of high school, didn't try college and settled for working for his wife's family at their dairy. They were dirt-poor, but that's not why Tisha didn't try to leave Robby with them. Even Tisha, as jaded as she was, knew that it didn't just take money to raise a happy and healthy child. Tisha's parents were also the most unhappy people in the state. Bad luck, bad choices and hard work had taken a toll on Allen and his wife.

He'd been left half of what was now Natalie's ranch, but sold it to Natalie's dad before she, or any of his children, were born. Her dad always felt somewhat guilty about it because while Allen had been paid good money, the value had skyrocketed a decade later, and he could have had so much more.

They'd come to hear the reading of the will. Robby had thought it great fun to have five second cousins, once removed, in the house. It didn't phase him that they spent their time either in front of the television or playing video games.

What Natalie remembered most was how Tisha's parents weren't surprised to find that the money was gone.

Allen no longer had a gambling problem; he now had an I've-given-up-on-life problem.

Natalie's dad had left them money. Since, at the time, there appeared to be no money, they'd left without it. Now, Natalie considered, she could make good on her dad's intention. She could send them the money. She'd address the envelope and check to Allen's wife.

"It's time to pray." Patty's husband was standing up again, and the video no longer provided insights into birth order. Looking over at Lucky, Natalie watched as he finished penciling a note into the margin of his already well-scribbled-in Bible and bowed his head. He looked peaceful. In the back of the room, Allison closed her notebook. She no longer looked exhausted. She looked serene, even happy.

On Natalie's other side, Patty was smiling, but Patty smiled most of the time. Before bowing her head, Patty reached over and took Natalie's hand. Up in front of the room, Patty's husband prayed about the coming Thanksgiving holiday, about the sick and about the lost. Everyone else looked content.

Natalie had never felt so lost.

Lucky's mother chatted happily as they pulled away from the Main Street Church. Her bright red nails beat a frantic tap, tap, tap against the door handle. She was as excited as he'd ever seen her, and his mother excited easily.

Nothing compared to this evening.

She wanted to buy Robby a pony. She wanted to decorate a room for him at her house. She wanted to buy a second home here in Selena so she could be easily accessible should she be needed. She wanted so much Lucky almost felt out of breath just keeping up with her.

He wanted a few things, too.

He wanted not to be around when his mother fell back down to Earth. No way would Robby be getting a pony anytime soon. The empty barn was a testimony to Natalie's fear. His mother decorating a room was fine, but Lucky didn't want to be around when she mentioned the idea to his father. As for buying a second home, Lucky figured that argument would be won or lost about the time his mother mentioned decorating a bedroom for what his father would consider a "surprise" grandson.

His mother was having trouble staying true to the short-term, and boy could she dream about the long-term. Lucky was more a realist. More than anything, he wanted Natalie to realize she wasn't losing Robby but gaining family.

No, more than anything, Lucky wanted his father to be open to the idea of Robby, wholeheartedly accept him and support everyone involved.

If the prodigal son had had a son, he'd have been welcomed in his father's home.

Lucky's father didn't welcome any son who went against his wishes. Ever.

"Mom, what have *you* told Dad?"

The tapping fingers stilled. "After you came home from the meeting yesterday, I decided to call Henry. It's not fair to keep this from him. I told him there was something I needed to tell him, but he sounded busy so I didn't tell him what." She stared out the window instead of at Lucky. He didn't blame her. Her whole life she'd learned to approach her husband from the side and never straight-on.

Well, maybe not her whole life. He and Marcus had found pictures from when their parents dated. There'd been a time when their father smiled, laughed and spent time with family.

That part of his dad no longer existed by the time

Lucky came along. Maybe if it did, his mother wouldn't be angst-ridden and maybe Marcus wouldn't be—

No, don't go there.

His mother took a deep breath and finally looked at him. "You didn't tell him, either." Her words were somewhat accusatory.

Sometimes Lucky wondered how his mother kept her sanity. He and Marcus left at age eighteen. His mother stayed, and this year she'd be celebrating twenty-eight years of staying.

"I'm going to call him tonight."

The evening shadows made the town an eerie gray and black. A wind sent the trees shivering. His mother shivered, too. "We have to," Lucky said, "and the sooner the better. We probably should have told him before we negotiated our visitation requests."

"What do you think he'll do?" Mom asked.

For the first time in years, Lucky truly didn't have an answer. His father was fast approaching sixty and Lucky couldn't remember the man ever having fun, ever being open to new ideas. There were rodeo clowns past sixty who knew how to embrace life. How to have fun. Some of them worked harder than Lucky; some of them played harder than Lucky. They epitomized fun, and most of them initiated new ideas. Never, not in Lucky's memory, had Henry Welch given permission for anyone—not himself, not his children—to take a risk, make a poor choice or live down a mistake.

The father Lucky knew would demand paternity tests, consider Robby an embarrassment, and then he'd still turn his back on Marcus's son.

The way he'd turned his back on Marcus.

Risks, poor choices and mistakes had no place in Lucky's dad's life.

"What do you think he'll do?" Lucky's mother repeated softly.

"I'm not sure, Mom, but it doesn't matter. Robby is what matters."

She nodded and went back to staring out the window. Her bubbly mood was gone.

Bernice had beaten them home. No surprise since Lucky's mother had to escort her grandson to the car, had to say "Bye" fifteen times and had to contain herself and her words because the little boy didn't know the woman cooing over him was his grandma.

The porch light was on. Lucky's mother went up the stairs and into the house without a word. Lucky followed slowly, nodding a greeting to Bernice's family and then heading upstairs. Mary's room didn't look inviting, and the grays and blacks outdoors deepened. It was nine at night. His dad would be in his office, books open, not even remembering that for the rest of his family, it was church night.

Lucky went straight to the table by the window and set his Bible down. He didn't need to open it. The scriptures he needed swirled in his mind like bumper cars connecting, detaching and jarring.

Honor thy father and thy mother. Lucky had always honored his mother, figuring out at an early age that she more than any other person on Earth was on his side. After he'd moved out, honoring his father became much easier because he could honor at a distance.

Until coming to the Selena rodeo, that is.

But humility comes before honor. For the first time, Lucky considered just who should experience this humility. He wanted it to be his earthly father, but, Lucky knew this time, yet again, it would be him. He picked up the phone. It took only two rings before Henry Welch barked a hello, managing to sound harried.

"Dad?"

"Your mother about to come home?"

No doubt Dad wanted home cooking.

"I don't think so. That's why I'm calling."

His father was silent, which was unusual enough to give Lucky hope. But then, his dad was canny. He had to know something was going on.

"Go ahead," Dad finally said.

"I've met a woman here. Her name is Natalie Crosby."

Lucky heard a book close and a chair creak before his dad stated, "Crosby? That was Tisha's last name."

Surprised his father remembered, Lucky hurried on, "Yes, she's Tisha's cousin, and apparently she dated Marcus, too."

His father's snort indicated no surprise. Lucky winced. So far, he was making Natalie sound a whole lot like Tisha, and nothing could be further from the truth. Still, Lucky continued, wishing the words sounded better, wishing his gift of gab hadn't failed him at the worst possible moment. "Dad, she has a son. He's three years old. His name is Robby and—"

"She's claiming the boy belongs to Marcus?"

"She doesn't need to claim. One look at Robby and there's no doubt."

"There's always doubt," Dad insisted. "What does she want?"

Lucky felt the pressure lifting. "She doesn't want anything." It was true, too. Not once during their negotiations last Tuesday had she brought up money. He had, and she'd explained about the will, the missing money and then the discovery of the bank bonds.

"Dad, I'm just letting you know that here in Selena, you have a three-year-old grandson. His name is Robby Crosby. His name should be Robby Welch. Mom and I met him, and we already love him."

"You stay away from this woman, and tell your mother I said get home now."

"Dad, this is something you need to tell Mom yourself. But I'm staying in Selena. Robby is Marcus's child, my nephew, your grandson, whether you like it or not. I'm going to help take care of—"

Lucky needn't continue. His father had hung up.

Good thing, too, because Lucky might have accidentally given away that not only did he intend to become a permanent fixture in Robby's life, if his heart was any indication he intended to do the same in Natalie's.

Chapter Seven

Natalie felt even more lost on Saturday morning as she stood in the front doorway watching as Robby piled toys in the backseat. He was convinced that Miss Betsy needed to see his train collection. He was convinced Lucky needed to see his trucks and broomstick horse.

All Natalie really needed to do was toss in some food and clothes, and they'd be good to run away for at least a week.

She shook her head, clearing the cobwebs and fantasies. "Come in, Robby. We need to get a sweater on. It's cold."

"Nooooooooo."

"Yeeeeeeees."

While he truly believed that Miss Betsy and Lucky needed to see his toy collection, he didn't think Miss Betsy and Lucky needed to see his warm clothes. He chose cowboy boots, shorts and a torn white T-shirt. He wasn't happy when Natalie changed him into a warm red sweater and a pair of heavy-duty jeans. That she let him keep the cowboy boots went unnoticed.

"I hot," he insisted, so Natalie changed him into a

long-sleeved T-shirt, tucked the sweater in his backpack and, finally, with only ten minutes to spare, buckled Robby into his car seat and crawled behind the wheel.

She imagined herself driving to Canada. It was a straight shot north.

"Mommy, choo-choo," Robby whined. Usually, Natalie worked hard not to reward such behavior, but this morning, no way did she want to show up at Bernice's with an unhappy, screaming kid and a disheveled look. She jumped out of the car and headed into the house to retrieve yet another train. She knew just the one he wanted. She'd put it on top of the refrigerator last night when Robby decided that playing on the kitchen floor with his train was more important than eating.

Hopping back in the car and handing Robby his beloved favorite train, she hoped he didn't do the same today. Natalie didn't need Mrs. Welch demanding an account of what, when and where Robby ate, and why he thought throwing himself on the kitchen floor was okay.

Bernice lived twenty-five minutes away, on the other side of town, in a house that looked lived-in. Natalie parked behind a red Sebring. Checking the child mirror, she saw Robby's anxious face and forced herself to calm down.

"We're going to have fun today."

Robby nodded and went for his seat belt. Since Natalie didn't want him to master unbuckling yet, she made it around the car and to his side quickly. To her relief, he ignored the stash of toys and simply held on to his favorite train. They'd barely taken a few steps when the front door opened and Lucky came out.

"The star attractions!" he called.

"You mean attraction," Natalie corrected.

Robby pulled his hand from hers and ran toward Lucky. "See my choo-choo."

"I see your choo-choo," Lucky said. "And, I meant attractions. We're glad that both of you are here. Come on in. Most everybody is either in the kitchen or around back."

Natalie had actually been here a few times as a teenager, but back then she'd been here for the horses and hadn't noticed the down-home look. It was a kid's dream. Scattered toys, soft furniture, and most breakables were out of Robby's reach.

Small things, but they helped Natalie relax.

She didn't need to ask Lucky directions to the kitchen. The aroma of fried chicken led the way. Then came the sounds of laughter and raised voices.

"Mary's here. Do you know her?" Lucky asked.

Bernice's oldest daughter, nine months pregnant and ever the high school cheerleader, raised a Popsicle in greeting.

"Everybody knows Mary," Natalie finally said as Robby pressed against her leg and herded her toward all the noise. Clearly, he wanted to be in the thick of things, only he wanted to make sure she was near. "I was three years behind her in school."

"Natalie!" Bernice turned from the oven when they walked into the kitchen. "I'm proud of you and mad at you at the same time."

"Mother," Mary warned. She was placing plates on the table. Natalie did a quick count—eleven.

Hmm.

Bernice aimed a large spoon at Mary and shook it.

"I'm supposed to fade into the background, I've been told. Still, we're so glad you're here. Most everyone is in the backyard."

Lucky looked relieved to get out of the kitchen.

"I want kicken," Robby said. He headed for the stove.

Bernice blocked the oven door, spoon at the ready. "Well, of course you do," she said. "I've saved a leg just for you. I'll bet your mother's taught you the word *hot*. Am I right?"

"I think she has some six-legged chickens hidden away because she always offers legs to my two children," Mary added. "Rachel is Robby's age. Shall we introduce them?"

The backyard was even better than the living room. A swing set beckoned. The door to the barn was open enough so Natalie and Robby could see horses, hay and farm tools. Even better than that, right in front of the barn were the beginnings of something.

"What that?" Robby asked.

Lucky crouched down so he was eye level with Robby. "Howie Junior's been bugging me to help him learn to ride bulls. I put together a mini-arena. I've been making him jump on the bales of hay, and I've been helping him with balance. See?" Lucky pointed. He'd tied a metal barrel to four trees. "With just a pull on a rope or two, Howie gets to ride a pretend bull."

"Oh," Robby said. He'd stopped paying attention after the first three or four words. He took two steps toward the barrel.

"I don't think so," Natalie said.

Lucky shot her a look, but echoed, "I don't think so."

Robby looked ready to let out a healthy three-year-old whine, but luckily someone laughed behind them. Robby turned and saw kids his own age. He took two steps in their direction, looked at his mother questioningly, decided he was brave enough to leave her side and ran toward Howard, Bernice's husband, and Mary's two children. A little boy bigger than Robby stayed near his grandpa, but a little girl just Robby's size ran toward him.

"Robby, wait!" Natalie called, but it was too late.

They met hard in the middle, looking like two tiny sumo wrestlers. Both fell to the ground. Robby sat up first, grinned and said, "Okay?"

The little girl nodded, "'Kay."

"I'm thinking about making her a bull rider," Lucky said after both children brushed themselves off and ran toward the swing set. Lucky smiled as the little girl scampered up the slide with Robby right on her heels. For the first time, Natalie noticed how his smile seemed to reflect in his rich brown eyes.

Lucky continued, "So far today, Rachel's fallen off a chair, hit her head on a door handle and pulled a bowl on top of her head. Not once did she cry. She did ask the bowl if it was ''kay.'"

"Rachel must be two."

"Yup."

"Robby was forever hurting himself when he was two. One night I heard him. He'd fallen out of bed. When I got to him, he was already back to sleep, on the floor, clutching a shoe. He had a knot on his head. I stayed by him for hours afraid that he shouldn't be asleep, but also afraid to wake him up."

"And Marcus missed all those things," Lucky said sadly.

"Yes, he did." There was no sense sugarcoating it.

"I just find that so strange." Lucky sounded amazed. "He loved children. When we were teens, he was the one who worked at a special-needs camp for three summers in a row. It had some kind of animal therapy with horses that Marcus helped with. The kids loved him. He still gets letters."

Natalie opened her mouth, but the words didn't come. She'd never really met Marcus, and Tisha had only had negative things to say.

"I still wonder. How did you meet?" Lucky started.

"Where's your mother?" Natalie interrupted.

Lucky sobered. "She's not here. I planned on telling you but was hoping to let you settle in first. We called my dad Wednesday after church. We told him about Robby."

Natalie's stomach clenched. Lucky's dad was the one who knew high-dollar lawyers. Lucky's dad even scared Tisha. Tisha wouldn't say what it was about the man that frightened her. She left Natalie with the idea that not only did Marcus want nothing to do with his dad, but that his dad wanted nothing to do with them.

"Dad made her come home. He doesn't believe Robby is a Welch."

"And your mother went?" Natalie had trouble fathoming the concept.

"She went. I drove to Lubbock and put her on a plane Thursday. She cried the whole way."

"Oh, my." Natalie sat on a bale of hay.

"I promised her I'd take lots of pictures today. I hope you don't mind." Lucky took out his cell phone, punched a button and aimed it at the children.

It would be a lovely picture, Natalie thought. Mary's

daughter's blond hair shimmered in the sunlight as she tried to climb up the slide instead of using the steps. Robby's brown hair stuck straight up in the air. He followed the little girl's lead. Looking back at Lucky, Natalie watched as his hand went to his own hair, smoothing it back, making sure it didn't stick up. The smile had gone out of his eyes. He was probably thinking about what his mother was missing.

Natalie had spent the day, the week, the last two weeks regretting what her rash announcement at the rodeo had done to *her* Robby, *her* world, *her* life.

She'd forgotten there were other people, other worlds, other lives involved.

And they were hurting just as much as she was.

Lunch went great, except for his mother's absence. Robby sat between Mary's children. He mimicked the older boy and bowed his head in prayer, even saying Amen, and then took care of little Rachel. Robby moved her drink so it wasn't too near the edge of the table. Lucky took a picture. Robby said "Nooooo" when she reached for Grandpa Howard's butter knife. Lucky took a picture. The little boy seemed to think he had a job taking care of Rachel, and he intended to do it. Lucky's mother would have been mesmerized. Lucky was. He hadn't been around kids much, except at the rodeos, and there they all seemed to want autographs or cotton candy.

Looked like Robby was a good kid.

Natalie relaxed after her second piece of fried chicken. It was only the second time Lucky had seen her without a pinched and somewhat panicked expression. He took another picture, this one of Natalie.

She'd almost relaxed with him Wednesday night during church, when he'd confessed that he was the baby of the family.

He caught Bernice's eye and smiled. This was her doing. Marcus had always accused Bernice of putting a truth serum inside her chicken because it seemed the whole family loosened up and came clean during one of her meals. Except for his dad, of course. Henry Welch had only made it to Bernice's table a handful of times during his marriage to Lucky's mother, and Lucky had grown up wishing Bernice's husband, Howard, were his father. Howard not only seemed to enjoy spending time with his family at the meal table, but also he wasn't above refilling a tea, cleaning up mashed potatoes from the floor or even doing dishes while his wife and her best friend simply sat on the front porch and talked.

"You going to stay at the ranch now that your dad's gone?" Howard asked Natalie.

"Yes. It's a perfect place to raise a kid. Plus, how could I leave? That place has been in my family more than a hundred years."

"Sure is a big house for one little girl," Howard said.

"Yes, but the little girl's lived there her whole life." Natalie didn't miss a beat. Lucky liked what he saw. She knew what she wanted, and she went after it.

He sat up and leaned forward, watching her face, her expressions, her mannerisms. She was a lady through and through. Amazing. And not Marcus's type at all. Natalie was Mary Ann. Marcus liked Gingers.

She continued, "Not much about the house or the land I don't know. I'm going to offer MacAfee more grazing land, and then the only thing I'll need to worry about are the four acres around the house."

Lucky watched the interchange. These were questions he'd wanted to ask, but didn't know how. When he'd first come to town—had it really only been two weeks ago?—everyone was talking about Natalie's lack of money.

Just last Tuesday, when he'd sat across from her at the diner, she'd let him know money was no longer a problem.

"Place the size of yours takes a lot of upkeep," Lucky said. He almost added that it would be hard enough for a man to take care of the grounds and chores, but he choked back the words. They sounded too much like his father's.

"For emergencies I have Patty and her husband. My dad's friend Walt calls almost every night."

"Uncle Walt gave me a lollipop," Robby added, letting them know that while he didn't follow the conversation, he knew it was going on.

"I like lolpops," Rachel agreed, nodding seriously. Mary's older son paid no attention to the conversation.

The fried chicken was that good.

Howard nodded. "There's not much about the financial dealings here in Selena that Walt doesn't know." Turning to Lucky, he said, "Walt owns the bank. He's turned the reins over to his son—"

"Who Natalie used to date," Mary interrupted.

"Lord, I forgot about that," Bernice said. "That was how many years ago?"

Natalie was blushing. "Too many to count."

Mary turned to her mother. "How many kids does Timothy have now?"

"Three, and his wife's pregnant with the fourth."

"Peter, Timothy's middle boy, is Robby's age," Natalie said. "We belong to a playgroup that meets every Monday morning. I haven't been since my father died."

"You need to go again," Mary said gently. "It's good to get out. I'd go nuts if not for the time we spend with friends who have kids my kids' ages."

Natalie looked at Lucky, and he saw her eyes go liquid.

"There's just been so much going on," she said softly.

"Some of it is good," Bernice reminded. "You're keeping the ranch." Then Bernice looked at Lucky and said, "Robby needs a father figure more than he needs other little kids. Who better than Lucky?"

"Mother!" Mary gasped.

Lucky might have gasped himself, but he was lost suddenly in Natalie's shimmering blue eyes.

"Mother," Howard said gently and looked at Robby. "Little pitchers have big ears."

Bernice took a bite of chicken and chewed while trying to, pretending to, look contrite. "Okay, okay, I've never understood that saying, but I know I promised not to interfere."

"What do you do besides the playgroup?" Mary asked. "My kids like it best when the toddlers from church get together. It only happens about every three or four months but—"

"I'm not a toddler." Johnny spoke for the first time.

Mary reached over and tussled his hair. "Of course you're not."

"Last summer we did the Mother and Toddler swim class. Robby was the best one there. He jumped in the first day. The lifeguard was impressed. If he could listen and follow directions, they would have moved him up a class."

"I a good swimmer." Robby held up his plate. "More?"

"I'll get you more," Bernice offered. "He has a good appetite, Natalie. What's his favorite meal?"

"Spaghetti, but he usually winds up wearing more of it than he eats."

"Johnny was like that," Mary said.

"Was not!" Johnny said it loud enough that both Rachel and Robby stopped eating.

"No yelling at table," Robby instructed.

"Table," Rachel agreed.

"One time," Natalie said, "when Robby was about eleven months and I wasn't looking, he managed to load most of his spaghetti into the back of one of his toy trucks. I noticed about two days later. Yuck."

Everyone laughed, and finally Lucky was able to tear himself away from her eyes. What he couldn't seem to do was forget Bernice's "father figure" remark. No one else seemed to be dwelling on it, though, not Natalie, and not Mary, who was laughing as she said, "Oh, Johnny did that, too, only with macaroni and cheese."

Johnny squirmed. "Did not."

Lucky shook his head. His mother had a similar story about both him and Marcus. She would have loved hearing what Natalie had to say. Bernice did a great job of making everyone feel comfortable. Still, she kept giving Lucky side looks, as if she blamed him for his mother's absence. Or maybe she blamed him for not jumping up and demanding more time with Robby.

He needed to assess what he was doing here. He'd made his list, but despite the long-term on it, had he really thought beyond the next six months? The list only offered the basics. It didn't deal with just how much Lucky might want to *add* to the list.

Lucky put his third piece of fried chicken down and thought back to what Marcus had said about Bernice's chicken and truth serum.

In truth shimmering blue eyes made him want to stay in Selena as much as seeing Robby did.

"Lucky!" Mary said.

"What?"

"You're doing that staring thing again. You know, like you did when you were in high school and had better places to be than at our table."

"I never," Lucky insisted, "had better places to be than in front of Bernice's fried chicken."

Inviting Mary and her family was a stroke of genius on Bernice's part. Not only did having other young children make it more comfortable, but also as the meal continued on to dessert, Mary and Natalie shared a few memories. Natalie knew about Mary's exploits, and Mary knew about Natalie's barrel-racing skills.

By the time lunch was over, Rachel and Robby were nodding off, and Bernice was pushing everyone out the door so she could do dishes. Alone.

"It's easier," she insisted.

Natalie pulled Robby from his chair. He curled his arms around her neck and murmured, "Mommy, no sleep."

"Yes, sleep," Natalie said gently.

Mary was gathering Rachel up. Her blossoming

figure didn't hinder her at all. "Let's put them on my mother's bed."

Lucky followed, watching the two women. Rachel was asleep; Robby was not. The moment Natalie laid him down, he popped back up. Natalie leaned over and whispered something in his ear. He looked at Rachel, nodded and settled into the pillow.

After she pulled the blanket over Robby, Natalie followed Mary out into the hall and managed a smile at Lucky.

"What did you whisper in his ear?"

"I told him to stay with little Rachel for a few minutes to make sure she's okay, and then I'll come and check on him."

"So he's not going down for a nap?"

"He'll be asleep before I make it to the bottom of the stairs."

About the time he and Natalie reached the back door, Johnny and Howie Junior were running toward the mini-arena. Mary trailed by just a few feet. Howie Junior turned on the radio and Van Halen blasted.

"You choose the music?" Mary asked.

"Yes," Lucky said, thinking he should direct his answer to Mary but unable to take his eyes away from Natalie. "When you're teaching young bull riders, 'Kum Ba Yah' just won't do."

Natalie put a hand over her heart. "I'm appalled."

"Honey!" Mary's husband called.

"Coming," Mary yelled. She studied Natalie and Lucky. "You two be good."

They both watched as Mary walked away, singing to the classic rock lyrics of Van Halen and looking every bit like she belonged onstage.

Lucky waited until she was out of earshot and shook his head. "That girl."

"Has a vivid imagination," Natalie agreed. "Give me a minute. I'm going to run upstairs. I promised Robby I'd check on him."

She hurried back to the house.

Lucky enjoyed the view. She didn't exactly run, more like scooted, and her shoulder-length hair bobbed with each step.

She told Robby she'd come back to get him, and even though she knew the little boy was probably asleep, she was keeping her word.

He admired that.

He knew the power of the Word. He'd taken on the role of preacher more than two years ago. First, helping his mentor. Then, filling in when no one else was willing or available. Finally, he'd stepped up to the plate, accepted God's calling and started organizing the services at the rodeos he attended. Cowboy Church filled a necessary void. Demand, not only among the rodeo participants, but also among the fans, increased every year. If he wanted, he'd have a pulpit, be it a tree trunk, every week, and he'd have listeners. Of course, Cowboy Church was nothing like the church here in Selena. Lucky sometimes wanted a regular church. Other times, the thought of trying to meet the needs of a diverse congregation scared him to death. Cowboy Church meant a certain breed of people. It didn't mean singing, one preacher, a chance to repent and then a prayer before goodbye. It meant lots of people coming forward and confessing their sins, both to relieve their hearts but also to encourage others. If there needed to be a baptism, they had to find a place to do it. Watching hearts heal had done a lot for Lucky because he'd seen firsthand what havoc loss of hope did to individuals, families, lives.

Maybe if Marcus had tried a littler harder, stayed with Natalie a little longer, then his life would have been different.

What little time Lucky had spent with Natalie certainly inspired him to want to try a little harder.

Stay a lot longer.

You two be good. He, unfortunately, had a vivid imagination, too, and wasn't entirely opposed to what Mary was thinking. Watching Natalie hurry down the back steps and toward him, he tried to remember that she was the mother of his *brother's* son. Instead of choosing the necessary path, the questions he needed to ask about Marcus and Natalie's past, Lucky queried, "You ever been here before?"

"Yes, but it's been years. Looks like they've done quite a bit to the place."

He started with the barn, noticing how she dragged her heels when they came near the stalls. He took her through the fields and down to a creek. At first, he talked about the land, comparing it to his grandfather's place. Then, he moved on to his career.

"Marcus always seemed to make the top fifteen. Me, I managed to stay in the top forty-five, which means, actually, that I made good money. Not as good as Marcus, but good enough to keep me in the game. This year, I'll be lucky to be in the top hundred. I'll probably break even this year. That is, if I don't skip any more rodeos where I've already paid the entry fee."

She shuddered. "I can't even imagine jumping off a bull."

As much as he wanted to, he couldn't tell her what she wanted to hear, because while she couldn't imagine jumping off a bull, he couldn't imagine doing anything else.

Yet.

"Most jobs are dangerous. We bull riders just have to acknowledge that the bull is bigger than we are and know how to get out of the way. It's the know-how that makes the difference. You take most people, they go to work, and if something dangerous pops up in front of them, they haven't any know-how."

He looked down at her.

"Nice try," she said. "But I design Web pages for a living, and there's nothing you can compare to the bull in my profession."

He grinned. She had him. Now, if she'd used her father's profession, owner of a stockyard, he'd have had an argument. If she'd used Howard Senior, or Mary's husband or...

"A computer could fall on your head. You could be electrocuted," Lucky offered.

"I use a laptop, it weighs eleven pounds. I also have a surge guard."

"I won't be a bull rider forever. Someday, I want to retire, have my own church and maybe a place like this." They'd circled the perimeter of Bernice's house. "I'm just not ready to throw in my hat, change my life, yet."

The breeze suddenly took on a colder feel, one that had Natalie studying him intently before turning back at the house. Lucky didn't know if it was truly the weather that clutched at his heart, his declaration that he could retire someday or the look on her face.

It was the first time he'd uttered the word *retire* aloud. He looked down at Natalie, blaming her for his change of heart, and noted how the top of her blond head came to just under his chin. He noticed how she kept her hands in her jacket pockets and how she watched Howie Junior and Johnny practice falling off the bales of hay. Funny, until he had Natalie at his side, he hadn't noticed how they always playacted writhing in pain.

He wasn't ready to throw in his hat yet. But if he made Selena his home base, and he fully intended to, Natalie Crosby just might help him get there sooner.

Chapter Eight

Natalie looked out the window for the tenth time. Any minute now, per their agreement, Lucky would drive up and load Robby into his truck, into the car seat he'd borrowed from Mary, and off they'd go to church. Natalie would be in the house alone for the first time since her father's death. She could work on Web pages uninterrupted. She could sit in a comfy chair and read uninterrupted. She could maybe clean out a closet or two uninterrupted.

It was going to be a long, boring day, uninterrupted.

As if affirming her assumption, Robby crawled on the couch next to her and peered out the window, too. "Here yet?"

"Not yet."

"You come?"

"Not this time."

"Okay."

It was that easy for Robby to accept Lucky and a boys' day out.

Not that Lucky Welch could be described as a boy.

No, he was a man, bigger than life, who was upsetting the applecart as her dad would say.

"Church fun," Robby remarked.

"I'm glad you think so."

Lucky's truck bounced into sight right then, and Robby was off the couch and tugging on the front doorknob before Natalie had time to smooth her hair and make sure her shirt was tucked in.

"Morning," Lucky called, stepping down from his truck and heading up the walk.

Yup, bigger than life. He wasn't a cowboy this morning. No, in a black suit, white shirt and gray tie, he was definitely a Sunday-go-to-meeting man. Natalie couldn't say why she was surprised. Maybe because on Wednesday night, he'd been relaxed in jeans and a flannel shirt. Looking down at Robby, she rethought his black jeans and blue sweater.

Lucky must have read her mind because when he got to the front porch, he said, "Robby looks fine. I'm all dressed up because this morning the preacher's wife called. Seems Tate's not feeling too good. They asked me to preach."

"Then Robby will be in the way. I can keep him home, and you can take him some other time." She'd meant to sound helpful instead of hopeful, but no such luck.

Lucky chuckled. "Mary's still in town. She's been bribing Rachel all morning with getting to see Robby again. She'd have my head if I showed up at church empty-handed. Robby will sit with them during the beginning minutes of service, then there's a children's hour."

"A children's hour?"

"Kids ages two to ten have their own service, down in the basement. There's puppet shows and singing."

Again, Natalie considered that the church Lucky was describing was not the church she remembered. It was more a church she wished she remembered.

Robby held out his hands, and Lucky picked him up. "You weigh as much a baby bull," Lucky teased, hoisting the little boy high into the air. Then, he did something Natalie didn't have the strength to do. He flew Robby in the air all the way to the truck. Robby chipped in by making plane sounds. A moment later, Lucky deposited Robby in the child's seat and then started fumbling with the buckle.

"I do it," Robby offered.

"Oh, no, no, no." Natalie left the safety of her porch, where she'd been watching her son too willingly go off without her.

She nudged Lucky aside and took the harness and first attached it at the chest and then between Robby's legs. She could feel Lucky practically pressed against her. She wanted to say, *Hey, preacher man, isn't there, like, a two-fingers rule about how close you can stand to the opposite sex?* But she knew he was just studying her every move, watching her buckle Robby in, so he could buckle Robby in safely, without her assistance. Knowing that, she didn't mind if he stepped on her toes.

Truth was, she didn't mind how close he was at all. He was warm and smelled of soap. The bottom of his chin brushed the top of her head. If he were anybody else, she'd think he was invading her space on purpose.

"We'll probably go out for lunch after services, so

I'm thinking we'll be gone about three or four hours. Okay?"

"You'll need his bag." Natalie quickly returned to the house, grabbed Robby's diaper bag and hurried back to Lucky. "If he says potty, take him right then. We're getting it right about ninety percent of the time."

She almost wished Lucky's cell phone was within grasp. She needed a camera because the look on Lucky's face was priceless.

"Mary will know what to do," Natalie assured him, holding out the bag and almost enjoying his unease because it was so comical. "There's a diaper just in case, but I doubt you'll need it."

Lucky looked skeptically at the bag and didn't make a move to take it.

"Trust me, you need it."

Finally, Lucky took the bag. He placed it in the front seat.

"We go!" Robby urged.

"We go," Lucky agreed, slipping into his truck and into three-year-old lingo easily. He paused, then turned around to check out his backseat. Clearly having second thoughts, he said to Natalie, "You want to come with us?"

"To church?"

"That's where we're going."

"We go, Mommy!"

No, she didn't want to go to church. She didn't want to sit still for an hour, didn't want to answer the questions as to why she was suddenly attending and who she was attending with, and most of all, she didn't want to hear a sermon about sorting out right from wrong.

Because right now, Natalie was doing wrong. This

preacher man deserved to know the truth: that Robby was Marcus's son but *not* Natalie's. The urge to tell him almost made her dizzy. It was the right thing to do. It was the scariest thing in the world to contemplate doing. She caught the handle of his truck in a firm grip. No way did she want to have to explain to Lucky exactly why she was feeling faint.

"Natalie!"

She looked up at him, blinked and opened her mouth. Words didn't come.

"You either need to let go of the door handle or, even better, jump in and come to church with us."

"Yes, Mommy, come church."

"No, I can't go to church."

"Can't or won't?" Lucky asked.

"Both work." She stepped away from the truck, surprised by how much she wanted to go with them. If only she'd borne Robby, if only…

Lucky started the truck, the wheels turned and he slowly drove away. He waved, and in the backseat, Robby tried to turn. The safety harness only allowed so much movement. Still, his little head bobbed up and down as he tried to see her while trying to wave, too.

Her knees almost buckled. Her little man was going off without her. Taking a deep breath, she regained her composure and looked back at the house. For a month, she'd been daunted by how empty it was without her dad. Empty didn't begin to describe how it would feel without Robby.

She took one step, two, back toward the porch. Actually, this was good. She and her dad had always agreed that Robby shouldn't be coddled, and since her dad's death, Robby had been nothing but coddled. At church, he'd be with Rachel, who at the moment was his favorite person, and he'd see Patty and her kids. Realistically, this was a good separation.

Good for Robby.

Not so good for her.

Glancing back, she watched as Lucky's truck got smaller and smaller. So this was what "shared custody" felt like, like a best friend moving away, promising to write, but it's never the same.

When the truck finally disappeared from sight, Natalie opened the front door and went in. Evidence of Robby was everywhere, more so now than when her father was alive. Back then, she'd tried to keep things picked up. Now, the toys lay at the ready, and in some ways it was a maze to get through the living room and to the kitchen.

With hours to kill, she started cleaning the living room, worked her way to the kitchen and did both bathrooms, then her and Robby's bedrooms. The guest room simply needed airing out.

The door to her father's room had been closed for almost a month. It needed more than an airing out; it needed emptying out. Walt had offered to help more than once. Standing in the hallway, in front of the room that had belonged to her father, Natalie figured the room felt and looked much like she did, lonely and dusty.

She checked her watch. Church should be ending right now. Lucky planned to take everyone out to lunch. She'd love to be a fly on the wall for that venture. If he blanched at the diaper detail, he'd also be bewildered when Robby refused to eat, crawled under the table and wanted to run around greeting the other diners.

Pop Pop called Robby a future Wal-Mart greeter.

She had more than an hour. The knob turned in her hand and the door pushed open, almost without her consent. Lately, she seemed to be doing more things she didn't want to do than things she wanted to do.

She needed to change that.

Her father's scent of Old Spice and down-home comfort lingered in the room. She missed him. Oh, how she missed him. She'd never felt like a single mother with him by her side. She'd felt like a family. And three seemed such a great number. It had been she, her mom and dad, three. Then, it had been she, Robby and Dad, three. Now it was Robby and she, two.

Three was a much better number.

She stepped into the room, thinking she'd wash the bedsheets and then grab some garbage bags and start packing her father's clothes.

The phone saved her.

In the quiet of a house that had not three, not two, but one lonely individual, the phone was loud, distant and welcome.

She hurried downstairs and picked it up.

It was Lucky. "Robby's crying, and we can't get him to stop."

"Did he fall?"

"No," Lucky said slowly, "I went to pick him up from Bible hour, and when I peeked in, he was just fine. He was sitting by Rachel and holding up his finger and singing *'This Little Light of Mine.'* Rachel spotted Mary and ran right to her. Robby just looked at us, and when I told him to come on, his bottom lip quivered, and he started sobbing."

"Put him on the phone," Natalie ordered.

"Mommy. You no here."

Natalie knew just the expression Robby wore on his little face. He had eyes pooling with tears. He had a bottom lip that not only quivered but also stuck out. And he wasn't exactly crying, more like keening.

"Robby, what's wrong?"

"Mommmmmmmy."

"Mommy's at home. You'll be home soon."

"Mommy home?"

Lucky took the phone then. Natalie had to give him credit for parental instinct. A phone call with Robby could take an hour and consist of mainly two-to-four-word fragmented sentences. Lucky, obviously, was too hungry to wait an hour. "Should I bring him home?"

"You can."

"Better still, why don't you drive over and meet us for lunch? We're going to The SteakHouse." She heard muffled sounds, and then she barely made out Lucky saying to Robby, "Mommy is coming to the restaurant."

"Eat!" Robby replied. No more keening, no more quivering bottom lip. "We go eat. Mommy eat."

She had no problem hearing Robby.

And she had no problem figuring out that the opportunity to say "yes" or "no" to the restaurant was gone. Robby missed her; Robby expected her at the restaurant. She'd meet them at the restaurant.

Part of her wondered if Lucky knew he'd worked it so she had no opportunity to decline the luncheon invitation.

Lucky came back to the phone. "It will take us about twenty minutes to get to the restaurant."

"Since it's Sunday," Natalie said, "you'll have about

a thirty-minute wait. I'd call ahead, get your name on the list and then drive around a bit. Robby's a handful in a crowded room with no toys and no place to roam."

"Bernice already called, but I'll take your advice about driving around."

After she hung up the phone, Natalie looked down. She no longer felt lonely, but she still looked dusty. When Robby was a baby, she'd mastered the eight-minute shower. It served her well this morning. Unfortunately, there was no such thing as an eight-minute blow-dry. She took the full ten minutes needed, wanting to look nice, and worried that she was trying to impress the big cowboy more than the little cowboy.

Remembering what Lucky looked like, she chose an outfit she didn't get to wear often enough. Hmm, come to think of it, the last time she'd worn the black, satiny pants and matching black-and-white-striped jacket had been for an evening out back when Robby had been four months old and her father arranged the blind date.

That said something—her father trying to play matchmaker. The date liked Natalie, but he was about fifteen years too old. She'd never been willing to settle, which might be the reason she hadn't had a real date in three years.

Hurrying to the car, she checked her watch and figured she just might arrive in time for dessert.

But her hair would look great!

Natalie chuckled. Her father had bemoaned Natalie's attention to her hair. Of course, back when he was teasingly complaining, she hadn't mastered the eight-minute shower, and ten minutes would never do for a decent styling. For the first time in a long time, when she checked her image in the mirror, she felt like a woman more than a mother.

She could fool herself and say it was for Robby, but Natalie was no fool.

The day was taking a turn for the better, and maybe, just maybe, when she got back home she'd tackle her dad's room with a better attitude. Surely after a lunch with her little man, Lucky and Bernice's whole crew, loneliness would take a holiday.

In a way, the drive to The SteakHouse felt like a holiday. The weather was perfect, and Natalie was looking forward to being a part of something, something like a family. She turned on the radio and hummed along with a country station all the way to the restaurant.

The SteakHouse used to be a barn. It belonged to a family her father referred to as entrepreneurs. They had ten children and realized not all wanted to farm, thus the family restaurant.

It worked, Natalie remembered, as she pulled into the parking lot. Five of their ten children worked the land. Five worked the restaurant.

Natalie's timing couldn't be better. She walked into the restaurant just as Lucky and everyone were being seated.

"Mommmmmmmy!"

As she stretched out her arms, Natalie overheard a diner say, "Kid sure is happy to see his mommy, but he looks just like his daddy."

Natalie's step faltered.

Every time she started thinking she could do this, share Robby, something reminded her that at heart she was, indeed, an only child, and she didn't share well. Worse, the diner's words, *"Sure looks like his daddy,"* reminded her that what she wasn't sharing didn't really belong to her in the first place.

Robby skidded to a stop and held up a piece of paper. "Look, Mommy. Look what I made."

It was a white piece of paper with cotton balls and craft sticks glued to it.

"Um, that looks really nice," Natalie said, guiding Robby to the table and helping him into the booster chair. Rachel was in a booster chair also, across from Robby, and she was holding on to a similar piece of paper.

Johnny, feeling the power of being the oldest, solemnly filled Natalie in. "We had a lesson in Bible hour about being sheep."

Natalie looked at Robby and made a quizzical face. "I thought you wanted to be a horse."

"No, sheep. Baa."

Everyone laughed. The hostess showed up, passed menus around, and before Natalie had time to worry about Robby's behavior, she found herself sitting between him and Lucky, who'd pulled out her chair. Robby was making a liar out of her by behaving like a little adult. He held the kids' menu as if he were reading it. Rachel did likewise.

Lucky leaned over. "You've eaten here before?"

"Many times."

"What's good?"

"You'd better say everything," the waitress walked up and said. She was still tying her apron. After she finished the knot, she retrieved a tablet from her pocket and said, "Is this all one check?"

Bernice said no; Lucky said yes.

It only took a wink from Lucky to encourage the waitress that one check was all that was necessary.

Natalie was impressed.

So impressed that she had a hard time keeping her eyes off him while he led the prayer. She noticed that he watched her, too, while she cut Robby's hamburger into small pieces. Luckily, little Rachel then insisted that Natalie cut hers and no, Mommy wouldn't do, it had to be Robby's mother. Natalie not only cut the meat but also arranged it in a happy face. She then made sure Robby ate six bites of his hamburger, three fries, and drank his milk.

When the last dessert was cleared away and Robby finished his milk, Bernice's husband stood. "We need to be getting home. There are still chores to do."

Howie Jr. was the only one to groan. Mary's husband, casting a worried look at Mary's bulging stomach, pulled a sleeping Rachel from her chair. Robby put down the toy train Natalie had pulled from the diaper bag and scooted to the floor. Natalie retrieved the train, Robby's sippy cup and two crayons from the table before taking Robby by the hand.

"Need help?" Lucky offered.

"No, I'm going to get him home and put him down for a nap. I have some work to do."

"Need some help with the all that work? Or better yet, how about if I come along and distract Robby after he wakes up?"

Natalie opened her mouth, but no words came out.

Her cell rang, saving her from making a decision.

Lucky tucked Robby under his arm, snagged the backpack from Natalie's hand and mouthed, *I'll wait for you outside.*

It was nice to have help.

Natalie flipped open her phone and listened to Sunni's normally calm voice rise a few octaves.

"Slow down," Natalie advised.

Over the line, she heard Sunni take a breath. Then, the lawyer said, "Natalie, the private detective just called. He started with Tisha's last known address and has been working his way backward."

"Has he found Tisha?"

"No, but he found someone else."

Lately, Natalie had gotten used to imagining worst-case scenarios. "Another baby?"

"No, he found another private detective."

Chapter Nine

Monday morning when the alarm clock rang, Natalie rolled out of bed with purpose. She'd tossed and turned all night, and in the gloom of midnight had made a decision. The private detective she and Sunni hired had not located Tisha. The private detective her father had hired had not found Tisha.

At least now they knew where her father's missing money had gone and why he'd put his business at risk. His private detective charged sixty dollars an hour plus expenses. Natalie's father had paid for airfare, hotel bills, gas…the list went on. It added up quickly.

And still no Tisha.

Her dad's private detective did know why he'd been hired. When Natalie's dad heard that Marcus had died and how much money Marcus had, he'd worried that Tisha might come around. He, like Natalie, intended to do everything in his power to keep Robby with them.

Her father's main goal, like Natalie's, had been guardianship papers.

Both Sunni and Natalie agreed. The private detective needed to keep looking for Tisha. Until all parties came to an agreement, Robby's future was at stake.

The minute Tisha was located, Natalie was telling both Robby and Lucky the truth.

It was the responsible thing, the right thing.

She tugged on gray sweats and a pink T-shirt. Then she checked on Robby, grabbed a glass of milk, snagged a handful of cookies and headed for her office. The world as she and Robby knew it was about to change, and it was important for both of them to keep some things the same.

Like routines. Their routines had been disrupted when Pop Pop died. Then, their routines had been completely destroyed when Natalie challenged fate and lost. If she were honest with herself, she'd known Lucky was a good guy, which was why she'd approached him for money. But she'd never expected Lucky to turn out to not only be a good guy with a good family but also a good guy who wanted to be part of their lives.

Natalie booted up her computer and opened her calendar. So far the e-mail about her father's death had garnered lots of sympathy from her clients. All claimed to understand if she was a bit slow with updates, but a month had passed, and even the most patient of clients had to be having second thoughts. She'd been slowly getting back into routine; today was the day routine returned for good.

First, she sent out a blanket e-mail letting her clients know that she was back in the saddle and to please send new updates. She also attached a sample trailer, a cost breakdown, and offered her clients what she called "a new opportunity." She'd managed to catch up on just two clients when—

"Morning, Mommy!" Robby stood in the bedroom door, grinning. Clutched in his left hand was a pair of fresh, clean pajamas he'd gotten from his dresser drawer.

"Good morning, my favorite little man. I am so glad you're awake. You wet?"

"Uh-huh."

Ten minutes later, Robby sat at the table in jeans and a sweater, eating a waffle, or pretending to eat a waffle—one bite didn't really count as eating—and looking out the window.

Natalie looked out the window, too. Robby, she knew, was hoping for a cowboy. Natalie was hoping for a miracle.

Too bad she didn't believe in miracles.

"Mommy? What we do today?"

"I thought we'd go back to playgroup."

Robby's eyes lit up. "Playgroup? Yeaaaahh!"

The playgroup they belonged to met at the community center. Natalie had missed so many sessions she no longer had a current monthly calendar. After cleaning up the breakfast dishes and bundling Robby into a coat, they left the house. Robby insisted on walking by himself, climbing into the car seat by himself, and even trying to buckle.

Any other day, she'd feel proud. What an independent little guy, and was he growing up! Much too quickly. Today she wanted that small hand in hers. She wanted to smell the baby shampoo in his hair. She needed to know that she was the most important person in his world, the one who put batteries into trains and bandages on boo-boos, the one he'd call for in the middle of the night.

But what was best for Robby?

The community center was down from the church. Robby sat up straight as they drove past. He held up his finger and twirled it. "Little light of mine," he sang over and over. He looked at her, as if expecting her to join in, but she didn't know the words. She managed to hum the tune a bit as they pulled into the parking lot of the community center and parked. Robby was still singing when she pushed open the door to the preschool room. She ushered Robby in and to a seat. Today, seven toddlers sat around two tables while parents or caregivers helped them trace their hands. Two stopped what they were doing, put their finger lights in the air and started singing.

Natalie shook her head as she watched Jasmin, Allison's little girl, glue eyes to her turkey. Would Robby be that careful and artistic when he hit four? Right now his turkey looked more like a ham, and it looked like green would be the color of choice. One of the assistants was reminding the children about the pilgrims and the first Thanksgiving.

Thanksgiving!

The kids were making turkeys because, of course, Thursday was Thanksgiving. She'd had her calendar open this morning and hadn't even noticed. Patty had invited her weeks ago. Had she said yes? Better make a phone call and soon. Luckily, holidays were on the long-term portion of Lucky's list.

Robby dropped his green crayon and grinned at all the "Robby!" and "Hi, Robby" greetings he received. He even received one "Hi, Thawobby." Playing the strong—make that short—silent type, he neglected to do more than give a tiny "Hi" in return. The lady in charge touched Natalie's arm in welcome. Funny, up until two weeks ago, Natalie assumed every touch, every nod, every tearful look was an act of sympathy because of her father. Now, she worried that they knew something else.

Which was why Natalie needed to deal with it before someone said the wrong thing in front of Robby.

He'd gone to her place, but she wasn't home. Yesterday, she'd been about to invite him over. He knew it. Whoever was on the phone had upset her. He wanted to know why because his gut feeling was that right now everything that was upsetting her in some way, shape or form came back to him.

They had to get past this.

He found her at the park next to Selena's town square. She was sitting on a bench dividing her time between reading a paperback and watching Robby.

Lucky sat down next to her, enjoying her look of surprise, but then feeling empty when her eyes darkened to suspicion.

She'd been pleased for all of a nanosecond.

He didn't have time to ask why.

"Lucky!" Robby launched himself into Lucky's arms. Lucky stood, twirled the boy and then chased him across the playground. Lucky realized his mistake two minutes into the game. Sitting astride a bull was an eight-second ride; chasing a three-year-old was a much lengthier investment of time and energy. By the time Lucky climbed the slide, slid down, circled the swing set and jogged twice around the length of a park that rivaled a football field, Robby finally fell to the ground giggling. Lucky landed beside him. When Robby's giggling stopped, Lucky heard an echo. No, not an echo. What he heard was Natalie laughing at him.

Okay, so he was a bit winded.

Standing up, he managed to limp toward Natalie. She'd put her book down because he and Robby were much more entertaining.

"Again?" urged Robby.

"Oh, Lucky's got to rest," Lucky said. "You play on the slide and in a minute, I'll join you."

"I wish I had a camera." The November wind whipped Natalie's hair across her face. She brushed it back and looked up at him. The sting of winter put red in her cheeks, but still the laughter didn't quite reach her eyes.

"And I wish I had an eraser."

"What?"

"I wish I had an eraser so I could get rid of all your suspicions about me."

She shook her head. "It would need to be a pretty big eraser."

"I'll buy it if you'll use it," Lucky offered.

She looked up at him, somewhat frightened, but also managing a brave smile. He went down on one knee in front of her and said, "Natalie, I promise. We can make this work out so everybody's happy."

She nodded, silently, and then waved Robby over. "It's time for his nap. You offered to come over yesterday. If the offer still stands, how about today?"

"Best offer I've had all day."

Natalie's house hadn't changed since his first visit, except this time the "Welcome" on the front mat was literal. He followed her into the living room, where she turned on the television before ordering him to sit down. Then she and Robby marched up the stairs because Robby had announced in the driveway, "I wet."

Lucky followed orders, because resisting orders might result in him assisting with diaper duty. He sat down in what was definitely a man's room: beige walls, tan carpeting and heavy, brown leather furniture. The walls displayed a hodgepodge of pictures with no definite design. Some were of family, primarily Robby and Natalie. Standing, he started walking the room, really studying the pictures, the lives depicted on the walls. He saw Natalie as a small girl, in pigtails and missing teeth. He saw Natalie and her parents—she looked like her mother—in studio poses. Then he saw Natalie with Robby and Natalie's father.

They looked happy.

Interspersed between the family photos were the pictures of the property, from the beginning when it was a true working ranch to today when it, at best, could be called a house on a very large piece of unused property.

It seemed a waste. Natalie had mentioned her father's love for this land. She'd mentioned how the earliest house resembled an outhouse. It took him a minute, but he found the picture she'd been describing and almost laughed. She'd nailed it. Based on size and design, the first house had all the earmarks of an outhouse. The people of this era cared more to preserve land than faces. If an ancestor of Natalie's appeared, they were in the distance, on horseback or leaning against a fence. He glanced out the window. She still had plenty of room for horses and such. Really, this place was about the same size as Bernice's. It could easily be a working ranch again, maybe not Bonanza, but definitely a smaller version of Southfork. He looked at the pictures on the walls again. Nope, not a single one of Natalie on a horse.

They existed; he knew it.

He turned off the television. On Monday afternoons, soap operas, judges and home shopping salespeople ruled. Lucky'd rather live in an outhouse than watch.

Actually, he'd rather think about the lovely Natalie Crosby, who, by the way, muttered. The whole drive over here, she'd been talking to herself. From his vantage point directly behind her, he could see an occasional nod of her head. Every once in a while she made gestures, both fists of anger and then one quick open hand signifying exasperation. In the backseat, Robby's head turned right or left. He didn't seem to care that his mother was having a virtual conversation. Robby knew that Lucky was following them. Obviously, Robby intended to make sure Lucky didn't get lost.

Lucky had no intention of getting lost, ever.

After a moment, Robby and Natalie came down the stairs. Robby headed right for a leather chest in the corner of the room. He pulled out two or three trains and immediately started changing the look of the room. The oversize coffee table became a world with trains and accidents. He immediately started having a conversation. Lucky figured he was the recipient, but he definitely wasn't needed.

Natalie headed for the kitchen. "You can come with me if you want. I'm making peanut butter and jelly."

The kitchen looked a lot more like it belonged to Natalie. It didn't have the heavy browns of the living room, but more hues of burgundy and pink. It fit her personality. It smelled of cinnamon and Kool-Aid. It wasn't the smell, though, that made him look twice. It was the woman, standing at the counter opening a jar of peanut butter.

She took bread from the cupboard and started talking, almost more to herself than to him. The apple didn't fall far from the tree. "Before my father died, we had Robby pretty much potty trained. In a matter of days, right after the funeral, he was back to having accidents and wanting his bottle."

"Makes sense," Lucky said. "After Marcus died, I was all messed up. I wasn't hungry. I couldn't sleep. I kept waiting to hear him snore or have him wake me from a solid sleep because he suddenly remembered a joke."

"I thought you guys had stopped traveling together."

"We had, but when he was alive, it was like I knew he was out there somewhere snoring, saving up jokes to tell me. When he died, I knew it would never be the same again. There was this empty feeling I couldn't seem to get rid of. I think it was then that I really understood why some people give up hope."

He watched her, waiting. Surely she'd flinch, look sad, or something. The memory of Marcus's death should inspire some emotional response from her.

Nothing.

Not a tear, not a dirty look, nothing. She didn't mutilate the sandwich bread or fling jelly.

Nothing.

"Eat!" Robby ran into the room before Lucky could start to question.

"Yes, we're going to eat," Natalie said calmly. "Why don't you help set the table."

Robby headed toward the pie safe and took a handful

of paper plates. Lucky followed the boy and watched as he set the table. "Pop Pop sat here." Robby pointed to where Lucky would be sitting.

"Thanks for letting me know."

"Otay." Robby ran to the counter, holding out his hand, and then dashing back to the table once the sippy cup full of cherry Kool-Aid was secure in his grasp.

Lucky took his seat, make that Pop Pop's seat, and waited. If he were a bit more comfortable, he'd be helping with napkins and drinks, but there was something disquieting about knowing he was sitting in Pop Pop's chair and doing what Marcus apparently never got to, *maybe never wanted to do.*

Robby picked up his sandwich and took a bite. Natalie stared at hers.

"Maybe we could say a quick prayer?" Lucky suggested.

"Okay," Robby agreed.

Natalie didn't bow her head, but she didn't object. Lucky made it short and easy. "God, thank you for this food. Amen."

"Amen," Robby echoed.

Robby took over the conversation. Good thing because it didn't look like Natalie intended to talk much. She stared out the window while Lucky listened to Robby talk about Lucky's truck—he wanted to ride in it again; to Robby talk about playgroup—he was glad they were going again; and to Robby talk about "Tanksgiving"—the boy liked turkey.

"Where are you going for Thanksgiving?" Lucky asked.

Robby looked at his mother; an exaggerated expression gave away that he knew the word *Tanksgiving* but not the meaning, yet.

"We're going to my friend Patty's." She finally focused on what was in front of her. Maybe what she was seeing out the window was not the wind in the trees but the past.

"Patty's," Robby echoed, like he really knew. "For turkey." For the rest of lunch, Robby turned his peanut butter sandwich into a train and then a horse. Lucky followed suit by turning his peanut butter sandwich into a plane and then a bull.

Natalie managed a tiny smile before reminding Robby that if he didn't eat his sandwich there'd be no treat.

"For you, either," she told Lucky.

"And you," he responded pointedly.

He and Robby finished their sandwiches in record time.

When the last crumb was accounted for and the last potato chip put back in the bag, Robby scooted from his chair and took his paper plate to the trash.

"Mommy, nooooo," he immediately whined.

"Robby, yes," Natalie countered. Looking at Lucky, she said, "It's nap time and because you're here, he really doesn't want to go."

"Nap time! Wow, I wish I could take a nap," Lucky said.

Robby didn't look convinced.

Glancing at Natalie, Lucky suggested, "How about if I go with you two? I'd like to see your room."

Robby's eyes lit up. "I have choo-choo room."

The stairs creaked under Lucky's weight. Robby

made it to the top first with Natalie right behind. It didn't take a genius to figure the positioning was on purpose. If Robby tripped, Natalie would stop the fall. Judging by the three-year-old's sure-footed scampering, falls didn't happen often.

"Hurry," Robby urged.

Robby's bedroom, like the kitchen, showed Natalie's touch. Trains ruled. "I started with Winnie the Pooh," Natalie said, "but when Robby got old enough to choose, it quickly became apparent that he liked trains."

Robby climbed in a train tent and choo-chooed for a minute. Then he scooted out and hopped on his train-shaped bed.

"Under the covers," Natalie ordered.

"But—"

"Under the covers," Lucky echoed, surprising himself. His words surprised Natalie, too, judging by her expression. They worked wonders on the boy, though. He crawled up to the top of the bed, put his head on the pillow, pulled up the covers and closed his eyes.

Then, he opened one.

When he saw they were both still in the room and still staring at him, he giggled and closed it again, this time covering his head with the blanket.

"Go to sleep," Natalie ordered.

"Lucky here awake?" Robby peeked out.

"I don't know if Lucky will still be here when you wake up," Natalie said, "but if you don't go to sleep, I'm asking Lucky to leave now."

"Go to sleep," Lucky echoed sternly.

"Otay."

This time he closed his eyes fiercely and pretended to snore.

And Lucky knew he intended to be there when Robby woke up.

Closing the door to Robby's room, Natalie turned to Lucky and said, "Go on downstairs. I have one thing to do and then I'll join you."

He left without arguing, continuing to be the one sane, reliable person in her world. She leaned her head against Robby's closed door.

Changes were coming, and if Lucky was any indication, Robby would benefit. There existed a family who was so thrilled with the little boy they'd probably bring a boxcar into their backyard if Robby wanted it.

"Natalie." Lucky's voice was low. He was standing at the bottom of the stairs.

"Can you see me?" she whispered.

"Yes."

Great. First of all, what man can hear a whisper? Her father certainly never heard her whisper, but then, he was hard of hearing. Natalie had called it his selective hearing. Worse, since Lucky had answered yes, it meant he'd been watching her lean against Robby's door.

She turned, heavy hearted, and headed for the stairs. When she reached him, he didn't move. He simply said, "Are you all right?" She was forced to look up at him, feel his warmth, and he was warm. He made the house feel alive again, like when her dad moved through the rooms.

No, she wasn't all right. Her world kept spiraling out of control, and everywhere she turned, here was this man offering to make it better, offering to help. The kicker, what made it all so frustrating, was that not only was he the most willing to help, but also he was the most qualified. "I'm all right," she finally said. "I was just thinking about all the decisions I have to make."

He nodded, and it looked like he started to reach for her but stopped himself. Natalie wanted to sit on the bottom step and cry. Since meeting Lucky, time and time again he proved that he was someone she could rely on, lean on.

"When I woke up this morning," she admitted, "I decided today was the day I'd tell Robby about his relationship with you."

He smiled and she noticed that he was one of those guys who had a half smile. She'd never realized just how appealing half smiles were.

"Good," he said. "Can I help?"

She led the way to the kitchen; he willingly followed.

"Natalie," he said when he sat across from her at the kitchen table. "You know what I like best about you?"

She looked at him suspiciously. "What?"

"You bounce back good," Lucky said.

Natalie blinked. Her father used to say that, until she fell off the horse that last time. "What?"

"You bounce back good. No matter what life throws at you, you meet it head-on, and no matter what, you're keeping Robby as the most important aspect of your life. I admire that."

She swallowed. If this were a Lifetime movie, she'd be the one with the secrets, the one the audience pushed to tell the truth. She was the one lying, Lucky was the hero, and every day he seemed to grow even more heroic. Yet here he was saying he admired her. Truth was, she didn't bounce back; she fell flat.

"How well did you know Marcus?" Lucky asked suddenly.

"Not well at all," she admitted.

"Did you love him?"

"No, I didn't love him." In some ways, though, she was starting to have warmer feelings toward Marcus. Surely any brother of Lucky's couldn't have been all bad.

"Why didn't you?" Lucky asked slowly.

"He belonged to Tisha," Natalie said simply. Desperately, she tried to think of a way to change the subject.

"Would you even know Marcus if not for Tisha?"

Natalie shook her head.

"Marcus used to be my hero," Lucky admitted. "He could do everything, and he did it well. He made the top forty-five in just three years. I'm in my sixth and still haven't gotten there. This might have been my year, but truthfully—" his grin disappeared "—my heart's not in it."

She wanted to say, *Tell me about your brother*. But that would give her away. Even more, she wanted to say, *Tell me about you*. Still, he'd finally given her a chance to change the subject. "Why did you become a bull rider?"

"When you're not raised on a ranch, bull riding's the event to get into. Neither Marcus nor I had the hours in the saddle to become a bronc. We're city boys."

"You don't act like a city boy."

"That's because we spent summers with my grandparents over in Delaney. Grandpa had us in the saddle, but two months every summer didn't make cowboys out of us."

She understood. For years, Allison's mother gave riding lessons. Natalie and Allison had watched as kids here for two-week vacations thought they were *riding* horses. What they were doing was holding on to horses, usually *holding* on to the saddle horn like it was the only thing between them and the ground. In most cases, it was.

"I'll bet you were a natural," she said.

"Marcus was the natural, and Grandpa had been a bull rider. He had us on barrels from the time we were little. I could show you pictures. Made my mother worry and my father threaten to keep us home summers."

"But still you became a bull rider."

"I think my brother and I did everything we could to do exactly the opposite of what my father wanted."

"I loved riding," Natalie said. Boy, had it been a long time since those words had come from her mouth. "Dad was what you'd call a more-than-gentleman farmer. His dad ran a working ranch, and so did my great-grandpa before him. Dad remembered when this place really thrived. But the 1940s were really hard, and my great-grandpa started selling off parcels. My grandpa managed to keep it as a working ranch, but even he had to sell off a few plots. He realized that if anything was going to remain for his two sons, he'd need a career change."

"The stockyard?" Lucky said.

"Yup. Grandpa managed to buy back a few pieces after the stockyard made good. Dad took over after he got out of college. He married my mother and almost immediately started buying horses and a few cows. Mom kept chickens and, from what I hear, she was partial to mules."

"When did your mother die?"

"I was eight. Dad got rid of the chickens, cows and such because without her help, he just didn't have the time. He kept the horses. I was already a big help taking care of them."

"What about your uncle, Tisha's dad?"

"Dad bought Allen out. It's kind of a sad story."

"What's he do for a living?"

"He works on his wife's family's dairy farm. He still has five children living at home. He…" Natalie stopped. Just how much did she tell Lucky? If she opened her mouth, used Tisha's name, wasn't she getting that much closer to saying something she'd regret, something she wasn't ready to share?

Oh, what a tangled web we weave.

"Natalie?" Lucky encouraged.

"Allen's never been known for having much luck in life."

"Are all his kids like Tisha?"

Natalie had to give Lucky credit. Most people, once they'd met Tisha, had all kinds of opinions. He asked the question everyone thought but didn't have the courage to address. He even managed to look thoughtful.

"No, none of the other kids are like Tisha. She, like your brother, was the oldest. She took off at eighteen, and I don't think she's ever been back."

"So, she had a rough childhood and that's why she's the way she is?"

"What she had was a childhood without all the extras and without happiness. They just never had money.

I'm not sure her parents even had the desire for things like cable or designer jeans. She came to spend the summers here, at my dad's request, and when it was time for her to go back home, she'd cry and cry."

"Because you had cable and designer jeans?"

"Cable, designer jeans, entry fees for rodeos and all the fast food we wanted just a fifteen-minute drive away."

"She came every summer. Were you friends?"

"Friends? No, not really. I had friends, Patty and Allison. Even more, I had my dad and I had horses. Dad wanted to keep me from being lonely, but I was never alone. I think by the time he realized that her spending the summer with us wasn't good for me and wasn't good for Tisha, he didn't know how to stop it."

Lucky scooted his chair closer to the table and reached across to touch the top of her hand. "I think every family has issues. Some work them out as a family. Others never work them out."

She nodded, noticing that his hand remained on top of hers, noticing how light his touch was, how caring.

Who was she? Was she someone who could work through this with Lucky? Or was she someone who would never work it out?

Was she like Tisha?

Looking across the table at Lucky Welch, Natalie again realized the power of a lie and how much a lie cost everyone involved.

For a while, she'd only thought of losing Robby, but now she realized that once the lie escaped, she'd be losing Lucky, as well.

Chapter Ten

It was a two-bedroom apartment with horse privileges. If it were any other place, it might have worked. The bedrooms were small; he could live with that. The kitchen and living room were combined. No problem. The bathroom only had a shower and not a bath. Again, no problem. The only problem, besides that it was the second story of a barn and his comings and goings would be public because this was a working ranch, had to do with the rancher's wife. The landlord, Richard Dunbar, was friendly yet all business. He discussed responsibilities, price and lease. No wonder this was one of the more successful cattle and hay ranches in the area. He also mentioned having seen Lucky at church.

For a moment, Lucky was convinced he'd found temporary lodging. He couldn't stay at Bernice's forever.

Then Patty Dunbar had entered the apartment. A curvy blonde, whom Lucky remembered well from the rodeo and from church, she was Natalie's best friend—something Lucky hadn't realized when he saw the ad in the paper. She was also a mama bear. Natalie didn't need any help; she'd been taking care of Robby just fine for three years. He had everything a little boy would ever need.

With a baby on her hip and a single purpose, Patty demanded, "So why are you thinking about signing a six-month lease? You have the travel trailer. Selena, Texas, is not a central location for a bull rider. Surely it's about time for you to be heading out again?"

"I'll get to the rodeos," Lucky assured her, even though he now had no intention of renting the place, "and it's time to settle down."

"Honey, I think I hear someone crying," Richard Dunbar suggested.

Patty gave her husband the I-know-what-you're-trying-to-do look and said, "If that were true, I'd be hearing the sound and not you."

"Maybe this is a bad idea." Lucky put his hat back on and stepped toward the door.

"Yes," Patty agreed.

Lucky almost smiled, but he didn't think Miss Patty would appreciate it. Too bad Richard Dunbar hadn't provided a last name during the phone query Lucky made, but then, why would he? Richard provided directions and agreed to meet Lucky at the barn. They'd been in the apartment all of five minutes when Lucky heard a screech, which was followed by someone pounding up the stairs.

"Look, Mrs. Dunbar, I didn't realize this was your place and I'll tell you what I keep telling Natalie. I only want to help."

Richard looked lost. He opened his mouth as if to say something, then wisely closed it.

A wail came from down below. It was followed by a "Mommy, I fell!"

"Wolf in sheep's clothing," Patty muttered before taking off.

Richard waited a moment. "I probably owe you an apology. I knew my wife wouldn't consider having you for a tenant, but I've been mulling something over for the last couple of days and it involves you. When you called, I figured it was God giving me the go-ahead."

"The go-ahead for what?"

"I've heard you preach," Richard said. "I mean, besides this past Sunday. It wasn't at that Cowboy Church you're so involved in. It was at a little congregation in Van Horn, with barely twenty-five members."

"I remember." Lucky remembered all too well. He'd gotten little sleep, had to drive more than two hours round-trip on top of preaching, and when he finally got on the back of his draw—a bull named ThrowAway— he'd made just three seconds. "A friend of my mother's attends there. She got my mother to ask me to preach. I about broke my neck trying to get everything done that day."

"I was visiting my cousin." Richard motioned toward the apartment door. "Let's head downstairs. I was only there that one day. My cousin doesn't attend church, so I went to the congregation closest to his house. I was in for a surprise. You gave a great sermon."

"Thanks." Lucky followed Richard out the door and down the stairs.

"So, whether or not you're renting this particular apartment, you're still settling down in this area?"

"Yes, absolutely."

Richard shook his head. "Most of the town didn't know Marcus was Robby's father. I'm not sure Natalie's father even knew. Judging by my wife's behavior, she knew. She'll also get over it if you do right by Natalie."

"I plan to."

"Good." Richard headed for the house with Lucky following. When they reached the bottom step, Richard turned around. "Have you given any thoughts to renting in Delaney?"

"No."

"Come on in. I'll get us some ice tea, and I have a proposition for you."

"Are you sure your house is safe?"

Richard laughed. "Patty's bark has always been worse than her bite."

"She threatened to hit me with her purse at the Selena rodeo. I'm thinking she has more heavy-duty weapons here."

"The ice tea is cold, and Patty makes the best chocolate-chip cookies this side of Lubbock. I'll go lock up her purse. You coming in?"

"I guess with that kind of incentive, I'd be a fool to say no."

Patty had one of her kids sitting on the kitchen counter. She was putting a bandage on his knee while he cried and said, "Ooooww. Oow. Ow." The baby crawled on the kitchen floor, seemingly fascinated by an errant paper towel.

Richard headed straight for the kitchen, said a few words to his wife that Lucky couldn't hear and then came back carrying two glasses of tea and a plate of cookies.

"Good balance," Lucky complimented him.

"Comes with helping the wife with the kids."

Lucky took one of the teas and followed Richard's example by sitting down, taking a drink and then placing his tea on the coffee table.

The living room was about the same size as Natalie's, but this living room showed a successful marriage of two styles. There was still an abundance of browns, tans and beiges, but here there were also frilly lamps, watercolors on the wall and no heavy furniture. The couch was red.

Richard took two cookies, offered one to Lucky and sat back. "Patty tells me that your mother was one of the Selena rodeo queens and that your grandparents lived in Delaney."

"I spent summers in Delaney."

"You still have friends there?"

"No, not really."

"Still like the town?"

Lucky thought back to the too-enthusiastic sign, the café and general store, and the playground. He thought about the empty church. "Yeah, I still like the town."

"I'm an elder here. Did you know that?"

"No, my mind's pretty much been on other things since I arrived."

Richard nodded. "I can sure understand that, but there's going to be a time when things settle down, much like you're planning to settle down."

Lucky leaned forward, took another cookie and said, "Mr. Dunbar, why don't you just say whatever it is you're trying to say."

"The church in Delaney has been without a minister for five years. Some of the men of the congregation tried to keep things going, but they all work long hours and, besides preaching on Sunday morning, none of them had the time or the know-how to do all the other things a preacher does. The church is in good condition."

"It's a historical landmark," Lucky remembered.

"For the last three years, many of its members have driven all the way to Selena to attend services. Others, though, have stopped attending altogether. There's a whole community hurting for a local congregation, and we can't seem to find someone to put behind the pulpit."

"And," Lucky said slowly, "you think I'm the one. As much as I appreciate the suggestion you're about to make, I'm a bull rider. Sundays are not a day of rest for me."

Richard leaned forward and, in a voice much too decisive, said, "Your brother was the bull rider."

Lucky leaned back. Nothing like having someone malign your talents after they offer you a job preaching. "No." Lucky shook his head. "I'm not ready to give it up yet. This would have been my year if my brother hadn't died. I'm in good shape, only a few injuries this year—"

Neither Richard's expression nor posture changed. "I've seen you and your brother ride. You've got a good seat, Lucky, I'll give you that, but with bull riding, you either give it your all or you give it up. I've never seen you give it your all."

"You've got a point—" Lucky stood "—but, as you said, I've got a good seat. Now I just need to ride better. I'm not ready to quit, and I don't think you can judge my skill on what you saw at the Selena rodeo."

Richard looked like he wanted to say something

else, but a soft "ahem" came from the doorway separating the living room from the kitchen.

"I've overstepped," Richard said. "I tend to do that when I get excited about an opportunity, and I think you're just what the church in Delaney needs. You'd help restore a lot of souls. Surely that's more important than buckles and purses."

"I'll keep your offer in mind." Lucky finished his tea in one gulp and headed for the door. He may not have been hit over the head with a purse, but he'd been hit over the head with an offer. The offer packed more of a wallop.

As Lucky jumped in his truck and started the engine, he couldn't help but think that God was telling him in more ways than one that it was time to really think about his future and where his priorities were.

What he'd done in the past was good, but maybe not good enough.

Maybe that was the kind of bull rider he was.

Good, but not good enough.

His worry, though, was maybe he was that kind of preacher, too.

Good, but not good enough.

"Mommy, I hungry."

"Hmm," Natalie said noncommittally. She glanced in the rearview mirror. Robby should have fallen asleep the moment they left Patty's. No wonder. He'd missed taking a nap; he'd played almost nonstop, and he'd been cuddled and hugged by every adult there. Patty had a huge family, and they'd always counted Natalie as one of their own. Richard's family wasn't quite as big as

Patty's, but what they lacked in numbers, they made up for in size.

Natalie's Thanksgiving had been something else. It had been melancholy. She'd sat in Patty's living room and laughed with the family. At Patty's table, she'd bowed her head in prayer and this time she understood why. She'd eaten the traditional turkey, stuffing and pumpkin pie. She'd played Monopoly with the young people, and she'd taken Robby to the potty.

The whole time she couldn't shake the fact that in her entire life, this was the first time she'd not cele-brated Thanksgiving at home.

A home that now felt so empty.

"I'm so full I can barely fit behind the steering wheel," Natalie said. She turned the windshield wip-ers on as a gentle rain began.

Robby giggled.

"How can you be hungry?"

"I no know."

Glancing again in the rearview mirror, she couldn't help but enjoy the sight of Robby grinning at her. His hair was a mess, and he'd spilled something blue on the front of his shirt, but oh, was he happy.

"Good day?" she asked.

"Good day," he mimicked.

"Do you want to stop at the café and have some ice cream?" The rain increased. It was almost a perfect end to a busy day. Rain meant staring out windows, touch-ing paned glass and waiting for a rainbow.

"Ice cream, yeah!"

The family who owned the café up until two years ago never opened on major holidays, but some out-of-staters had purchased it, and now the blinking neon light didn't seem to recognize the Sabbath or holidays. To them, Thanksgiving was just a day at the cash register. Natalie might grump about progress, but today it didn't keep her from taking a prime parking spot and hoisting Robby out of his seat and inside. She let go of his hand for just a minute while she shrugged out of her coat. That was all it took.

"Lucky!" he shrieked, and across the diner he went.

He had a clear shot since the diner was pretty much empty. Lucky Welch sat in a booth by himself, eating a turkey sandwich and reading the Bible.

He looked up just in time to catch Robby to him, and then he uttered words that only cemented what Natalie already knew. They'd be joining him.

"Looks like my prayer's been answered." Lucky grinned.

She was an answer to a prayer. Wow. Well, at least Robby was an answer to a prayer.

"I'm glad you're here. I was feeling pretty lonely."

"Can't have that," Natalie said.

"Did you get my message yesterday?"

"The one inviting Robby and me to church?"

"That's the one."

"I got it." Natalie stared out the window. Rain tapped the glass, giving her an excuse not to look at Lucky. "I've been busy catching up with work, and I've also been cleaning out my dad's room. It's past time."

Lucky was silent as he took the last bite of his sandwich. "I had to clean out Marcus's trailer."

"My dad's boots were on the side of the bed. His glasses were on the table. There was even a shirt tossed on the end of the bed. The room looked like it was waiting for him to come back."

"Yeah, I know that feeling, and it's harder around holidays. Did you go to Patty's?"

"Yes," Robby said, sounding all the world like a little grown-up.

"Why aren't you at Bernice's? They always have a huge Thanksgiving." Natalie snagged a menu from between the ketchup and mustard bottles and stared at it. No way was she going to order food, but she was having a hard time not staring at Lucky. If she kept it up, he might notice that she was staring *with interest*.

"Mary went into labor. The whole family packed up in ten minutes flat and were out the door. They invited me to come with them, but I've spent more than my share of Thanksgivings in hospitals."

"Mary's in labor? Why have you spent Thanksgivings in hospitals?"

"Hospitals?" Robby repeated.

The waitress showed up at that moment, took both Robby and Natalie's ice cream order. When she left, Robby took the salt shaker and stuck it in his mouth.

"Robby, no." Natalie took it away, and Robby screamed.

Lucky looked surprised.

"This is parenthood, too," Natalie said. "It's not all grinning boys in car seats and playing at the park and getting hugs." With that, she scooted Robby from the booth and took him outside. The crisp November air was a slap in the face and just what Natalie needed. She'd overreacted in there a tiny bit. Robby was acting like a typical three-year-old who'd missed his nap. She was afraid of getting too close to a man who threatened her lifestyle in more ways than one.

"Mommy, we stand here? Get wet?"

"We're standing here getting wet because I'm about to put you in the car and drive home. You don't get to scream in restaurants. Do you hear me? If you scream again we're going home."

He nodded, but then, he nodded a lot. Sometimes he nodded when she told him the man in the moon liked green peas. One time he nodded when she told him she was going to buy him pink cowboy boots with pretty sequins on them.

Lucky was eating the last of his mashed potatoes. He was also doing that half-smile thing that disarmed her the other day.

"So," she said, sitting down and returning to the conversation exactly where she left off, "Mary's in labor? And why have you spent more than one holiday in the hospital?"

"Mary's in labor. Nobody's worried. I expect there will be a new grandbaby any minute, and, Natalie, think, what do I do for a living?"

"Oh, yeah."

"What you do?" Robby questioned.

"I ride bulls."

"Oh, yeah."

Robby's "Oh, yeah" sounded exactly like Natalie's. Lucky choked a bit on a spoonful of mashed potato, and then burst into laughter. Robby did, too. Laughter that brought tears to his eyes and also brought the waitress running to make sure everything was okay. Finally, Natalie allowed herself to laugh.

"That sounded good," Lucky said when everybody finally settled down.

"Robby's 'Oh, yeah'?" Natalie asked.

"No, you laughing. I don't think I've heard it before. You know what they say?"

"What do they say?"

The ice cream arrived as Lucky flipped his Bible open. "Here, in Ecclesiastes, it says, *'There is a time to weep and a time to laugh.'*"

"I've heard that line before," Natalie said.

"Good, that means you're open to the Word."

"I don't know about that." Natalie stirred her ice cream for a minute, not taking a bite but not pushing it away. Sometimes what she wanted wasn't good for her.

Like Lucky.

"I just happened to hear that line somewhere," she finally said. "I don't remember where. Probably television."

"I've been sitting here studying the Word. The answers have always been here. Many are in Ecclesiastes. Solomon also says there is *'a time to be born and a time to die.'* I've been angry with God for letting Marcus die. But he didn't *let* Marcus die. Marcus chose a dangerous profession. Every bull rider knows the risks. I was angry at God, and I was angry at Marcus. Truth is, I just need to grieve."

"My father was too young to die," Natalie said. "And he wasn't in a dangerous profession."

The doctors mentioned cholesterol as the major cause of his heart attack, but lately Natalie had wondered if worry about Tisha, about what would happen after the private detective found her, had somehow contributed.

Maybe Tisha contributed to Natalie's father's heart attack.

The thought had rocked Natalie's world one more time.

"Is it in the Bible, the phrase, *'And the truth will set you free'*?" Natalie asked.

"I know that one by heart. John 8:32."

"So it really is in the Bible?"

"It really is." Lucky reached across the table, took her hand from the ice cream she wasn't eating and covered her fingers with his. His palm was rough, but there was that warmth again.

"Mommy, you 'kay?" Robby asked.

"I'm okay." Natalie wanted to jerk her hand away from Lucky's, but the truth was, she liked the warmth there. She liked the thought that he kept reaching out to her, wanting to help.

"Mommy, mo ice ceam?" Robby broke into Natalie's thoughts, reminding her what truth she was hiding and why. Her little man wore more ice cream on his face than was left in the bowl.

"You're right," Natalie told Lucky as she pushed her dish of ice cream over to Robby. He'd have a killer sugar rush, but she needed him to be quiet, entertained. She needed to talk with Lucky.

Lucky tapped his Bible. "He said it first. I just repeated it."

"Money," Natalie whispered. "I've never been in want. After Dad died, it was the first time I ever really worried about what it would be like without it." She looked up at Lucky. "It's what drove me to you, asking for help."

"I'm so glad." The half smile returned in full force. Lucky bowed his head. It took Natalie a moment to realize he was praying. With his hand resting on top of his Bible, he was praying. She looked at his Bible. It obviously meant a lot to Lucky. It was dog-eared and pieces of papers marked pages.

"What were you praying for?" she said when he raised his head.

"I was actually thanking God for sending you and Robby here. I'm glad Mary went into labor and I wound up eating here with you and Robby."

He looked at her. "You're why I'm in Selena."

"Robby's why you're in Selena."

"Maybe at first."

Funny, the whole time at Patty's, she'd felt like there was someplace else she was supposed to be. Here, at the diner, she didn't have that feeling. Natalie looked at Lucky's Bible again. "What does He say about sharing children?"

Lucky laughed. "When we first met and everything was going so fast, and you were so afraid and I was so mad, I turned to the Bible. The first story I considered was about Solomon. Two mothers were claiming a child to be theirs. Solomon pretty much said to cut the child in half and let each woman have a part."

"You're kidding," Natalie said.

Even Robby looked interested, like he was following the story.

"No, not kidding. Solomon was a very wise man. The true mother said to give the child to the other woman, to spare his life. The woman who was not the mother said nothing. Thus, Solomon knew who to give the child to."

"Maybe we need Solomon."

"Maybe," Lucky agreed.

"Who Solman?" Robby asked. He really wasn't interested in Natalie's ice cream; right now he was more interested in playing with it.

"A very wise man," Natalie said. Lucky's spoon inched over, and he snatched a spoonful of Robby's ice cream.

Natalie took her spoon and helped herself to Robby's ice cream.

"Moooommmm." He snatched up his spoon and took a quick bite and then another and another.

It was gone in a matter of moments.

"Fun, Mommy, this fun."

"Marcus never ate all his ice cream," Lucky said. "It always went to waste. But if I tried to take it, he'd gobble it up."

"You have lots of good memories with Marcus, don't you?"

"Yes. To me, he was larger than life. Your friend Patty's husband made me realize something this last Tuesday."

"Patty told me you looked at her apartment. I told her to rent it to you."

"I'm considering something else now. Anyway, Richard offered me the church in Delaney, and when I told him I wasn't a pulpit minister but a bull rider, he said, 'No, Marcus was a bull rider.'"

"You're a great bull rider. I was mesmerized at the rodeo."

"Great? No. Good, yes. I am a very good bull rider, but not like Marcus. Growing up, I did everything he did. I wonder if he ever got tired of a little brother tagging along. Don't get me wrong, I love bull riding, but I wonder…would I be a bull rider if not for Marcus?"

"You would have been. Something like that, it's in

your blood. You can't fake it." For the first time in years, Natalie thought about what she'd given up when she'd refused to get back on her horse. Maybe if she had, she'd be remembered for what happened after the fall instead of remembered for the fall.

"The sport's changed so much since I was barrel racing. I almost fell off the bench when I saw the first bull rider wearing a helmet instead of a cowboy hat."

Lucky chuckled. "Change is good."

Natalie slowly nodded. "Some change." She rearranged Robby, who was now falling asleep. "That being said, and since this little guy is telling me it's time to go home, let me tell you what else I've been doing since Monday. I've been reading articles on the Web about telling children the truth about their heritage."

Lucky's eyes lit up. It looked like he was about to say, *And you're going to tell him?* but he looked at Robby and instead said, "What have you decided?"

"Seems like the experts agree. Trying to keep the truth a secret is unrealistic over time. It's traumatic to the person hiding the truth, and it can harm the person who doesn't know the truth." She looked down at Robby. "Harming him is the last thing I'd ever do. I thought about telling him Monday, but so much happened that day. We went to the library Tuesday, and I checked out books about this. I've been reading them to him at night and emphasizing how special he is. I'm ready to tell him tonight, while you're here with us."

"He's asleep," Lucky pointed out.

"He's dozing. He's not all the way asleep. I can tell by his eyes. Robby, sit up."

"Otay, Mommy."

"Robby, you know how Lucky's been hanging around a lot, trying to get to know us, being our friend."

Robby nodded.

"Well, he's going to be around a lot more."

"Otay."

"A lot more, Robby, *for you*," Natalie emphasized.

Robby nodded again. "Otay."

"Look over at Lucky. Notice how he looks a lot like you?"

Robby was through nodding. She had his interest, and while he wasn't understanding everything, he was understanding enough to know something important was going on.

Lucky started looking uncomfortable. "Maybe we should be somewhere else, like a counseling office or with my mother or something."

"I thought about the counselor," Natalie admitted, "but Robby knows you, he likes you, and adding a stranger to the mix would only take away from what we're trying to tell him." She pulled Robby onto her lap, noticing how big he was getting, and how soon he wouldn't fit on her lap while they sat in a booth. "Lucky is your daddy's brother. You know, like Patty's children are brother and sister."

Robby no longer looked sleepy. He stared at Lucky for a long time. Then he leaned back against Natalie. "He Daddy?" Robby questioned.

"No, he's your uncle," Natalie responded. "A very special uncle.

"Not daddy?"

"Not daddy," Natalie said again. "He was your daddy's brother."

"Sometimes," Lucky said, "uncles act like daddies."

"Daddy," Robby tried the word. Then, he nodded again. "Daddy for keeps."

Chapter Eleven

"Yes, I'll be careful. No, I won't be gone long. Yes, I'll come right over to see you when I get back." He was talking to Natalie, but she was merely acting as a go-between for Robby. Robby had all the questions, but they were in a three-year-old lingo that Lucky still needed help translating.

Robby finally got on the phone and said his own, "Bbyyyyeee."

"Bye," Lucky said.

Natalie took the phone as Robby ran back to the kitchen to grab a snack. Not even Lucky could compete with the cookies they'd just made. "He talked about you all the way home. He's not bothered by the truth a bit. He thinks it's great to have a daddy for keeps. I'll work on the uncle thing while you're gone."

"This time I'll only be gone for two days. You know, when I first found out about Robby, I skipped a few rodeos. I felt like I had to. Now that Robby knows I'm his uncle, his special uncle, I really don't want to be away. This weekend, for the first time, I really want to skip rodeos. But I've already paid the entry fees. Although

I've been hit or miss this year, there's still time to earn some money, at least break even. Plus, with Cowboy Christmas Week coming up—"

"Cowboy Christmas Week?"

"The busiest week a bull rider has. I've paid entry fees for more than twelve rodeos, and they all happen in just five days. None of them are next to each other. Usually by this time, I'd either have a driving buddy—" he paused and Natalie knew that he was remembering Marcus "—or I'd have arranged plane fare when I could still get it cheap."

"Where are you going?"

"This morning I'm flying to Greeley, Colorado. I'll ride this afternoon and then either catch a ride or hop a flight to Steamboat Springs, Colorado. I'll ride Saturday night, and then I'll somehow find a red-eye from there to you. I'll stop by Sunday morning, take you two out for breakfast, before church. You will go with me?"

"I'll think about it."

"Have you taken a look at my Bible?"

Natalie thought about the book sitting on the table beside her bed. Last night, Lucky had carried a sleeping Robby to the car, buckled the boy in with a little assistance, and as he held open the door so she could easily slide into the front seat, he'd handed her his Bible.

"Take this home," he'd said. "Look at some of the passages I've highlighted. You'd be amazed at how much they help."

She started to hand it back, but he closed the door before she could.

He sure had a way of getting her to do what he wanted. First, getting to know Robby. Next, coming to church. Now this Bible thing. "I've looked at a few passages," she admitted. "It's more interesting than I imagined, but it's also confusing."

"I'll help you understand the confusing parts. Now don't say you'll think about it. Say you'll go with me."

Her heart sang. *Say you'll go with me.* He wanted both of them. Then, she stilled. Her heart had no right to sing. Yes, telling Robby the truth had somewhat set her free, but she had one more secret.

Lucky rambled on, "We'll discuss Robby, my parents and some other things. I'll be home for four days, and then the show begins. The truly good news is that the first rodeo I'm entered in for Cowboy Christmas Week is in Odessa."

"Why is that good news?"

"Because you and Robby can come."

Natalie didn't answer. She couldn't. She heard the exuberance in Lucky's voice, all because he wanted them to attend, and suddenly she wanted, more than anything, to be there with him.

"I have a hard time at rodeos," she said, hedging for time.

"I know, but I'll be with you."

Natalie paused. *I'll be with you.* That seemed to be the dominant theme of most of the scriptures Lucky had highlighted.

"Okay, I'll really think about it," Natalie agreed.

Then Natalie had another thought. She'd screamed in both excitement and terror while watching Lucky and the others ride their bulls during the Selena rodeo. She's been fascinated, but she hadn't cared for any of them.

She definitely cared for Lucky, so much that it was starting to hurt. "Tell you what, I will go to church with you Sunday morning, breakfast, too, and I promise to think about the rodeo."

"Robby loves the rodeo."

"You're going to have to come up with something better than that," Natalie teased before saying goodbye.

She thought about the rodeo as she took Robby to the park and then over to Patty's for a Friday-night movie. She thought about it Saturday morning while she worked on Web sites, signed on two new clients, and even did a keyword search for Tisha. She thought about it while she made Robby breakfast and started both laundry and dishes. She thought about it when the doorbell rang and Robby, a little boy in footed pajamas, ran in front of her to open the door. They were greeted by the local florist who was actually delivering flowers himself.

Roses.

Red and white.

From Lucky to her.

Oh, wow.

"I don't usually deliver flowers myself, Natalie, but after writing down the message on this card, I just had to follow through."

"Writing down the message?"

"Yes, most times when I'm filling out the cards for people online or over the phone, it's just the standard message. You know, 'Thanks for a wonderful evening.' 'Thinking of you.' 'I'm glad you're in my life.' Your young man, however, gives quite a message."

Natalie took the flowers, pulling a section of baby's breath off for Robby, and then opened the card.

I've never wanted a home until I met you and

Robby. Every day I'm on the road, I'll be thinking of you and counting the minutes until I come home. Remember what the book of Ecclesiastes says in the third chapter: There is a time to love and a time to hate. Thursday night I realized it was time to love—and I'm falling in love with you. Yesterday morning, I realized it was time to hate—I hated leaving Selena and you and Robby. Call me Lucky in Love.

"Wow," Natalie said.

"I usually only allow thirty words, but I got so busy listening to your cowboy that I let him go over. Not sure what I would have cut, anyhow."

"Mommy! It broke!" Robby's baby's breath was shredded. Natalie pulled another section off, handed it over and after setting the vase on a table went to get her purse for a tip.

She realized she was still holding the card as she watched the florist drive away.

"Wow."

Before this went any further, before her heart was fully vested, she needed to tell Lucky the truth. She had a feeling, however, that for her heart it was already too late.

Colorado had been cold, cold, cold. Lucky took fifth in Greeley and third in Steamboat Springs. The cowboys who'd teased him about going to Selena instead of Lubbock were no longer teasing. They were too intent on keeping their standing, knowing their place in line, and Lucky was no longer in the line. No matter how he scored, he wasn't going to be in the top forty-five. It was too late. At most, if he sat down and tabulated his winnings, he'd find the earnings equal to his spending.

And he didn't care.

He intended to finish out the year, do one last Cowboy Christmas, and then if the position at the church in Delaney was still open to him, he was taking it.

"Your toes okay?"

"Doc said I broke two." Lucky opened one eye and checked on Travis Needham. The boy had wasted no time after getting his feet wet in Selena. Apparently, he'd been doing a rodeo near Colorado Springs while Lucky had been doing Greeley, but they'd wound up next to each other in Steamboat Springs. "Don't worry. If I had to break something, it might as well be toes."

Travis nodded, and Lucky wondered if the boy really understood that bull riders rode with broken ribs, collapsed lungs and fractured skulls. Lucky thought about telling him, but didn't. Travis wouldn't listen. Lucky hadn't. Marcus hadn't.

"What time do you think we'll land?" Travis asked, looking out the window of the Cirrus SR20. They'd lucked out and met up with a wealthy cowboy out of Abilene. He'd fly them to Abilene, and then they could rent a car or catch a bus to Selena.

"We've got decent weather except for this wind," Lucky said when the small plane hit turbulence. "I'm thinking maybe four or five in the morning."

"I hate the bus. I took it from Lubbock to Colorado Springs. I thought I'd be saving money, but all I did was lose time and money. The bus was so late I almost missed the rodeo."

"Yeah, the bus definitely is a last resort, but we'll only be three hours from Selena, so it won't be that bad.

We'll get home around eight." That would give Lucky enough time to get to Natalie's, take her and Robby to breakfast and then make it to Sunday school. He'd be exhausted but happy.

Travis was already exhausted and happy. He'd come in last at both of his rodeos, meaning he got on the bull, wrapped his bull rope around his left hand, shouted "GO!", burst out of the chute and promptly lost the bull and found the ground.

After an hour of listening to Travis relive the rodeo, Lucky closed his eyes. His toes hurt, and he needed to sleep because he wanted to be wide-awake during his time with Natalie and Robby.

At best, it was a guarded sleep.

The sun had no intention of making an appearance in Selena this late November morning. It was a gray-and-black dawn. Travis's dad was waiting for them at the bus station. He shook Lucky's hand and took Travis's bag. His "How'd you boys do?" was answered with a solemn "Placed third and fifth" from Lucky, followed by an enthusiastic "Dead last, Dad!" from Travis.

Travis's dad dropped Lucky off at Bernice's and drove away. Dark, gray clouds filled the sky and seemed to reach for the ground. One ray of blue sky heralded their way. Lucky stood in Bernice's front yard a moment, thinking that for one bull rider a beginning lay ahead, but for him, he'd reached the end.

Bernice had given him a key when she realized he planned on staying. She wouldn't hear of letting him hook his travel trailer up to the barn and live out there.

"How'd you do?" Howie Jr. jumped up from the kitchen table and all but ran Lucky down.

"I did good, third and fifth."

"Why didn't you come in first?"

"I broke two toes in Greeley, still stayed on. The toes still hurt in Steamboat Springs, and I still did my eight seconds. Guess my form was a bit off, though. I slipped two spots."

"You want breakfast?" Bernice asked.

"No, I'm going to take a quick shower—" he glanced at the clock "—quicker than I like, and then I'm picking Natalie and Robby up."

Bernice beamed. She was worse than his mother in some ways.

He showered, dressed and was out to his truck in just twenty minutes. It was another twenty minutes to Natalie's house, and she was definitely worth the effort. Natalie answered the door, dressed in a silky red dress that emphasized curves and invited him to imagine the future. A future for the three of them.

Yes, he could spend forever with this woman.

Natalie stayed by Lucky all during church. Already he seemed to know everybody, and everybody seemed to know him. Some of them seemed intent on emphasizing that they were from Delaney and mentioned the drive. They all either shook Natalie's hand or hugged her. She'd never been hugged so much in her life. Robby, on the other hand, liked getting his hand shook, but he wound up with even more pats on the head.

Sunday school was easy. Lucky found a class for newcomers, and the preacher himself was the teacher. It was a small class. There probably really weren't that many beginning Bible students in Selena. In many ways, Selena, Texas, could be called the starting point, or maybe the stopping point, of the Bible Belt. It depended on which way you were traveling.

This morning's topic was the prodigal son. Natalie almost wished the preacher had attended the birth-order class. It would have been interesting to marry the older son to the characteristics of a firstborn, and the younger son to the characteristics of the baby.

When class ended, Natalie was surprised. It had been an hour but felt like minutes.

"What did you think?" Lucky asked. He took her arm and guided her out into the hallway.

"Interesting and painless," she answered.

"Painless?"

"I've always figured church was boring. I'm just surprised that it's not."

"The Word is never boring." Lucky looked a bit forlorn. "Sometimes it's painful, knowing family members are lost and such, but there's hope for those who seek."

They fetched Robby from class and took him to Children's Bible Hour. He was in his element, unable to decide whether he wanted to sit with Patty's kids or Mary's. He chose neither and sat right between two older girls who thought he was cute.

"He's a charmer," Lucky whispered.

"Like you," Natalie whispered back. She almost giggled when he stopped in his tracks.

They stopped at Selena Café after church. The waitress brought the correct drinks without being asked and didn't even blink when they ordered four bowls of ice cream. Then, without even discussing it, they went to Natalie's house. While Natalie changed into jeans and a T-shirt, Lucky, mindless of his good clothes, carried out the boxes containing her father's stuff. He stored them in the back of his truck. He knew some retired bull riders exactly Natalie's dad's size.

The minute he was done loading the truck, Robby insisted on a movie, which he fell asleep halfway through. Lucky carried him to bed.

When he came back downstairs, he sat next to Natalie on the couch. It reminded Natalie of high school and first dates and how good it felt to be nervous.

Lucky definitely made her nervous. Especially after that card had said he was falling in love with her. Neither of them had brought it up yet, but the chemistry between them was electric.

"I'm leaving Thursday night," Lucky said, gazing at her. "I'm taking my travel trailer. Travis Needham's going with me. That gives me three days to be with you and Robby. I've got two things I need to do. One, find a place to live, and two, deal with my father."

"I'll help you pick out a place to live," Natalie offered. "I think Patty will be a little more open to renting to you now."

"I was thinking," Lucky said slowly, "about heading over to Delaney."

Natalie was silent. Patty had already told her about the offer of the Delaney church, and more than one church member this morning certainly had mentioned it.

"Delaney's not that far," she said softly.

He put his arm around her, pulling her close, and whispered, "Could it be you don't want me that far away?"

"Could it be I want you even farther away?" she countered.

"I don't believe it."

"Good, because it's not true."

Lucky laughed, didn't remove his arm, and said, "Finding a place to live probably isn't the biggest issue. If push comes to shove, I can rent from Patty for a while, or even stay with Bernice a bit longer, and then take my time picking out a place in Delaney if everything works out. I've never been a pulpit minister, and quite frankly, the thought terrifies me."

"If it terrifies you, why are you doing it?"

"Because God is calling me to."

"You've been doing Cowboy Church for years. Why are you terrified?"

"Cowboy Church is me preaching to peers. And, really, there's very little for a preacher to do. Most of the time it's anybody who feels like it either witnessing or confessing. Their problems are no surprise. I've lived their problems. In Delaney, I'll have to do funerals, baptisms and weddings."

"Weddings," Natalie whispered. "I never imagined you doing weddings."

"Basically, I'll be a servant to every member of the church, whether I understand the way they live or not."

"You're a natural," Natalie encouraged. "Look how well we're doing, and what a start we had. When I met you I wished you off the face of the Earth, and today…"

"Today…?"

"Today," she said slowly, amazed at the words and how much she wished them to be true, "I wish I'd met you four years ago."

"I wish that, too," he said.

"But then I wouldn't have Robby."

The silence that followed should have been uncomfortable, but it wasn't. The flowers Lucky had sent were on one of the end tables. The red and white petals delicate, joyful. Everything could be right, *if only*. For a minute, Natalie worried he'd bring up Marcus, ask the all-important question that had simmered under the surface for weeks. *If you didn't love Marcus, how did you have his child?*

Next time he asked, she would tell him the truth. She was just happy that he wasn't asking today.

"Robby's a big reason for needing to meet my father head-on. This is killing my mother, and she doesn't deserve it. My father has acted irrationally more than once. There's no excuse for his behavior."

Natalie didn't have a response because if Marcus had been an involved father she'd not be a mother.

"Anyway," Lucky continued, "I was thinking about driving to Delaney tomorrow, and I wondered if you'd come along. I want to check out the church and see if there are any rentals."

"If you're willing to go later in the day, we'll go," Natalie said. "I'm working hard on catching up my Web business. I took too much time off after Dad died."

"Would eleven be good?"

"Delaney's just an hour away," Natalie said. "How long were you thinking of staying there?"

"Two or three hours."

"If we leave at eleven, we're talking about being gone during Robby's nap time. He's usually—"

"How many hours do you work?"

"I try to put in five hours a day."

Lucky thought for a minute. "Let's go at eight. I'll

get us back here about two. Robby can go down for a nap, and when he wakes up, I'll babysit until you've done your work."

It was like being with her dad again, organizing their lives so both of their needs were met. It was a feeling of not being alone. She could get used to it.

"Tuesday," Lucky said, "I'm taking on my father. I don't care where it happens, here or there. We're going to add Grandma to Robby's life with or without Grandpa."

"Are you flying to Austin?"

"Maybe. You wanna go with me?"

"No, I'm not ready for that."

"Then I'll try to get them here."

"Oh, goody."

"Natalie, I admit, I'm not sure taking you to meet my dad is a good idea, but I'm thinking that once he meets you, he'll have to realize just how wonderful you are."

"I'm not wonderful."

He shook his head. "Just look in the mirror. All you'll see is wonderful."

Skeptical was too tame a word to describe the look she tried to give Lucky.

He responded with the familiar half smile, before sobering up to say, "You're right, though, it might be too early to introduce you to my dad. I'll fly out alone on Tuesday morning and fly back Tuesday night. What do you want to do on Wednesday?"

"Me? What do I want to do?" She was surprised by the question. Lately, she hadn't been doing anything but planning on how to get her life back to normal.

There was nothing normal about Lucky Welch,

brother of Marcus Welch, asking her what she wanted to do on Wednesday.

"Are we starting to date?" she asked carefully.

"I hope so."

"It's happening awfully fast."

"Not fast enough," Lucky said. "I've already admitted how I feel about you."

"There's a lot you don't know about me."

"I'm going to enjoy finding out."

"What if you find out something you don't like?"

"We'll work through it."

Yeah, right, Natalie thought. Before she had time to dwell on the seriousness of the conversation and its repercussions, he went on, "We're doing what I want on Monday. Tuesday I'll be gone. Let's do something you and Robby would like on Wednesday."

"Like look for a Christmas tree?" Her eyes lit up.

"Hey," Lucky cried, hugging her close. "You're making me feel, well, like Santa. I've never really looked for a Christmas tree," he said. "I'm assuming you're not talking about going to a store."

"Of course not! Only the real thing will do."

"My mother grumbled every Christmas about not having a real Christmas tree. My father mentioned pine needles on the carpet and the time and energy to get rid of the tree, let alone the cost of buying a new one every year, getting the permit…"

"I already have the permit. My dad…" Her voice tapered off. Then, she managed to get it back. "My dad applied for it before he died. It came in the mail a few weeks ago."

"Okay, we'll get a Christmas tree. Isn't December second a little early?"

"I'll keep it watered." Her eyes sparkled, and she looked so beautiful that he leaned down toward her, his lips meeting hers in a gentle kiss that he hoped would go on forever.

The doorbell rang, and Natalie pulled back, seeming dazed. She shrugged out from under his arm, and Lucky grumbled. "I hope it's something important because I'm not crazy about interruptions."

Natalie wasn't crazy about interruptions, either, especially interruptions like Lucky's parents, Mr. and Mrs. Welch, suddenly standing at her front door.

Chapter Twelve

"Where's Robby?" Lucky's mother managed to beat her husband into the room. Lucky came off the couch in a fluid motion that quickly had him standing between his dad and Natalie.

His dad glanced around the living room, the couch Lucky had been sitting on, the Disney movie still playing, silently, on the television and the pictures on the wall. He edged around Lucky, both men looking wary, and walked over to the fireplace. A huge photo of Natalie, her dad and Robby was above it.

"Yes, where's the boy?" Henry Welch demanded.

Natalie felt like she'd lost her breath. "He's sleeping. He went down about an hour ago."

"This is a charming house," Betsy complimented, first shooting a look at her husband. "Perfect for raising a child. If you could pick up our house and move it to the country, it would fit right in."

"Dad, this is not a good time. I was planning to come visit you on Tuesday, talk this over and—"

"And make sure I didn't ruin everything?" Henry raised an eyebrow.

"Well, yes."

"I don't plan to ruin anything."

"Dad, I want— What? What did you say?"

"I don't plan to ruin anything. I accept that Robby is Marcus's son."

Natalie didn't have strength enough to go weak in the knees. Did Mr. Welch know?

Natalie doubted it.

"Lucky, your dad and I had a long talk last night. I told him about your list, the short-term and long-term visitation limits—"

"They're not limits," Natalie said. "They're guidelines."

"Reasonable guidelines," Lucky put in.

"We agree," Betsy said seriously. She looked at her husband. For a moment, Natalie thought she saw fear, but then she saw hope mingled with love, both tinged with doubt. "Your dad and I realized that finding Robby is a gift. We want to get to know him."

Natalie looked at Lucky.

He wasn't buying it, either.

Betsy turned to Natalie. "I won't buy him a pony, I promise. I won't buy a second home here in Selena. But I will make a room for him at our house."

Natalie felt the tears form.

"Please," Betsy said, "may I look at him?"

Natalie led the way, Betsy on her heels. Lucky came third, with Henry slowly taking the rear. They all crowded in the doorway. Betsy only had eyes for Robby. Henry seemed to have eyes for Robby, Natalie and Betsy.

Finally, Natalie saw it. The look a man has for the

woman he loves. Henry may be hard to get along with, but he loved his wife.

It gave Natalie a brief moment of hope. She peered into the bedroom. Robby lay facedown, his feet on the pillow and his head by the baseboard. He snored slightly. A tiny train was clutched in his hand.

"Oh, he's precious," Betsy breathed.

"He's not going to be precious if we wake him up before it's time," Natalie said gently.

Back down the stairs they went. Henry led. He went right back to studying the photos. Betsy did the same, oohing and aahing at every change in Robby.

Lucky went to stand by his father, taking a stance Natalie was starting to recognize. It was the same stance he'd used after jumping off the bull at the Selena rodeo when he'd known he was a winner. It was the same stance he'd taken when he stood in her front yard insisting that he wanted to be included in their lives.

He hadn't needed to use that stance with her lately; the half smile worked just as well.

"So, Dad, why the change of heart, really?"

Natalie saw, then, something Lucky probably missed. Glancing at Betsy, Natalie knew she'd seen it also. Henry aged right in front of their eyes. In the flicker, he'd gone from powerful my-business-is-my-business-and-my-family-is-my-business Henry Welch to an I'm-about-to-lose-everything father.

"Lucky," Natalie said gently.

"No, I want to know. What made you change your mind?"

"Go ahead and tell him," Betsy urged. "You told me. It probably saved our marriage. Maybe you admitting you were wrong will save your relationship with Lucky."

"I was wrong," Henry admitted.

Lucky looked like he was about to say something stupid, something a preacher would never say, like "Big surprise" or maybe "Duh" or even "I don't care."

He didn't say anything. He kept his stance, staring at his father in a way that made him more equal than son.

His dad seemed to recognize the stance as something to be reckoned with. He made a huge effort to regain his power, but the effort didn't reach his eyes. They were sad, so sad.

"I've lost your brother," Henry admitted. "You never come around. Your mother stopped talking to me." He glanced at his wife. "Two solid weeks and not a word, not even a 'Pass me the salt.' Then, on Friday, Bernice sends me an e-mail."

"An e-mail got you here," Lucky said, amazement edging his voice.

"She sent pictures of Robby at her house. She got him eating a piece of chicken, swinging, chasing Mary. They were beautiful. There was one of him on that pretend bull you made over at Bernice's," Lucky's dad said. His voice broke a little. "It was Marcus all over again, at Betsy's dad's place, riding that stupid pretend bull.

"Robby is Marcus's child. I'm a grandparent. I sat all afternoon at my desk, ignoring my secretary, ignoring the phone, ignoring the paperwork gathered in front of me.

"I never harmed you or Marcus," Henry choked. "Not physically, anyway, and for the life of me, I'm not sure why or how I lost you. I've provided—"

"Money," Lucky supplied.

"Yes, a good home, food, the best schooling."

It was father versus son.

"I'd rather have had time, Dad. I'd rather have had your time."

"I… Maybe I—" Henry stuttered.

"Mommy, who dat?" Robby entered the room, rubbing his eyes and staring at Henry.

The room remained silent. Henry didn't look away from Lucky. Betsy was still holding her head in her hands.

"This is Lucky's daddy and mommy," Natalie supplied.

"Oh." Robby looked around the room, finally seeing Betsy. He went right to her, crawled on her lap and settled down.

"Natalie," Lucky suggested, "why don't you and my mother take Robby into the kitchen for a snack or something?"

"Oh, no," Betsy said. "I'm not leaving. There's probably more I need to hear."

"No, Mother, there's not." It was Henry, calling his wife Mother, in that soft voice that denotes love. For all his faults, the man loved his wife. He loved both his sons, too. He just didn't know how to show it.

"Mr. Welch," Natalie said. "Maybe it's best we don't try to change everything today. Why don't you just get to know Robby, and then when both you and Lucky calm down, maybe you can have a conversation that is not heated?"

"My dad—" Lucky began.

"Is here admitting he made some poor choices," Natalie finished.

She waited to see what Lucky would do. Would he turn and march out the door, refusing to even listen? Would he demand that his father leave? Was there hope for forgiveness? Because if Lucky couldn't forgive his father for making poor choices, how would he forgive Natalie for not telling him the truth about Robby's birth?

If Robby hadn't entered the room, Lucky didn't know where the conversation would have gone. Robby simply looked from grown-up to grown-up and finally asked, "What going?"

"Nothing, baby," his mother said. "Just a bit of a family discussion."

"It loud," Robby remarked.

Loud? Lucky thought. The discussion could have been loud, should have been loud, but it was just his father, one more time, proving he didn't see what was right in front of him.

Time was more precious than money.

The only thing different about this confrontation was his father was actually admitting errors.

He studied his dad until he realized he had to make the first move. Again. And he would be the bigger person if he did.

"Natalie's right," he said. "We need to take this slow."

Slow turned out to be the whole family attending the evening church service. Robby didn't make it through the whole service, and for the first time Lucky understood why parents of toddlers seemed to miss evening services. Natalie didn't miss any of the service, though, because Grandma Betsy, with her very willing assistant and best friend, Bernice, was quite happy to sit in the foyer and watch Robby explore every nook and cranny.

Sitting between Natalie and his father, Lucky could only shake his head at the irony. His dad sat all stiff and stern, clearly out of place. Natalie was pale and fidgety, nothing like this morning. Both of them so needed the Word.

What had Natalie been asking about the other night at the café? John 8:32.

"...and the truth will set you free."

Judging by his father's posture, he wasn't feeling free. Judging by Natalie's posture, she wasn't as free as she should be.

After church, his parents headed for their motel after deciding that they would all travel to Delaney the next day to see the church Lucky was considering, and Lucky drove Natalie and Robby home.

He got a kiss from both of them.

Robby's kiss more or less hit his ear. Natalie's landed right where it was supposed to and didn't last nearly long enough.

He wondered, as he drove away, whether he should be kissing a woman whose faith didn't match his, the woman he'd fallen in love with anyway, the woman who should have been his brother's wife! *Oh, God,* Lucky prayed, *you promise us hope and a future, but please, God, let Natalie and Robby be my future.*

Natalie's dad used to moan, "I never get enough sleep," and Natalie had more or less tuned him out. Now she knew what he meant. It was four in the morning, and she was wide-awake. The outside was pitch-black; even the moon was hiding its face. The house was quiet. She padded down the hall and turned on the kitchen light, turned the radio to a country station and dropped a Pop-Tart into the toaster.

Even through her slippers she could feel the coldness of the floor. Winter had stopped knocking on Selena's door. It had arrived.

She went and adjusted the thermostat, then poured a glass of milk, retrieved the Pop-Tart and sat at the kitchen table for a minute. Pure happiness was just out of reach, so close her fingers were skimming the edge of its jacket.

Lucky was wearing the jacket.

She'd allowed herself to get complacent. She'd allowed herself to believe that maybe everything would be all right.

Maybe it would be.

Lucky had not turned on his father. Who knew? Maybe the two of them were out having breakfast right now. Natalie took a bite of her Pop-Tart and signed on to her laptop. This morning, first thing, she had to deal with a hosting issue. Then, she was updating the last of her current clients, and finally she had received signed contracts and initial payment from five new clients. She had lots to do.

None of her tasks took her mind fully off Lucky, his family or her problem. At seven-thirty, she woke Robby up, got him dressed and in front of a bowl of cereal, and went to her bedroom to get herself ready for the day.

When Lucky showed up, he wasn't alone. The trip to Delaney was eye-opening. Betsy was a gem. Not only was she a willing travel guide—she could write a book about the town—but also she took Grandma duty seriously. Robby's coat was quickly zipped, his runny nose wiped and his hand held ever so vigorously. Within hours, she owned the title "Grandma," and Robby said it often.

Grandpa was a different animal. Natalie wasn't one to believe a leopard changed his spots, and in Henry Welch's case, the spots really weren't changing.

Lucky's dad was none too pleased about being a passenger, but Natalie had argued that her car would seat four adults and already held Robby's car seat. Lucky willingly took the front passenger side. Betsy crawled in the center of the backseat and promptly began talking with Robby. Henry sat by the window.

The drive to Delaney wasn't bad, mostly because Henry spent his time talking into his cell phone instead of to his family. Natalie glanced over at Lucky. His lips were thin, and he was staring out the window.

If her dad were in the car, they'd have already stopped for treats and jokes would be rolling off his tongue.

Yeah, she missed her dad.

They arrived at the church about the time Betsy said, "Henry, put away the phone." Except for Robby, it was a pretty solemn group. Robby skipped across the barren parking lot and up the church steps. Lucky was right behind him, key in hand, not quite skipping but moving pretty quickly. A turn of the lock, and they all went in. Natalie liked it on sight. It was clean, small and quaint. A century of memories called out to her. Lucky had mentioned baptisms, funerals and weddings.

"This just might work." Lucky said exactly what she was thinking. Of course, he also said a lot more. "At most, this church holds eighty. I can deal with eighty. What a great opportunity."

The half smile turned to a full smile as he looked around the main auditorium. Natalie followed his scrutiny. She almost smiled, too. He was that excited; it was that contagious. The Delaney church was maybe a third the size of Selena's. The auditorium was a perfect square. Up front was a baptismal and a podium. Two small pews flanked the podium.

Pews took up the lion's share of the auditorium. There were ten on each side. Robby ran between them, his feet sounding too loud in the quiet church.

Suddenly, Natalie realized churches weren't like libraries. Churches were only alive when people crowded their halls.

"Mommy, wook!" Robby held up someone's long-forgotten toy train. He and Betsy promptly sat down and started playing choo-choo.

Henry shook his head. "Eighty doesn't mean eighty putting in the offering. It won't pay rent. It won't pay for insurance. What will you live on?"

"The elders talked to me for a little while last night. If I accept the position, a house comes with the job."

"What kind of a house?" Henry asked.

The house was next to the church. It looked as old as the church, too. One story, two bedrooms and a kitchen the size of Natalie's bedroom closet. A family was renting it. They had three kids and were trying to appear inviting. Clearly, they were terrified at being evicted on account of a preacher.

"I can live in the travel trailer if I decide to stay in Delaney," Lucky said. "Or I'll go ahead and rent the apartment at Patty's. Her husband talked about hiring me on as a cowpoke if I wanted."

He looked at Natalie. "Of course, you'll need to convince her you approve."

Natalie nodded, swallowing her emotions, and also watching Betsy and Henry. Betsy looked like she wanted to move in with Patty, too. Henry looked like he'd just swallowed the world's biggest lemon.

Before returning to Selena, they drove by Lucky's grandparents' place. Betsy wanted to stop, introduce herself to the people living there, but Henry checked his watch often enough to convince Natalie that this was not the perfect time for a social visit.

"We'll do it next time," she promised Betsy. In essence, she was promising Betsy a next time with Robby. It was okay, because already there had been lots of next times with Lucky.

Natalie reached across the seat and took his hand. She didn't care if his dad saw. She only cared that Lucky knew. She was there for him.

"Drop us off at the motel," Henry instructed. "We need to get back to Austin today. I can only afford to take one day off."

Natalie stole a peek at the rearview mirror. So this Monday counted as a day off for Lucky's dad. He'd spent most of it on his cell phone, the rest spent looking disappointed in his son's choice of a profession, followed by shooting down his wife's desire to visit the home she'd grown up in.

He hadn't really tried to get to know Robby. And, as if sensing it, Robby seemed fascinated by him.

Natalie almost felt sorry for Henry Welch.

There were two motels in Selena, one on each end of the town. The Welches had taken the one closest to the side of town Bernice lived on. Natalie pulled up be-

side a car with a rental bumper sticker, and Henry had
the door open before the car completely came to a stop.

"Mommy, go in?" Robby asked.

"He can come in for a minute?" Betsy asked, following her husband out of the car.

Lucky hopped out, too. "Mom, Natalie needs to get
home. She works out of her home and—"

"And I woke up at four this morning and got three
hours in, so we can stay a minute." Natalie turned off
the ignition. It was Betsy's face that prompted the
words, but Henry's face said even more.

Betsy unbuckled Robby, and together Grandma,
Grandpa and Robby walked into the motel room. Natalie opened the car door and got out. Lucky followed.

"Your father tried," Natalie said gently. "He's here."

"He tried on his terms."

Inside the motel room, something dropped. Natalie
froze. Had Robby knocked something over? Was she
about to hear her son wail? Or would she hear Henry
Welch's angry voice?

Instead she heard laughter.

Robby came out of the motel room wearing Henry
Welch's jacket, a tie, and carrying the man's cell phone.

"I spilled suitcase, Mommy. He picking it up now."

Natalie hurried into the room, intent on helping, but
both Betsy and Henry were bent down and chuckling.

"He went for my best tie. I brought three, in case I
wound up having to leave Betsy and attend a meeting
in Dallas. He didn't want one of my everyday ties, no
sirree. He had to have my best."

"The boys never did that," Betsy offered. "They
dressed up in my father's clothes."

Some of the leopard's spots faded when Henry managed to say, "Betsy, you want to stay in Selena a few days?"

"I do."

"Then let's pack up your things and get you over to Bernice's."

"Yeah!" Robby said.

"Yeah!" Betsy echoed.

Natalie thought she saw the barest trace of a smile on Henry's face.

Betsy, Robby and Lucky went into the motel room. Natalie didn't move fast enough. She wound up alone with Henry Welch.

As if on cue, Henry's cell phone rang. He reached in his pocket but instead of answering it, he turned it off.

Natalie heard Robby squeal, and she heard Lucky say, "If you're going to jump on the bed, you have to take Grandpa's clothes off it."

She took one step toward the motel door, but Henry's voice stopped her. "Robby's really not yours," Henry said quietly.

She couldn't move. Her legs had turned to cement. She managed to turn, face Lucky's father, and the only words she could manage to squeak were, "How did you know?"

"I've always made it my business to know where my sons were. I know Robby's birthday. I know where Marcus was at that time, and I know you weren't around. Your cousin Tisha was."

Natalie was silent.

Henry looked at her. "Quite frankly, I don't understand. Why would you drop out of college, give up a dream, and all for a boy who really doesn't belong to you?"

"Oh, well, that's the kicker," she said sarcastically. "Tisha pretty much left Robby with me when he was just two weeks old. By the time he was two months and I realized she wasn't coming back, my dad and I stopped looking. He belonged to us."

Natalie nervously studied the motel door. If Lucky came out now…this would be the worst time…there really would never be a good time.

"They can't hear me," Henry said. "And I don't plan on telling them. It would be just one more heartache after Marcus's death. Betsy has her grandchild, and unless I miss my guess, pretty soon she'll have a daughter-in-law."

To someone else, not someone who'd spent a month going back and forth with a horrible untruth, maybe this would be the answer to the prayer.

Answer to a prayer? Lucky was the answer to her prayer, one she didn't even know she'd been uttering. In front of her, what this man was offering had nothing to do with answering prayers.

Henry Welch was still trying to manipulate his family.

Three years ago Robby had changed her life. Three months ago Lucky had swooped in, done the same thing, and also started changing her heart.

Looking Henry in the eye, she said, "I thank you for not telling Lucky, but I intend to tell him."

Because if she didn't, she was just like Henry Welch.

"I'm not like you," she whispered.

His cheeks reddened, and for the first time, she saw where Lucky got his looks. They were the same. Maybe at one time Henry had even owned a killer half smile. It might explain why Betsy married him.

He shoved his hands in his pockets and turned toward the motel. "Good, because I wouldn't wish being like me on anybody."

Chapter Thirteen

"What did you say to my dad?" Lucky couldn't believe the change. Not only had Henry agreed to take Betsy to Bernice's, but also he'd decided to stay on an extra day at Bernice's, as well. In all their years, he'd never stayed at Bernice's, preferring a motel, or even preferring to go home while Betsy stayed.

Henry Welch claimed he wanted to get to know Natalie and Robby. Robby didn't seem to mind. Betsy was overjoyed. Lucky was speechless. And Natalie, well, she turned pale, fidgety, and Lucky could tell the main thing on her mind was escape. She and Robby stayed at the motel for a while, but didn't seem inclined to stick around or head to Bernice's.

Tuesday, Natalie dropped Robby off for a whole day with Lucky and his parents. She'd begged off staying, mentioning work and some chores. Lucky, sensing something was amiss, especially since she wouldn't look at him or his father, let her go. He'd get to the bottom of whatever was bothering her—and he sure hoped it wasn't his father—after his parents left.

Yesterday, his parents had taken Robby Christmas shopping and then picked him up again to attend Wednesday night services at the church. They left Thursday morning, and the first thing Lucky did was call Natalie and remind her of their Christmas tree date.

She might have begged off again, but Robby caught enough of the conversation to get excited. In the background, he could hear Robby wanting to see Lucky, wanting to see Grandma, wanting to see Henry.

It wasn't lost on Lucky that Robby referred to Henry Welch as Henry instead of Grandpa. When Natalie told Lucky to hold on and reminded Robby that Grandma and Henry were gone, wails erupted.

So here they were in the middle of a winter wonderland, Robby all smiles, chopping down their own tree. Lucky was having trouble getting Natalie to tell him what was bothering her, and something sure was.

"So, what did you say to my dad?" Lucky repeated. "He not only held my mom's hand yesterday—and I've never seen that—but also he turned his cell phone off for a whole afternoon."

She bit her lip, not something he'd seen her do before, and not something he really wanted to see. It took away from the joy of the day together.

"I guess the real question is, 'What did my dad say to you?' Come on, you can tell me."

The tears spilling from her eyes made him back off. Whatever happened had really upset her.

Anger, pure and hot and white, much more intense than Lucky had felt in years, caused him to step back and let the ax fall to the ground. The snow, as if sensing the intensity of the moment, fell even more heavily.

"What did my dad say?"

She looked at him, and he was reminded of a deer

in headlights. He recognized the look from the day at the courthouse. She'd had the look again on the church steps the first day his mother met Robby. Now, she had it again.

He'd take the blame for the first time only.

"Tell me what my father did."

"Nothing. Your father is not the problem. I am."

She busied herself with helping, making sure she was not looking at him, and also that she was as far away as possible. If he ventured near, she immediately acted as if Robby needed something.

It was a strange dance and not one Lucky was used to. He preferred to deal with things head-on. You draw a bull, you consider the bull's history and you ride the bull. You either win or lose. To Lucky's way of thinking, he'd drawn Natalie; he just needed to get past her connection with his brother. He knew Natalie's history, where she lived, went to school and who she dated, but every time he thought they were a team, something came between them. This time it wasn't a rodeo clown. This time it looked like it was his father.

What he needed was to get Natalie alone on a real date and woo her.

Together, the three of them carted the tree—Robby more a hindrance than a help, but an oh-so-enthusiastic hindrance—to Lucky's truck.

Lucky looked at her. The cold had rosied her cheeks. Her parka only intensified her curves.

This draw was for life. *Please, God, let it be for life.*

"I accepted the church in Delaney," he said. "This time next week, I'll be done with Cowboy Christmas Week. Then I'm also done being a bull rider. I can't imagine anywhere I'd rather be than with my own church, close to you and Robby."

He hoisted the tree in the back of the truck, secured it and then hopped down next to her. "Please tell me what my dad said."

"Nothing I didn't need to hear," Natalie said, walking to the passenger side and helping Robby into the back of the extended cab. It already looked like a dad's truck. The child seat was permanent, toys littered the floor and fish-shaped crackers were smashed into the seat. Natalie brushed some crumbs off Robby's knees before admitting, "Your dad didn't do anything but talk about Robby. Let's drop it. Today is for Robby."

"For me!" Robby echoed.

"No, today is for all of us," Lucky said as he started the engine.

His cell phone rang just as he hit the edge of Selena. His mother's excited voice, too excited for a greeting, immediately jumped into the middle of what she was trying to say "…And there's going to be a Santa Claus, and a Christmas village, and presents for the little ones, and crafts. Your father's the one who saw the sign. We were just driving through Delaney for old time's sake. He said we could stay one more day."

Lucky glanced at Natalie as his mother rambled on. Natalie remained tense.

"I'll call you right back, Mom." He hit the off button and laid the phone in his lap. "Do you know about the Christmas village in Delaney?"

"No," Robby said.

"Yes," Natalie said. "We took Robby last year. He had a great time."

"My parents were driving through Delaney for old

time's sake and saw the advertisement. My dad suggested they stay one more day and take Robby."

"Your dad?"

"Yes, I think we're all surprised."

"Another family gathering?"

"Yes!" Robby called from the backseat. Lucky checked the rearview mirror. The little boy understood way too much. Lucky needed to train himself to watch what he said.

"No," Lucky said. "This would be a grandparents' night out with grandson. Which would leave tonight open for us."

"For us?"

"Yes, a date. A real date. You and me."

She didn't look nearly as excited as he wanted her to look. Usually, when he asked a woman out, she started talking about time, what to wear and what to do.

Natalie just looked at him as if she was terrified.

"Here's what we'll do," he said quickly. "We'll pretend it's a first date."

"What?"

"You can thank Mary for the idea. When we were kids, she'd make Marcus and me play this stupid thing called the 'dating game.' She'd get three chairs. Marcus would sit in one. I'd sit in one. She'd usually put a stuffed animal or a cat in the third. Then, she'd ask us questions before she'd pick who got to date her. Come to think of it—" his words dropped off "—I always got picked."

"I'd have picked you," Natalie said, thawing a little.

Lucky chuckled. "Glad to hear it. Back then, our pretend date was always at a restaurant, and Mary made Marcus be the waiter. I remember being served empty cups of tea and lots of plastic food."

He looked at her, wanting so much and afraid of losing it all. "If we go out tonight, we can pretend it's our first date. We'll act as if we're just getting to know each other because… Well, because you picked me."

Yes, she'd picked him, all right, Natalie thought, staring into her closet. Unfortunately, he believed that she'd picked Marcus first.

Tell him tonight. Tell him you never even met Marcus.

Only that wasn't the most important thing to tell him. She had to tell him that although she was Robby's mother, she hadn't borne him.

She had quite an agenda for a first date.

First things first. Natalie pushed aside some cotton shirts. She'd worn her best outfit that Sunday she'd met them for lunch after service. Everything else added up to Mommy clothes, and there was no time to go shopping.

Great, tonight might be the worst first date of her life and she was worried about what to wear.

She pulled out the outfit she'd worn to church, tossed it on the bed and headed for the shower.

An hour later, she woke Robby from his nap, dressed him warmly, gave him a banana, and together they sat on the swing on the front porch and waited for their dates. A light snow fell. Robby would only make it a minute, but there was something magical about sitting on the swing in a winter wonderland.

Last December, there'd been strings of lights, sparkling reindeer with movable parts and a helium-filled snowman in their front yard.

This year, only the snow signaled Christmas.

"Where going, Mama?" Robby's words came out in white puffs.

"You want to go back inside and wait? Are you cold?"

"I fine. Where going, Mama?"

"You're going to Delaney with Grandma and Henry, remember?"

"Oh, yeah. Mama go, too."

"No, your uncle Lucky and I are going somewhere else."

"I go with you?"

"No, you go with Grandma and Henry."

"I wanna go with you."

Music to her ears. Unfortunately, at that moment, Grandma and Henry arrived. Robby flew from the swing and into his grandmother's arms.

Natalie switched the car seat to their car and gave Robby a big hug as she strapped him in.

"Is there anything he shouldn't eat?" Betsy asked.

"No, he can eat just about anything."

Mundane words, and the type of back-and-forth she could now expect, no, that she prayed she'd be using for years, until Robby grew up and no longer needed Mommy.

Henry got behind the wheel and Robby waved, but still Betsy Welch stood alongside the car, looking at Natalie. Then, as if someone had given her a push, she ran around the car and came at Natalie, crushing her in a tight embrace. "Talk about an answered prayer. Oh, thank you for all this. Thank you."

Natalie felt the tears swell. She swallowed them back and nodded.

* * *

He had no idea where to take her.

Usually, on first dates, it was dinner and a movie. But this really wasn't a first date, and this date deserved to be set apart from all others.

The other first dates were with women he might want to get to know. This first date was with a woman he already loved.

Dinner and a movie weren't good enough.

But he absolutely could not come up with any other ideas.

His parents and Robby waved as they drove down the driveway.

Was that a smile on his dad's face?

No, definitely not. Couldn't be, could it? Lucky grinned.

Coming around a curve, he saw Natalie sitting on the porch swing. She had on brown boots, black pants and a sky-blue parka with white edging. Her hair was covered with a matching blue hat.

Imagine coming home every night to this.

He parked and walked toward her, wishing she'd raise her head, look at him and smile.

But she was looking at her hands. He made it all the way to the third step on the porch before she looked up.

"You should be wearing mittens." He took the space next to her and reached for her hands.

She let him.

They were red, cold and felt like heaven.

"What's wrong?"

"Oh, Robby just drove off with your parents, and I'm feeling a little blue."

"It's good for him to be with other people. And

you need some adult company. Feel like dinner and a movie?"

She looked at her hands, only this time they were still encased in his. He tightened his grip. No, this was not a first date. First dates didn't feel this good.

"I don't know. I think I've lost my appetite, and I don't know if I'd be focused enough to stay with a movie."

"Okay," he said. "What would you like to do?"

"I don't know."

"Hey, that's the guy's line," he protested.

She smiled, thawing a bit, and took her hands from his and stuck them in her parka pockets.

"So, what is there to do in Selena on a Thursday night?"

She laughed, thawing even more. "Dinner and a movie."

He shifted, stretching his legs out and looking at the land. It was gorgeous. Snow, glistening and perfect, pelted the front yard and stretched across the empty grazing land.

"Last year at this time, what were you doing?"

"Decorating for Christmas."

"Why aren't you doing it this year?"

"With Dad gone..."

Of course, Lucky felt like slapping himself on the forehead. He'd have done it, too, if he had been with a riding buddy or church friend. He was falling in love with Natalie, but he kept forgetting, or at least he was trying to forget, her past. In his defense, he still had trouble thinking of her with Marcus.

"What kind of decorating did you do?"

"Since Robby turned one, we've had lots of stuff

in the yard, a big tree. We used to do a little tree. I have singing Santas and sparkly reindeer with movable parts, and I have a blow-up snowman."

"Well," Lucky said. "I didn't really feel like dinner and a movie, either."

She looked at him. The deer-in-the-headlights look gone.

"Robby would be really impressed if the house was all lit up when my parents dropped him back home."

Her face lit up.

He wished it were more from the idea of decorating with him than the idea of pleasing her son, but he'd take what he could get.

Then, her face fell. "He'll be asleep."

"This would definitely be a good reason to accidentally wake him."

She didn't look convinced.

"I have to leave at eleven tonight, and I'll be gone all weekend. I'd like to say goodbye. Waking him up would mean a lot to me."

"Another rodeo?"

"In Odessa."

"The weather's bad," she argued.

"So…"

Finally, she laughed and affectionately muttered, *"Cowboys."*

The Christmas stuff was stored in the barn where the horses should be. It took him about ten trips to cart the plastic bins—all labeled—either to the front porch or inside the house.

"You do the labeling?" Lucky asked.

"Yeah. Dad had a bad habit of throwing stuff wherever it would fit. Ornaments stayed on the tree, candles melted and when the treetop angel lost her halo, I took over the packing up."

Whatever her father had used to secure the Christmas lights to the rafters was now missing in action. Lucky wound up driving in nails while Natalie handed up oversize paper clips. Thanks to her heavy mittens, she dropped more than she handed. Thanks to cold, bare hands, it took him a lot longer than it should have. Finally, she ran in and got him a pair of her father's gloves. Except for when he also dropped the paper clips, things speeded up. There was some daylight when they finished the porch.

He'd do the roof when he came back.

Because he intended to come back again and again.

By the time the movable reindeer were nodding their heads, it was almost dark. Fifteen minutes later, the inflatable snowman became a glowing beacon in blackness.

It was time to move inside.

Natalie had already positioned the tree in a stand close to the front window. She had it in water. Lucky checked to see if it was near a heat register. It wasn't.

"Robby should be here for this." Natalie opened a box of ornaments.

Outside, they'd been moving, laughing and tossing an occasional snowball at each other.

Inside, their fingers ached from the cold, and if Lucky guessed correctly, Natalie was suddenly remembering other Christmases—Christmases that involved Robby, her father—and Robby's father? He shook the thought away.

"Do you want to stop?"

She didn't answer.

"I am hungry." He gave her an out.

"Oh!" She looked up, chagrined. "You're right. We needed to eat hours ago." She closed the box of ornaments.

Lucky felt oddly disappointed. He hadn't decorated a tree in years. His mother still did, but if he made it home for Christmas it was just that one day. He really no longer even noticed the tree.

He noticed this one because he noticed the woman it belonged to.

She moved to the kitchen, and he watched her walk. No limp. No stress?

"How about grilled cheese and tomato soup?" she called.

He looked out the window, the one somewhat blocked by a tree waiting for decorations. Snow was starting to fall; the Christmas lights blinked away the darkness. On the wall next to the tree was a photo of Natalie and Robby.

"Perfect."

He wasn't talking about the meal choice.

"Good, give me a minute," she called.

He had no intention of sitting alone in the living room. He moved to the kitchen and watched her.

"Want me to set the table?" he asked.

She looked at him. A few strands of hair fell in her eyes, and she blew them away. "Sure."

It was a nice meal. Just Lucky and Natalie, sitting at the kitchen table, staring out the window at a tiny winter wonderland they'd created. Then they'd stare at each other. Each time Lucky tried to turn the look into something more than innocent appraisal, she looked away.

"Robby should be home any minute," she said.

She was telling him to wait.

Why? He wanted to know why!

"Did you see that?" He pointed out the window. "A shooting star."

"You can't see shooting stars during a snowstorm," she said pragmatically.

"Who says?"

She didn't have an answer.

"When I was little," Lucky said, "Mom and I used to make wishes on shooting stars."

"Yeah, so did I."

"If you could make a wish, right now, what would it be?"

"I'd wish that there were no secrets between us. That this custody battle was over. And that we were still doing things like visiting churches, eating at the diner and decorating for Christmas." Her answer was so quick, so honest, that it surprised him.

"Natalie, that wish can come true."

She shook her head.

"Natalie, we need to talk."

She put down her spoon and frowned. "You said this was a first date. We are talking. Probably too much."

He raised his hands innocently, halting the conversation. He was halfway relieved because had the conversation continued, he'd have had to share his wish.

I wish that I'd met you first before my brother did.

"Okay, okay. So, the rodeo tomorrow in Odessa. Why don't you and Robby come?"

"I don't do rodeos."

"You met me at a rodeo."

She wrinkled her nose. "Yes, but I had an ulterior motive for being there."

"If you come to the rodeo tomorrow, I'll be glad to give you another ulterior motive for being there."

"Like what?"

"Like I'll take you and Robby out for steaks afterward."

She shrugged. "You gotta try harder than that."

He leaned forward, reaching across the table for the hand she had loosely wrapped around a glass of milk. He entwined his fingers with hers. "I'd really like you to come. Just once, I want my girl in the audience. I've never really had anyone other than fans or my mother cheer me on. It will be something we can tell our children."

"Our children!"

"Don't sound so surprised."

"Lucky, we're pretending this is a first date! We haven't known each other long enough for commitment."

"How long did you know my brother?"

She jerked her hand out of his.

He sat back, studying her. Why was she so skittish? Why didn't she want to talk about his brother? Maybe, if they could work through Marcus, they could both heal—together.

Lucky started to say something, thought better of it and concentrated on eating. He finished the last of his soup and pushed the plate away. The grilled cheese was long gone.

So was his heart.

He didn't want this to be a first date. He wanted it to be a last date. Truthfully, he wanted to be setting a date. But it was much too soon and there was baggage between them. Baggage she didn't want to talk about yet.

"I'm leaving soon. I need to get to Odessa and settle in. The event starts at five. You'll have fun."

"What if you get hurt?"

"I could have slipped off the ladder when you kept throwing paper clips at me."

"You know what I mean. Bulls are even more dangerous than horses. One wrong turn and—"

"Won't happen. I promise."

"You can't promise."

"It didn't happen last time you watched me ride."

"Last time I watched you ride I didn't…"

"Didn't what?" Lucky urged. "Didn't love me?"

"I don't love you, but Robby does." She looked out the window. "I sure hope this eases up before tomorrow. I don't want you driving all the way to Odessa in bad weather."

He smiled. It was all he needed. She worried about him.

The phone rang, loud against the silence of their once again locked stares.

She started. Good, she was just as befuddled as he was.

He could hear her in the living room and decided to impress her with his domesticatedness. He cleared the table, rinsed the dishes and wiped up all the crumbs. He got to the living room in time to hear her say, "So, she'll sign the guardianship papers?"

If that didn't peak his interest, then the sentence she uttered next did. "What do you mean she's going to have another baby?"

Definitely a private conversation. He started to head back to the kitchen, but paused.

Why would Natalie need guardianship papers?

He stayed, not wanting to eavesdrop, wishing she'd turn and see him and hoping she was talking to Patty about a mutual friend.

She did finally turn. Gone was the deer in the headlights; here was the stunned deer staring down the barrel of the gun.

"Tell Tisha that I'll do my best not to let her current boyfriend find out about Robby."

"Find out what about Robby?" Lucky asked.

"Goodbye." Natalie hung up the phone.

Silence, falling heavily like the snow outside, enveloped the room.

He'd learned from his mother—who had to deal every day with his father—to ask easy questions. "Who was on the phone?"

"The private detective my father hired."

"What did he have to say?"

She didn't answer.

"Did he find out what happened to your father's money?"

"He happened to my father's money," Natalie said.

"What? Oh."

In the distance, the sound of a car rose above the wind of the storm. Lights flashed briefly in the window. His parents were in the front drive. A door opened; a door slammed. Robby squealed.

Natalie said softly, "Ever since your brother died, my father's been trying to find Tisha. He was afraid Tisha might come hunting for Robby. He was afraid your family would find out about Robby. He was afraid you'd want Robby."

"What does Tisha have to do with this, with Robby?"

She cried silently, tears streaming down her face and

not a single sob. Her breaths came out in jerks, and he could see her chest heaving. He thought about going to her, but his feet wouldn't move.

They wouldn't move.

"I didn't know your brother," she said. "I never met him."

Lucky felt stupid, slow. This wasn't something he could fix with a hammer, nail and paper clip. This wasn't something an eight-second ride would wipe away. This wasn't something the Good Book had an immediate answer to. At least not one he could think of right away.

"You mean, Marcus isn't Robby's father?"

"No." Natalie shook her head. "No, I mean *I* didn't give birth to Robby. Tisha did."

Chapter Fourteen

"Mommy! Dere's lights. Everywhere!" Robby burst through the door.

Natalie tore her gaze from Lucky's. Five more minutes. That was all she'd needed. Maybe then Lucky would have stormed out of the room, letting her know all her worries were justified and had just tripled. Or maybe he'd have listened to her, listened to how afraid she was, how much she wanted to tell him the truth, but how vulnerable she felt.

Instead, she saw him wince when Robby said *Mommy*.

Surely, the bull rider some called "The Preacher" knew sometimes the best mommies were not only the ones who gained weight for nine months, not the ones who went through labor, not the ones who...

Oh, who was she kidding?

There were no words to tell the man, his family, either, just how much Robby meant to her and her dad.

"Mommy here," Natalie said, looking at Lucky when she said it.

He nodded, but it didn't really look like a yes. He

took his coat from the hook by the door, looked at her
and no one else and then he walked out.

"You told him," Henry Welch accused.

"Mommy, come look at lights!" Robby raced for her
hand, tugged at it. "Pease."

It was impossible to say no to Robby. He practically
jumped up and down. Not only was he excited about
the lights, but also it was hours after his bedtime. He
had antlers on his head, bits and pieces of broken candy
cane in his hair and chocolate smears on his shirt.

"Mommy," he reminded. "Lights."

She didn't stop for her coat. Nothing would chase
the chills away tonight. The cold slapped her in the
face and she started to hurry after Lucky, but Robby
was looking up at the lights. "You do dis?"

"Lucky and I did it."

"Unca Lucky!" Robby called.

Lucky paused at the truck door.

Robby carefully went down the front steps and then
raced toward the driveway.

"What's going on?" Betsy said.

Neither Natalie nor Henry answered. Lucky bent
down and said something to Robby, gave the boy a hug
and then hopped in the truck and drove away.

"Henry, are you going to tell me—"

"I will tell you, Betsy," Henry said. "Natalie, we're
going to Odessa tomorrow for Lucky's rodeo. Did he
already invite you?"

"Rodeo!" Robby whooped as he ran toward them.
He stopped in the yard and kicked the oversize, glowing snowman.

"Robby!" both Natalie and Betsy scolded.

"He did invite me," Natalie said once Robby

switched his attention to the reindeer, "but that was before I told him about Tisha."

Betsy Welch dropped her purse. She didn't bend to pick it up.

"We're leaving at about three," Henry repeated. "Let's just leave the car seat in the Cadillac."

"No, I'm not going."

"Henry, what's going on?" Betsy Welch didn't sound happy. Natalie didn't blame her. Tisha had that effect on people. After Henry told Betsy the truth about Robby's parentage, Natalie would have that effect on Betsy.

And Lucky.

Robby stomped up the porch stairs, studied the overhead lights again and said "Wow" one more time.

"Mommy," he started. He didn't continue. He stopped to rub his eyes, apparently got snow in them and started to cry. He immediately raised his hands to Natalie. "Up."

"We're coming by at three," Henry said.

"I—" Natalie bent and picked Robby up. He gave her a wet kiss and then turned so he could watch Henry and Betsy.

"I'm not bossing you. I'm giving you an opportunity. You're a strong woman—" Henry looked around, his perusal ending when his eyes met his wife's "— like my Betsy. You're raising a son, you're keeping a home, and for the last few months you've managed to not only make my youngest son fall in love with you, but also enraptured his mother."

"Oh, Henry, hush," Betsy said.

"On top of that, Bernice approves of you." He chuckled. "She sure doesn't approve of me."

Neither Betsy nor Natalie said anything.

"If you decide to attend the rodeo tomorrow, we'll be glad to drive you."

"Rodeo, Mommy, I wanna go rodeo."

"Of course you do."

Natalie did, too.

It was a good day to come in last place. Lucky'd gotten no sleep, and if you looked up *foul mood* in the dictionary…his picture was on the page. Half of him wanted to jump for joy. Natalie hadn't been with his brother. The other half wanted to punch holes in a wall. Why hadn't she told him? Well, he knew why, really, but the knowledge didn't make the truth any easier to stomach. The last two months had been based on a lie. And because he was naive, he'd bought into the whole facade.

Next to him a foul-mouthed contestant cussed his draw. "Stupid bull. He's rank, and I drew him. Not what I need right now. Not what I need."

Lucky managed to look sympathetic. He wasn't thrilled with his draw, either. He'd wanted the big orange-and-brown-striped bull. In Steamboat Springs, the cowboy on the orange and brown took first place. But there were worse things than WannaBee, the bull Lucky had drawn, and Lucky had as much chance of doing eight seconds on a known bucker as he did a spinner or jumper. Of course, today, what he really needed, to make sure he at least made a second, was to draw a bull named Whimper.

"You keep looking at the stands. You finally got a girl?"

Lucky scowled.

"That explains why you're not doing so hot," the cowboy said.

He scanned the crowd one more time. It was stupid, really. No way was she coming to the rodeo. No way did he want her to come. He'd left her with his parents. According to his cell phone, his mother had called ten times and his dad twice. Twice meant his dad was serious. She'd told them something, and he wasn't ready to find out what.

Natalie hadn't called.

And he hadn't called her.

He had found a scripture, but it did more to soften his heart than harden it.

He thought of Proverbs 3, *"Never walk away from someone who deserves help; your hand is God's hand for that person."*

He'd gotten Natalie to church.

And she wasn't much of a liar. The whole time he knew she was keeping something and it was eating at her.

He'd invited her; he'd left her standing on the porch; it was over. She wasn't there.

He headed for the metal chute. WannaBee? Stupid name for a bull. The name should be WannaYouOffa-MyBack.

"Want some help?" the other cowboy said. Lucky finally recognized him. Billy Sam, out of Albuquerque. Not a bad sort, really.

"Yeah, that'd be great."

Billy wrapped the rope around Lucky's wrist, leaving room for it to slip, just slightly, upon the animal's departure. Lucky wondered if time was going as slow as it felt. He walked toward the bucking chute. The smell of sweat, both human and bull, permeated the air. Even though time was standing still, Lucky managed to make his way to WannaBee's back. His legs dropped to WannaBee's side, and he slid toward the rope holding him to the bull. His other hand was in the air.

Yet again, since Marcus died, Lucky was doing the circuit alone. It had never bothered him as much as it did today.

Lucky wanted Natalie, and Robby, to see this, see him ride, see him win! *See that he wouldn't fall.*

"Go!"

The man at the gate flipped the handle, loudly, and the gate flew open. WannaBee snorted in anger. Power, speed and air rushed across Lucky's face. Whoa, everything happened so fast. The bull was fast, maybe faster than Lucky. He turned, bucked and ducked his head toward the ground. He spun left, again and again and again. WannaYouOffaMyBack, yup, that's what his name should have been. WannaBee knew the game, but so did Lucky. A buzzer sounded. Lucky reached for the tail of the rope, pulling it to untie the tangled hand that kept him secure on the back of the bull, and with one last burst of energy—Lucky couldn't say where it came from—he hurtled off WannaBee, landed on the ground, thought about his broken toes and tumbled. WannaBee, spent, ran off.

The crowd cheered.

Eight seconds.

And in the crowd, standing up, clapping, was Natalie.

She'd been enjoying for the first time in years the true meaning of rodeo, of rooting for someone, and thinking maybe she could get on a horse, maybe, maybe, maybe, when she'd felt a shift next to her.

"Dat was Unca Lucky?" Robby asked.

"That was Unca Lucky," Natalie responded. The man who'd held on to a steaming locomotive and jumped off its back was Lucky. Their Lucky.

"He okay?"

Betsy pulled Robby onto her lap and buried her chin in the top of his hair. "He's okay." She looked at Natalie and then bowed her head. "Everything is going to be okay."

Her lips were moving; Natalie knew a prayer when she saw it. What a surprise. According to Henry, Betsy had barely flinched when Henry told her the truth about Robby's birth. She'd called Natalie five times since breakfast, and each and every time thanked Natalie for being Robby's mommy.

God is with me.

Natalie squirmed. Where did that thought come from? It was definitely more a Lucky thought than a Natalie thought, and it was straight from the Bible he'd lent her.

The message was as straightforward as the man who'd lent her the Bible.

"God is with me," Natalie whispered.

He'd been with her as she worked this morning, as she cared for Robby, as she made lunch, and as she dressed them both for a rodeo she had no intention of attending.

Lucky, fresh from a winning ride and full of raw power, came and sat beside her, so close she could feel the heat from his body. "I didn't fall."

The fans who were following him stopped. No one

asked for an autograph. They seemed to sense this was a private moment. They faded from sight.

"No, you didn't fall."

"And if I had, I'd have picked myself up, bleeding, broken, and I'd have made my way over to sit by you."

"Betsy," Henry said, "this might be a good time to take Robby for a potty break."

"Even after last night?" Natalie whispered.

"Especially after last night."

"I made up my mind to tell you the truth weeks ago, but the right moment…there never was a right moment."

"Natalie," Lucky interrupted, "I didn't fall *in* the arena, but I did fall outside of it. I fell for you."

"I love Robby," Natalie whispered.

"Well, good," he said, almost chuckling.

How could he chuckle at a time like this?

"I'm not his biological mother," she said. "Ever since the day I approached you at the rodeo, I've been so afraid. I probably have no claim on Robby, not compared to you."

"You've got quite a claim," Lucky said gently. "You've got a whole town full of people who've watched you mother him."

"But—"

"Natalie, you've been worried this whole time that I could take Robby away from you. I understand that. Oh, it shocked me last night. I cannot tell you how I wish I'd known the burden you carried. We wasted a lot of time dancing around the wrong issues."

Natalie patted her leg. "I can't dance."

"Well, darling, you're going to have to learn because I don't want to take Robby away from you. As a matter of fact, I want to stand beside you, raise him as my own. Just think of what we can do *together*."

God is really with me, Natalie thought. Then, humanity knocked. Natalie felt her hands drop to her sides; she felt weak and scared. Stupid tears, they spilled over as she looked up at Lucky. "I don't deserve this."

"You're right," Lucky agreed. "You deserve so much more. But I'm hoping I'll do. With God, all things are possible. I'm the luckiest man I know. Don't you know?" He pulled her into his arms. "How can you not know...? All this time I was worried about what really went on between you and Marcus. As much as I loved my brother..." Lucky choked up. "I was sitting in my truck last night, in the dark, looking at the sky where we saw the shooting star, and I was thinking about my wish. I wished that I'd met you first. I had my Bible open, and I was searching for a scripture on how to deal with you not being Robby's mother, with you not telling me the truth. Finally, I realized I didn't need a scripture to tell me God had answered my prayer."

Natalie buried her head in the crook of his neck for a moment and then looked up at him, knowing she never wanted to look away. It was there, close enough she could touch it. This man was offering her the chance for a family. She saw it in his eyes, she felt it in his touch, and right there in front of a stadium of rodeo fans, right now, she cherished it in his kiss.

His fingers finally slipped away from her cheeks, and his lips left the warmth of hers. She immediately wanted them back.

"You know," she said carefully, "it's really not that

far from my place to Delaney. Maybe the first thing we should have in that new church of yours is a wedding."

"Ours?" Lucky said hopefully.

"Ours," Natalie agreed.

* * * * *

Dear Reader,

What fun to write a story with not only a faith element, but also with a rodeo, roots and romance. Natalie and Lucky, the heroine and hero in *Daddy for Keeps,* are special characters who had to overcome self-doubt, the judgment of others and secrets.

Natalie, whom I thought of as a mother bear, quickly became someone who spoke to me. First, she was dealing with an issue that is near and dear to my heart: raising a child. She happened to be raising a child she didn't give birth to, and for most of the story she dealt with the fear of perhaps losing the child, who, by every thought, memory and deed was hers. My parents dealt with the same issue. I am an adopted child, and an adopted *only* child, and my parents, by every thought, memory and deed, let me know that adoption was just a word and that the words *Mommy* and *Daddy* were more than just words.

Then there was Lucky, a rugged hero who managed to be a diamond in the rough. He's a man of faith and character. I know many Luckys, and in real life, I even managed to marry one!

Thank you for reading *Daddy for Keeps.* I love hearing from my readers. Please visit my Web site, www.pamelatracy.com. You may also contact me c/o Love Inspired Books, 195 Broadway, 24th floor, New York, NY 10007.

Pamela Tracy

QUESTIONS FOR DISCUSSION

1. At the beginning of the novel, Natalie is worried about money. She has to make decisions that affect not only the way she's raising Robby, but also *where* she raises Robby. What is the catalyst that sends her to Lucky? Would you have made such a choice?

2. From the beginning, Lucky is very careful in how he deals with his parents. Does he make the right choice in waiting to tell them about Robby?

3. Lucky's brother caused a lot of grief. We know some of the things Lucky did to try to "save" Marcus. None of them worked. What scripture could help Lucky deal with the loss of his brother? Could the same scripture help his mother? His father? Or, what scripture might they need to turn to?

4. Natalie simply lets people believe Robby belongs to her. Why? Is this what you would do? Name some benefits to this approach. Name some negatives to this approach.

5. When Natalie first has to "share" Robby, what is her biggest fear? How does she deal with it? What is your biggest fear? How do you deal with it?

6. During Natalie's visit to Wednesday-night services, she hears about birth order. She thinks about being an only child, and Lucky talks about his position.

Are you an only? A oldest? A middle? A youngest? How has your placement in the family affected your life?

7. What are Lucky's mother's strongest points? Weakest points? Is there a spiritual change she needs to make? What are Lucky's father's strongest points? Weakest points? What change does he make by the end of the story? Will it last?

8. When does Lucky start to fall in love with Natalie? What is it he likes best about her? When does Natalie start to fall in love with Lucky? What is it she likes best about him? Think of someone you love. What do you like best about them? Now, tell them.

9. Is there any hope for Tisha's redemption? What do you think shaped her? What will it take to change her? If she finds the Lord and repents, what should be her role in Robby's life?

10. Lucky decides to leave the rodeo and take a congregation. What are some of the obstacles he will face? Natalie will go from being unchurched to being a preacher's wife. What advice would you give her?

WE HOPE YOU ENJOYED THESE TWO

LOVE INSPIRED®

BOOKS.

If you were **inspired** by these

uplifting, **heartwarming**

romances, be sure to look for

all six Love Inspired® books

every month.

Love Inspired®

Love Inspired®

Save $1.00

on the purchase of any
Love Inspired® book.

Available wherever books are sold, including most bookstores, supermarkets, drugstores and discount stores.

Save $1.00

on the purchase of any Love Inspired® book.

Coupon valid until July 31, 2018.
Redeemable at participating retail outlets in the U.S. and Canada only.
Limit one coupon per customer.

52615199

Canadian Retailers: Harlequin Enterprises Limited will pay the face value of this coupon plus 10.25¢ if submitted by customer for this product only. Any other use constitutes fraud. Coupon is nonassignable. Void if taxed, prohibited or restricted by law. Consumer must pay any government taxes. Void if copied. Inmar Promotional Services ("IPS") customers submit coupons and proof of sales to Harlequin Enterprises Limited, PO Box 31000, Scarborough, ON M1R 0E7, Canada. Non-IPS retailer—for reimbursement submit coupons and proof of sales directly to Harlequin Enterprises Limited, Retail Marketing Department, 225 Duncan Mill Rd., Don Mills, ON M3B 3K9, Canada.

U.S. Retailers: Harlequin Enterprises Limited will pay the face value of this coupon plus 8¢ if submitted by customer for this product only. Any other use constitutes fraud. Coupon is nonassignable. Void if taxed, prohibited or restricted by law. Consumer must pay any government taxes. Void if copied. For reimbursement submit coupons and proof of sales directly to Harlequin Enterprises, Ltd 482, NCH Marketing Services, P.O. Box 880001, El Paso, TX 88588-0001, U.S.A. Cash value 1/100 cents.

5 65373 00076 2   (8100)0 12313

® and ™ are trademarks owned and used by the trademark owner and/or its licensee.

© 2018 Harlequin Enterprises Limited

LICOUP0318

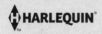

HARLEQUIN®

Save $1.00

on the purchase of any

Harlequin® series book.

Available wherever books are sold, including most bookstores, supermarkets, drugstores and discount stores.

✂

Save $1.00

on the purchase of any Harlequin® series book.

Coupon valid until July 31, 2018.
Redeemable at participating retail outlets in the U.S. and Canada only.
Limit one coupon per customer.

52615203

Canadian Retailers: Harlequin Enterprises Limited will pay the face value of this coupon plus 10.25¢ if submitted by customer for this product only. Any other use constitutes fraud. Coupon is nonassignable. Void if taxed, prohibited or restricted by law. Consumer must pay any government taxes. Void if copied. Inmar Promotional Services ("IPS") customers submit coupons and proof of sales to Harlequin Enterprises Limited, PO Box 31000, Scarborough, ON M1R 0E7, Canada. Non-IPS retailer—for reimbursement submit coupons and proof of sales directly to Harlequin Enterprises Limited, Retail Marketing Department, 225 Duncan Mill Rd., Don Mills, ON M3B 3K9, Canada.

U.S. Retailers: Harlequin Enterprises Limited will pay the face value of this coupon plus 8¢ if submitted by customer for this product only. Any other use constitutes fraud. Coupon is nonassignable. Void if taxed, prohibited or restricted by law. Consumer must pay any government taxes. Void if copied. For reimbursement submit coupons and proof of sales directly to Harlequin Enterprises, Ltd 482, NCH Marketing Services, P.O. Box 880001, El Paso, TX 88588-0001, U.S.A. Cash value 1/100 cents.

5 65373 00076 2   (8100)0 12314

® and ™ are trademarks owned and used by the trademark owner and/or its licensee.

© 2018 Harlequin Enterprises Limited

HSCOUP0318

Get 2 Free Books,
Plus 2 Free Gifts—
just for trying the
Reader Service!

LOVE
Harlequin
romance?

Join our Harlequin community to share your thoughts and connect with other romance readers!

Be the first to find out about promotions, news, and exclusive content!

Sign up for the Harlequin e-newsletter and download a free book from any series at

www.TryHarlequin.com

CONNECT WITH US AT:

Harlequin.com/Community

 Facebook.com/HarlequinBooks

 Twitter.com/HarlequinBooks

 Instagram.com/HarlequinBooks

Pinterest.com/HarlequinBooks

ReaderService.com

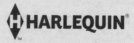 **HARLEQUIN**®

ROMANCE WHEN YOU NEED IT

HSOCIAL2017